"DOES THIS HURT?" HE ASKED.

Because it was hurting him.

Beneath his hands, her breathing quickened. "N-no." She stared at him, eyes wide but unafraid, and her soft, pink lips parted slightly. "It feels . . . nice."

He was braced over her now, his body stretched alongside hers, so that he had only to lower his head to touch his lips to hers. Thoughts of the Heirs, the Primal Source all dissolved like vapor beneath the sun of his and her shared awareness. Her gaze flicked down to his mouth, as well, and the dropping of her lashes and flush spreading across her cheeks revealed that not only had she shared his thought, but wanted it, too. What would she taste like? Both the scientist and the man within him needed to find out.

Slowly, slowly he bent lower, suspended in liquid time. His heart slammed within the cage of his chest, and he was tight and hard everywhere. He cradled the juncture of her neck and jaw, feeling the rush of her pulse at that tender convergence. Such delicacy. Combined with remarkable strength.

"You're a very courageous woman," he breathed, close enough to count freckles.

She brought her hand up to curve around the back of his head. "I know," she answered.

He smiled at that, a small smile. And then he stopped smiling, because he kissed her.

The Blades of the Rose

Warrior

Scoundrel

Rebel

Stranger

Published by Kensington Publishing Corporation

STRANGER
The Blades of the Rose

Zoë Archer

ZEBRA BOOKS
KENSINGTON PUBLISHING CORP.

http://www.kensingtonbooks.com

ZEBRA BOOKS are published by

Kensington Publishing Corp.
119 West 40th Street
New York, NY 10018

All Kensington titles, imprints and distributed lines are available at special quantity discounts for bulk purchases for sales
promotion, premiums, fund-raising, educational or institu-
tional use.

Special book excerpts or customized printings can also be created to fit specific needs. For details, write or phone the office
of the Kensington Special Sales Manager: Attn. Special Sales
Department. Kensington Publishing Corp., 119 West 40th
Street, New York, NY 10018. Phone: 1-800-221-2647.

Zebra and the Z logo Reg. U.S. Pat. & TM Off.

ISBN-13: 978-1-4201-0682-4
ISBN-10: 1-4201-0682-1

First Printing: December 2010
10 9 8 7 6 5 4 3 2 1

Printed in the United States of America

For Zack,
sometimes strange but never a stranger,
my heart will always know yours

ACKNOWLEDGMENTS

Thank you to superagent Kevan Lyon and wondereditor Megan Records for loving my crazy adventurers as much as I do. And thank you to the many people whose support and encouragement helped make the dream of the Blades of the Rose a reality: Andy and Christina Blaiklock, Lorelie Brown, Pauline DiPego, Jerry DiPego, Gene and Janice Fiskin (hi, Mom!), Kathy Harmening, Carolyn Jewel, Carrie Lofty, Tiffani McCoy, Julia McDermott, Courtney Milan, Martti Nelson, Elyssa Papa, Jeffrey Silber (hi, Dad!), Liz Thurmond, and Lisa Zalokar.

Chapter 1

Shipboard Meetings

The steamship Antonia, *two days from Liverpool, 1875.*

Three guns pointed at Gemma Murphy.

She pointed her own derringer right back. Two shots only. Maybe she could get her hands on one of the revolvers aimed at her. Hopefully, it wouldn't come to that.

A sane person would have fled the cabin. But Gemma wasn't sane. She was a journalist.

So, instead of running, she confronted three faces ranging in expression from curious to outright hostile. And their guns.

The culmination of weeks of hard travel. On the trail of a story, she had journeyed all the way from a small trading post in the Canadian Rockies, across the United States, to New York, where she boarded the *Antonia*. Horseback, stagecoach, train. Clapboard boardinghouses with thin mattresses and thinner walls. Food boiled to inedibility. Groping hands, speculative leers. Rats and dogs.

She'd faced them all, pressing onward, always a day

behind her quarry—but that was deliberate. She couldn't let them see her. To be seen was to risk being recognized. Maybe she flattered herself to think that any of the people she followed would remember her. After all, she had only seen them twice, and spoken with one member of their party once. Weeks, thousands of miles, had passed since then.

But there was a strong disadvantage to being a redhead. People with bright copper hair and freckles had a tendency to be remembered—like a flare's afterimage burned into the eye. Sometimes Gemma used her appearance and gender to her advantage. It always helped a reporter to have an advantage. Other times, her looks and sex were a damned pain in the behind.

As soon as she learned that her quarry had booked passage on the *Antonia*, bound for Liverpool, Gemma also reserved a cabin on that same ship. To follow at sea, even a day behind, meant the possibility of losing them. So, for the past week onboard the ship, she'd led a nocturnal existence. Staying in her cabin during the day, to avoid being spotted. In those close confines, she wrote articles until her hands cramped. She had little to go on but speculation. That did not stop her from piecing together events with her own prodigious imagination. Night saw her skulking about the ship, getting some much-needed fresh air. And, once the other passengers had retired for the evening, listening at doors.

Her quarry met in one another's cabins. Often, their conversations held no information. But tonight had been different.

"When did the Heirs activate the Primal Source?" The woman's voice. Her English accent was refined, but her words were tough and strong.

Gemma pulled from her pocket her notebook and began scribbling furiously in it.

"Some two and a half months ago." Another English voice. One of the two men. His voice, so impeccably British in its accents, was deep and sonorous. Even now, with a door between them, his voice played havoc with her normally reliable sensibilities. She remembered the impact his voice had on her at the trading post, and ruefully reflected that none of that impact had been lost in the intervening time and distance. "But they haven't the faintest idea what to do with it."

"That's why they came for me in Canada," said the woman.

"If the Heirs can't use the Primal Source," the second man noted, "then there shouldn't be any danger." The accents of western Canada marked this man's voice, yet he held a natural authority in his tone.

"It does not work that way," the woman answered. "The Primal Source has the power to grant and embody the possessor's most profound hopes and dreams."

"Even if said possessor does not actively attempt this?" asked the Canadian.

The woman replied, "All the Primal Source needs is to be in close proximity to the one who possesses it, and it can act on even the most buried desires."

Good gravy! What could this Primal Source be?

Just then, a sailor on watch walked through the passageway. He looked at Gemma, standing alone outside a cabin door, with a curious frown.

"Can I help you, miss?" he asked.

"Just looking for my key," she murmured, careful to keep her voice down. Her notebook was concealed in the folds of her skirt. "I'm such a ninny—I can never remember where I put it."

"The purser can get you another one."

"Oh, no," Gemma said. She made some wave of her hand, the universal sign of a woman who doesn't want to be a bother. "I'll find it. Please, carry on with whatever you were doing."

"Are you sure, miss?"

Blast these polite sailors. "Yes, quite sure." She

smiled and, God help her, fluttered her lashes. Gemma
never considered herself a beautiful woman—red hair
and freckles weren't often considered the height of
female loveliness—but she did know that batting her
eyelashes generally worked as a distracting device.

Correct. The sailor, hardly more than a boy, flushed,
stammered, and then ambled away. The moment he disappeared down the passageway, Gemma pressed her ear to the
cabin door, notebook at the ready.

"And what are the Heirs' deepest desires?" This was
asked by the Canadian. He was the newcomer in the trio,
she deduced.

The reply came from the Englishman, an answer arising
from long experience. "The supremacy of England. An
empire that encompasses the entire world."

Gemma pressed her hand to her mouth, horrified by the
idea. It seemed the stuff of a despotic nightmare, to have
one country in control of the whole globe, with one set of
laws. One monarch. The American in Gemma rebelled at
the idea. Nearly a hundred years ago, her country had been
forged in blood, fighting to free itself from the tyranny of
oversea rule. Thousands of lives lost to secure freedom for
its citizens. And to lose it all again? Just as every other
nation would lose its independence?

The woman added, in hard, bleak tones, "Somehow, the
Primal Source will embody this. Which means destruction
and devastation on a global scale."

"Unless the Blades stop the Heirs' dream from manifesting," said the Englishman.

"I pray to God we aren't too late." This, from the woman.
A grim hope.

On that somber note, the voices within wished each
other a good night. Gemma scurried away, into the shadows, to watch from a safe distance. Peering around the
corner of the passageway, she saw the door to the cabin
open, yellow lamplight falling into the corridor. A woman

and man emerged, holding hands. The woman was fair in coloring, slight of build, but she radiated a steely strength matched by the bronze-skinned man beside her.

When they stepped into the passageway, the man tensed slightly. The change in his posture was so subtle, Gemma barely saw it, but the woman felt the change at once.

"What is it, Nathan?" she asked.

He peered around, much the way a wolf might search for prey. "Thought I sensed something . . . familiar." He gazed up and down the passageway with sharp, dark eyes, and Gemma could have sworn he was actually *smelling* the air.

She flattened herself against the bulkhead, hiding, heart knocking against her ribs. She'd come too far to be found out now, so close to the story.

She heard the man take a step in her direction, then stop. "It's this damned sea air. Can't get a bead on anything."

"We'll get you on land again soon. Come to bed," murmured the woman, and Gemma knew from the throaty warmth of the woman's voice, bed was precisely the destination in mind. Gemma's own face flushed to hear the husky promise in the woman's words. Words one would speak to a lover. And it affected the man, most definitely. Gemma thought she heard him literally growl in response, before their footsteps hurriedly disappeared toward their stateroom.

Once they had gone, Gemma poked her head around the corner again. She saw the third man in the group standing outside the cabin, locking the door. He was a tall man, and had to bend a little to keep from knocking his head into the low ceiling. Gemma recognized his long, elegant form immediately, and would have lingered longer to observe him, but she did not want to risk being spotted. So she pushed back into the shadows, listening to him lock his door. It seemed to take rather a long time, but at last he straightened and began walking.

Straight in her direction. On feet well used to keeping silent, Gemma hurried away.

She waited in the stern for several minutes. Once she felt confident she wouldn't encounter any of her quarry, she jogged quickly back to the cabin. She pressed her ear to the door. No sound within. Bending low, she looked at the small gap between the door and the deck. Dark. The lamps inside were extinguished. He wasn't inside—unless he'd come back within minutes of leaving and immediately gone to sleep. Unlikely.

Now was her chance to do some investigating. Surely she'd find something of note in his cabin. A fast glance up and down the passageway ensured she was entirely alone.

Gemma opened the cabin door.

And found herself staring at a drawn gun.

Damn. He *was* in. Working silently at a table by the light of one small lamp. At her entrance, he was out of his chair and drawing a revolver in one smooth motion.

She drew her derringer.

They stared at each other.

In the small cabin, Catullus Graves's head nearly brushed the ceiling as he faced her. Her reporter's eye quickly took in the details of his appearance. Even though he was the only black passenger on the ship, more than just his skin color made him stand out. His scholar's face, carved by an artist's hand, drew one's gaze. Arresting in both its elegant beauty and keen perception. A neatly trimmed goatee framed his sensuous mouth. The long, lean lines of his body—the breadth of his shoulders, the length of his legs—revealed a man comfortable with action as well as thought. Though Gemma had not been aware *how* comfortable. Until she saw the revolver held easily, familiarly in his large hand. A revolver trained on her. She'd have to do something about that.

"Mr. Graves," she murmured, shutting the door behind her.

Behind his spectacles, Catullus Graves's dark eyes widened. "Miss Murphy?"

Despite the fact that she was in danger of being shot, it wasn't until Graves spoke to Gemma that her heart began to pound. And she was absurdly glad he did remember her, for she certainly hadn't forgotten him. They'd met but briefly. Spoke together only once. Yet the impression of him remained, and not merely because she had an excellent memory.

"I thought you were out," she said. As if that excused her behavior.

"Wanted to get a barometric reading." Catullus Graves frowned. "How did you get in?"

"I opened the door," she answered. Which was only a part of the truth. She wasn't certain he would believe her if she told him everything.

"That's not possible. I put an unbreakable lock on it. Nothing can open it without a special key that *I* made." He sounded genuinely baffled, convinced of the security of his invention. Gemma glanced around the cabin. Covering all available surfaces, including the table where he had been working moments earlier, were small brass tools of every sort and several mechanical objects in different states of assembly. Graves was an inventor, she realized. She knew her way around a workshop, but the complex devices Graves worked on left her mystified.

She also realized—the same time he did—that they were alone in his cabin. His small, *intimate* cabin. She tried, without much success, not to look at the bed, just as she tried and failed not to picture him stripping out of his clothes before getting into that bed for the night. She barely knew this man! Why in the name of the saints did her mind lead her exactly where she did not want it to go?

The awareness of intimacy came over them both like an exotic perfume. He glanced down and saw that he was in his shirtsleeves, and made a cough of startled chagrin. He reached for his coat draped over the back of a chair. One hand still training his gun on her, he used the other to don his coat.

"Strange to see such modesty on the other end of a Webley," Gemma said.

"I don't believe this situation is covered in many etiquette manuals," he answered. "What are you doing here?"

One hand gripping her derringer, Gemma reached into her pocket with the other. "Easy," she said, when he tensed. "I'm just getting this." She produced a small notebook, which she flipped open with a practiced one-handed gesture.

"Pardon—I'll have a look at that," Graves said. Polite, but wary. He stepped forward, one broad-palmed hand out.

A warring impulse flared within Gemma. She wanted to press herself back against the door, as if some part of herself needed protecting from him. Not from the gun in his other hand, but from *him*, his tall, lean presence that fairly radiated with intelligence and energy. *Keep impartial*, she reminded herself. That was her job. Report the facts. Don't let emotion, especially *female* emotion, cloud her judgment.

And yet that damned traitorous female part of her responded at once to Catullus Graves's nearness. Wanted to be closer, drawn in by the warmth of his eyes and body. An immaculately dressed body. As he crossed the cabin with only a few strides, Gemma undertook a quick perusal. Despite being pulled on hastily, his dark green coat perfectly fit the breadth of his shoulders. She knew that beneath the coat was a pristine white shirt. His tweed trousers outlined the length of his legs, tucked into gleaming brown boots. His burgundy silk cravat showed off the clean lines of his jaw. And his waistcoat. Good gravy. It was a minor work of art, superbly fitted, the color of claret, and worked all over with golden embroidery that, upon closer inspection, revealed itself to be an intricate lattice of vines and flowers. Golden silk-covered buttons ran down its front, and a gold watch chain hung between a pocket and one of the buttons.

Hanging from the chain, a tiny fob in the shape of a knife glinted in the lamplight.

On any other man, such a waistcoat would be dandyish. Ridiculous, even. But not on Catullus Graves. On him, the garment was a masterpiece, and perfectly masculine, high-lighting his natural grace and the shape of his well-formed torso. She knew about fashion, having been forced to write more articles than she wanted on the subject. And this man not only defined style, he surpassed it.

But she was through with writing about fashion. That was precisely why she was on this steamship in the middle of the Atlantic Ocean.

With this in mind, Gemma tore her gaze from this vision to find him watching her. A look of faint perplexity crossed his face. Almost bashfulness at her interest.

She let him take the notebook from her, and their finger-tips accidentally brushed.

He almost dropped the notebook, and she felt heat shoot into her cheeks. She had the bright ginger hair and pale, freckled skin of her Irish father, which meant that, even in low lamplight, when Gemma blushed, only a blind imbecile could miss it.

Catullus Graves was not a blind imbecile. His reaction to her blush was to flush, himself, a deeper mahogany staining his coffee-colored face.

A knock on the door behind her had Gemma edging quickly away, breaking the spell. She backed up until she pressed against a bulkhead.

"Catullus?" asked a female voice on the other side of the door. The woman from earlier.

Graves and Gemma held each other's gaze, weapons still drawn and trained on each other.

"Yes?" he answered.

"Is everything all right?" the woman outside pressed. "Can we come in?"

Continuing to hold Gemma's stare, Graves reached over and opened the door.

Immediately, the fair-haired woman and her male companion entered.

"Thought it was nothing," the man said, grim. "But I *know* I've caught that scent before, and—" He stopped, tensing. He swung around to face Gemma, who was plastered against the bulkhead with her little pistol drawn.

Both he and the woman had their own revolvers out before one could blink.

And now Gemma had not one but *three* guns aimed at her.

"Astrid, Lesperance," said Catullus Graves as though making introductions at a card party, "you remember Miss Murphy."

"From the trading post?" demanded the woman. Gemma recalled her name: Astrid Bramfield. She had exchanged her mountain woman's garb of trousers and heavy boots for a more socially acceptable traveling dress. Yet the woman had lost none of her steely strength. She eyed Gemma with storm-colored eyes cold with suspicion, an enraged Valkyrie. "Following us all the way from the Northwest Territory. She must be working for them."

Them?

"Let's give her a chance to explain herself," said the other man, level. Though he didn't lower his gun. Nathan Lesperance, Gemma recalled. He wore a sober, dark suit, as befitting his profession as an attorney, but the copper hue of his skin and sharp planes of his face revealed Lesperance's full Native blood.

A white woman, an Indian man, and a black man. Truly an unusual gathering. One Gemma was glad she'd followed.

"I retrieved this from her," Graves said, holding up the notebook.

"What does it say?" Astrid Bramfield asked sharply.

Graves glanced down at the notebook. A frown appeared between his brows. Gemma nearly smiled. Her handwriting was deplorable, mostly because she deliberately made it illegible to anyone but her. No sense letting other reporters read her notes. She may as well give those buffoons in the newsroom all of her bylines.

"I don't know," he answered.

At this, Astrid Bramfield looked surprised, as though Graves admitting a deficiency in *any* knowledge was shocking.

"If I may translate," Gemma said, holding out her hand. She did not miss the careful way in which Graves returned her notebook, avoiding the contact of her skin.

Wanting her own distraction, she looked down at her notes, although she hardly needed them. Every word of the conversation she'd overheard was inscribed permanently on the slate of her memory. She recited everything she had heard.

"Eavesdropping," snapped Astrid Bramfield.

"I prefer to call it 'unsupervised listening,'" Gemma answered.

A corner of Graves's mouth twitched, but he forced it down and looked serious.

Gemma closed her notebook and slipped it back into her pocket. "All very strange and bewildering, you must admit."

"We need not admit anything," Astrid Bramfield replied.

"You're a journalist," Graves said with sudden understanding. His keen, dark eyes took note of her ink-stained fingers, the tiny callus on her right index finger that came from holding a pen for hours at a stretch. "That's what you were doing at the trading post in the Northwest Territory."

Gemma nodded. "I had planned on writing a series of articles about life on the frontier. But when you crossed my path, I knew I would find a hell of a story. And I was right."

"A journalist," Astrid Bramfield repeated, her tone revealing exactly how she felt about reporters.

No doubt most members of Gemma's profession deserved their reputation. But Gemma wasn't like them. For one thing, she was a woman. Not an automatic guarantee of integrity, yet it was a small mark of distinction.

Something that looked suspiciously like disappointment flickered in Catullus Graves's eyes before being shuttered away. "You'll find no story here, Miss Murphy." He took a step back, and she found, oddly, that she missed his nearness. "It is in your best interest, when this ship docks, to turn around and go home."

Back to Chicago? She would never do that—she had crossed a continent and an ocean for this story.

"Who are the Heirs?" Gemma asked.

Graves, Lesperance, and Astrid Bramfield all tensed. None of them spoke as a sharp silence descended. Very surprising, considering recent developments. Then—

"They're called the Heirs of Albion," Lesperance said.

"Nathan!" Astrid Bramfield exclaimed, and Graves looked alarmed.

Yet it couldn't be stopped now. "A very powerful group of Englishmen," Lesperance continued. "They want the entire world as part of the British Empire, no matter the cost. But Astrid, Graves, and I are going to stop them. With the help of the other Blades of the Rose."

"Lesperance, enough," growled Graves.

Astrid Bramfield was at Lesperance's side in a heartbeat, alarmed and concerned. Though she still held her pistol pointed at Gemma, her other hand cupped Lesperance's face with tender anxiety. "What are you doing, revealing such secrets? This woman is a stranger."

Frowning, Lesperance murmured, "I don't know. I only know that we can trust her."

"But she's a *journalist*," was Astrid's reply. Her words fought against a sense of betrayal by one held so deeply within her heart. As Gemma had seen thousands of miles ago in the Northwest Territory, the connection and bond between Astrid Bramfield and Lesperance was palpable, enviable.

She'd never had that connection, that bond. And never would, given the choices in life she had made.

Gemma shouldered aside that familiar loneliness. "Don't blame him," she said quickly. "It's an . . . ability I have. To get answers."

"Ability?" Graves repeated, raising an eyebrow.

She did not want to dwell on something that might derail the entire conversation. "But Mr. Lesperance is right. You *can* trust me."

"There is no such thing as a trustworthy reporter," retorted Astrid Bramfield.

"You *did* say you were after a story," Graves added, somewhat more gently.

Gemma thought quickly. "I can write about these Heirs of Albion and expose them. Stop whatever it is they plan on doing."

Astrid Bramfield, despite her refined English accent, gave a very unladylike snort of disbelief. "It would not be so easy as that."

If Gemma was to find an ally, it would not be with this tough, guarded woman, so she turned to Catullus Graves. He watched her carefully, commingled caution and interest in his expression.

"Exposure in a national newspaper can bring even the most powerful men down," she said, meeting his gaze. Even behind the protective glass of his spectacles, his eyes were a dark pull. He observed her as if not entirely certain to what species she belonged.

"Astrid is right," he answered. "If it was simply a matter of publishing an exposé, such a thing would have been done long ago. A few printed words would not even dent the Heirs' armor. They are above trifles such as exposure and public opinion."

"Surely no one is *that* powerful."

"Miss Murphy," he said, holding her gaze, "you have no idea."

The gravity of his words, the seriousness of his handsome face, shook her like the deep tolling of a bell. Which meant she needed to know more.

"What could they possibly have at their disposal that gives them so much influence?"

Again, that tense silence fell, and Gemma could feel them all struggle against it, against her question.

"Magic," Astrid blurted, then clapped a hand over her mouth. She stabbed Gemma with an angry scowl.

Over the course of her life and professional career, Gemma had been the recipient of more than one angry scowl, and Astrid Bramfield's could not upset her. Gemma was much more interested in what the Englishwoman had just revealed. "Magic," Gemma repeated.

This was not a question, and so no one spoke.

With a deliberate gesture, Gemma put her derringer onto a nearby table, then gave it a small shove so that it moved out of her immediate reach. Now she was entirely unarmed.

Graves saw the move for what it was: a sign of faith. Theatrical, but effective. He tucked his own revolver into his belt, never taking his eyes from hers.

Lesperance followed suit, but Astrid Bramfield put away her gun only with great reluctance. Clearly, some great injury lay in her past, to make her so cautious.

Gemma's attention moved back to Graves, drawn to him as if by some inescapable force. He had been watching her, assessing her, and she prayed she would not blush again under his scrutiny. God! She was hardly an innocent child, and had seen—and done—rather a lot in her twenty-seven years. Yet nothing and no one made her blush as Catullus Graves could with just a look.

He narrowed his eyes. "Yes, magic, Miss Murphy." He spoke lowly as though recounting to a child a tale of terror.

"There exists in this world actual magic. It is too dangerous for any civilian reporter to confront—and live."

"I know."

"You might scoff, but—wait. You *know*?"

"Yes."

"About magic?"

"Yes."

"That it is *real*?"

"Yes."

He gaped. As did Astrid and Lesperance, who traded looks of disbelief with one another. Obviously, everyone had anticipated that she would *not* believe in magic. And, had she been anyone else, perhaps she wouldn't have.

"How—?"

Gemma turned to Astrid. "Assist me with something."

Guardedly, the Englishwoman approached.

"Please, stand out in the passageway."

"Why?"

The Englishwoman's caution grated. Gemma said, teeth gritted, "Just . . . please. I promise I won't seduce or kill anyone while you do."

With one final, suspicious glance over her shoulder, Astrid opened the cabin door and stood in the passageway. Gemma shut the door in the woman's face. A yelp of outrage penetrated the door.

Lesperance strode toward Gemma with a dark scowl, as ferocious as a wolf protecting its mate.

"I'm not going to harm her," Gemma said, raising up her hands. Without question, Lesperance would utterly annihilate anyone foolish enough to try to hurt Astrid. "Just a brief demonstration."

Barely appeased, Lesperance held himself back. A pulse in her throat proved to Gemma that she had narrowly avoided danger. "Now," Gemma said, turning to Graves, "lock the door."

A small frown knitted his brow, but he came closer to do

so. His boots brushed past the hem of her skirt, and, even though the gesture could not have been less intimate, Gemma's heart sped into a gallop. She'd spent months in the Canadian mountain wilderness, living close with trappers and miners and men of every stripe, the raw and the refined. Almost nothing any of them did or said affected her the way a simple brush of Catullus Graves's boots against her skirt could. And he seemed equally flustered, despite the fact that he was well past boyhood and most definitely a grown man.

Gemma made herself focus on the lock. It wasn't an ordinary lock on the door, but a small device that clearly was his own invention—an intricate network of metal fittings that looked as if it was assembled by tiny, industrious Swiss watchmakers. Graves's long, agile fingers worked quickly over the lock, and she heard a click.

"There," he said, straightening. He cleared his throat and stepped back, and Gemma realized that she had drifted closer to watch him at work.

"Now, Mrs. Bramfield," Gemma said through the door, "try to come in."

The doorknob rattled, but the door remained closed. "I can't," came the muffled reply.

"Use a little force."

This time, the knob rattled harder, the door shaking a bit, but it still remained shut. "Still can't," Astrid said. "I could try to kick it in."

"Not necessary." She turned to Graves, watching avidly. "You agree that I didn't *kick* the door open when I came in a short while ago." When he nodded, Gemma said, "If you would, unlock the door and let Mrs. Bramfield in."

He did so, and the Englishwoman strode back into the cabin, looking puzzled. "What did that prove?" she asked.

"That, when the door was shut and Mr. Graves's lock was set, you could not open the door." Gemma walked to it and opened the door again. "I'm going to stand in the passageway, and I want you to lock the door behind me. Just as you did with Mrs. Bramfield."

Graves, still frowning, gave a short nod. So Gemma did exactly as she said she would, going out into the passageway and letting Graves close and lock the door.

"All set?" she asked through the thick wood.

"Yes—all set," he answered.

Gemma placed her hand on the doorknob. And opened the door.

Instead of being met by a gun, three stunned faces greeted her entrance into the cabin.

She shut the door behind her again. "You asked how I might know of magic, Mr. Graves? There it is."

"Could be a trick," Lesperance noted.

"No," said Graves. "Nothing can open that lock except the key that I made." He gazed at her with a mixture of admiration and surprise. "Nothing, but magic."

"It's called the Key of Janus," Gemma explained. She felt a strange little glow of satisfaction to amaze not just Astrid and Lesperance, but a clearly brilliant mind such as Catullus Graves. "Something that's been in my mother's Italian family for generations. Dates back to ancient Rome. With it, we can open any door. Doesn't matter how strong the lock, how heavy the door. The Key opens them all." Though lately, even that had changed. But there was no need to mention that now.

"How did your family keep from becoming thieves?" Graves asked.

She grinned. "Many didn't." Then sobered. "But even more remained honest, despite the temptations to do otherwise. So you see"—she opened her hands wide—"I know that magic exists, since it's been in my family for hundreds, if not thousands, of years."

Astrid muttered something that might have been, "Blimey."

Graves thoughtfully rubbed his mouth. After staring at

her for a few moments, he strode toward the porthole and, bracing his hands on either side of the small window, gazed out at the moon upon the water.

"You can't scare me with tales of magic, Mr. Graves," Gemma said to his broad back. "Because I know all about it."

"Not *everything*," he corrected, turning back to face her. "The magic that's in your family, that is just one small, and relatively innocuous, part of the limitless magic that exists in the world. It can be found everywhere, from the most populous cities, to the farthest reaches of the wilderness."

"Including the Northwest Territory?" Gemma asked. According to Gemma's investigations at the trading post, Astrid Bramfield had been living alone in the Canadian mountains, until Catullus Graves and another man—now dead—had come to find her. Graves had returned from the wilderness with Astrid and Lesperance before setting off for England, with Gemma in pursuit.

"Exactly." His hands clasped behind his back. He had, at that moment, a professorial air, much more comfortable discussing such subjects than being in touching distance of her.

"Is that what those other Englishmen at the trading post were looking for? Magic?"

"You remember them?" he asked, taken aback.

Gemma's mouth curved, wry. "Hard to forget. A bigger bunch of pompous asses I never met—and, believe me, I've known quite a few." Especially in the newsroom of the *Tribune*. "They came in the same day that Mr. Lesperance arrived, looking for guides, and managed to insult everyone in the trading post."

Lesperance stood even straighter. "You," he said, staring at her. "I saw you there that day, too. Out of the corner of my eye. You were lurking behind some buildings. I went to follow—and then the Heirs grabbed me."

She *did* do rather a lot of lurking in her work, but couldn't feel too embarrassed about it. Being polite and proper never made anyone into a good journalist. "Heirs," she repeated. "You mentioned them before. Those Englishmen at the trading post were called Heirs?"

"The Heirs of Albion," Graves said, grim. "As we said, they want everything for England's empire, and that includes the world's magic."

Gemma blanched. "That's . . . awful." A sudden thought struck her. "Does that include *my* magic?"

His somber expression showed that he had already considered this possibility. "Very likely. Either it will be stripped from you or—" He broke off, frowning deeply.

"Or?" Gemma prompted.

"Or your magic, and you, will be enslaved. At any given moment, you could be summoned and forced to open any lock, any door. A vault holding a nation's wealth. A chamber guarding royalty, leaving the monarch vulnerable to an assassin's bullet."

A whooshing in her ears, the sound of her blood rocketing through the vast network of her body. Saint Francis de Sales, that would make her an accomplice to murder! Her stomach churned in disgust and revulsion.

"The Heirs wouldn't do that," she averred, then undermined her own certainty by adding, more faintly, "would they?"

"They have and they will." Graves's tone left no room for uncertainty. He stepped closer, his eyes containing experiences beyond Gemma's substantial imagination. "Which is exactly why you cannot be involved in anything to do with them. Even if the magic they wield is itself benign, their use of it is incredibly dangerous. Especially to someone like you."

Now that he stood in front of her, Gemma had to tilt her head back to look him in the eye. If the intent was to intimidate her, in that regard, the gesture didn't work. What his nearness *did* do, however, was make her aware of his warmth and scent—a mixture of bergamot, tobacco, and the intangible essence of him, his flesh and self.

"I don't mind a little danger." Her voice sounded husky to her ears.

His velvet-dark eyes moved over her face, lingering on the freckles dotting the bridge of her nose, before traveling down to idle on her mouth, and then lower. The dress Gemma wore was modest as a schoolmarm, with a high, buttoned collar and not a single bit of flesh exposed, save for her hands. But even in the most demure dress ever sewn, there was no concealing Gemma's figure. Not only had she inherited her mother's magic, but her hips and breasts as well. While Gemma had a mind for journalism, fate and family had given her the body of a burlesque dancer. Between her figure and her flaming, bright hair, Gemma's pursuit of professional legitimacy was an uphill battle.

Sometimes she resented her curvaceous figure and saw it as nothing more than an impediment to being taken seriously. And other times . . .

To see frank male admiration in Catullus Graves's face as he looked at her . . . she couldn't deny a certain . . . gratification.

When his gaze met hers again, his voice came out somewhat raspy. "It isn't a little danger. It's a lot of danger. And I refuse to imperil you at all by having you anywhere near the Heirs—or us."

A difference, she sensed, between his protectiveness and the condescension she endured back home. The male reporters at the *Trib* smirked and told her the life of a journalist was too perilous for a woman—her delicate constitution, her fragile sensibilities. Never mind that she could hold her liquor better than any of them, including Pritchard. Gemma could also swing a mean left hook and shoot a rifle. But, no, as befitting a woman's disposition and health she was supposed to be writing harmless little articles about putting up summer beans or the best ways to get grape stains out of a baby's pinafore.

Catullus Graves's concern for her safety had nothing to

do with whether or not he considered her capable, and everything to do with the fact that these Heirs of Albion were ruthless, murderous men. Men hell-bent on controlling the world's magic for their own selfish desires.

She recognized the danger was real. Just as she understood that she *had* to write this story. Joseph McCullagh knew reporting on the Civil War from the front lines could cost him his life, but the risk to himself was nothing compared to the need for the public to know about the horrors of war.

"I will still write about this," she challenged.

"No one will believe a word of it," he answered.

"Then tell me more! What harm could it do, if no one will believe what I write?"

Graves, still holding Gemma's gaze, shook his head. "The answer is no. Any more information will only jeopardize you further." His expression darkened. "Lives *will* be lost, Miss Murphy. Of that, there is no doubt. And I swear that yours will not be one of them."

"Will *your* life be lost, Mr. Graves?"

"Very possibly." Not a trace of fear or exaggeration in his voice, just a simple statement of fact. He might die soon, violently, and he accepted that.

Her heart plunged to contemplate his death, even though he was a stranger to her.

Gemma started when Catullus Graves's large, warm hands curved over her shoulders. Even through the layers of her clothing, she felt his touch move in swift, heated currents through her body. Temporarily stunned, she let him gently guide her backward. Then he took one hand from her, opened the door, and then lightly conducted her into the passageway.

"Forget everything you've heard here tonight, Miss Murphy," he advised.

"You know I can't do that."

"Much as it pains me to say so," he said, "that is your concern, not mine. But forget it you must."

"But—"

"I know you can open any door, but I will trust you not to open mine again." Regret seemed to cross his handsome, thoughtful face. "Good night, Miss Murphy. And, for the last time, good-bye."

With that, he closed the door. Leaving her alone in the passageway.

Gemma stood there for a moment before heading back to her cabin and vowing to herself that, whatever the costs, whatever risks to herself, she would have her story. There were still so many questions unanswered, and she would find those answers. Not even the formidable force of Catullus Graves could stand in her way.

Chapter 2

Tenacity

It amazed Catullus. He had been on board the ship for over a week and, during that time, not once had he seen Gemma Murphy. Now, he could not take a step outside his cabin without running into her.

Not literally—she maintained a respectable distance. But he had only to turn his head, and there she was. Across the dining room. Striding briskly past deck chairs and their blanket-swathed occupants as he took one of his own daily walks. Peering at him from behind a week-old newspaper in the reading room. Even the smoking lounge, the province exclusively for men. Catullus had gone in to indulge in an occasional pipe, and she entered the room right after him. Took a cheroot from an astounded steward, then lit up and cheerfully smoked, while Catullus and everyone else in the lounge gaped like guppies. No one had ever seen a respectable woman smoke before. It was . . . disturbing. Alluring.

He thought perhaps she might badger him with questions. Yet she never did. Whenever he saw her, she would smile cordially but preserve the space between them.

He couldn't tell if he was glad or disappointed that she had not entered his cabin again. Every step outside in the passageway had made his pulse speed. But she never came to him privately. Only hovered in the public parts of the ship like a brilliant phantom.

Catullus now stood upon the prow, watching the ship cleave the gray water as it neared Liverpool. Sailing directly to Southampton hadn't been an option, since the next steamship traveling to that town wouldn't depart New York for two weeks. Far too long a wait with so much at stake. So, he and Astrid and Lesperance had booked passage to Liverpool, with the intent to hop immediately on a train heading to the Blades' Southampton headquarters.

If he could, he would get out and tow the ship in, if only to get them to Liverpool faster. The ship docked tomorrow morning, and he was in a fever of impatience to reach their destination. What Astrid had revealed about the Primal Source—that it could actually embody the dreams and hopes of its possessor—had to be brought to the other Blades' attention. At headquarters, they could discuss strategies, formulate a plan. Catullus enjoyed plans.

Wind and sea spray blew across the prow. Not as cold as those Canadian mountains, but he took pleasure in the soft black cashmere Ulster overcoat he wore, with its handsome cape and velvet collar. Too windy for a hat—but he was alone and so there wasn't a breach of propriety.

Or *had been* alone. Catullus sensed, rather than saw, Gemma Murphy as she stepped onto the prow. His heart gave that peculiar jump it always did whenever he became aware of her. It happened the first time he saw her, at the tatty trading post in the Northwest Territory, and it happened now.

"Don't be an ass," he muttered to himself. She had said quite plainly that what she sought was a story. Nothing more.

He tried to make himself focus on the movement of the ship through the water, contemplating its propulsion mechanisms and forming in his mind a better means of water displacement. No use. His thoughts scattered like dropped pins when flaming hair flashed in his peripheral vision.

Bracing his arms on the rail, Catullus decided to be bold. He turned his head and looked directly at her.

She stood not two yards away—closer than she had been since the night in his cabin. That night, they had stood close enough for him to see all the delicious freckles that scattered over her satiny skin, close enough to see those freckles disappear beneath the collar of her prim dress, close enough to wonder if those freckles went all the way down her body.

God, don't think of that.

Like him, she now had her forearms resting upon the rail, her ungloved hands clasped, and her face turned into the wind, little caring, as other women might, about the unladylike color in her cheeks called forth by the wind. She stared out to sea, watching the waves and the seabirds drafting beside the ship, a little smile playing upon her soft, pink mouth. Something secret amused her.

Him? He told himself he didn't care if she found him amusing, terrifying, or wonderful. The division between them was clear. He was a Blade of the Rose on the most important mission ever undertaken. The fate of the world's magic, and freedom, lay in the balance. Pretty redheaded reporters with dazzling blue eyes and luscious figures were entirely, absolutely irrelevant. Dangerous, even.

But he watched her now, just the same. She wore the same sensible traveling dress, a plain gray cotton that had seen several years of service. So thoroughly was it worn that the fabric, as it blew against her legs, revealed that Gemma Murphy had on a very light petticoat and was most likely not wearing a bustle.

He found himself struggling for breath.

Keep moving upward, he told his eyes. And they obeyed him, moving up to see that the truly magnificent bosom of Miss Murphy was, at present, marginally hidden by a short blue jacket of threadbare appearance. The elbows were faded. She must move her arms quite a bit to get that kind of wear. An active woman.

What he wouldn't do to get that delectable figure and coloring into some decent clothing! Silk, naturally. Greens would flatter her best, but there were also deep, rich blues, luxuriant golds, or even chocolate browns. And he knew just the dressmaker, too, a Frenchwoman who kept a shop off Oxford Street. Madame Celine would be beside herself for the chance to dress a pre-Raphaelite vision such as Miss Murphy. And if he could see Gemma Murphy slipping off one of those exquisite gowns, revealing her slender arms, her corset and chemise . . . or perhaps underneath the gown, she would wear nothing at all. . . .

Catullus shook himself. What the bloody hell did he think he was doing, mentally dressing and undressing a woman he barely knew? A woman who made no secret of her ambition to expose the world of magic that Catullus, his family, and the Blades had fought so hard to keep hidden.

But instead of marching back to his cabin, as he planned, he simply remained on the prow, close, but not too close, to Miss Murphy.

He glanced over at her sharply, realizing something. Then swore under his breath.

Gemma Murphy blinked in astonishment when Catullus strode over to her. Clearly, she hadn't anticipated him approaching. He said nothing as he pulled off his plush, warm coat and then draped it over her shoulders. The overcoat was far too big for her, naturally, its hem now grazing the deck.

She also did not speak, but stared up at him. Her slim, pale hands held the lapels close. Catullus cursed himself again when he saw that she was shivering slightly.

"Don't you have a decent coat to wear?" he demanded, gruff.

"It got lost somewhere between Winnipeg and New York." Her voice, even out here in the hard wind, resounded low and warm, like American bourbon.

"Then get another."

Again, that little smile. "Lately, I haven't had the funds or time to see a dressmaker."

He had the funds, thanks to the Graves family's profitable side work providing manufacturers with the latest in production technology. And, even though time was in short supply, Catullus had managed to squeeze in an hour with one of Manhattan's best tailors, where he'd purchased this Ulster and three waistcoats. He usually avoided ready-made garments, but an exception had been made in these unusual circumstances, and the coat had been modified to his specifications. Catullus didn't patronize bigots, either, but if the color of his skin had bothered the tailor, the color of Catullus's money won out.

"Then perhaps you oughtn't stand out on the coldest part of the ship," he suggested dryly.

Looking up at him with her bright azure eyes, she said, "But I like the view."

Did she mean the sea or him? Damn it, he never could tell when a woman was saying something flirtatious or innocuous. Catullus didn't have his friend Bennett Day's skill with women—nobody did, except Bennett, and now Bennett was happily married and miles away. So all Catullus could do was blush and clear his throat, wondering how to answer.

Flirting was a skill he never mastered, so he plowed onward. "Why do you keep following me?" he asked.

"That's cocky," she answered. "Maybe *you* keep following *me*. This isn't such a large ship."

"I've been followed enough to know when it happens." And he'd had just as many bids on his life. Though he doubted Miss Murphy would try to stick a knife into his throat, which happened far too regularly.

Her eyes did gleam, though. "Have you been followed before? How many times? By whom? How did you elude them?"

"No one ever forgets you're a reporter, do they?"

Her laugh was even more low and seductive than her voice. "*I* never do. Why should anyone else?"

True enough. "As I said before," he pressed, "you will get no more from me, nor from Astrid or Lesperance. *There is no story.*"

"There most definitely *is* a story, Mr. Graves," she corrected smartly. "And either you tell it to me, or I'll conduct the investigation on my own. But I *will* get everything. I'm quite tenacious."

"So I've observed." In truth, tenacity was a quality he had long prized in others and tried to cultivate in himself. Most inventions took persistence to perfect. Almost nothing came together with merely a whim. If a mechanism wasn't working precisely right, he kept at it, refining, reassessing, until he created exactly what he intended.

In the case of stubborn American reporters, he could do with a little less tenacity.

This American reporter suddenly sank her hands into the front pockets of the overcoat and sighed with appreciation. "What a lovely coat! I've never felt anything so soft. What's it made of?"

"Persian cashmere."

"Bless me, how wonderful." She rubbed one creamy cheek against the velvet collar. "And so many pockets." She examined the inside of the coat and found that, indeed, it was lined with a multitude of pockets, and all of them holding something.

"I requested them added when I purchased the coat," Catullus said, watching her slim fingers trail over the pockets in a quick cataloguing.

"It's so nice and warm—though," she added with a sparkle in her eyes, followed by a lowering of reddish gold lashes, "you did me a favor by warming it for me."

With the heat of his body. Now sinking into hers. The

idea dried his mouth as a bolt of desire ran straight to his groin.

Catullus clenched his jaw in consternation. Either the woman was an extremely accomplished flirt and manipulator of men, or she simply had a knack for saying things that roused his normally restrained libido. Neither of the possibilities pleased him.

"Keep the coat," he muttered. "Have it sent to my cabin later." He started to stalk off.

"Wait, please!"

He turned at her words, knowing he was scowling and being altogether ungentlemanly, but finding it hard to stop himself. Being played with like a puppet on a string did little to coax him into good humor.

The flirtatious cast of Miss Murphy's face evaporated, leaving behind an expression he suspected was more true to the woman. Instead of deliberate charm, her eyes were alight with intelligence and determination. She gazed at him steadily, not a coquette but a woman with intent.

"I've been doing some thinking," she said, "since the other night in your c-cabin." She stumbled a bit over that last word, as if remembering the few moments they had been alone together. More playacting?

"I often think," he replied. "And find it to be a highly underutilized pastime."

A brief, real smile flashed across her face, and Catullus saw to his dismay a minuscule dimple appear in the right corner of her mouth. Precisely where a man might place the tip of his tongue before moving on to her lips.

"We're in agreement on that." She stepped nearer. "But what I've been thinking about, and can't seem to get out of my head, is the Heirs of Albion's goal."

The mention of his old foes brought Catullus's mind fully back into the present, and future. "A British empire that encompasses the globe."

"You're British, aren't you? Wouldn't such a goal work to your benefit?"

"I don't believe *any* nation should have that much power. And I don't believe one government should dictate how the rest of the world conducts its business." Warming to his topic, he forgot to be angry with Gemma Murphy, and instead spoke with unguarded feeling. "Further, capturing the world's magic to ensure that kind of despotism is abominable."

"And your friends, Mrs. Bramfield and Mr. Lesperance, they and others share your feelings. Mr. Lesperance called them . . ." She thought back for a moment. "The Blades of the Rose. Are you one of these Blades?"

At her question, he felt a subtle pressure, a force working upon him, coaxing him. *Tell her. She's trustworthy. Just open your mouth and speak the answer.* But he shoved that force away. An odd impulse, one he was glad he didn't give in to.

"This conversation is over, Miss Murphy." Before he could take a step, she reached out and took hold of his arm with a surprisingly strong grip.

"I'm sorry," she said quickly. "I won't ask more about them. Only—don't go."

He rather liked hearing her say that. Somewhat too much. Yet, despite his brain telling him to do just that— leave and never speak with her again—he stayed.

"I also think that what the Heirs are doing is horrible," she continued. "Not just because they might steal or use my magic. My Irish family in America fought against the British in the War of Independence. Some lost their homes. Others died." Her voice strengthened, grew proud. There was no artifice here. "It's always been a source of honor for the Murphys, myself included. We stood up and fought for freedom, regardless of the price."

"A justifiable sense of pride."

She accepted this with a nod. "I can't be a soldier—

I don't want to be one. But I can do something to help, something to stop the Heirs."

"Miss Murphy, your help *is not wanted*."

She did not flinch from his hard words, even as he regretted having to say them. She pressed, "Tell me everything. About the exploitation of magic. About the barbarity of the Heirs. Let me write about them."

With a sharp movement, Catullus turned to go. Yet she dogged him, putting herself in his path.

"You say no one will believe what I write," she said insistently, "but I don't think that's true. The public *will* believe, Mr. Graves. And they won't stand for such wickedness. They will rise up and—" She stopped, because he was laughing.

Not an amused laugh, but a harsh and bitter one. "Newspapers mean nothing to these men. They couldn't care less if you published their home addresses and bank accounts, plus a detailed description of every crime they had ever committed. A fly's buzzing, nothing more." He stepped closer, and, judging from the slightly alarmed look on her face, he must have cut a menacing figure. Good. She needed to be afraid.

"And do you know what they do with flies?" He pounded one fist into his own palm. "Crush them. Destroy them utterly."

"But the public," she foundered, "the government—"

"Can do nothing. Not the president of your United States, and not even the Queen. The Heirs serve her Empire, but neither she nor the prime minister nor all the damned members of Parliament can touch them. They answer to no one but themselves and their greed. And they will take a tender morsel such as yourself and make you wish *all* the Murphys had died in the Revolution so that you might never have been born."

The pink in her cheeks was gone entirely. Her freckles

stood out like drops of blood upon her chalky face. Catullus realized he had been shouting. He *never* shouted.

He collected himself, barely. A tug on his jacket, a straightening of his tie. "I do not like yelling at ladies," he said after a moment. "I don't like yelling at *you*. But the moment the Heirs of Albion become aware of your presence is the day you become one of the walking dead."

"Like you?" Her voice did not tremble.

"Pardon?"

"Are the Heirs aware of your presence?"

"Yes." More than aware. They hated him and his entire family. Considering that the Graves clan had been supplying the Blades of the Rose with inventions and mechanical assistance for generations, the Heirs would prefer if every single member of the Graves family were cold in their tombs.

"Yet you're still alive."

"Because, in this war of magic, I am a professional soldier. And you are a civilian."

"Civilians can fight. They did in the War of Independence."

"This isn't flintlock muskets and single-shot pistols, Miss Murphy. It's magic that can literally wipe a city off the face of the map. And I am telling you now for the last time"—he jabbed out with a forefinger—"you are not to get involved."

He spun on his heel and stormed away. This time, she did not try and stop him.

Several hours later, he was bent over the cramped desk in his cabin, adjusting the tension in some steel springs, when a tap sounded at his door. He found a steward outside, holding his coat.

"The lady said I was to give you this, sir," the young sailor said.

Catullus gave the lad a shilling and, after taking back the overcoat, sent him on his way.

With the door to his cabin closed, Catullus found himself holding the coat up to his face, inhaling. He pictured her in the coat, how deceptively delicate she appeared in its voluminous folds.

There. The scent of lemon blossom and cinnamon. Her scent. He could smell it all day and never grow tired of it. Even this small sense of Gemma Murphy thickened his blood.

A small square of paper was pinned to the lapel. He adjusted his spectacles to peer at handwriting, ruthlessly tamed into a semblance of legibility.

> *It* is *a beautiful coat, but you look much more dashing in it than I. Thanks for the loan.*—GM

He ran his thumb over the scrap of paper, picturing her ink-stained fingers. Perhaps he should write her a note. Apologize for his rudeness.

No. What he did was for her own protection, whether she believed him or not.

He dropped the beautiful Persian cashmere coat upon the floor and went back to work.

After the relative quiet of life aboard ship, the noise and commotion of the Liverpool docks threatened to knock one down to the floor. Catullus, Astrid, and Lesperance joined the rest of the *Antonia*'s passengers as the steamship approached the dock. From their vantage at the rail, they saw how the docks seethed with activity. Sailors, stevedores, and passengers all crowded along the waterfront in a chaos of sound and movement. Merchandise of every description was being hauled back and forth—American cotton, Chinese tea, African palm oil.

But slaves had made Liverpool. Not with their hands, but with the sale of their bodies. As Catullus watched the bustling dock draw closer, it didn't escape him that Liverpool—and England—once grew wealthy from the slave trade. Ships had sailed from the Liverpool docks, laden with guns and beads, to trade for men, women, and children ripped from their West African homes. Those same ships then made the grueling voyage to the Caribbean and the American South, and there sold their surviving human cargo—including Catullus's own family, generations ago. Then back to Liverpool with sugar, rum, cotton, and profit.

The slave trade had been officially abolished in England almost seventy years past, but Catullus felt its presence as the steamship approached the thriving docks.

All this, built by blood. Blood that ran in his veins.

Yet, despite this, he felt glad to be back in England again. It was, in all its conflicting existence, his homeland. His friends, the Blades, and his family were all here. He missed his workbench, and his tools, and the smell of oil, metal, and electricity. His workshop, nestled in the basement of the Blades' headquarters, remained his truest home.

He glanced over at Astrid, who was also watching the dock come closer. Her mouth was pressed into a thin, tense line, and her hand was threaded tightly with Lesperance's, her knuckles showing white.

"Back again," Catullus said gently.

She gave a tight nod. Four years ago, a grieving Astrid had fled England, and the Blades, after her husband had been killed on a mission. She had exiled herself in the Canadian Rockies, until Catullus had been forced to bring her back. But she wasn't returning with a broken heart.

Lesperance spared not a look for the bustle of the docks. His focus remained solely on Astrid, a concerned frown between his brows. "You can face this," Lesperance murmured, knowing what tumult she must feel. "It's only a pile of rocks. Nothing compared to the strength of you."

The thin press of her mouth softened as she turned to Lesperance with a small smile. Despite the fact that they stood in full view of everyone on the ship and the docks, Astrid leaned close and kissed Lesperance. Such unguarded warmth and tenderness in that kiss, returned passionately by Lesperance, who clearly didn't give a damn that anybody was watching.

Catullus looked away, fighting a quick pain, a sudden loneliness. Astrid had somehow been blessed to find love not once but twice, both times with good men. At forty-one years old, love still eluded Catullus.

His gaze alit upon Gemma Murphy, standing some distance down the rail. A group of passengers separated them, but he met her vivid blue eyes across the crowd.

In that crowd, amidst the cacophonous din rising up like a fist from the docks, Catullus found himself aware of only her. The brilliant gleam of her eyes, alive with intelligence and humor and will. A quick, potent flare of desire answered within him. More than desire. Something else, something deeper than a body's wants. And, in the way she suddenly drew herself up, widening those astonishing eyes, she felt it as well.

"Haunted still by your redheaded ghost," Astrid said behind him, her voice hard with suspicion.

Catullus came back to himself, who and where he was. He broke from Gemma Murphy's gaze to watch the dock.

"No amount of silence on my part will exorcise her," he said.

"Determined," Lesperance noted, admiring. Astrid shot him a glare.

Catullus made himself shrug with indifference. "We'll lose her once we come ashore."

"I wouldn't be so sure," said Astrid. "That bloody girl's resolved to attach herself to us—or rather to *you*."

He scrupulously avoided looking at Astrid and her sharp

eyes. "I'm the unattached male in our party. For a woman like her, I present the easiest target."

"For a huntress, she's damned fond of her prey," Astrid replied, heated.

The ship finally docking gave Catullus a reprieve. He, Astrid, and Lesperance joined the chattering, excited passengers as they disembarked. Somewhere in the crowd behind him was Gemma Murphy. But ahead of him was the most important mission of his life. He would forget her, as he must.

A few satchels made up their minimal luggage. As soon as it was collected, they started toward the train station. Everywhere was thick with people and voices and heavy drays loaded with cargo. The cheerful chaos of commerce.

Which made for hard going to reach the station on foot. It wasn't far, a quarter mile, and hiring a cab was impossible in this bedlam. Yet each step found the trio buffeted by movement. At this rate, they would reach the station by nightfall.

"Bugger this," Catullus muttered under his breath. He signaled Astrid and Lesperance to a narrow side street off the busy dock, blissfully empty.

They both nodded. It might not be a direct route to the station, but they'd reach their destination faster. And, in these circumstances, time was all. They had to reach Southampton as soon as possible.

So the three of them ducked into the side street. The only occupants were a few crates and a dog. The dog noticed Lesperance and trotted forward to him, tail wagging. Lesperance gave the animal a good scratch under the chin before striding briskly onward. The dog scampered away, cheerful in its existence.

"Always making friends," Astrid murmured.

"*They* aren't friends," Catullus said. He stared ahead, where the large figures of three men swiftly blocked the narrow street. He, Astrid, and Lesperance stopped, tensing. The men loomed nearer. All of them held knives.

"Heirs," growled Lesperance.

"No—they won't get their hands dirty here," Catullus said. "Thugs hired by the Heirs to watch the docks. Should have expected this."

He started to reach for his revolver before checking himself. This was civilized England, where men didn't wear guns in the streets, including himself. His pistol and shotgun were both packed away in the bags he carried. And, even if he could get to them quickly, firearms were too conspicuous, too noisy, too problematic for close-quarters fighting.

Evasion was a better option than engagement. Only fools raced into battle, if it could be avoided.

Catullus turned, thinking to lead Astrid and Lesperance back to the main dock. They might have a chance to lose their pursuers in the throng.

He cursed as two more men blocked the other end of the street. One of them pulled a cudgel from beneath his heavy coat, and the other, smiling brutally, brandished a dockworker's hook.

"Hardly ten minutes ashore, and already in a fight." But Astrid smiled coldly as she spoke, shifting into a ready stance. Meanwhile, Lesperance growled, half in warning, half in frustration. Even this side street was too public for him to truly unleash what he was capable of. His hands curled into fists as a substitute.

"I'll take the two behind us," Catullus said lowly.

"We've got the other three," answered Lesperance. A shared, clipped nod, and they broke apart.

Lesperance and Astrid sprang toward the advancing threesome. The thugs stood motionless for a bare second, stunned that those who were supposed to be the victims had, in fact, become aggressors. Catullus had a brief impression of Lesperance's swinging fists, and Astrid's own expert fighting skills as she dodged and struck. But Catullus's attention had its share of distractions and he focused on the two toughs coming at him.

He couldn't use his guns, but pulled a shotgun shell from a side pocket on a satchel, then dropped the bag. He kicked an empty crate at the advancing men. They ducked, and the crate shattered into planks and splinters. The bloke with the cudgel recovered faster than his comrade, lunging forward and swinging out with his heavy club. Catullus neatly sidestepped the blow. Then the cudgel hit a brick wall lining the street. The bricks exploded with a flash of blue light.

Catullus shielded his eyes from the glare. He leapt back to see a hole the size of a door where the cudgel had hit. The man wielding it laughed, a guttural rasp.

"That's right, guv," he chortled with a Liverpudlian roll to his words. "Got me a little something extra, thanks to the gents what hired us." He held the club up, and Catullus saw a small mark branded into the wood. Catullus had seen that lion brand before on other clubs, knives, and even the wooden handles of guns. It imbued whatever had been branded with the Heirs' particular variety of dark magic— including a hired tough's cudgel.

The man swung the club again, this time hitting the ground. Another blast of light. Catullus staggered from the concussion as the pavement split apart into gaping fractures.

As he struggled to gain his footing, the other thug pounced, hook swinging. Catullus blocked the wicked curved gaff, then planted a foot in the man's gut and shoved him back.

His comrade plowed toward Catullus again.

"I have a little something extra, as well," Catullus said. Gripping the brass shotgun shell, he slammed its bottom down onto a nail sticking from a shattered crate.

The small blast shook him, ran in shock waves up his arm, but it was enough to shoot a little ball of glinting material from the cap. The ball spread into a wire net, which tangled itself around the advancing thug.

For a few moments, the tough could only flounder and swear, snarled in the net, his cudgel useless against the snare.

"Never tried that by hand before," Catullus murmured to himself.

His companion shoved past and came at Catullus. The hook swung. Catullus lightly stepped back, then grabbed the man's arm. It was difficult, since Catullus's hand still buzzed with the aftereffects of the shell's blast. They grappled, fighting for footing and control of the gaff. Catullus was taller than the thug, but the man was heavier and furious that the intended target wasn't going down easily. They wrestled, careening back and forth between the walls lining the street. A hot trail of pain gleamed as the hook caught the top of Catullus's cheekbone.

With a sudden grunt, the man collapsed against Catullus. Peering over the unconscious man's shoulder, Catullus saw something rather amazing.

Gemma Murphy held a heavy rope, one end tied into a large, weighty knot. The stain of red and clump of hair attached to the knot testified to how hard she had hit Catullus's assailant.

"Dead?" she asked.

Catullus shoved at the man heavily against him. The man crumpled to the ground. "No, but he smells like it." He strode to where the cudgel-wielding tough still struggled against the net. With one quick punch, Catullus knocked the man unconscious. Like his associate, the thug collapsed to the ground.

"Deft," Catullus murmured, glancing between the rope she held, then up at Miss Murphy.

She looked back at him with a gleam of triumph hidden beneath careful sangfroid, then turned to the net, still covering the insensate thug. "What are you doing with a net inside a shotgun shell?"

"I had planned on using it for fishing. It has a much smaller charge than with a typical shell." Which had kept him from blowing his own hand up. He shook it out, losing the last traces of the reverberations.

"Diabolical," she added, eyeing the intricate wire net.

Catullus smiled modestly.

Then Gemma Murphy glanced behind him with a frown. "Your friends—"

Hell. He'd been so amazed at Miss Murphy's appearance, he had almost forgotten Astrid and Lesperance. He turned to them now. One of their assailants lay upon the ground, unconscious or dead Catullus could not tell. The other two were giving a hell of a fight. Lesperance bared his teeth as he and his attacker traded punches, while Astrid sent a flurry of deliberate kicks toward the stomach and legs of the thug advancing on her.

The man bearing down on Astrid glanced over to see Catullus standing with Gemma Murphy. His watery little eyes took stock of everyone in the alley, as though cataloguing them for a future report to the Heirs. Yet the thug not only saw Catullus, Astrid, and Lesperance, but Gemma Murphy as well, including her in their ranks. Too late did Catullus step in front of her, shielding her from his gaze. Astrid also darted a glance in Catullus's direction, giving her attacker a tiny opening. But instead of launching an assault, the man spun on his heels and darted away. He'd calculated the odds and found them decidedly not in his favor. So he fled.

His comrade wasn't so lucky. Lesperance punished him with punches until the remaining thug slid in a boneless, bloody heap to the grimy pavement.

"Everyone all right?" Catullus asked.

Astrid nodded, and Lesperance grunted an assent, gingerly adjusting his jaw.

"And you?" Catullus turned to Miss Murphy.

She also nodded, though she held up one slim hand, revealing red, chafed fingers "Little bit of rope burn." She shrugged off this small injury.

"What are you doing here?" Astrid demanded.

Miss Murphy was not fazed by Astrid's harsh tone. "I had a feeling that trouble might follow you off the ship." She glanced over at the huge hole and fissures left by the cudgel, and raised a brow. "I see I was right."

Catullus took advantage of the brief lull to retrieve the cudgel. With a knife, he scratched off the lion brand, rendering it just a piece of heavy wood. He tossed it to the ground and was gratified that it only rolled along the pavement, rather than cleave a gaping hole in the street.

Miss Murphy still had her questions. "How did they know to find you in Liverpool?"

"The Heirs must have hired men to watch all the major ports," said Catullus. He was all brisk business as he collected his bags. "Bristol, London. Southampton, of course. And Liverpool. We have to leave immediately. Before more Heir hooligans arrive."

"One of them got away," Lesperance rumbled. "I can give chase."

"How?" asked Gemma Murphy. "He's probably long gone by now, lost in the crowd."

"I've got a few ways of tracking someone," Lesperance said, with a small, dark smile.

Miss Murphy didn't understand, but this wasn't the moment for explanations.

"No time," Catullus said. "The authorities might be here any minute and we have to get out of Liverpool *now*. Grab your bags." He strode toward Gemma Murphy and wrapped a hand around her slender, strong wrist. She glanced down at the sight, then up again, a question in her eyes.

"What are you doing?"

He began to pull her toward the end of the street, toward the train station. "Keeping you alive."

Chapter 3

Miss Murphy Makes the Leap

Gemma hurried to keep up with Catullus Graves's long-legged strides as they cut through the streets of Liverpool. She had no idea where he was taking her, but he seemed to know exactly where to go. Gemma darted a quick glance behind. None of the thugs followed, though Astrid and Lesperance remained vigilant as they trailed after her and Graves.

"Those men," she panted. Damn those weeks of travel, leaving her softer and less conditioned. "They were sent by the Heirs?"

"Yes." Clipped and alert, he didn't spare Gemma a glance. But he didn't release her, either. His hand was an unbreakable hold around her wrist. "And they saw you." This he said with anger hard in his voice. Anger at her? She had just *helped* him.

When a train station loomed into view, Gemma tried to dig her heels into the pavement. "Don't send me away."

He didn't slow, her resistance proving useless against his strength. "I'm not," he growled. "We are taking a train to Southampton, and you're coming with us."

So prepared was she to argue her case, she thought she misheard him. "What?"

On the steps leading into the station, he finally did stop, swinging around to face her. Behind his spectacles, his eyes were deepest brown, gleaming with fury and resolve. "I was a damned idiot," he snarled. "I let one of those bastards see you, and now your life isn't worth tuppence."

His anger was for himself, not her. But she couldn't allow that. "He only saw me for a second. Surely that's not enough."

"For the Heirs, it's all they need. It won't take much for them to learn who you are, and know that you fought on the side of the Blades. That means your life is imperiled." He paced up the stairs to the station, with her still in tow. "The safest place for you now is with me."

A fast chill ran along Gemma's spine to think that she was now the target of a ruthless band of powerful, magic-wielding men. She'd experienced danger before—including a trio of unruly fur trappers desperate for female company, though they were less inclined to pursue her after she shot one in the hand and nearly emasculated another. There had been many other brushes with risk. But nothing like this. Nothing where she truly felt her life was threatened.

Graves would keep her close, keep her safe. There was no doubt in him. While she was in his care, he would ensure no harm would come to her.

Inside, the station teemed with activity, almost as chaotic as the docks. Gray sunshine poured in from large skylights, illuminating the cavernous station and people swarming along platforms, where huge, shining black trains waited and steamed. None of the thousands of people here had any idea that a war was being fought for the world's magic. But they might learn, when she wrote of it.

If she lived.

Graves stopped in the middle of this industrial and

human maelstrom. Astrid and Lesperance caught up, and the Englishwoman shot Gemma a suspicious glance.

"She's coming with us, then?"

"One of them saw her."

Astrid nodded with grim understanding, though it was clear from her severe expression that she didn't care for Gemma's presence.

Well, Gemma didn't much like Astrid Bramfield, either. "You aren't the only woman who knows how to fight." She had proved it, minutes ago.

"Good." But there was no faith or gratitude in the Englishwoman's silver eyes.

"Miss Murphy's shown she can be trusted," Lesperance said.

"She's demonstrated she can swing a rope," countered Astrid. "That doesn't mean she's trustworthy."

"She's still coming with us," said Graves.

"And standing right here," added Gemma. She didn't care for being talked about like a unmatched, smelly shoe.

"I'll purchase the tickets." Graves finally released Gemma's wrist to move toward the ticket counter, and she found she wanted his touch again.

"Wait!"

He swung around at her cry. She closed the distance between them. When she reached up to his face, he pulled back with a frown.

Gemma licked her thumb and rubbed it over his cheek, where the thug's hook had cut him. The contact of wet skin to skin was a visceral charge. "You had a little blood on your face," she breathed in the close space between them.

The air of hard authority fell away from him for a moment as his frown disappeared. He swallowed, tried to speak, then, finding no words, turned and strode toward the ticket counter. His long, dashing coat billowed behind him as he paced away.

Gemma watched him, saw the crowds part ahead of him,

deferring to his natural air of command. She had seen the swift, confident grace of his movement in combat, the speed of his mind and body working together to create a man of devastating potency. Yet, with her, he became cautious, uncertain. What a paradox, one that fascinated her not as a journalist, but as a woman.

She broke her gaze to find Astrid Bramfield studying her. Gemma sent a challenging look right back. Yet, for some reason, the Englishwoman's gaze was more contemplative than critical.

A few minutes later, Graves returned and handed each of them tickets. "We'll have to change trains a few times, but we should reach Southampton by tonight."

"And then?" asked Gemma.

"And then," he said, "we will convene with the rest of our friends, plan our attack strategy. Nothing can be gambled when so much is at stake. And you will remain in Southampton under guard whilst we battle the Heirs."

"Under guard," she repeated, glowering. "You mean, held prisoner."

He did not blink at her accusation. "Call it what you like. But you *will* be safe." He turned away. "We have a train to catch."

The world rushed by, smokestacks and suburban developments giving way to farmland and fields. Gemma sat at the window, watching England as it unfolded around the rushing train, her mind filling with images and words as it always did whenever she observed something new.

A tame place, she decided, compared to home. Everything she saw out the train's window seemed old, weighted down with millennia and history. Green, gentle hills and low stone walls. Farmhouses and biscuit-tin villages. She tried to picture the magic that must exist beneath this cultivated country, the magic the Heirs of Albion would seize for themselves to ensure England's dominance.

Yet when Catullus Graves sat opposite her in the train carriage, thoughts of secret wars for magic fled from her mind. She couldn't look away from him. He'd cleaned the cut on his face and now presented the image of an elegant gentleman traveling. One would hardly suspect that not an hour earlier, he'd been fighting in a Liverpool street like a born warrior. But Gemma saw the small powder burns on his left hand and knew that his outward sophistication made up one small part of the whole.

Gemma openly studied him now.

He was abstracted, deep in contemplation, with that ever-present line between his brows. She wondered what he thought about: The Heirs? A new invention? Her?

His distracted gaze drifted to the window, then, restless, moved over her. And as soon as that happened, he suddenly remembered that she was in the carriage, too, and his demeanor changed.

He focused on the landscape speeding past, almost as if too shy to look at her. He'd been so imposing at the train station, and then, moments earlier, he'd been the picture of a brooding general on the eve of battle. Now he was diffident. They were alone in the carriage, Astrid Bramfield and Lesperance having gone to the dining car for something to eat. The air, as it often did when she and Graves were alone together, became charged.

A somewhat awkward silence stretched between them, with the clatter of the train as a steady undertone.

"Did you really make that shotgun shell with the net in it?" she asked.

He turned to her, guarded. "I did."

"I've never seen anything like that. It was remarkable."

He flushed slightly at her praise, and tugged at the cuffs of his perfectly aligned shirt. "A very simple device, I assure you."

"Not to me."

"Inventions and mechanical devices are something of a family trade."

She was amazed at his genuine humility. "They should be proud of you, then."

He gazed at her with hooded eyes. "You are still going to remain in Southampton, Miss Murphy."

Gemma snorted. "I'm not trying to *flatter* you into letting me stay with you, Mr. Graves. My compliment is sincere."

"Ah." He was abashed. "Well . . . thank you. And, if I may say, Miss Murphy—"

"Go ahead and call me Gemma," she said. "Calling me 'Miss Murphy' is too formal, especially after I saved your bacon today."

"You didn't 'save my bacon,'" he said, indignant. "I was perfectly in control of the situation. But," he added at her noise of protest, "you *did* lend a hand in that fight, and for that, I do thank you." He made a small bow, one hand pressed to his chest.

She found herself mollified. The man *could* speak so beautifully. Gemma felt she could listen to him describe the digestive systems of jellyfish and she would be enthralled.

"In fact," he went on, "I cannot think of another woman, who wasn't a Blade, who could handle herself as admirably."

The variety of blandishments Gemma received from men often involved her looks. All surface, no substance. Her appearance had nothing to do with *her*, or who she was, not truly.

"I don't think anyone's ever complimented me on the way I swung a heavy rope in a brawl." When he made choked noises of apology, she added quickly, "It's the best compliment I've ever been given."

"Really?" He blinked at her.

"Usually I get some nonsense about my eyes or my hair

or other trifling things." She made a dismissive gesture with her hand. "But, to be praised for how I fight—*that* means something. So, thank you."

"Oh." He fidgeted with the lapel of his coat. "You're . . . welcome."

Then, because she had come so great a distance for so much, she went on. "That's not the first time you've mentioned these people I believe you called the Blades of the Rose. Who are they?"

He tensed, either because she was prying into secrets or because her question had reminded him of the ever-present threat.

Whichever it was, she wanted an answer. "Mr. Graves—Catullus—"

Her using his given name startled him. And, judging by his indrawn breath, it wasn't entirely unpleasant to hear Gemma call him thusly. She actually liked it, herself. The shape and feel of his name in her mouth, with its hard opening consonants falling into a soft ululation. A metaphor, perhaps, for the man who bore the name? A hard exterior concealing something much more sensitive beneath.

"You have told me about the Heirs of Albion," she said. "You have told me about the world's magic. But there is more. I know that the Blades of the Rose, whoever they might be, are also involved."

Still, he hesitated.

Gemma leaned forward, earnest. "You say you want to keep me safe—"

"I do." His voice was firm with resolve.

"Then prove it, and tell me all. How can I begin to protect myself if I do not know everything? Without full understanding, I'm just fumbling around in the dark, at risk from the Heirs as well as my ignorance." She refused to play the flirt and charm information from him. If Catullus was to open up to her, it must be because he saw something within her to trust and value. She could not respect herself to resort to cheap ploys, and she needed that self-respect. Without it, all that she worked so hard for was valueless.

For some long moments, they stared at each other. She watched him assess her, his perceptive gaze held with hers, as if he sought to delve into her innermost thoughts.

Strangely, she did not resent this. For the first time in years, she actually welcomed a man into her mind, knowing instinctively that if anyone was to truly understand who she was as a person—not a woman, not a journalist, but the true and most essential part of herself—it would be *this* singular man, Catullus.

So she let him look, holding herself open to his scrutiny.

Peculiar. She hadn't realized she needed this kind of openness until now. Hard lessons had taught her to keep her deepest self in reserve. Too many times, she'd left herself open, vulnerable, and been wounded by careless, heedless men. Men like Richard. She evolved into a hard-edged reporter and thought herself all the better for it.

She'd been wrong. Some part of her still yearned for closeness, for connection. And that need revealed itself now as she let Catullus Graves gauge her.

After many lifetimes, he gave a barely perceptible nod, reaching an internal decision. Gemma's breath left her in a rush, and she only then realized she had been holding it.

"Magic exists in many forms," he said with his rich, deep voice. "Sometimes it's in families, such as yours; sometimes a single person can possess it. But it is also found in objects that are scattered across the globe. They are potent objects whose powers can run the gamut from the benign to the malevolent."

"Like the club that thug was using in Liverpool," she volunteered.

"No—that was a simple charm on an ordinary item. The objects I am speaking of hold vast power. These objects," he continued, "are known as Sources, and Heirs search the globe for them, seeking to add the Sources to their arsenal, crushing anything and anyone who stands in their path."

The idea was beyond horrible. "Something has to be done to protect the Sources," Gemma objected.

"Something is done," Catullus said. "By me and Astrid. And people like us. The Blades of the Rose."

The name on his lips sent a shiver through Gemma, as though hearing a long-forgotten enchantment.

Catullus saw the name register with her, then went on. "It is the sworn mission of the Blades to safeguard Sources around the globe from the Heirs, and others like them. This battle we're heading into now with the Heirs . . ." He watched his hands curl into fists. "It will be the biggest any of us has ever faced. We've never gone up against the Primal Source, but we have to before the Heirs solidify their power. We have no idea if any of us will survive. But we have to fight. All Blades fight not just for magic, or England, but for everyone."

"A noble calling," Gemma murmured, but her blood was chilled. He spoke so easily of the possibility of being killed! "Like frontier lawmen."

"Or errant knights." He allowed a small smile to tilt his mouth, amused either by the accuracy of their descriptions, or their complete misread. Yet, given the inherent nobility in his bearing, Gemma hopefully suspected the former.

"But the Primal Source I heard you speaking of," she continued, "what, exactly, is it?"

"The Source from which all other Sources arise. The origin of magic, and repository of mankind's imagination. Whoever possesses the Primal Source has at his or her disposal the greatest power ever known."

"And now the Heirs of Albion have it," Gemma recalled.

"Have it, and unlocked it." Catullus scowled out the window, mind almost visibly churning. "Several months ago."

She saw the focus in him, the determination and intent.

This war with the Heirs was his life—and possibly death. "Unlocked?"

"Accessed the Primal Source, allowing its power to be felt all over the globe, in all magic."

"That explains it, then," Gemma murmured. When he raised an eyebrow in a silent question, she explained, "Around the same time you said the Primal Source was unlocked, something changed with the Key of Janus. I could open more than just physical doors."

"Meaning what?" he asked.

"Mental doors." Gemma pressed a fingertip to her temple. "When I ask someone a question, they *must* answer me. That's how I was able to follow you three all the way from Canada. I asked anyone you might have met along the way, and they told me exactly what I needed to know. Including the ticketing agent at the New York harbor, and"— she cast a slightly apologetic glance at Catullus—"your friends, I'm afraid."

"Ah," he said, mouth wryly tilting. "That's what I felt when you asked me questions. As if a gate inside my mind wanted to spring open and reveal itself to you."

"What I don't understand," she wondered, "is how you were able to resist it. No one has, until now."

"I have been a Blade of the Rose for years," he answered, dry with understatement. Gemma could see plainly in the way he held himself that he was a veteran of at least two decades. She had seen him fight just that morning, with the skill of a hardened soldier. "I have been exposed to magic many, many times. No doubt I've developed something of both a sensitivity and resistance to it."

"Or perhaps your mind is simply too strong."

He raised a wry brow. "Entirely possible. However," he added, stern, "I don't want you to use that magic on me, Astrid, or Lesperance again."

"I won't," she said at once, and felt for the first time stirrings of misgivings about the usage of her magic.

Dwelling too much on her own use—or abuse—of magic wasn't a pursuit Gemma wanted to engage in overmuch. She steered the conversation back to more relevant topics. "Tell me more about what I . . . overheard . . . outside your cabin, that the Heirs sought Astrid because of her knowledge of the Primal Source. They don't know how to use the Primal Source?"

"Not fully," answered Astrid, coming with Lesperance into the carriage. The Englishwoman sat down beside Catullus, with Lesperance lowering himself down next to Gemma. Even though Lesperance's attention was fully given to Astrid, Gemma could feel from the man waves of energy, as though he was barely containing some great force within. He did not speak much, but still cleaved a presence into the world.

She would have found him fascinating, this Canadian Indian in European clothing, far from his own home. He clearly loved the flinty Englishwoman, Astrid Bramfield, as she loved him in equal measure. Doubtless Lesperance had a story to tell, one she would have gone to great lengths to discover. Yet, even this intriguing man could not hold her attention when Catullus Graves was near.

She forced herself to focus. They were discussing the Primal Source.

"But," Astrid went on, "as you heard when *eavesdropping*, that doesn't mean the Primal Source will not work on its own. Even without direct guidance, the Primal Source will act upon the Heirs' wishes."

"Which means disaster." Gemma felt herself turn ashen and cold, thinking about what that meant. If the Primal Source was as powerful as these people believed—and Gemma didn't doubt their veracity—then whatever it unleashed upon an unsuspecting world would be devastating. Just the scale of lives that could be lost in the ensuing catastrophe turned her stomach.

"Whatever is coming, the Blades will face it," Catullus said, resolute. "We'll fight until the threat has been eradicated."

"Or until there are none of us left," Astrid added. Lesperance, grim-faced, reached across to grip her hand, but did not deny this possibility.

Gemma stared at Catullus, no doubt eyes wide as apples. "With your own magic?"

Astrid and Lesperance shared a quick glance before Catullus said, "Not precisely. One of the ways in which Blades protect magic is to use none of it themselves, not unless it is given to them by birth or gift."

"That's ridiculous!" Gemma protested.

His gaze frosted. "Ridiculous or not, it is our code. To use magic that isn't ours is to risk becoming like the Heirs, greedy for more power. So we take pride in our difference."

She knew something of pride. "There are only three of you," she noted.

"There are more of our numbers. Not as many as the Heirs, but enough to make a go of it." He nodded toward the window, where the countryside sped past. "They're gathering in Southampton now."

"Where I'll be held captive," Gemma added.

"Only for your protection," he clarified. As if that made it better.

"Until when?"

"Until it is safe."

"When might that be?" she pressed.

His eyes fixed on her before sliding away. "I don't know."

Taking risks was something she did as if by biological compulsion. As a child, she alone out of three sisters and four brothers dared to go inside the abandoned house on their street. Later, at the age of eighteen, after giving her virginity to Robby Egan, instead of accepting his offer of marriage, Gemma left home and moved into a boardinghouse close to the *Tribune* offices, determined to become a journalist and not a young wife. She once followed a fire engine on horseback when several huge warehouses went up in flames so she might report on the destruction firsthand. She disguised herself as a charwoman to observe the late-night dealings in a local politician's office.

Hell, she even trekked out to the Northwest Territories in search of a story, and then journeyed alone all the way across the continent and the Atlantic Ocean. She could no more stop herself from taking a risk than most people could keep from sneezing. It was a necessity.

Yet when Catullus insisted that she must go to and remain at the Blades' Southampton headquarters, she knew better than to try to evade his escort. Only someone picklebrained would attempt to slip away. The Heirs were aware of her. She had already seen a minuscule portion of what they were capable of. Gemma had no desire to be confined in Southampton, but she had even less desire to be dead.

So, when she announced that she was heading to the dining car for a bite to eat, and Catullus insisted that he join her, she didn't take umbrage. In fact, she was glad for the company.

For *his* company, in particular.

They sat at a neat little table spread with a white cloth, and, at Catullus's direction, plates of cold sandwiches and cups of hot tea were brought by a solicitous attendant. Gemma watched with badly concealed amazement as the attendant eagerly jumped to accommodate Catullus's wishes.

"You seem shocked by something, Miss Murphy," he remarked.

"Gemma," she corrected.

"Gemma," he said, and gave a little smile at her name.

She felt herself dissolve like a sugar cube in tea. Then shook herself to awareness. "It's very different here in England than it is at home."

"How is that?"

No way to be delicate about it. "You wouldn't have been seated in a dining car on an American train."

Yet he did not look angry or surprised by her blunt comment. He tipped a small silver pitcher of milk into his tea, and it looked like a child's toy in his large hand. Yet, for all that, he had a precise, polished way of moving.

Still, when he spoke, his voice was reserved, almost cool. "And you prefer the American policy."

"God, no!" Gemma stared, horrified. "I find it . . ." She couldn't find a word strong enough. "Disgusting." That barely covered the depth of her feelings. "What damned difference does it make what the color of someone's skin is?"

A man and a woman, seated nearby, gasped at her coarse language and vehemence.

She ignored them. Other people's opinions didn't matter. But *his* did.

Relief, then, to see his gaze thaw. And restrained approbation take the place of coldness.

"I'm glad you don't share your countrymen's views," he said.

She felt compelled to defend her home. "Not *all* Americans are like that. But," she conceded, "some are. And their intolerance disappoints me."

"I experienced it when I was in America." He took two meticulous spoonfuls of sugar and stirred them into his tea. She could watch his beautiful table manners for hours. "Not only on trains, but in hotels, restaurants. And I had to book passage on a British ship to come home. Almost all the American companies wanted me to travel third class or steerage."

"I'm . . . sorry." She reddened, embarrassed by her countrymen's bigotry.

"It stunned and upset me, at first," he admitted. "I'm not used to that kind of outright prejudice."

"It hasn't been that long since the War." Ten years, though that didn't make it right.

"Yes, but this was in the civilized North," he said, but there wasn't any rebuke for her in his voice.

"I do love my country," Gemma said, looking out at the passing English landscape, a rush of green and gray so unlike the wide cornfields of Illinois. "And it also embarrasses the hell out of me, sometimes."

He raised his teacup and smiled over its rim. "I know a little about conflicted feelings for one's homeland." His expression darkened. "We're on a train speeding toward a battle with men who claim to uphold Britain's finest virtues. The Heirs say they want the advancement of our nation—but the cost is too high. The world may pay the price. Soon. Within days. If the Blades cannot stop them."

She shuddered, thinking of how close everything was to disaster. Days. And yet she and Catullus sat on a train, passing towns and farms that had no idea what war brewed. Her family in Chicago—they were wholly unaware that their lives could be completely torn apart. But Gemma knew, and she felt the weight of responsibility begin to settle on her shoulders.

"Do the Heirs truly want everything to become English?"

"To them, the height of civilization is England. And I don't believe that this country should serve as the world's model."

"So there isn't perfect equality in England?"

A rueful laugh, and then a sip of tea. Despite the many turbulent thoughts filling her mind, she could not help but watch his mouth upon the delicate porcelain. He closed his eyes for a moment, the clean angles of his face lit with sensuous pleasure. The sight entranced Gemma, made her imagine things she had no business imagining. To distract herself, she took a bite of her sandwich. How did they get the ham so incredibly thin?

"Ah, even on a train," he sighed, opening his eyes, "one can't get a finer cup of tea than in England."

"I like coffee better," she said.

He shook his head over her barbarism. "No wonder our nations made war against each other. Twice. But, to answer your question, there is no perfect equality. Even here. It's not as overt as in America, but, trust me"—and here his expression sharpened again—"skin color *does* make a difference. I'm judged before I speak, before I act."

"I know a little about being prejudged," she said, echoing his earlier words.

He fixed her with an inquisitive look. "Female journalists are so uncommon?"

"Not so rare if they want to write about *feminine* things—clothes, food, babies." She felt her mouth twist, though she fought against bitterness. Gemma had no quarrel with clothes, food, or babies, but she didn't want to write about them. So many other things snared her interest. Richard hadn't understood that. Hadn't understood her, despite his claims to the contrary.

"And if they write about the Northwest Territories?"

"There is no 'they.' There's only me. So far, I'm the only one." She leaned forward, lowering her voice as if letting him in on a secret. "Most people think I'm a bit crazy."

Catullus leaned forward as well, velvety eyes dancing as he whispered back, "Me too."

They shared a smile, something for the two of them alone. They remained like that for a small while, warming themselves with this unforeseen gift. The ever-present threat faded briefly as they discovered unexpected similarities linking them, a connection neither of them could have predicted. Outwardly, they had nothing in common, nothing bridging the sizable gap between them. Yet Gemma learned well from her journalist's work that most things of value did not dwell on the surface, but took a careful eye and patience to uncover.

58   *Zoë Archer*

Here, then. This man—inventor, adventurer, his skin a different color than her own—he spoke to her and of her work without judgment, as though they truly were equals.

Suddenly, Catullus pulled back, glowering. Gemma thought that his forbidding expression was for her, until she saw his gaze fixed behind her. She turned slightly in her seat to see what angered and alarmed him.

Two men were coming into the dining car. Gemma quickly assessed them. One was of average height, a bit stout, with a neatly trimmed moustache. The other was taller, dark haired. Both had the pale skin of the upper ranks, with the snooty demeanor to prove it. Even on the steamship, none of the other passengers belonged to this class. This was her first time ever seeing the British gentry. They moved into the dining car as if it, and everything they saw, were their possessions.

Gemma, democratic, disliked them on sight.

An attendant approached them, gesturing toward an empty table. They began to pepper the man with questions, which the attendant stammered to answer.

She turned back to Catullus, and now he looked downright dangerous. He tore his gaze from the men and forced himself to look out the window, as if the view fascinated him. "Get up slowly," he said between gritted teeth. "Don't draw attention to yourself. Make for the other exit and head straight to our compartment."

Gemma's heart kicked. "It's them, isn't it? The Heirs."

"Yes, now *go*. While the attendant has their attention. And don't look at them."

She rose up from her seat as casually as she could, all the while aware of the men behind her. Catullus followed suit, and set a handful of coins on the table. Gemma almost smiled. They were trying to evade the deadly Heirs of Albion, and he was *still* leaving tips. A true gentleman.

She and Catullus had just reached the door at the other

end of the car when a man's voice hissed loudly, "It's Graves and that woman!"

Neither Gemma nor Catullus wasted any time. He threw open the door, pulled her through to the next car, then slammed the door. Through the glass, she saw the men running toward them.

"Blast," Catullus growled. "Can't lock the door. Run."

Gemma went as fast as she could, plunging down the aisle of the second-class car as confused passengers watched from their seats. She heard Catullus close at her heels.

Through another carriage, and another. At her back came the sounds of the adjoining doors opening and slamming shut, men's footsteps hurrying toward her and Catullus. She glanced quickly at some of the passengers watching the spectacle. Couldn't someone help?

She reached another door. Two cars down was their compartment. Once they reached it, she wasn't sure what was going to happen, but reach it they must. At the least, Astrid and Lesperance could lend a hand. Four against two offered better odds.

Gemma pulled open another door and started up the aisle, but turned when she did not hear Catullus behind her. He stood on an empty seat beside the door, bending to keep from knocking against the luggage rack overhead. She saw at once what he meant to do. His position kept him hidden from the advancing Heirs.

The men entered the carriage, and Catullus leapt. He slammed a fist into the jaw of the stout man, who stumbled back and into the path of his companion. The two Heirs tangled for a moment, lurching.

"What the devil?" cried a middle-aged passenger, observing. "No brawling on the train!"

"My apologies," Catullus said, sprinting toward Gemma. He took her hand, and they both ran together.

Within a moment, they arrived at their private compartment. Astrid and Lesperance, huddled close, hands interlaced and speaking in low, intimate tones, broke apart at the entrance of Gemma and Catullus.

Lesperance looked at both their faces and rose to standing. "Heirs," he said immediately.

Astrid swore, also seeing the truth. She too leapt to her feet.

"Must've gotten on the train at Shrewsbury." Catullus grabbed his baggage as well as Gemma's battered little carpetbag. "Have to get off *now*."

No one argued. With movements so swift as to be almost instantaneous, all the bags were collected and the compartment vacated.

"That way." Catullus indicated they move toward the front of the train.

As everyone hurried away, Gemma dared to venture, "The train's *moving*, you know."

"Counting on it." Catullus kept throwing glances over his shoulder, to see if they were being followed. And, damn it, they were. The Heirs had recovered their footing, though one of them already sported a swelling jaw, and cut through the narrow, rocking passages of the first-class compartments.

Gemma didn't know how long English trains were, and was afraid to find out. Once she and the Blades reached the engine, she had no idea what they planned on doing. Maybe throw the Heirs into the furnace?

She collided with Lesperance's solid back as he stopped short. Gemma braced her hands against him to right herself.

"Accident," she muttered when Astrid glared at her.

"What's the matter, Astrid?" Catullus asked behind Gemma. "Why'd you stop?"

Astrid rattled the solid door in front of her. It didn't even have a window. "Locked."

They all glanced back to reverse their course, but just then the Heirs appeared at the other end of the carriage. No way back, couldn't go forward. Trapped.

"Get to the side," Catullus growled. "I'll kick it open."

But Gemma's restraining hand held him back. "Not necessary." She quickly edged forward until she stood in front of the locked door.

And opened it.

Both Catullus and Lesperance chuckled in appreciation, and then they all hastily entered the carriage ahead. Catullus slammed the door shut behind them right before the Heirs caught up.

The two Heirs pounded on the locked door, shouting threats so crude, even Gemma blanched. And then one of the Heirs began to throw himself against the door. It rattled hard, threatening to open.

Gemma looked around. She and the Blades were in what appeared to be a mail coach, with heavy canvas bags filled with letters lined up on the floor and on racks. No windows, no external doors. Two hinged hatches were set into the ceiling, allowing thin slivers of sunlight to filter into the tightly crammed coach.

"And now?" she asked Catullus.

"Now," he answered, looking up, "we make our departure."

"Sod this," snarled Draycott. He drew his pistol and shot the lock off the door.

"Careful!" Forton threw up his arms to shield himself from flying wood and metal.

But Draycott didn't spare Forton a glance as he threw open the door. He stepped into the coach with his pistol ready.

He and Forton found themselves in a mail coach crowded with sacks of letters and wrapped parcels. And no Blades.

"Where are they?" Forton bleated.

"How the bloody hell should I know?" Draycott scowled

at the empty coach. When he reported back, Edgeworth would be furious. Two of the most important Blades had been in their grasp, and slipped away. Again.

And *where* the devil had they gone to? They had disappeared, and Draycott almost believed that the Blades had broken their own fool directive to never use magic. With an oath, Draycott shoved his way past Forton out of the coach, never seeing the unlocked hatch above him.

"Tuck in your arms and legs," Catullus shouted to her. "And let yourself roll."

Gemma, balanced on the junction between the mail coach and the next carriage, eyed the speeding ground with a combination of terror and excitement. The bags had already been thrown off, and both Astrid and Lesperance had leapt off soon after. If they'd survived, she had no way of knowing.

Her choice was either to go back into the mail coach and risk the Heirs, or throw herself off of a racing train.

At her hesitation, Catullus took her hand and gave it an encouraging squeeze. "I'll be right beside you," he shouted. "Trust me." And he actually winked at her before tucking his spectacles into an inside coat pocket.

She actually *did* trust him, and having him beside her *did* give her confidence. So, with a nod and a smile, she crouched, readying herself.

Her movements made him smile, admiring. Then he, too, prepared himself to leap.

"On my count," he yelled. "One . . . two . . . three . . . *jump!*"

Gemma threw herself into the air.

Chapter 4

Unfamiliar Territory

The only thought careening through Catullus's head as he flew through the air was, *God, please let her be safe.* Jumping off speeding trains wasn't something he did daily, but he had enough experience with it to feel confident about landing without being hurt. Gemma, however, was new to his world. She could be hurt. Or worse.

He hit the ground, pulling his arms in close to take the impact. Rolling, he tumbled down a low hill. He smothered a curse as he bounced over a rock, but then, mercifully, the hill ended and he came to rest in a ditch. He heard the distant sound of the train speeding away, but no Heirs in pursuit.

The Blades and Gemma had gotten away. For now, they were safe. Or maybe not.

His eyes opened to find himself staring up at a curious sheep. It stared at him with black, ovine eyes before trotting off with a bleat. Catullus took a mere moment to be sure that all his limbs were still functioning before sitting up. He looked around quickly; then his heart pitched.

Gemma lay on the ground, a few feet away. And she wasn't moving.

He scrambled over to her, a litany of swearing tumbling from his lips. She lay on her back, one arm flung overhead, the other resting on her stomach. Tiny cuts and scrapes dotted her face and hands, and her hair had come down into a mass of copper waves.

He knew better than to try to move her right away, but he had to restrain himself from gathering her up in his arms.

"Gemma?"

No answer.

He said her name again, then bent low to her mouth, where, saints be praised, he felt the stirring of her breath. Gently taking up her wrist, he felt for her pulse, and it came steadily against his fingertips.

Catullus brushed strands of her satiny hair from her face. "Gemma?"

Then, she moaned softly, and her eyes flittered open. He thought he might shout with joy to have those sapphire eyes on him again.

"Catullus," she whispered. "The Heirs?"

"Gone, for the moment."

She blinked, coming back into herself, then tried to push herself upright.

"Careful. Don't move. Are you hurt anywhere?"

She shook her head slightly, but the motion made her gaze unfocused. "Dizzy."

"Rolling down a hill tends to do that to a person." He felt anything but droll, however. "I'm checking you for injuries. Let me know if anything pains you."

His hands moved over her, impersonal—or he tried to be. He tested her arms, her hands, and gained his first true understanding of her slim, strong body. When he progressed to her feet and legs, he struggled to remain objective. This was simply a matter of field doctoring, the same as he'd done hundreds of times in his life for himself and other Blades.

Except it wasn't. Gemma Murphy was not a Blade, and his

body somehow knew the difference. He tested her slender ankles with gentle attention, trying like hell to dampen his reaction to her. "Does this hurt?"

"No."

Her legs needed to be checked for breaks or sprains. Over the skirt, or under it? He had to be thorough. "I'm sorry, but—" His hands slid under her skirt to touch her calves.

Some mystic in India once taught Catullus special breathing techniques to help gather his thoughts, calm his mind and body when the world grew too present. Catullus drew upon every drop of that training to help him now.

Good God, she had gorgeous legs. He could not see them, but he could feel with a greater sensitivity. The muscles of her calf were sleek and lithe beneath the coarse knit of her stockings, not the calf of a leisured lady who reclined upon a chaise all day, but the kind that attested to an active life full of motion and purpose. And, damn him, if he didn't find that unbearably arousing.

He wanted so badly to take his hands up farther, over her knee, across her thighs to feel those muscles and the band of bare flesh above her stockings. But he could not. That would be a violation.

He pulled his shaking hands away, and carefully smoothed down her skirts. "Try moving your legs."

Her skirts rustled as she did this. He set his teeth against the sound.

She said, "They're fine."

"What about . . . your ribs? Are they bruised?"

She made to bring her hands up to feel them, but the movements were fitful as she struggled to regain her strength. "I don't know."

"May I?" He was a tongue-tied boy again, simple words stuttering in his mouth.

"Yes, please."

So he lowered himself beside her, and, at her nod, ran his hands along her sides. Her dress was worn thin, and he felt beneath the fabric the material of her corset, each individual lace and hook that constrained her body. It was a corset for traveling, lightly boned, so that he knew now, to his deep joy and dismay, that the curves of her waist were entirely hers and not the result of a corsetmaker's art.

What he wouldn't give to slide his hands up higher, cup those exquisite, full breasts in his hands. He had large hands, but she would spill from them with their abundance. He wanted to touch her so badly, his own breath sawed through him, louder than a steam engine.

"Does this hurt?" he asked, hoarse. Because it was hurting him.

Beneath his hands, her breathing quickened. "N-no." She stared at him, eyes wide but unafraid, and her soft, pink lips parted slightly. "It feels . . . nice."

He was braced over her now, his body stretched alongside hers, so that he had only to lower his head to touch his lips to hers. Thoughts of the Heirs, the Primal Source all dissolved like vapor beneath the sun of his and her shared awareness. Her gaze flicked down to his mouth, as well, and the dropping of her lashes and flush spreading across her cheeks revealed that not only had she shared his thought, but wanted it, too. What would she taste like? Both the scientist and the man within him needed to find out.

Slowly, slowly he bent lower, suspended in liquid time. His heart slammed within the cage of his chest, and he was tight and hard everywhere. He cradled the juncture of her neck and jaw, feeling the rush of her pulse at that tender convergence. Such delicacy. Combined with remarkable strength.

"You're a very courageous woman," he breathed, close enough to count freckles.

She brought her hand up to curve around the back of his head. "I know," she answered.

He smiled at that, a small smile. And then he stopped smiling, because he kissed her.

Soft, at first. Just the brush of lips. Then more. Her mouth was silken, yielding, yet had its own demands. When he deepened the kiss, she met him with an equal need, opening her lips to take him inside, her tongue touching his without hesitation.

Heat tore through him with the strength of a firestorm. He'd never experienced in his life a kiss this potent, over-whelming him with desire. Catullus, rousing even more, took the kiss further, slipping from the reins of his control. Had he some sense of himself, he might have been shocked at the way he was devouring her. But she devoured him, in turn, and so he had no sense of himself. No sense of any-thing but his need for her, the taste of her, which, he learned, was the taste of summer fruit warmed in the sun. Sweet and ripe.

And so damned responsive. As they kissed, she moaned softly into his mouth, her fingers gripping tighter on the back of his head. His free hand began its ascent, tracing the curvature of her ribs, and then higher, until it brushed the underside of her breast.

Sweet heaven, yes.

"I see you survived the jump."

Catullus broke the kiss and looked up with hazy eyes to see Astrid and Lesperance standing some five yards away. Lesperance trained his gaze studiously on a nearby farm outbuilding, as if it was truly fascinating. But Astrid stared at Catullus with her arms crossed over her chest, wearing a distinctly frosty expression.

Catullus felt like a boy caught just before supper with a mouthful of plum cake.

He edged back from Gemma. "Yes, well . . . Gemma . . . Miss Murphy had, ah, taken quite a tumble—"

"Or was about to," Lesperance said, *sotto voce*.

Catullus glowered at Lesperance, but had recovered enough to get to his feet. Thank God he had on his overcoat, or else he'd treat Astrid, Lesperance, Gemma, and the sheep grazing nearby to the sight of his aching erection. The cashmere coat provided a welcome bit of privacy.

He held out a hand to Gemma. "Can you stand?"

She nodded, and slid her hand into his. The feel of her skin against his own ensured that he'd have to wear his coat for a good while longer.

Catullus helped her to standing, and he couldn't stop himself from noticing her lips, red from kissing, and the riotous mass of her unbound hair cascading over her shoulders. She looked like a woman moments from being ravished.

He felt both exhilarated and appalled by his behavior. The Heirs could, even now, have reached the next station and be heading back to finish what they'd begun on the train. Meanwhile, Catullus had been caressing and kissing a woman in a ditch—a *ditch*!—as if powerless to stop himself from the pull of desire between them. He'd never done anything like that, not once, in the whole of his existence. Why, after forty-one years, would he do something like that *now*?

It was her. A woman unlike any other he'd ever met. Gemma Murphy, watching him with her crystalline eyes and flushed, freckled cheeks.

"Are you truly all right?" he asked her lowly. He'd flog himself before hurting or taking advantage of her.

"I really am," she answered. "And this has been one of the most interesting days of my life," she breathed for his ears alone. A tiny smile bowed the corners of her mouth.

Her smile held both a woman's experience and a girl's freshness, and Catullus, a rational man of sober temperament and restraint, felt against reason a small gleam of happiness.

But reality set in. And his happiness winked out, like a doused lamp.

"The day isn't half over. And neither is the danger."

* * *

They would have to keep to bridle paths and game trails. The main road was far too trafficked for safety. If the Heirs knew enough to put some of their men on the correct Southampton-bound train, they'd have the roads watched, too. Time, always in short supply, became even more scarce.

So, collecting their strewn baggage, Catullus, Gemma, Lesperance, and Astrid quickly made their way to a narrow, seldom-used path running parallel to the main southern road. Horseback would be faster, but more conspicuous, leaving the party one option—to proceed on foot.

Catullus tried to calculate the number of miles to Southampton, how long they would be vulnerable on the road, on foot. England's great forests were mostly gone under the plow, or felled to make room for yet more urban development. Wide fields and roads were fine if one didn't mind traveling completely exposed. He missed the forests of Canada, or the wild barrens of the Gobi Desert. At least there one could journey hidden in the landscape. England's sedate pastures left him, Astrid, Lesperance, and Gemma far too open to attack.

He wanted to stay vigilant, but his mind kept fogging. It probably wasn't a good idea to have Gemma walk in front of him. He was mesmerized by the unconscious sway of her hips as she moved, as well as the way she looked about her, taking in the landscape with an alert and eager eye.

He rather wished she would put her hair back up. But she hadn't, and he became equally enthralled by the gleaming mass as it trailed down her back in brilliant waves.

Catullus made himself study the surrounding land, the familiar world of hedgerows and paddocks, stiles and hay-fields. Underneath all these quotidian sights lay ominous threats. The Heirs could be anywhere, and had many means of spying.

He and the others couldn't reach Southampton fast enough. He hated having Gemma vulnerable in any way, and could not fail her when it came to her protection. And he needed to focus all his faculties on the issues at hand. There were so damned many issues: the Heirs and the Primal Source, the inevitable battle that could very well determine the fate of the world. He couldn't allow his thoughts to be muddled by overwhelming, surprising desire for a female American journalist. Once she was safe at headquarters, he could devote himself fully to the mission.

It did not help that whenever he turned his gaze from Gemma, he found Astrid staring at him with concern. He and Astrid were good friends, and he'd worried about her terribly when she'd retreated into the Canadian wilderness. Now it was her turn to worry about him—though he wasn't entirely sure what she protected him from. Certainly not Gemma Murphy. Or, did Astrid see something in her that Catullus didn't?

He couldn't believe that Astrid was jealous. Not with her heart so fully given to Lesperance. Only two other times had Catullus witnessed such a powerful bond between lovers: Thalia Burgess and her husband, Gabriel Huntley; and Bennett Day and his wife, London Harcourt. Astrid loved Lesperance just as deeply. Further, Catullus and Astrid had always been strictly platonic friends. So she did not resent Gemma for a romantic reason. But why, then?

"How wide a net do you think the Heirs have over this area?" he asked Astrid, to keep his mind on track.

"There's no way to know," she answered.

"We could be walking right into them," said Lesperance.

"Perhaps it would be wise to do some reconnaissance, before moving on." Catullus wished he had more than a spyglass with him, but he'd had to leave behind his larger pieces of equipment in the haste to return to England. He might be able to fashion something—though the surrounding farmland didn't leave him much to work with.

Nearby, a shaggy pony at the edge of a field looked up from cropping grass and watched them. It wore a halter. Perhaps he could salvage some of the leather and metal. . . .

Astrid halted, bringing the whole group to a stop. "How do you suggest we attempt that?"

Catullus scanned the surroundings, then spotted a densely wooded dell to the west. "Astrid, you're one of the Blades' best scouts." She did not contradict him. "You can take that pony and reconnoiter. Lesperance, you can . . . provide aerial assistance."

Gemma frowned in confusion, but Lesperance understood.

"And you?" asked Astrid.

"Gemma and I will find shelter in that dell."

Astrid raised a brow.

"I can help, too," Gemma objected.

But Catullus shook his head. "Scouting is too dangerous for a civilian, and I don't want to leave you on your own and unprotected."

He wondered to himself how much of this was truth, and how much was an excuse to be alone with her again— something he both craved and dreaded. He decided he didn't want to investigate his motivations.

Thank God no one pressed him on this. With promises to convene at the dell within an hour, the party broke into two. The late autumn day had only a few more hours of daylight, so time was vital.

"Is all of England like this?" Gemma asked as they tramped speedily through a soggy field. She refused to allow Catullus to carry her little bag, so she slung it over a shoulder and marched onward with a lively stride. Likely the result of having such wonderfully long legs.

Stop it. Get her safely to Southampton and then move forward. Stay alert.

But, damn it, he liked talking to her, even as he kept his eyes in constant motion, assessing for threats. "You don't fancy our English pastoral?"

"Oh, it's fine, I suppose," she said airily.

"Just *fine*?"

"Well," she said, "if you have to press." She gazed around as she walked. "It's pretty enough. But there's no drama. It's very . . . tame."

Oddly, her words stung, as if she was criticizing *him* and not the sodding landscape. "There's nothing wrong with being cultivated."

"But not everything should be contained and tidy. Without a little mess and wilderness, things would be so dull."

"There is wilderness in England. The Lake Country. The moors. The Cornish coast." Why did he sound like a priggish geography professor? "All quite wild, I can assure you."

She sent a playful smile over her shoulder. "I've got no doubt that beneath England's civilized exterior, there's a good deal of wildness."

His footsteps faltered briefly before he regained his pace. *This*, he discovered, was where he got into trouble with women. When it was a matter of letting the body do as it demanded, he followed instinct and need. But this interaction, this banter and play, reading subtle cues, artful compliments and deft, intriguing evasions, here his admittedly gifted brain left him at an utter loss.

So, like an ass, all he could say to Gemma's teasing was, "Ah."

It had been much simpler kissing her. He liked that. He liked it very much. Very, *very* much.

They reached the dell, a little wooded niche whose steep sides and rock-strewn bed kept it safe from cultivation. Autumn had already stripped the branches of their leaves, but tree trunks offered ample camouflage. Catullus found a large fallen chestnut tree and guided Gemma to sit in its shelter.

"Just a moment," he said before she sat, and produced a square of tartan flannel to lay upon the ground. "To keep you from getting dirt upon your clothing."

She murmured her thanks before settling down. For himself, he couldn't sit quietly, not when the Heirs could be near. So he paced. And thought. When he reached Southampton, he'd go straight to his workshop and begin raiding his arsenal and supplies. What might he need for a massive battle against the Heirs? Ammunition, his demolition kit for urban combat, the wireless telegraph device he'd been developing. Blades out in the field would need to communicate with each other, and the devices could be incredibly helpful for transmitting information between distances. He'd also have to consider—

"I'm getting dizzy."

He froze at Gemma's words. "Is it the jump from the train? You might have hit your head rather hard—"

"From watching you pace."

Heat crept into his face. "Sorry."

She brushed aside his embarrassed apology. "Don't fret. I like watching you think. I just wish you'd do it in a more stationary way."

She liked to watch him *think*? "It's difficult for me to remain static when I'm ruminating." Even now, he struggled to keep from tapping his foot, restless both from the need to think as well as being the subject of her frank interest.

"You must have worn a trench in the floor of your office."

"Very nearly." He felt himself almost vibrating with tension.

With a low laugh, she waved a hand at him. "You look like you're about to spontaneously combust. Please, keep pacing."

He started to move, then forcibly stopped himself. "But—"

"I'll try to avert my gaze." Her eyes glinted with wry amusement before she drew up her legs and rested her head upon her knees. "But it won't be easy."

Oh, God, was she teasing him? If he had Bennett's skill

with repartee, he could think of something clever and urbane, perhaps pay her a compliment with a hint of suggestiveness. Like what? What could he say? He'd *kissed* her passionately not that long ago, and she'd enjoyed it. Words should not be so difficult after a devastating kiss.

"Erm, thank you," he muttered, and resumed his pacing.

"When did you become a Blade?" she asked. When he hesitated in his answer, she added, "This can be, as we say in journalism, 'off the record,' if you're worried I might write about you."

"I would appreciate that." He scanned the afternoon sky for any suspicious avian activity. The Heirs often made use of birds' sensitivity to magic, binding them with spells and forcing them into service as surveillance. Catullus wondered if Lesperance was having any difficulty on that front. However, considering how well Lesperance had handled himself in Canada, Catullus shouldn't be overly concerned. That didn't stop Catullus's mind from whirling, though.

"So . . . ?"

He snapped out of his thoughts at her prompt. No wonder he could never sustain a relationship with a woman. Always spinning off into the kingdom of his own mind. No woman could tolerate such perceived neglect. His arrangement with Penelope, the wealthy mercer's widow in Southampton, worked because they expected only bodily gratification from each other. Their usual pattern had him arriving between eleven and eleven thirty in the evening, after most of her staff had gone to sleep. He and Penny barely exchanged pleasantries. Once in her bedroom, they silently took off their clothing and had sex, sometimes in bed, sometimes elsewhere in her room.

He made sure Penny felt pleasure, and she gave it, as well. But the truth was, the whole process bordered on mechanical, stripped of real connection. Half the time they were together, his thoughts drifted to current projects and

inventions. Penny wasn't offended. She only wanted his
cock. Not his mind, not his heart.

What would Gemma want? Would she be bothered by
his straying thoughts? She did not appear impatient now,
nor did she seem unconcerned, like Penny.

Gemma patiently waited for his response.

"I became a Blade at eighteen," he answered. "On a mission to protect a Source in the Åland Islands."

"Seems awfully young!"

"Not for my family. We've been providing mechanical assistance to the Blades for generations. It was simply a matter
of time before I became an official Blade of the Rose."

"Generations," she repeated. She raised her head, frowning in confusion.

He saw the source of her bewilderment. "Great-great-
grandmother Portia came to England from a sugar planta-
tion in Jamaica. She came with her owner as a gift to his
daughter in London."

The implication of that statement widened Gemma's eyes.

"Yes. She was a slave." He didn't stop his pacing, though
he slowed, out of consideration for Gemma's balance.

"Oh, Lord, Catullus," she gulped. "I'm so sorry."

"Why? You had nothing to do with it."

"I know, but . . . it's awful to think about. Someone in
your family actually being considered . . . property . . .
instead of a human being."

He shrugged, long inured to this. "Great-great-
grandmother Portia wasn't the only one. A third of my
male relatives were slaves in the British Caribbean at one
point in their lives."

"No one would blame you," she said slowly, "if you
hated England."

"My skin's pigment does not define me, no more than
your freckles define you. Although," he mused to himself,
"I am extremely fond of freckles."

He wasn't actually aware that he had spoken this last bit aloud, until Gemma said with a smile, "That's good news, since I have quite a lot of them."

He blinked at her response, and then repressed an urge to yell his triumph. He'd done it! He'd said something flirtatious, and received a very encouraging reaction! That should be recorded in one of his journals, like an experiment.

Though his response to Gemma had little to do with science. Perhaps biology. And something beyond the body. Was there a science of the mind, of the heart? There ought to be.

His attempt at flirtation had been purely accidental, so he couldn't repeat the procedure. Gemma looked up at him with those sparkling eyes, fringed with red-gold lashes, and he didn't know what to say. The volley ended with him, like a missed tennis ball whiffing past a racquet. He forged onward, taking up his pacing again so that he wouldn't have to dwell on the fact that he was not, and would never be, a rake.

"But, ah, to return to great-great-grandmother Portia." He turned in slow circles, his eyes on the horizon for any possible hazards. "She displayed a tremendous talent for mechanical devices of all kind. Fixing clocks, perfecting the springs on carriages, even making adjustments on the fireplaces so they burned more efficiently."

"She sounds quite remarkable," she said, thoughtful.

Despite his relentless scrutiny, nothing loomed in the distance, except his increasing interest in Gemma Murphy. "Never met her, myself, but all accounts described her as a singular woman. Eventually, her mistress freed her, and Portia found work in a household in Southampton. That household was, in fact, the headquarters of the Blades of the Rose. And that's how the long association began. So it continues to the present day with myself and my sister Octavia."

"Is Octavia married?"

"Yes, and a mother, but she continues to develop devices for the Blades, when she has time."

"And you?"

"I'm always developing devices," he answered abstractedly, preoccupied by a shape on the horizon. He ought to have his shotgun ready, and cursed himself for not thinking of it sooner. But as he bent to retrieve the firearm from its case, her softly stated question caused him to freeze like a startled fox.

"I mean, are you married?"

He bolted upright, weaponry forgotten. "Good God, no!" Catullus swung to her, plainly appalled. "You don't think that I'd . . . that I would even consider . . ."

"Kissing me," she filled in helpfully. He remained mute, stunned into silence, so she shrugged. "Married men have been known to kiss women who weren't their wives."

"*I* would never do that!"

She contemplated him for several long moments, while Catullus's heart threatened to burst from his chest and find its own way to Southampton. "No," she said after some time. "I don't believe you would. And, *on* the record," she added, "I don't kiss married men."

"Well . . ." he said, "that *is* a relief."

The candor of her gaze revealed that she found them both, at that moment, a little ridiculous.

He'd traveled all over the civilized world, and battled his way through the uncivilized one, as well. Polar seas, barren deserts, obscure jungles. Glittering world capitals and villages that could fit inside a rabbit hutch. And yet the exotic country of Gemma Murphy left him lost. It was easier to dwell in action than dwell on the conversation they were now having.

Catullus hefted his shotgun, but saw the shape on the horizon turn into nothing more than a collection of sheep meandering across a pasture. A pity. He'd rather brawl with the Heirs than fumble his way through another attempt at flirtation with this sharp-eyed, forthright woman.

He whirled around with his shotgun ready as he became aware of a close, noiseless presence. Gemma gave a small yelp when Astrid appeared, like a dryad, from behind a nearby tree. Yet there was no magic in Astrid's stealth, only a lifetime of experience that had taught her hard lessons. Catullus's heart ached for the pain she'd had to endure. There wasn't a Blade or soldier, however, who could match Astrid for strength and skill. Suffering had forged her. Now she was ready for combat.

"The main road is watched," Astrid said without preamble. She strode toward him and a rising Gemma. "I saw a coach stopped and searched just outside the nearest village. Apparently, the Heirs have convinced the local law that we're fugitive thieves."

Catullus feared as much. The authority of the Heirs easily awed village constables and magistrates. "We stay off the arterial roads, then."

"Getting all the way to Southampton will be a challenge."

"But we must manage it."

"I found an inn ten miles from here," said Lesperance, also emerging silently. Catullus saw Gemma's observant gaze fix on Lesperance's necktie, which showed itself to be not completely knotted, as if only just put on, and a few buttons undone on his waistcoat. She did not miss much, this journalist.

"Safe?" Catullus asked.

"Looks like it was built before the train line, and the village it's in isn't on the main road."

The man had done his reconnaissance well. Meanwhile, the sun traced its path closer to the horizon. Nightfall approached. They needed shelter. Catullus had spent countless nights sleeping on the ground, but he'd try like hell to spare Gemma that discomfort. For all her strength and bravado, this world—the world of Heirs and dangerous magic and pushing oneself to the brink of physical collapse—wasn't hers but his.

"Good," Catullus said. "We need to reach there before the sun sets."

Lesperance's information proved correct. The village they walked into was barely more than a handful of cottages, the high street unpaved, without even a church or grocer. Catullus saw not gas lamps but candles burning inside the houses that lined the street. Some of the cottages stood dark and moldering, and weeds pushed their way through cracks in walls. The few people out were, to a one, elderly and dressed in the fashions of King George.

The technological glories of the century meant nothing in this forgotten little town. Catullus could well imagine that he and his traveling companions had somehow penetrated the veil of time, journeying at least fifty years into the past.

Some misfortune had befallen the village to see it slowly grind into nothingness. Within a decade, the streets would stand empty, and no one would mourn the village's surrender to obscurity. The deepening shadows of dusk crept through the lane, sweeping the small town further into darkness.

Yet, amidst this quiet and decay, stood an inn. It seemed so perfectly incongruous that the four travelers could only stand outside and marvel for a moment.

"Is this place real?" whispered Gemma.

"Let us hope so." Catullus strode through the open door, with everyone following. "For I've need of food, ale, and a bed, in whatever order they are given to me."

He and the others stood alone for several moments just inside the doorway, until, finally, Catullus called out, "Hallo the house."

A wiry man with equally wiry white hair scampered forward, hastily donning an apron. He stood gaping at them, momentarily shocked to have actual guests.

"We'll need three rooms for tonight," said Catullus.

The innkeeper started. "What's that? Rooms?"

"Three," said Catullus again.

"Oh, sir"—the innkeeper wrung a handful of apron in his hands—"only two are available."

Catullus glanced around, dubious. It wasn't a large inn, or even medium-sized, but it boasted two floors and a tap-room, where three equally white-haired men were sitting and watching the new arrivals with no attempt at disguising their interest. No one had the look of a traveler, save for Catullus and his companions. "Surely there are more than that."

The innkeeper smiled in embarrassment. "Yes, there are four guest rooms in all, but one of 'em, it's full of things. When the Denbys moved away, they sold us the lot of furniture. Chairs, tables, Sarah Denby's loom—though me and my wife can't use it. And then the Yarrows moved to Gloucester, so we took *their* furniture. Same with the Cliffords, only they moved to Birmingham, not Gloucester. But we didn't know where to put everything, so it all got shoved into one room, you see. And it'd take days to clear it out."

"And the other?" Catullus asked, fighting weariness. The day had been long. He wanted an English beer, and he wanted it now.

"That's where we keep the cheese."

"The cheese?" Gemma repeated.

"My wife's cheese. She makes it herself," the innkeeper said with pride, "and the room is cool, so it works quite nicely as a pantry. So you see, sir"—he made an apologetic shrug—"there are only the two rooms." Seeing their expressions, he added hastily, "But each of 'em has a nice, big bed, so they can sleep two all nice and comfy."

At the mention of beds, it took more self-control than

Catullus knew he possessed not to glance over at Gemma. The possibility of sharing a bed with her lay waste to his fatigue, his entire self sharpening with alert awareness.

"So, will you be staying, sir?"

Catullus, after a silent conference with Astrid, nodded, and the innkeeper leapt forward to take everyone's luggage. "Put the ladies' bags in one room," Catullus said.

The innkeeper froze as he bent to retrieve the baggage, startled, then regained his professional demeanor. "Very good, sir. If you all will follow me, I'll take you up right now. And there's supper, if you'd like it. 'Tis plain country food, not the sort of fancy stuff you might get in the city," he said with a concerned look to Catullus's stylish, though now somewhat travel-worn, clothing.

"I'm sure whatever you serve will be more than delightful. Especially the cheese."

The innkeeper ducked his gratitude and pointed them up the stairs. "Just this way, please."

As everyone climbed the steep stairs, Gemma asked, "Do you get many guests?"

"Gramercy, no!" The innkeeper chuckled. "You fine folks are the first guests we've had in four months."

"Isn't that hard for business?"

"'Tis," came the cheerful answer as he stopped on a landing, "but this inn's been in my family for four generations. It stayed open after the mail route changed, taking most of the travelers—and townsfolk—with it. And then when the trains skipped this corner of the shire, well"—he smiled, fatalistic—"that about killed us, it did. I reckon the inn won't be able to stay open after me and Sarah pass on."

Gemma gently touched the old man's hand. "I'm very sorry."

"Ah, obliged to you, miss." He reddened to be the recipient of a pretty young woman's sympathy. "But 'tis the way of things. We all must leave this world at some point, even inns. And, now," he continued, taking the stairs again, "just a little farther, and here we are."

A single, narrow corridor ran the length of the story, floorboards warped by the passage of years, a framed drawing of London Bridge the only adornment on the walls. Four doors faced each other across the passageway, two on the left, two on the right.

"The ladies will take the free room on the left," the innkeeper announced. "And you gentlemen will have the one on the right."

Astrid, after sending Lesperance a glance of parting, took her bag and went into one room. Lesperance looked unhappy to be without her for even a moment, but he found his way into the other room.

"I'll leave you to get your supper ready." The innkeeper bobbed, but Catullus stopped the old man before he headed down to the kitchen and gave him a florin.

"Thank 'ee, sir," the innkeeper chirped, brightening, then hurried away.

For a minute, Catullus and Gemma stood alone in the corridor. The narrow space forced them to stand close to one another, and all around them came the sounds of life— Astrid in her room, Lesperance in the other, the innkeeper downstairs happily chattering to someone, pots banging in the kitchen—everything quite ordinary, quite domestic, like any other inn Catullus had visited. Yet here, standing with his body very close to Gemma so that he saw the flutter of her pulse just beneath her jaw as she looked up at him, nothing was ordinary or domestic, but charged and fraught with possibility.

"Collecting material for your article?" he asked softly. He cast a quick look to the staircase, down which the innkeeper had walked.

"No." She faintly frowned at the idea she might exploit the innkeeper's tale for her own benefit. "I just like to hear people's stories."

He didn't doubt that. Gemma Murphy was, he continued to learn, exceptionally inquisitive. Not only for her work as a journalist, but for herself, because she loved knowing and learning and exploring for their own sakes. She imbued even the proprietor of a dying, tiny country inn with gravity and worth, where others—more thoughtless—might dismiss such a man.

This woman is very dangerous. Not in the common way dangerous, ready with a knife or betrayal, but danger of another sort. A well-guarded heart might not be as fortified as previously thought. And a body that had gone far too long without pleasure and release could not resist her, with her lush, seductive curves, her freckled, warm skin, her nimble hands.

But he would. He knew self-discipline, and good manners, and a lifetime of loneliness that could not be eradicated within the span of a few days. So, despite everything within him demanding that he close the small space between him and Gemma, and press her against the wall as he kissed her thoroughly, he said, instead, "See you at supper, then."

Catullus thought he saw a look of disappointment cross Gemma's face, but it vanished before he could make certain. "Yes, at supper."

Then she turned and went into her room, and Catullus stood by himself for many moments afterward.

Chapter 5

Sleeping Arrangements

Once inside the room she was to share with Astrid, Gemma looked up, expecting to find hams hanging from the rafters or perhaps goats gnawing on the coverlet. But the room was only that—simply furnished with a washstand, a chair, a chest of drawers and, of course, a bed. As the innkeeper had promised, the bed looked wide enough to easily accommodate two.

Astrid paced the room, taking its measure. She checked the one small casement window, making sure it opened, then glancing down to the road a story below. Checking for escape routes, Gemma realized. Astrid moved with precision and purpose, a battle-hardened veteran who also happened to be a woman. Gemma could only speculate what variety of adventures and hardship the Englishwoman had endured.

While Astrid surveyed the pitched-ceiling room, she continued to glance at Gemma with caution, as though Gemma were a variety of spider that leapt on and bit its unsuspecting prey. The source of Astrid's circumspection could be any number of possibilities. What might it take to win her trust?

In any event, it seemed unlikely that Gemma and Astrid would spend the night exchanging whispered confidences and giggling beneath the blanket.

Gemma rifled through her little satchel, desperate to find a brush for her disobedient tangle of hair. She wasn't especially vain, but knowing that she would be sharing supper with Catullus in a few minutes made her more attentive to her appearance. Maybe it was for the best that the room's only mirror was both tiny and fogged with age. Leaping off moving trains tended to wreak havoc on one's hair and clothes, and Gemma was sure she looked as though she'd not only jumped off a train, but landed in a sty and then rubbed handfuls of forest in her hair. Looking at herself in a mirror would only confirm her suspicions.

Astrid's gasp sounded behind her.

Gemma ran to her side, supporting Astrid as she staggered. The Englishwoman wore an expression of both pain and acute concentration.

"Are you all right?" Gemma tried to usher Astrid to the bed, but found herself waved off.

Astrid regained her footing, and shook her head to clear her mind. She looked at Gemma, her eyes sharp and determined, and just a little frightened, which scared Gemma. Astrid Bramfield feared nothing, or so Gemma believed. Then the Englishwoman's next words truly did alarm Gemma.

"It's beginning."

In the taproom, a supper of stew, bread, and cheese was laid out for the four of them, but none quite had the appetite, given Astrid's revelation.

"You're sure?" asked Catullus.

Astrid stared into her tankard of ale, her jaw tense. "Quite sure. The Primal Source is manifesting the Heirs' dreams. Very soon they will be embodied."

"When?" pressed Lesperance. He held Astrid's free hand between his own, as though unable to be near her without touching.

"A matter of days, if not sooner."

"How do you know this?" Gemma asked.

Astrid's expression darkened even further. "The Primal Source and I are . . . linked. I can feel its energy, especially the closer I come to it. And I felt its energy gathering. Coalescing. Even without the Heirs' direct manipulation, the Primal Source is materializing their desires. *Now.* And it has to be halted."

Catullus frowned at the worn wooden tabletop, his fingers drumming against the surface. "Damn," he growled. "There isn't time to get to Southampton. We have to stop it on our own." His look turned unreadable when he gazed up at Gemma, sitting beside him. "Which means, you will be coming with us."

Directly into the path of danger, he did not say. But they both knew it.

The prospect gave her some alarm, yet she couldn't quite stifle a thrum of excitement. But she couldn't decipher whether her excitement was because she would witness the upcoming battle or because she was to remain with Catullus. The thought of staying behind in Southampton while he went off to risk his life had been gnawing at her, creating a pit within her, empty and restless.

"I want to come with you," she said.

"Because you're a reporter," Astrid clipped.

Gemma turned from Catullus to meet the Englishwoman's unyielding gaze with her own. Words formed and tumbled from her, each one gleaming with a truth Gemma fully understood only at that moment. "Because I want to *help*."

Astrid's gaze tried to dismiss her. "What can *you* do? You're not a Blade. You aren't trained to fight. All you have is some parlor magic."

"Which saved you on the train today," Gemma noted.

Both Catullus and Lesperance watched this verbal sparring match with open interest.

"We could have kicked the door open."

"Then the Heirs could have gotten into the mail coach, and you would have been cornered."

The Englishwoman crossed her arms over her chest, unconvinced. "I still think you will be a liability."

"I'll prove that I'm not. I'll fight, right beside you."

"And write about everything after."

"Maybe." But she countered Astrid's immediate scorn. "But whether I write about this battle or not is immaterial if the war is lost. As I see it"—she leaned forward, bracing her arms on the table—"you Blades are outgunned and outnumbered. You can't afford to turn anyone away, not with so much at stake."

She addressed everyone at the table, her voice vibrating with barely banked fury. "The more I think about what the Heirs are trying to accomplish, the angrier I get. Who asked them to patrol and superintend the world? Why should they impose their values on everyone? And to steal magic—to steal *anything*—in order to achieve this . . . I can't pretend I'm a disinterested observer. I can't sit idly by and do nothing. I have to help . . . however I can."

For a moment, the only sound came from the fire in the hearth nearby. No one at the table spoke; no one moved. Gemma did not look at Astrid or Lesperance. Their opinion of her held no weight.

Richard never truly respected her—she'd realized that too late, after she failed to conform to his idea of who *he* thought she ought to be. That betrayal had hurt her, badly. Oh, she was used to the snide comments and dismissals in the newsroom. But Richard had been her lover, her confidant. She'd thought him unlike other men. His disappointment and dismissal cut her because she'd thought him different. She learned to prize her own opinion of herself.

She now discovered something, something faintly frightening: she wanted Catullus's respect. Because *he* was a man worthy of esteem.

Catullus did not smile at her, nor beam his approbation. But his night-dark eyes flashed behind his spectacles as he tipped his head in a regal nod. Confident in himself, *and* her.

Within her, this approval, more than anything, burned brightly. She felt momentarily giddy, as if she'd been spinning around the room and came to a sudden stop.

Yet she grounded herself with his eyes, velvety and bright eyes that saw and understood not just scientific theory, but the very real practicalities of what it took to survive.

"Nicely argued, counselor," Lesperance said, breaking the silence.

Even Astrid had to agree. "I hope you fight as well as you talk."

Gemma asked calmly, "So, now that that's settled, where are we going?"

"Wherever the Primal Source's energy is gathering." Catullus was all business now, which Gemma appreciated. This wasn't about *her*, after all, but the ensuing battle. He turned to Astrid. "Can you feel where it is collecting?"

Astrid snarled, frustrated with herself. "Somewhere south of here, but I'm not certain where."

Everyone moodily poked at their food. Gemma sifted and sorted through what she had learned about the Primal Source, knowing that a solution lay somewhere within grasp. "You said that the Primal Source is based on hopes and desires."

Astrid nodded after taking a drink of ale. "Its power, like all magic, comes from wishes, dreams, and imagination— that which makes humanity different from other animals."

"And we know that the Heirs' dreams are for a global English empire," said Lesperance.

"Because they believe England to be the apotheosis of human culture, the pinnacle of all that is good and right." Catullus's words, to his credit, held only a slight edge. "They wish England to be the world's champion."

"Champion." Gemma mulled this over. "That word has a very old-fashioned feel to it, as if it belongs in some child's book of fairy stories."

Slowly, Catullus drew himself up, his spine straightening even more than his usual faultless posture. His gaze sharpened further to knifelike perception. Gemma was surprised that the inn wasn't simply cleaved in two from the blade of his eyes.

"Not fairy stories," he said. "Chivalric romance."

"Chivalry, as in knights?" asked Gemma.

He turned to her, but his thoughts reached far beyond where she sat. "Exactly. Knights of the Round Table."

Understanding jolted them all at once, like a current of electricity through water. "Could it truly be?" Astrid whispered.

"Yes—yes it is." Catullus could no longer sit, energy and thought propelling him to his feet. The taproom's few other occupants watched him pace, confused and disgruntled that there should be so much commotion to break their evening's fireside drowse. The aged men helped each other to standing and then tottered out, muttering about strangers coming into town and making such a bustle.

No one paid the old men much attention. They would be back tomorrow, likely having forgotten this night's tumult. For her part, Gemma was riveted by the sight of Catullus fully consumed by inspiration, his body in motion as if to keep pace with the speed of his mind.

"Consider it," he said, hands clasped behind his back as he strode back and forth. "The glories of Camelot, when England emerged from darkness to serve as a model for governance and behavior for the world. Knights on quests, perpetuating and propagating the chivalric code—protecting the weak, spreading the faith and honor of their liege wherever they journeyed. A perfect kingdom ruled by one perfect leader, the best and most exemplary Briton, the ideal king."

As one, Gemma, Lesperance, and Astrid rose from the table, each drawn upward by the same thought.

"The king," Astrid breathed.

Catullus stopped his pacing to stand before the fire, and it formed a fiery corona around his tall, powerful body, turning him into a creature of shadow and light. "King Arthur."

"Was King Arthur real?" Gemma knew something of the legendary king, but the stories on which she'd been raised were Irish legends and Italian folktales. Kings were exactly what her family had fought *against*, in generations past. Who wanted a king when America offered at least the theory of equality?

"There's speculation," said Catullus. "Some think Arthur was a warlord of the Dark Ages who brought peace between tribes after Rome left England. Others think he was a Christian warrior king who stopped a Saxon invasion. None of this has ever been proven. But it isn't relevant," he continued, animated. "It's not the *real* Arthur that matters."

"Who, then?" Lesperance demanded.

"Arthur, as England wishes him to be. The Arthur of legend, of myth and imagination." Catullus spread his palms, encompassing the realm of collective dreams. "He is the best Briton, the finest example of what England once was, and what it might one day be—a beacon of light to the rest of the world."

"It makes sense," Gemma mused, "that the Heirs' shared desires could be embodied in such a figure. To them, Arthur must be the personification of everything they want."

"I can well imagine the Heirs believe themselves to be knights," growled Astrid, "setting off on quests for Sources, bringing the light of civilization to a savage world. And the Blades are the forces of chaos, undermining this noble ambition."

Gemma shuddered at the depths of the delusion. Yet it seemed far too possible.

Catullus resumed his pacing, unable to keep still. "The legend of Arthur posits that he would rise again when England had need of him."

"Returning from where?" asked Gemma.

"An enchanted sleep on the magical island of Avalon," Astrid answered.

Lesperance slapped his palms on the table in front of him decisively. "Then Avalon is where we should go, if that's where he'll appear."

Catullus's mouth formed a wry smile. "There's no such place."

"But you said that it isn't the reality that matters," Gemma noted, "so much as the legend."

"True, yet magic is tied to the physical world, the world of humanity. We can't simply *wish* ourselves to imaginary Avalon. If the Primal Source summons him for the Heirs, it will be here, in England. It's the *where* of it that confounds me." He pressed his lips tightly together, angry with himself for lacking any knowledge. He pushed himself, Gemma realized, much harder than anyone else, allowing no room for uncertainty or doubt.

She might not have the answers, but she could help guide the ship toward its destination. Being a journalist meant exploring every realm of possibility to get as close to the truth as possible. As well as using a fair amount of luck.

So she ventured, "There must be a real, physical place in England that is associated with Avalon."

Catullus stopped his pacing to glower out a window. His fists pressed into the stone wall surrounding the window as he leaned closer to the glass, searching for answers in the opaque night. It was a wonder the glass didn't shatter from the force of his churning mind. He held his wide shoulders stiffly, as if they bore a heavy weight under which he would not bow.

Avoiding Astrid and Lesperance's curious glances, Gemma edged around the table and came to stand beside Catullus. Gently, she lay her hand upon his forearm, felt the tense, firm muscles there beneath the exquisite fabric of his coat. Her touch served as reminder that he was not alone in this search.

He glanced over at her hand upon him, his expression gentling. Beneath this, she saw in his eyes a glimmer of something, something hungry and yearning.

No one ever touches him, she realized. *He's sealed off*— by design or circumstance, or both. To everyone, he was a perpetual stranger.

It broke her heart a little to think of it. Then realized she saw in him a mirror, reflecting her own solitude.

But now was about more than their shared isolation. So she said, "We will *all* think of the answer."

His gaze dropped away, as if embarrassed to have revealed so much, but he rallied in an instant, becoming again the incisive commander. "Several sites in England are associated with Avalon. Some say it lies in the mists off Cornwall's coast. Or near Wales."

"Astrid said she felt the Primal Source's energy gathering south of here. Surely there's some place south of . . . wherever we are . . . that's linked to Avalon."

She *felt* the inspiration hit him, as strongly as a silver wave coursing to shore. A physical sensation, but also deeper, more profound, a strange and strengthening bond connecting them.

"Glastonbury." He turned from the window, and Gemma's hand fell away as he surged back into motion. He stared at her, then at Astrid. "Glastonbury," he repeated.

Where or what that was, Gemma had no idea, but Astrid clearly did, because she changed from grim to energized in a moment. "God! I should have thought of that!" Astrid turned to Lesperance, watching with a puzzled expression that, no doubt, paralleled Gemma's.

"Glastonbury is an island?" asked Lesperance.

Astrid rushed headlong into her explanation. "No, it's a hilly town in Somerset. But it was once surrounded by marshes, which would give it the *look* of an island."

"One of the holiest places in England," continued Catullus. He began smiling now, everything within him brightening as the sun of understanding emerged from gloom. "Its abbey used to be the wealthiest, after Westminster. And in the twelfth century, monks claimed to have unearthed the grave of Arthur and Guinevere near the abbey. The bones disappeared, but the legend remained that Glastonbury was, *is*, Avalon."

Astrid pressed a hand to her chest, closing her eyes, focusing inward. "I can feel it now. The Primal Source is drawn to where myths are strongest, and there are so many swirling around Glastonbury, it would attract the Primal Source's energy. I sense it . . . gathering beneath the ground, taking shape, becoming real." Her eyes opened. "We have to stop it."

"How can we prevent something as powerful as the Primal Source from calling forth Arthur?" Gemma asked.

"I don't know," Catullus answered, and this dimmed his excitement but not his determination. "Yet we *must* try. If King Arthur is truly summoned, if he is imbued with the power of legend, then there will be almost nothing the Blades can do to keep him from achieving what the Heirs desire."

Rush headlong to stop a mythical king from being summoned by the world's most potent magic? It couldn't be done. It seemed to Gemma just then that the Blades had set for themselves an impossible goal, that they fought not to win, but because *someone* had to, regardless of the consequences.

* * *

The Primal Source was magic. They were human. Which meant their bodies demanded rest. Racing down to Glastonbury without a night's sleep went beyond the prospect of daunting to nigh impossible. And Catullus, the general in command of their army of four, ordered everyone to their beds so that, early the next morning, they could speed south without delay, refreshed and rested.

They had finished their supper, everyone barely restraining their sense of urgency and tension, and bidden each other a good night before retiring to their rooms.

By the light of a single taper, Gemma changed into her nightgown. Like all of her clothing, the height of its glory had passed many washings ago. She fought a sigh as she considered the worn cotton. If only a band of French lace adorned it, or a bit of dainty embroidery. Threadbare calico lacked the sophistication and sensuousness of ribbon-trimmed silk—which Catullus was no doubt more accustomed to.

As though it mattered what Catullus thought of her nightclothes! He'd never see her in them.

Gemma glanced over at Astrid, who sat on the edge of the bed they were to share that night. The Englishwoman hadn't yet changed for bed, but perched warily, fully clothed and ill at ease.

"Have you no nightgown?" Gemma asked. She, herself, had only the one, so nothing could be loaned.

"I don't wear anything when I sleep," came the strained reply.

Oh. "I promise I won't try anything fresh."

Astrid managed a taut smile, her gaze straying to the door. Across the hall was Lesperance, and through the inn's thin walls, the deeper voices of him and Catullus resonated in bass murmurs.

"You miss him," Gemma said quietly.

Astrid choked out a laugh, shaking her head at herself. "Absurd, I know. He's just across the hall. One night should not matter. I lived alone for years and didn't need anyone. Then he roars into my life and . . ." Her look grew tender, faraway. She was in a distant land Gemma had never truly seen—love. "We have not slept apart once since then."

What must that be like, to need someone so fully? Strange, too, witnessing the steely Englishwoman's vulnerability. Yet it didn't diminish her, but somehow made her even stronger, that she could hold such love and need for someone, and still fearlessly fight. It helped that Lesperance was a man of uncommon strength, as much a warrior as the woman who loved him.

Gemma ducked her head. "I'm sorry you have to be separated on my account."

At this, Astrid chuckled. "Catullus, for all his unconventional ways, can be something of a traditionalist. He wants to protect your reputation."

Now Gemma laughed softly. "That assumes I *have* a reputation."

"He's an optimist."

"I know you don't trust me," Gemma said, and Astrid did not dispute this, "but I want you to understand something. I will *never* manipulate or seduce Catullus to my advantage."

"I know you won't," Astrid said, "because, if you do, if you hurt him for your own gain, I will cut each and every freckle off of you with my skinning knife."

Gemma had no doubt Astrid would do just that. She refused to let the Englishwoman cow her, however. Blandly, she asked, "Which side of the bed do you want?"

Astrid smiled, not entirely without warmth. A kind of détente had been reached, an establishment of mutual respect that might not see bonds of eternal friendship forged, but at least created a foundation of wary esteem.

"It doesn't matter to me," Astrid said, standing. "I'm not

sure how much sleep I'm going to get. I've grown so damned used to having that wolf beside me every night."

Gemma furrowed her brow at Astrid's word choice, but didn't comment. Must be a pet name or term of endearment.

"The innkeeper said he had some whiskey," Astrid continued, moving toward the door. "Think I'll have a nightcap. That might help me sleep." She paused, one hand on the doorknob. "Want to come down and have a drink?"

This, absurdly, touched Gemma. "A shot of good whiskey sounds wonderful, but," she added with disappointment, "I can't creep about the place in my nightgown."

"As you like," Astrid shrugged, then left the room.

Gemma stood next to the bed for several minutes, heart thudding, mind awhirl. The men's voices across the hall had gone silent.

She drew a breath, summoning courage.

Before she could stop herself, she padded across the hall and opened the door to the other room. She stepped inside and shut the door behind her. A mirthless smile touched her lips. She was forever stepping on the wrong side of doors, into situations she should probably avoid. But then, if she did avoid those situations, her life would be indescribably dull.

And dull certainly did not describe the scene before her.

Catullus, dressed only in his trousers and an open shirt, rose up from the bed at her entrance. His hand reached for a nearby pistol, but stilled when he saw she was the unannounced visitor. Gemma's eyes moved from his shocked face to the sculptural planes of his chest, satiny skin lightly dusted with dark hair. She would have followed the causeway of ridged, defined muscles down from his chest to his flat abdomen, and lower, but the sound of claws scraping on wood snared her attention.

Gemma froze when she beheld the room's other occupant. Less than five feet from where she stood. Staring at her with topaz eyes as it uncurled from the floor to standing. A huge silver-and-black wolf.

"Wolf," she said absurdly.

And that's what it was. Not a large dog that had somehow wandered into the room. But a massive wolf looking right at her. She didn't have a lot of experience with wolves, had only seen a few at a distance when she'd been in Canada, but even someone of her limited experience knew that *this* wolf radiated power and deadly potential.

What in God's name was it doing in Catullus and Lesperance's room? And where *was* Lesperance, anyway? Downstairs, having a quick tryst in the taproom with Astrid before retiring to separate beds?

Not that any of this mattered. There was a damned *wolf* in the room.

She backed to the door. Her eyes never left the animal. She rasped to Catullus, "Move slowly. Just edge toward me and we can make an escape."

Catullus sighed. He was irritatingly calm about the presence of an enormous wild animal in his room. "Not necessary."

Her eyes flew to his. "But there's a—"

Before she could finish this thought, the wolf trotted forward and gave her motionless hand a friendly lick. Its tail wagged, briefly, then looked up at her with what she could have sworn was humor in its golden eyes.

Gemma managed to break the gaze to see a pile of men's clothing folded neatly in the corner. Sober, respectable clothing that an attorney might wear.

Understanding came with the loss of her breath. "Lesperance?"

The wolf gave a soft *woof*. It moved back and sat on its haunches.

Gemma's eyes shot to Catullus, watching her with a kind

of resigned amusement. Oddly, all she could muster was annoyance, not amazement that there were *humans who could turn into animals*. "You didn't tell me."

"Never seemed an appropriate time," he said. "'The Heirs are about to unleash a mythic power on an unsuspecting world, and we have to stop it, and, incidentally, Nathan Lesperance can change his form into a wolf, a hawk, and a bear.'"

"A hawk and a bear, too?" This aggravated her further. "What about you?" she demanded of Catullus. "Can you turn into a turkey or an anteater?"

His lips quirked. "No—I'm just a man."

She was, in truth, all too aware of the fact that he was a man. And she was in her nightgown. In his bedroom.

Which prompted him to ask, "What are you doing here, Gemma?"

Yes. Right. "Astrid's miserable." She addressed this to Lesperance. "Right now she's downstairs trying to drink herself into a good night's sleep without you."

Lesperance made a low whine of distress, getting to his feet. Or was it getting to his *paws*? She really had no idea.

"You need to be with her," Gemma continued. "The two of you are . . ." She searched for the most fitting word. "Bonded."

Lesperance rumbled his agreement. And Gemma realized she was having a conversation with a wolf. She doubted she could ever write such an outlandish scene.

She held the door open. When she'd left her room, she hadn't shut the door behind her, so now the empty room waited across the hall. "Go to her."

Making no noise of protest, Lesperance trotted out of the room and into the other. He even winked at her before nosing the door closed, as if they were two collaborators in Astrid's waiting surprise. Gemma shut the door of Catullus's room.

And now they were alone together. They both knew it with the powerful awareness of the rising moon, tidal.

"I think they would have survived a night apart," Catullus said dryly.

"But not well. I've never seen two people so connected." Which awed her, knowing that such love could truly exist in this world. "And," she added, willing herself not to blush, "I . . . heard them."

"Heard them?"

"On the ship. At night, when I would be . . ."

"Eavesdropping."

There really was no way to dispute that, since it had quickly become clear that Astrid and Lesperance weren't discussing strategy or secret plans in their cabin. "Yes. They're a very . . . passionate . . . couple." *Very* passionate, and Gemma had the singed ears to prove it. The sounds the two of them made would arouse a glacier.

Catullus lost the war against blushing, his own face turning a deep, burnished henna. "Ah," he said.

Without the distraction of a wolf in the room, Gemma allowed herself to look her fill of a partially dressed Catullus Graves. His crisp white shirt was undone and untucked, leaving a swath of bare skin from his neck to his stomach. A lone candle upon the nightstand illuminated the room, so his exposed flesh became a tantalizing play of gold and mahogany, planes and valleys of distinct muscle that revealed him to be not just a man of the mind, but also of the body.

No coat, jacket, or waistcoat hid the way his fine shirt clung to the breadth of his shoulders, the length of his arms. And his trousers, of course, fit him beautifully, the expensive drape of wool delineating the lengthy muscles of his legs. His feet, large and long, were bare. This, more than even the bare flesh of his torso, struck Gemma as unbearably arousing, strong yet vulnerable, and she swallowed past a lump of heat that had suddenly formed in her throat.

Likewise, his gaze traveled over her, from the tips of her

own bare toes, up along the expanse of threadbare cotton nightgown—lingering, it had to be noted, on her breasts—to her hair spilling over her shoulders, and then her mouth, her eyes. A thorough perusal, not a bit analytical. If anything, Catullus's gaze held the same haunted look of yearning she had seen before. Yearning, and desire.

He forced his eyes away from her, and his voice, when he spoke, was a growl. "It's not right for you to be here."

Which wasn't a rejection, exactly. But he didn't exactly cross the span of the room separating them and enfold her in his arms either. His kiss still resonated through her, many hours later, much more memorable than the leap and fall from the train, and she wondered with an almost detached desperation if such heat could flare between them again.

"Neither of us follow the rules," she said. "Now is no different."

Astrid could be heard outside, ascending the stairs. She moved lightly, but the timbers were old and creaked with little provocation. Both Catullus and Gemma held themselves still, listening, as Astrid opened the door to her room. The cry she made—a girl's shriek of unmitigated happiness—caused Gemma's heart to contract with bittersweet satisfaction. Lesperance gave a low laugh, said something, though his voice was too deep to distinguish words through the walls, and the door to Astrid's room shut quickly. Then came the unmistakable sounds of two people throwing themselves onto a bed, the headboard knocking into the wall.

The next few hours were going to be rather noisy.

Catullus turned from her to stalk the length of the room, but the chamber's small dimensions made him ricochet from side to side like a bullet in a cave. "I don't want you to go to Glastonbury."

She hadn't anticipated this abrupt turn in the conversation and struggled to gain equilibrium. "You've got no choice. But I *can* help, and I *can* fight—not as well as you and Astrid and Lesperance, but good enough."

He pulled off his spectacles and rubbed aggressively at the space between his eyebrows, as if trying to push her out of his vision and thoughts. "If anything were to happen to you . . ." His teeth clenched. "Blades do their damnedest to prevent any civilian casualties."

This stung. She had seen herself as more than a naive by-stander blundering into the path of danger, a foolish woman who needed constant protection. "I see. I'm just a civilian whose blood you don't want on your conscience. A liabil-ity." Maybe this was an unfair accusation, but she wasn't feeling entirely impartial at the moment.

His breathing changed, hitched. She thought, at first, that he had no response to her accusation. Deliberately, he set his spectacles on the nightstand. Gave them a little push with one finger so they aligned precisely with the table's edge.

"You're more than that to me," he said lowly. "Much more."

His words sent a deep, resonant thrill through her. Yet he did not move, ruthlessly holding himself back.

She drew a breath. She felt herself hovering in an ele-mental moment, the suspension between two worlds, with possibility on every side. A single movement from her would cause everything to shatter into shards and dust.

For almost a lifetime, he gazed at her. And then, some-thing snapped, broke within him. He stalked toward her, halting not a foot away, so that she felt the warmth of him radiating out, filling her senses to repletion. Even without the splendor of his elegant clothing, his presence was a pal-pable thing, the depths of his intelligence and dynamic force of his body.

He stared at Gemma, and without the protective shield of his spectacles, his dark eyes were piercing, sharply aware. His gaze delved into her, probing, as though she were a paradox to be solved, and he had but to stare long enough, pick her apart with the precise machine of his mind and a definitive answer would arise.

Yet she was no equation. No contraption of metal and wood and canvas. She had no single answer—or, at least, she *hoped* she was more complex than that.

"I want to know more about you," he said lowly, his voice a rumble of silk.

"It's the same for me," she answered. "You're a wonderful enigma I need to understand. Although I believe, in a way, we *do* know each other."

"But—"

"You think too much," she said, then stepped around him and doused the candle.

Chapter 6

Catullus in the Dark

The room pitched into shadow. After a moment, darkness separated itself into varying shades—the deep jet of the room and the softer, smoke-colored night sky framed in neat squares by the windows. The room itself became infinitely vast but also as private as two hands cupped together, a close and dark hollow.

Catullus understood. There was freedom in darkness. Without the candle's precise delineations of form and shape, he became, for a while, liberated. Gemma knew this with an instinct that stirred him.

He had to touch her, seeing in his mind's eye how she had looked in her exceedingly worn nightgown. The thin cotton did more than hint at the body beneath—it had revealed her curves, the slim lengths of her limbs, her slender waist, those generous, coral-tipped breasts that made his mouth water and his body hard. Those freckles that dusted her face and disappeared beneath the neckline of her nightgown. He saw all this now without seeing. She left a wake of warm, womanly scent and air as she had passed. He would pursue.

Catullus strode toward her; then his foot collided with

something heavy. A dresser. A bolt of pain shot up his leg. "Bugger!"

Gemma stifled a giggle, and Catullus wanted to slam his head into the wall. So much for smooth, effortless seduction. He was floundering around like a drunk, amorous rhino with a dockworker's vocabulary. Without question, Bennett Day would never have kicked a piece of furniture en route to a kiss.

He started as he felt Gemma's slim, agile hands take his own. "I've got excellent night vision," she murmured. "Just follow me."

He was a man unaccustomed to being led. The paths he took—mental, physical—he forged himself. Always better that way, with himself in control, confident in his own abilities to take him precisely where he needed to go. So it was strange for him now to surrender, just a little, and let Gemma guide him through the darkness of the room, through the maze of desire and duty.

His feet felt large and clumsy as he allowed her to pull him . . . somewhere. They stopped, presumably near the bed, but he couldn't be sure.

What he *was* sure of was the growing heat and need within. He and Gemma stood very close to one another, and, their hands still interlaced, palms pressed against each other, she brushed softly against him. He barely contained a groan to feel the lush fullness of her breasts graze his chest, breasts contained by nothing except unbearably thin cotton. His own skin became taut, hypersensitive, and the rasp of his crisp shirt combined with her soft nightgown and sumptuous, silky flesh drove him directly into the path of madness.

Her breath came quick and shallow, as did his. He felt her looking up at him. It made sense, that she could see in the dark. Here was a woman who saw no obstacles, only possibility. And that fearlessness inflamed him.

He struggled to think of another woman who'd ever affected him so strongly, so quickly. Found he could not. He wanted balance, the security of his own will, but it evaded his grasp.

"I'm not the sort of man who does this," he breathed.

"And I don't creep into men's rooms wearing my nightgown," she answered, but her voice was just as unsteady as his own. "Some things we just *have* to do, even if they don't make much sense at the time. Catullus—"

But he was done with words. They never served him well beyond his work for the Blades—he could command or explain or use logic to solve a problem. With women, though, words became a hindrance, and so he couldn't let words stop him now. The darkness within the room was complete, yet he was an explorer determined to discover the unknown, so he lowered his head and put his mouth to hers.

It started as a kind of experiment. He needed to know if the heat and pull he'd felt during their earlier kiss could be replicated, or if it was an aberration, never to be experienced again. He desired and feared both possibilities. But, as in all things, he was driven by the demands of knowing. A kiss now, and he'd have his answer.

The moment their lips touched, he understood one thing: He was an idiot to believe something so potent and wild could be reduced to the safe confines of an experiment.

She was soft, soft and excruciatingly delicious. The light brush of their lips gave way instantly to deeper, open kisses. Sharp hunger tore through him like a white-hot blade to feel the yield and demands of her mouth, acquiescing and challenging his own. She licked his mouth. He dragged his teeth along her bottom lip and was rewarded with her low involuntary moan. Oh, God. She was a flame, and he the moth hurling himself gladly toward a fiery death.

A gentle but firm tug on her hands, and he hissed when her body pressed fully against his. She might have a man's profession, but only one word burned into his mind now: *woman*. The embodiment of everything that was feminine and sensuous, contained within the seductive curves of Gemma Murphy. Full breasts, the nipples tight buds scraping his chest, the soft roundness of her belly cushioning the thick length of his erection, somehow still confined within the tightening fabric of his trousers.

Instinctively, their hips pushed against each other, and she made another soft noise at the contact. The slide of her nightgown as they rubbed together became an acute, wonderful torment.

"Not enough," he said hoarsely into her mouth.

He released her hands and brought one of his own to tangle in the tumble of her hair. Heavy, rough silk, her hair, and he curled his fingers into it to bring her mouth harder against his own. She went, willingly. She clung to him, gripping his shoulders. When her short fingernails dug through his shirt into his skin, he nearly exploded with release.

His other hand clasped her waist. No more corset, no stiff, concealing layers of clothing, only this whisper-light nightgown that sighed at his touch. And beneath. Sweet heaven, beneath burned her naked body. Her narrow waist flared out to hips designed to turn a man's rational mind to porridge. A goddess's hips.

Then his hand slid down and back, until he met the curves of her behind.

"Bloody, bloody hell." Catullus had little gift for poetry—none, in fact—yet he was seized but the inspiration to write odes and sonnets to Gemma's delectable arse. No wonder she didn't wear a bustle. It would be a crime against all civilization to hide this ripe, ripe peach in a cage of steel. He wished, just then, for an owl's vision, so he could see as well as feel this marvelous gift he now cupped in his hand. All he could do was touch, and growl.

He felt her smile against his mouth. "Thank you."

"Really," he rumbled, "it is *me* who should be thanking *you*." Because her body was a gift, and not simply for its shape, but because it was her, fearless and outspoken, the physical manifestation of a woman he was coming to know and admire.

He moved his mouth from hers, trailing his lips in questing kisses along her jaw and down the arc of her neck. As he did this, his other hand untangled from her hair and traced over her shoulder, along her arm, and then he thought he might lose consciousness because he had her breast in his hand, and there had never in the history of time been a breast like this, spilling over his large palm. Full, firm, luscious. His thumb brushed the pearl of her nipple, and her breath left her in a rush.

Through the worn cotton, he caressed her, and her throat's pulse raced beneath his mouth and her breast was perfect and satiny in his hand. Each touch was a new discovery, a realm of sensation whose threshold he had never crossed. Still, it wasn't enough. He needed—

"More," he rumbled, and could not recognize his own voice. Since when did he sound like a steam engine?

He began to gather up the fabric of her nightgown, collecting handfuls of it just enough to allow him to delve beneath and stroke the long, sleek expanse of her leg. He allowed himself the pleasure of touching her in slow strokes, up and down, learning the feel of her.

"I love your hands," she gasped. "So very . . . clever . . ."

"Always been good with my hands." To prove this, his hand drifted up her thigh and then—

His name exploded from her mouth as he found her, slick and hot, at the juncture of her legs. Nothing beneath his fingertips had ever felt so incredible, her liquid skin, the evidence of her desire for him. Catullus always felt his hands were his blessing; they could withstand the burning heat of a soldering iron, but had the sensitivity to detect minute differences between tissue-thin sheets of metal. Perhaps because his hands were large, he worked particularly hard to make them as precise as the finest tool. He'd thought this was a skill he needed for the workroom alone. God, he was happy to be proven wrong.

So he touched her, tracing and stroking the intimate flesh, and she writhed against him and made sounds of the most profound pleasure. Desire gripped him, tight and relentless. Never had pleasuring a woman been so arousing.

When her hand dragged down his cock, he thought he might explode from his skin into a molten mass to set the whole inn ablaze. Her touch was as deliberate and inexorable as his own. If he had trained his hands to precision, her skill was innate. Through the wool of his trousers, she slid over him, testing his length and girth.

Then her adept fingers unfastened his trousers to wrap around him, stroking him hard, lightly scoring her nails down his length, and he sucked in air like a man searching for his final breath.

"Too rough?" she murmured.

"No, no, *God* no."

Their mouths tangled again, and their hands fell into a rhythm as natural and perfect as seasons. He became concentrated into three points: mouth, hand, cock, three stars in a constellation of pleasure, obliterating all other stars. The gearworks of his mind shut down. He wanted, demanded her climax as much as, if not more than, his own.

So he caressed and stroked, and she did the same, and very soon, far too soon, he could hold out no more. Yet he had enough control to delay release a small while longer as he rubbed, coaxing and deliberate, the tight gem of her clit. She tensed, a living arrow, her hand stopped its motion, and he took into his mouth the noiseless sound of her release. Again and again it rocked her, with her pressed hard against him, shuddering.

Yet no sooner had the final tremor ceased than her touch upon him resumed with even greater purpose. This woman, who had been a stranger to him only a few days before, knew exactly what his body needed, and gave it gladly. All he knew was her hand was on him, drawing pleasure from him as though shaping currents of fire. He wished it could go on like this for hours, days, forever. No more thought. Sensation alone.

A futile wish. Because suddenly it took him—release, incredible release, that seemed to begin somewhere around his toes and continued on up until it reached the sky. He could only hold on, until he was certain he would collapse into a heap of ashes.

He and Gemma leaned against each other, panting raggedly, as they returned to themselves and their hearts slowed. She draped against him languidly. His shaking legs barely supported them both. The room was filled with the sounds of their breath, the musky scent of sex. Ecstasy receded. He became suddenly aware of himself, the liberation of darkness and pleasure dissipating to leave him to navigate a foreign sea without a chart or star for guidance.

Some minutes later, after her nightgown had been smoothed down and he had cleaned and returned himself to his trousers, he heard, rather than saw, Gemma's patent disbelief to his proposal. "You are *not* going to sleep on the floor while I take the bed."

"I don't mind."

"*I* do."

Stubborn—which he knew already. He exhaled. "Then I'll sleep on top of the blankets, and you sleep beneath them."

"For God's sake, why?"

"Us sharing a bed." He tried to turn away to pace, but knew that, in this darkness, he'd just slam into a table or knock into a wall, so he was forced to stay where he was. "It wouldn't be . . . proper."

A brief, incredulous pause. "Catullus, you just had your hand on my—"

"I know," he growled.

"And *I* was touching your—"

"I am aware of that, too." As if he needed reminding. Just her words alone called up a sudden rush of arousal that he struggled to batten down.

"Again, *why*?"

The barrier of words, once more. He didn't know how to explain it to her. Now that the tempest of desire had briefly passed, when he had been guided by instinct and need, he found himself mired in an all-too-familiar reticence. The conundrum of women. Their minds, their needs. He had a natural aptitude for mechanics, and none for the subtle, diaphanous realm of women. Inevitably, he said the wrong thing or could not properly anticipate a response, and was left floundering like a boy. His attempts at courting had been, at best, maladroit, at worst, depressing. He'd once accidentally overheard a woman he was trying to woo refer to him as "a gorgeous, gauche automaton." In a way, it was for the best. Something was inevitably missing, a connection, an understanding beyond immediate attraction, that left him as isolated as he'd always been.

Over the years, he'd had lovers—admittedly few—and there was Penny. Theirs was an uncomplicated arrangement. Neither of them wanted or could give the other anything beyond physical gratification. He left her bedchamber before things devolved into awkward attempts at a relationship or conversation. No trepidation, no uncertainty, precisely *because* he and Penny had no bond.

Gemma stared at him now, with her scent still clinging to his fingers. Catullus wanted to put his fingers in his mouth, savor her tastes. He wanted to crawl back into the shelter of darkness and desire.

"Because . . ." He struggled for words, sodding words. "Because I like you."

Another stunned pause. Then, slowly: "I like you, too."

"And that is why . . . that's why . . ." He would ruin it. He would want too much, seek something that wasn't there, and, because she was Gemma Murphy, because she was different from any other woman he'd ever known, the loss would be even greater.

Frustration and anger, for himself, welled. Life was easier in his workshop or out in the field. But not this. The complex, baffling architecture of the heart.

And surely his ridiculous circumspection would only drive Gemma further away. He started to turn, to blunder in the dark, but her hand on his arm stopped him.

"All right." Her voice was gentle. "It's all right, Catullus."

He stood, frozen, then heard the soft rustling of the linens. "I'm in bed. Come on." The sound of her hand patting the blanket. "Lie down."

Gingerly, he lowered himself to the bed, then reached out and found the shape of her leg beneath the coverlet. Twin impulses assailed him: to stroke her leg, feeling its lithe strength, or to snatch his hand away as though singed.

He did neither, instead slowly pulling his hand back and then stretching out carefully beside her, lying atop the blankets. Her presence beside him held the living energy of summer, radiating out warmth and possibility. The intimacy of a shared bed shortened his breath—he could not remember the last time he'd slept beside a woman, if ever.

"I should warn you," he began.

"You snore?" A trace of amusement.

"No! At least, I don't think so. But I usually don't . . . sleep much." Here was another obstacle. His inherited, bizarre insomnia. "Only a few hours at a time, and then I have to get up and . . . work."

"On inventions?"

"Yes."

"Do you go back to sleep after working?"

"Sometimes. Often, not."

He waited for her disapproval, or perhaps for her to tut and say that he simply needed a proper inducement to sleep.

When he was younger, he did try to fight the restlessness that always woke him. He used to exercise—box, swim, fence, run—until barely able to move. Or prohibit himself from doing anything related to work, even reading, at least two hours before bed. None of it succeeded. He had even tried drinking himself into a stupor. When he'd awakened four hours later, he was still drunk and miserable. And, during his earlier attempts at having lasting affairs, his lovers eventually banned him from their beds, saying his insomnia made *them* lose sleep.

"Is that all?" she asked.

He started. "I believe so."

"I'm a deep sleeper," she said, her voice already growing drowsy.

"Truly?"

"My mother said someone could operate a cotton gin beside me and I wouldn't notice." She yawned hugely. "I'm already halfway asleep. Been an"—*yawn*—"eventful day."

"It has."

Then she rolled toward him and gave him a quick, familiar kiss. "Good night, Catullus." Before he could return the kiss, she had rolled away again. Her hair made a silky scrunching sound as she adjusted her head on the pillow.

"Good night, Gemma."

A minute passed. Her deep, even breathing confirmed she was already fast asleep.

For some time, Catullus lay beside her, stiff and unmoving, his hands at his sides. His mind swam with everything that had happened that day, the ongoing threat of the Heirs, the Primal Source, King Arthur, thoughts of his distance communication device, but mostly thoughts of her.

It was a fair assessment to say that Catullus had seen a tremendous amount in his time as a Blade. He'd traveled more than most ten men combined. He'd battled frost demons and floods of fire, vicious creatures that defied logical definition, and sloe-eyed enchantresses. Yet never in his whole life had he met a woman like Gemma Murphy. And she fascinated and terrified him.

But, being a Blade meant he rather enjoyed being fascinated and terrified. And so he eventually drifted off to sleep, his mouth curving into a bittersweet smile.

Catullus met them all at first light. He waited for Gemma, Astrid, and Lesperance in the taproom, having already been up several hours. Yet he felt refreshed, ready to face anything.

Almost anything. When Gemma appeared before Lesperance and Astrid emerged from their room, she was properly dressed, hair pinned, and he found himself caught upon the rack of his self-consciousness. What, precisely, did one say to a woman whose hand alone created the greatest sexual experience of one's life? And whose own most intimate parts one had touched to her intense pleasure? Then he'd gone and made an ass of himself by insisting he sleep on top of the blanket out of some misguided sense of honor.

"Good morning." A fair start. "I trust you . . . ah . . . slept well." Too familiar? Not familiar enough? "That is, I hope I didn't wake you. When I rose. To work." Which only confirmed the fact that he was, and would always be, too idiosyncratic for any woman to accept.

Gemma, however, smiled, unperturbed. "Mm, I slept *very* well. Thanks to your very skilled hands." Her smile turned sultry.

Oh, Lord. "Ah. Thank you. Likewise."

Thank you? Likewise? Catullus squeezed his eyes shut, mortified by his ineptitude. He wondered if the innkeeper kept any hemlock.

But either Gemma did not notice his social clumsiness or did not care, because she asked smoothly, "Was it a productive night?"

"By 'productive,'" he began, cracking open his eyes, "do you mean—?"

"Work." She pointed to the small leather case that held his tools, resting atop a wooden table. He had, in fact, only just packed the tools up minutes before she appeared. "I imagine sleeping only a few hours a night gives you many more hours to work on your remarkable inventions."

He brightened. "Yes! Some of my best creations are constructed in the predawn hours, before everyone else is up."

"No distractions." She nodded with approval. "I'm too lazy to get up before the sun, but I'm sure it would make me a hell of a lot more prolific."

Scowling, Catullus said, "You're *not* lazy. Certainly no one who is lazy would have forged a career for themselves in a hostile environment, which is exactly what you've done."

She appeared momentarily taken aback by his vehemence, as well as his praise; then she smiled again and the lovely sight tugged hard on his chest. "Thank you," she said. "Likewise."

He hesitated, unsure whether she was mocking him.

She winked.

The tug on his chest turned into something else—a lightness with which he was unfamiliar.

Astrid and Lesperance chose that moment to stride into the taproom. Both wore matching expressions of alert focus, and, based on appearances alone, one would never have known that they had spent a goodly portion of the night engaged in some very—what was the word Gemma used?—*passionate* activities. Catullus, however, had been treated to their uninhibited sounds on and off during the night for the second time in his life. He flushed to see Astrid now, trying to block the mental images.

She was one of Catullus's closest friends, yet listening to her making vigorous, ardent love made him consider developing advanced earplugs, or soundproof wall material, or both.

Considering the speculative glance Astrid sent toward him and then Gemma, he wondered if maybe his old friend had heard a few things of her own last night. His flush deepened. He had never been an exhibitionist.

He found refuge in command. "Everyone rested? Good. We'll have a quick breakfast, and then we must leave. There's a hard day's travel ahead." He consulted his pocket watch, then shut it with a decisive snap. "Every minute not spent on the road means the greater likelihood of disaster."

Urgency meant they needed horses. Impossible to reach Glastonbury in time on foot. But the only horses to be found in the village were as old as its human inhabitants, so there was the loss of an impatient hour to reach a stable with horses to hire. Astrid was the best judge of horseflesh, and she selected three strapping, eager mounts.

They led the snorting horses away until they were a goodly pace down the road. A small wooded stand provided a bit of necessary shelter.

"There are four of us," Gemma noted, casting a glance at the three mounts.

"I won't need a horse," answered Lesperance. He had already begun loosening his clothing as he strode toward the cover of the trees. This had to be out of respect for Gemma, since Catullus and most definitely Astrid had already seen Lesperance unclothed in preparation for his transformation.

Catullus watched Gemma's face as she stared at Lesperance's retreating back. Lesperance had whipped off his jacket and his shirt was being tugged off to reveal the sharply muscled expanse of his shoulders. She blushed as her eyes widened. Catullus scowled.

Here was something new: jealousy.

Ridiculous for Catullus to be jealous of Lesperance. If ever a man was entirely devoted to one woman, it was Lesperance, whose love for Astrid obliterated everything. And the sentiment was returned with the same vehemence. Astrid had loved her late husband, but this bond she now shared with Lesperance glowed white-hot and eternal.

And Catullus and Gemma had spent only one night together. An incredible and awkward night, but just one. He hadn't even slept under the covers with her.

So there was no rational explanation for Catullus's surge of possessiveness. None at all. That didn't stop him from glowering and wanting to plow his fist straight between Lesperance's shoulder blades. Instead of falling to Catullus's imagined punch, Lesperance disappeared behind a tree.

With her own far-too-perceptive glance, Astrid took in Gemma's reaction to Lesperance, and Catullus's scowl. She raised a brow in silent question at Catullus, and he turned away, pretending to rifle through his bags.

Moments later, an avian shriek unfurled, and a red-tailed hawk flew from behind the tree. Astrid held out an arm. The bird perched there, accepting Astrid's strokes along its feathered throat with a series of soft chirps that could only be described as contented.

Gemma slowly approached, her wide gaze fastened on the hawk. "Is that . . . ?"

"Yes, it's Nathan." Astrid smiled warmly at the bird. "He'll scout for us, and if he sees any trouble ahead, he'll let us know."

The hawk chirped again.

"How will he know where to go?" Gemma pressed. "Has he ever been to Glastonbury before?"

"No," answered Astrid. "But I have, and so he'll know."

Gemma turned confused eyes to Catullus, seeking an explanation.

Still riled, disturbed by his own jealousy, he gritted, "The bond they share. It enables them to find one another."

Gemma nodded with growing understanding. Wonder lit her face, and she glowed with delight at this newest discovery. "Like a homing beacon."

"Something like that," Astrid murmured, scratching just beneath the hawk's beak. The bird's eyes shut, rapturous. "Ready?"

The hawk bobbed its head. Astrid gave a small push with her arm, and the bird took to the air with a few beats of its powerful wings. Everyone watched the ascent, until the hawk became a tiny, wheeling fleck against a pearl gray sky.

"That must be wonderful," Gemma breathed. "I've always wanted to fly." She turned to Catullus. "Have you ever built a flying contraption? Is such a thing possible?"

"I have and it is," he answered with a small sliver of pride. He might not possess magic, nor a younger man's physique, but no one disputed his ingenuity. "Bennett Day used it in Greece not too long ago. Still needs refinement, though."

And he felt a gleam of satisfaction when Gemma looked up at him with genuine respect. Different, too, from the usual looks he received, especially from women, who were occasionally intimidated. Often mystified, as if he'd wandered in from the bottom of the ocean to display his gills and drip on the floor.

"I'd like to see that," she whispered. "Maybe when this is over . . ."

Reality returned with a snap. There might not be *anything* after the battle with the Heirs. A battle they might be able to avert if they reached Glastonbury in time. He had his duty to Blades. And to Gemma, to keep her safe. Which meant there wasn't a moment to waste on his fumbling attempts at flirtation.

"You can ride astride?"

Gemma blinked at Catullus's abrupt change of topic, but recovered quickly. "Yes—there weren't many sidesaddles in the Northwest Territory."

"Good. Mount up." He gave a clipped nod and turned away, his mind already miles down the road.

* * *

Hard travel taxed the horses and the riders, but as the hours and miles rolled past, alternating between a run and a brisk trot, Catullus pushed everyone—especially himself—even harder. Glastonbury was still half a day away. He saw with a strategist's eye the familiar English landscape unfold around him: its gently undulating hills dotted with bare trees rattling in the late-autumn winds that offered little shelter against a possible attack, the exceedingly domestic villages and towns that had to be skirted, those stretches of road bound by hedgerows that left the travelers far too exposed for his liking.

Yet he wasn't alone in his vigil. Astrid was at all times aware of her surroundings, and Lesperance kept watch from the sky. Even Gemma, a stranger to the way of the Blades, never relaxed into complacency as she bent low over her horse's neck. Catullus allowed himself a moment's distraction to watch Gemma ride.

She had a natural confident grace in the saddle, despite her skirts bunching as she rode astride. Though she wasn't a toughened mountain woman like Astrid, Gemma commanded a supple strength all her own. He recalled lucidly the satiny, bright feel of her legs beneath her nightgown and cursed himself for his vivid imagination when his body responded to the mental image. Arousal and horseback riding made for a bruising combination.

Shortly before midday, a hawk's cry drew them all to a halt.

"Heirs." Astrid squinted up at the sky, where Lesperance wheeled and banked overhead in a sequence of intricate circles. Catullus at once detected a pattern in the hawk's movements. "One mile up, at the junction of two major roads. Three men on horseback. There's a bridge that spans a river, and they're on it."

Gemma also looked up, shading her eyes with her hand. "You worked out a communication system ahead of time."

"A simple code. Easier this way, so he needn't go

through the bother of landing and transforming into a man."
Astrid turned to Catullus. "Suggestions?"

Standing up in the stirrups, Catullus took in the surrounding landscape, gauging exactly what could get them past the Heirs without going too far out of their way. Rerouting even a few miles could cost time that wasn't theirs. Then he saw the solution.

"There." He pointed toward a narrow river cutting through the vale. "That's the river over which the bridge spans. The Heirs will be watching the roads, but not the water."

"Will we be able to sneak past them without being seen?" asked Gemma, but there was no fear edging her words.

Catullus smiled. "I've got a way to ensure their attention is elsewhere." He glanced at Astrid. "Tell Lesperance to land. I have a job for him."

"Don't think anyone can *tell* Nathan anything," Astrid murmured wryly. Yet she pulled from her coat pocket a heavy Compass, then used its polished surface to send a signal up to Lesperance.

Gemma peered at the Compass, curiosity illuminating her face. With her sharp journalist's eye, she couldn't have failed to notice the Compass's unusual design, its metal casing covered with fine engraving, the four blades that marked the cardinal directions. Catullus saw Astrid's use of it now as a sign of her growing trust in Gemma, for the Compass was closely guarded by the Blades.

"That's the Compass," Catullus said in answer to Gemma's unasked question. "All Blades carry one as a badge of office and means of identification."

"Including you?"

"Of course. It's our most prized possession. My great-great-grandmother Portia created the very first Compass."

Gemma chuckled ruefully even as she shook her head at Portia's innovation. "It's claimed my great-great-grandfather

Lucca created a fountain that endlessly poured wine, but no one was ever able to prove it."

"Endless, hm? I'll have to work on that. Could prove profitable."

"It wasn't for great-great-grandfather Lucca. They say that when he died, he owed money to at least seven men and three women."

"Women?"

"A handsome man, Lucca. A little *too* handsome."

They shared a smile just as Lesperance alit on Astrid's outstretched arm. Reluctantly, Catullus turned from Gemma to address the hawk—a process he *still* wasn't used to, speaking with an animal that wasn't truly an animal but a man. Sometimes, he thought with an inward sigh, it was deuced difficult to reconcile science with magic.

Nevertheless, he asked blandly, "Ever spooked a horse, Lesperance?"

The hawk gave a small cry that could only be described as eager. It seemed that Lesperance had lost none of his rebellious spirit.

Hidden behind a bend in the shallow river, Catullus, Gemma, and Astrid watched the bridge. It was a newer iron bridge, thirty feet above the river. Normally, Catullus liked to study bridges, contemplate what the engineer had attempted and whether the effort could have been improved. Not a few coins in the Graveses' coffers came from helping to build bridges just like this one. Bridges ensured that the grinding poverty of rural life could be alleviated through regular deliveries of food and modern convenience.

Today, however, Catullus wasn't scrutinizing the bridge, but the men on it. Three of them, mounted, their expensive horses gleaming with the obsessive care that only wealth and privilege could afford. The men surveyed the road, attentive to anyone who might pass. Catullus, mounted on a much more economical horse, watched the men through his spyglass.

"Are they really Heirs?" Gemma whispered.

"Costly clothing, *de rigueur* moustaches, autocratic posture, and aura of entitlement." Catullus ticked off a list of attributes. "Those are most assuredly Heirs."

"I don't understand how they knew we would be here."

"They knew we abandoned the train and likely have men scattered throughout the area."

"Do you recognize any of the bastards?" growled Astrid. She, more than any Blade, had a personal vendetta against the men who killed her husband and tried to capture and torture her years later. "Is Bracebridge or Gibbs with them?" Her hand strayed to her coat, where her revolver waited.

"No." *Thank God.* As dedicated as Astrid was to their mission, Catullus wasn't certain she wouldn't give their position away by simply shooting either Bracebridge, the mage who tried to kill Lesperance, or Gibbs, one of the two men personally responsible for Michael Bramfield's death. "And they all start to look the same after a while. Pompous and self-congratulatory." He shut the spyglass and returned it to his saddlebag. "There's Lesperance."

Sure enough, Lesperance swung his hawk form down from the sky and disappeared behind several buildings lining the road. Then, in a burst of silver and black fur, a huge wolf darted out and ran straight toward the bridge.

The Heirs' overbred horses sensed the wolf before their riders. At once, the animals began to rear up, whinnying in terror. The Heirs tried to rein in their horses, lashing them brutally with their riding crops as they shouted for control. Before the mounts could be restrained, the wolf snarled and charged. This proved too much for the poor, skittish horses, who had likely never seen a wolf, especially one so enormous. All three horses bolted, tearing off the bridge and down the road, their riders clinging to their backs. There wasn't even time for any of the Heirs to draw a weapon and fire at the wolf.

"Now!" Catullus commanded.

He, Gemma, and Astrid urged their own horses into a swift canter, darting through the river and underneath the bridge. Water splashed up as they sped down the center of the river, the horses' hooves clattering on the rocky river bottom. But it didn't matter how much noise they made. The Heirs would be halfway to Torquay before they regained control over their terrified mounts.

As Catullus, Gemma, and Astrid raced through the river, Lesperance appeared in hawk form to fly alongside them. He gave a victorious cry, and they all shared a brief smile of triumph. So many obstacles, many of them deadly, lay ahead. None of them truly knew what *did* await them. A consciously reckless plunge into the unknown.

Everyone needed to savor whatever victory they could, however transitory. And Catullus's gratification came not just from thwarting the Heirs, but also from Gemma's smile.

Chapter 7

Question and Answer

"We stop to eat and rest," Catullus said, hours later. He slowed his horse, and Gemma and Astrid did the same. There was one other member of their party. Gemma looked up to see the red-tailed hawk bank and then alight upon a tree branch. The hawk watched as the horses came to a stop in a sheltered glade.

She still could hardly believe that animal was actually Lesperance. She thought she knew about magic, but so much existed beyond what she was coming to learn was her own limited scope. A good deal of magic remained a mystery to her. But she had a feeling that she'd learn more, much more, before too long. The thought frightened and thrilled her.

Right now, however, she just wanted off this damned horse.

She'd been shipbound and idle for too long. Her bottom ached from nearly a full day in the saddle. She needed to relieve herself. She was hungry.

Her complaints went unvoiced. Whining never did anyone any good, and Gemma was determined to show the Blades of the Rose that she could be as tough and resilient as any of them. Astrid continued to warily scrutinize her. And Catullus . . .

As everyone dismounted—Gemma fighting not to wince—she gazed at Catullus. He moved with athletic grace, and surveyed the glade with a strategist's eye, sure and alert. Astrid asked him a question about distance and travel to Glastonbury, and he answered with a ready air of authority and command. When he caught Gemma looking at him, he smiled; then his smile faltered as if he became aware of himself. He glanced away, removing and polishing his spectacles with a spotless handkerchief. Once the already-clean lenses gleamed, he busied himself with tying up his horse, and wouldn't meet her eyes again.

This, from the man who'd touched her intimately, who'd given her a devastating climax with his extraordinary, wonderful hands! Such a damned puzzle.

Once her own horse had been secured, Gemma started toward the shelter of some bushes. Catullus appeared, blocking her path.

"Where are you going?" he demanded.

"To tend to my personal needs," she answered, level.

"Oh." He blinked. "Just . . . ah . . . be careful."

Tired and sore as she was, she didn't feel particularly charitable toward his shyness at the moment, and said dryly, "I mastered the task a while ago."

"Right. Of course."

Gemma stepped around him.

His voice stopped her. "The Heirs are out there, somewhere. So, please, be cautious. If you need anything just . . . call out."

Damn it—she couldn't keep up her temper when he was so gallant.

She hurried off to the privacy of the shrubs and, after ensuring that no one was about, relieved herself, sighing. Adventuring was all very well and exciting, but one's bodily needs didn't disappear just because the fate of the world's magic and freedom was at stake.

After she was finished, she knelt beside a nearby creek to freshen up. She dipped her fingertips into the water, then pulled them back, hissing. Too cold! But she needed to wash, so she forced her hands back into the creek to rinse, then splashed some water onto her face and the back of her neck. Her fingertips turned blue within seconds. On a brighter side, only a dead person could be unaffected by such a chilly bath. Gemma's senses glittered back to life.

As she knelt, she became aware of a presence behind her.

Her hand crept toward the derringer in her pocket.

"Only me," said a deep, Canadian-accented voice.

Gemma relaxed as Lesperance, clothed in trousers and an open shirt, feet bare, came forward silently and crouched beside her. A striking man, lean of body, with a profile that should be minted onto coins. Any sighted woman would enjoy looking at him, and Gemma definitely had eyes. She admired him the way one might admire any art—all theory and aesthetics, but nothing that stirred her desire.

Not the way a reserved, bespectacled inventor with dark eyes stirred her.

Lesperance plunged his hands into the frigid water. She waited for him to pull back or at least grimace from the temperature. He didn't.

"I thought my hands would freeze off," she noted. "You don't seem to be bothered, though. Is that a facet of being able to . . . change?" Only minutes earlier, he'd been flying overhead as a hawk. And before that, he'd run as a wolf. Catullus said that Lesperance could even take the form of a bear. Now she was *talking* with Lesperance.

What a story he must have.

He nodded, unaware that her journalistic impulses bubbled furiously. "Grew to like the cold, actually. Ever since my power to change showed, I run hot."

Oh, didn't Gemma know it, judging by the way he and Astrid carried on in bed.

Instead of voicing this, she asked, "When did your changing ability manifest?"

He tensed, then realized she wasn't employing the Key of Janus to force him to answer her question—just as she'd promised Catullus she wouldn't. Lesperance raised a brow. "Interviewing me for a story?" Before she could answer, he asked, "You like finding out people's secrets—is that why you became a reporter?"

"Cross-examining me, counselor?"

They met each other's gaze with cool challenge. Neither spoke. Until—

"A trade," Gemma proposed. "We each ask a question, we each have to answer."

"Well negotiated." He gave an appreciative nod. "All parties agree to the terms. As a show of good faith, I'll start. I discovered my ability to shift just after you saw me at the trading post."

She gaped. "That was only a few months ago!"

"Take that surprise you're feeling, then multiply it by a thousand." A corner of his mouth tilted up. "That's how I felt when I learned I was an Earth Spirit."

"But . . . how did it happen?"

He held up a finger. "Not your turn. Answer my question first."

Right. Her end of the bargain. "Ever since I was small, I wanted to be a reporter. Learning. Observing." She mulled this. "It's not secrets that interest me, but the truth."

"Once you discover the truth, what then?"

Now she held up a cautioning finger. "Not your turn, counselor. You owe me an answer."

"The Primal Source released a dormant power in me." His expression darkened. "Those son of a bitch Heirs tried to enslave my people."

"Tried, but didn't succeed."

"Because we fought back. The Earth Spirits, and the Blades." He scowled. "That's two questions you asked me."

"Technically, I didn't ask you anything. I made a statement, and you confirmed it."

He smiled, almost grudging. "You still have my question to answer."

She might have known that Astrid's lover would have a will of iron. "When I uncover the truth, whatever it is, I write about it."

He looked at her, his gaze hardening. "Not any of what I just told you. Not my people. Merely a few printed words about them would destroy their lives."

The stab of conscience in conflict with her journalistic instincts pierced her. Write and publish, giving full knowledge to the world, or remain silent to protect innocents. "Damned ethics," she muttered, "getting in the way of a good story."

"Try being an attorney sometime—*then* we'll talk about conflict with ethics." Yet his look didn't soften. "I don't want to threaten you, but I will do anything to protect my people."

"And I'm no threat to you, or the Earth Spirits." She pressed her lips together, then said, "They're safe from my pen."

He relaxed slightly.

Something occurred to her then. "She asked you to interrogate me."

He knew precisely who Gemma meant. "'Interrogate' is a word for criminals. But, yes, she's wary of you."

"She keeps looking at me as if I were a keg of gunpowder that could detonate at any moment."

Rather than look offended, Lesperance chuckled. "Protective."

This startled Gemma. "Blindfolded, drunk and asleep, that woman could take me apart. She has nothing to fear from me. I can't hurt her."

"It's not you she's protecting. It's Graves."

Surprise gave way to annoyance. "Catullus is a grown man who can take care of himself." She had direct knowledge, in fact, that he was fully an adult. Remembrance of the night before heated her cheeks as she glanced down at her hands. She'd touched Catullus with those hands, stroked him and felt him shudder with release.

"Astrid told me that Graves . . . he's brilliant, but bring women into the equation . . ." Lesperance shook his head. "Not the most worldly."

"I've never met a more complex man in my life."

"Doubt he's ever met anyone like you. I've only known him for a short while, but I know Astrid as well as I know the contours of my own soul. She sees how you affect Graves, what you mean to him. That makes her cautious."

Gemma rose to her feet, and Lesperance did the same. "I'm not that important to him." If she was, wouldn't he be more assertive? Catullus kept backing away.

Lesperance held her gaze steadily. "You *do* matter to Graves. Even I can see it."

She prided herself on being levelheaded. Journalists needed to present to the world an unflappable façade, needed to believe in their own sangfroid to be impartial to what they reported. Personal emotions clouded truth. So Gemma was implacable, even when presented with the most flagrant case of political corruption she'd ever encountered. She reported the facts calmly, objectively—until her editor took the story away from her and gave it to a male reporter, who then heaped adverbs, adjectives, and accusations all over the piece. Even then, she didn't let loose her scream of frustration, but calmly continued with her work as she inwardly seethed.

This time, however, she couldn't hide her amazement. Catullus felt something for her, something hidden by his reticence. And what she felt for him . . . whatever it was, burgeoning, taking shape, she knew it went beyond hunger for simply his body.

She'd thought the same of Richard, too. But once she and Richard had been sexually intimate, he had tried to change her, to impose himself on her. He assumed they would marry, but never went to the trouble of actually *asking* her. After they wed, Richard had said, she must give up journalism. It was the only respectable thing to do. Or, if she insisted on writing, perhaps she could write more suitable material . . . like children's books.

Shaken, it had taken Gemma too long to realize Richard truly believed she would give up everything she wanted, everything she was, to suit him and his needs. She returned the ring he'd once confidently put upon her finger. He fumed, then pointedly ignored her. He married a girl from his neighborhood six months later. The girl, Gemma learned from a friend, wrote nursery rhymes.

Catullus did not make demands. He seemed to like her exactly as she was. A tentative hope began to unfurl within her, hope for something she thought couldn't be hers.

"It's never been this complicated before. Not with anyone else." She gnawed on her bottom lip. "Nothing simple about Catullus." Or how he made her feel.

"Didn't trust Graves when I first met him," Lesperance said. "But he saved my hide a dozen times over. Aside from Astrid, there's nobody I'd rather have at my back in a fight. He's become a friend, and I don't want him hurt."

"Why does everyone think I'm going to hurt him?" Gemma demanded. "Maybe he'll hurt me!"

"Never willingly."

Gemma let out a frustrated sigh, uncertain of her next move. "Was it this perplexing with formidable Astrid?"

His sudden grin turned Lesperance from extremely attractive to devastatingly handsome. "A maze within a labyrinth. Kept me a shotgun's distance away, fighting the whole time. But I knew with every part of myself that we were meant for each other. I didn't give up, didn't let her fear of herself stand in our way. So I learned her—pushed when she needed pushing, gentled when she needed gentleness."

Gemma considered this, her mind churning. "Sounds like quite an experience."

"Still is." He laughed, rueful. "Damned skittish Blades. They can protect the world's magic, but when it comes to seeing to their own hearts, the lot of them are as baffled as a pride of lions in a library."

Gemma and Lesperance returned to the glade. Both Catullus and Astrid, standing close to one another and talking in low voices, looked up sharply at their approach. Astrid immediately came forward, seeing only Lesperance, while Catullus remained where he stood. He looked at Gemma as if nothing intrigued him more, yet he did not know where to begin his exploration.

Lesperance and Astrid took hold of each other's hands and drifted off to one side. Within a moment, they were deep in private conversation.

Thinking about what Lesperance had told her, Gemma walked toward Catullus. He held out an apple.

As she took the offered fruit, Gemma murmured, "From the tree of knowledge."

His brows snapped together. "Pardon?"

"Which makes me Eve, and you the coaxing Serpent." She bit into the apple, and smiled at the taste of sweet, crisp flesh.

Catullus watched her avidly. "Surely I'm not so devious."

She chewed, swallowed. "Maybe not, but you *are* tempting." Her gaze held his, and his dark eyes widened behind the glass of his spectacles.

"Ah," he said. Then, as though forcing the words from his mouth, he said, "You, also." A tentative smile, heart-breaking in its caution, curved his mouth. Then, his gaze sliding away from her as his smile faded, he removed his spectacles and began methodically polishing them.

Gemma, eating her apple, remembered what Lesperance had said. A careful dance, learning when to push forward, when to give ground.

"What were you and Astrid talking about?"

He exhaled in relief at the change of topic, replacing his spectacles. Vision restored, he glanced over his shoulder, as if confirming Astrid's presence. She and Lesperance continued to converse, their eyes locked, hands interlaced.

Turning back to Gemma, Catullus said, "We were discussing how much distance we've to cover. A matter of hours to reach Glastonbury, if we keep this pace."

"Once we get to Glastonbury, what then?"

Catullus rubbed his jaw with his large hand. Gemma's mind and body both recalled the feel of his hands on her, touching her intimately, drawing pleasure from her, as she'd done with him. Desire to kiss him—in front of Astrid and Lesperance and whoever might be watching—overwhelmed her.

She bit down hard on the apple. Sweetness filled her mouth.

He watched her lick juice from her lips, then shook his head to clear his thoughts. "We have to try to stop the Heirs' desires from summoning Arthur. But we might not be able to prevent that. Magic has momentum, like any force in nature. Once it has begun, it takes an extraordinary power to stop it."

"What will happen if they *do* summon Arthur?"

"There's no way to know." By the light gleaming in his dark eyes, she knew the prospect of unlimited possibilities exhilarated him. "He could return as a non-corporeal spirit."

"A ghost?"

"Possibly. Or Arthur could be a flesh-and-blood man that's terrified of the modern world—he could mistake a train for a fire-breathing dragon. He might rise up from the ground like a zombie." He gave a slight grimace. "Fought an army of those in Canada."

"An *army*? Of *zombies*?" She gaped at him.

He gave a dismissive shrug, as if battling the undead were perfectly mundane. "An Heir mage resurrected them. Disgusting. And messy." Which seemed to be the worst offense, judging by Catullus's tone.

"Did you fight them on your own?"

"Alone? No. Myself, Astrid, Nathan, and the Earth Spirits." He waved this incredible tale—one she desperately wanted to hear—aside. "Nevertheless, I hope we don't face more of that in Glastonbury. Zombies aren't merely revolting, they are *dangerous*." His expression turned grim. "I do not want any of those creatures near you."

She didn't want them near her, either, but Catullus's protectiveness warmed her.

"If I could just *speak* to King Arthur." Her imagination burst to life, considering this. "Think of it," she breathed, "the King Arthur of myth, made real. The stories he could tell—legends, histories. Fables and truths."

She had not realized she was smiling until Catullus shared in her smile. "You're so beautiful when hunting stories." Then he flushed, as if abashed at the husky words that had sprung from him without thought.

Embarrassment was *not* what Gemma felt at his candid, guileless compliment. Thrilled, more like. Catullus Graves wasn't a rake or flatterer, not a practiced seducer of women. What he said, he meant.

"I've a feeling," she said softly, "there are lots more stories ahead."

His flush deepened, but he didn't look away when their eyes met and held.

Astrid and Lesperance drifted over to them. Perhaps it was Gemma's imagination, but Astrid appeared less wary when the Englishwoman glanced at her. Almost . . . approving. Gemma wondered what Lesperance had said to his lover to cause this change of attitude.

From the pocket of his waistcoat, Catullus pulled out an exquisite timepiece. He consulted its face. "We can take fifteen minutes to eat, and then we have to press on to Glastonbury." He glanced at Astrid. "Can you still feel the Primal Source?"

"The connection I developed to the Primal Source when I studied it in Africa hasn't diminished, not in all these years."

"And now, is it gathering its energy?"

"It's growing stronger by the moment."

Grim, Catullus returned his watch to its pocket. "Ten minutes to eat. No more."

When the meal was concluded—eight minutes later—Catullus helped Gemma back into the saddle. His hands lingered at her waist, and she felt the warmth of him all the way to her core. For a moment, their gazes locked, fraught with significance.

And then they were off again.

Gemma considered Catullus out of the corner of her eye as everyone cantered through an open field. On horseback, his long coat billowing behind him, no man was as lethally attractive, so potent with movement and capability.

He drew up beside her.

"There's something else Astrid and I talked about." His words rumbled low, meant for her alone.

Her breath quickly deserted her. "Oh?"

"She reminded me that I don't need all the answers. That the process of discovery has its own . . . pleasure."

A sensuous word, made even more so by his rich, deep voice.

"A wise woman, Astrid," Gemma said.

Night drew on quickly as they rode. Barely a moment between twilight and full darkness, then, soon after, a round and shining moon breached the horizon. A strange, silver cast washed over the land. With the moonlight came a finely wrought tension, a harp string about to be plucked to sound an uncanny music.

Gemma sensed it—the change in her connection to magic. Her whole life, what she knew and felt of it kept itself limited to the small sphere of her family. Now she sensed it stretching, widening. Or rather she felt her own awareness growing. Sensing the waves of the world's magic lapping waves on the shore.

At that moment, she felt a growing presence, a perception, prickling along her skin. The others felt it, too. Catullus frowned deeply, and overhead, Lesperance let out abbreviated cries. But Astrid sensed the gathering magic more than anyone else. The Englishwoman almost vibrated with awareness as she bent over her horse's neck, plunging through the countryside.

Not a single traveler appeared; there were no carts or carriages on the road. It was as if everyone had sensed otherworldly power rising and stayed close within the perceived safety of their homes. Even the night sounds of animals were muffled.

Gemma, Catullus, and Astrid rode over flat country. Ahead rose the forms of hills, clustered together. Gemma knew without being told that this was Glastonbury. An ancient energy hovered over the place. She could well imagine that, long ago when swamps submerged the land, the hills appeared as islands—perhaps as Avalon.

Low-lying mists swirled around the bases of the hills, brightened into silver by the moon. Yet the mists weren't still. They shifted and eddied, without a breath of wind to stir them.

Everyone pulled their horses to a stop on the northern outskirts of what appeared to be a small town. The animals stamped and snorted, agitated. Gemma understood how the beasts felt.

"Where first?" asked Gemma.

"The abbey," Catullus answered. "That's where the supposed remains of Arthur were unearthed."

Astrid held out her arm, and the hawk sailed down to perch there. She stroked the feathers along his neck. "Any sign of the Heirs?" When the hawk shook out his feathers, she translated. "Nathan cannot see them nearby."

Catullus was not comforted. "Might be using some variety of magic to shield themselves."

"Cowards," Astrid snarled. Her hand lay atop a fold of her skirts, near her pistol.

"If they do not turn up," Catullus answered levelly, "we should consider ourselves fortunate. *None* of us need a fight." He glanced at Gemma, and she understood it was *her*, more than anyone else, that he protected.

She wasn't a liability. Gemma had a gun and her wits. "If the Heirs *are* around, we can beat them to the abbey." She brought her sidestepping horse under control, wheeling it around so it faced south. Her heels pressed into the animal's sides. It surged forward. "Tea party's over."

Behind her, she heard Catullus and Astrid also urge their horses into motion. A flap of wings as Lesperance took to the sky once more.

Catullus drew up beside her. A smile tilted one corner of his mouth. "Bravado has its place—but you don't know where we're headed."

True enough. No sense blundering around Glastonbury like a reckless tornado. She pulled up slightly, allowing Catullus to take the lead. He tipped his head in ironic gratitude before moving forward.

No one walked the streets, even though Glastonbury appeared to be a decent-sized town of both old and modern buildings. Had Gemma the time, she would have gladly studied the town itself—there was nothing like it back in the United States. Here, even man-made structures held the kind of history she had only read about. But this was not the moment for a journalist's inquisitive ramblings.

The hour wasn't late. Yet the shutters were drawn in the houses and storefronts lining the streets, the lamps doused.

None of this was nearly as strange as the mists that flowed over the pavement. They eddied around the cantering horses' legs, as swift and deliberate as streams of water, heading in the same direction. To the south. It had a will of its own, the mist. The air smelled of ancient fire.

Against the night sky loomed dark forms of crumbling walls with empty, arched windows. A ruin. In the middle of a town. She hadn't expected that.

Catullus held up a hand, and, silently, everyone slowed their horses to a walk. In a single, smooth motion, Lesperance glided down from the sky and shifted into a huge wolf. Gemma felt she ought to be used to that transformation by now. Yet she wasn't. She'd wandered out of her life and into a fairy tale.

A fairy tale with both light and dark magic—in which the intrepid hero, or heroine, might not live to see the happily ever after.

Gemma fought her fear, determined to prove to herself her own strength.

The wolf that was actually Lesperance padded alongside the horses as they all picked their way through the remains of what had been a medieval abbey. Maybe it was a sudden breeze pushing through the vacant gothic windows, or maybe something else, but the stone walls echoed softly with the sounds of chanting. Gemma looked up. The roof had long since vanished, so the moon shone down upon the ruins and the three people—and wolf—within. Vines, bare of leaves, climbed the walls as if trying to pull the remainder of the abbey into the earth.

Instinctually, Gemma brought her horse closer to Catullus.

"Where is Arthur's tomb?" she whispered.

He peered around the crumbling church. "There are two

sites. Where the tomb was originally found, and then where the remains were reinterred about eighty years later."

"We should investigate both."

He nodded. "Astrid, you and Lesperance go to the second site. It's in the chancel, near where the altar used to be in the church. Gemma and I will explore where the bones were first discovered."

Astrid agreed, and she and Lesperance moved deeper into the church, both tense as bowstrings.

When Catullus brought his horse around, leaving the church, Gemma followed. She sighed in relief as they left behind the looming, sinister walls. Catullus guided them toward a grassy field that appeared entirely empty.

"Nothing's here. Is this really where Arthur's bones were found?"

"This used to be the monks' graveyard, long, long ago. When excavations were done in the eleven hundreds, a stone slab and leaden cross were unearthed here. The cross bore an inscription in Latin proclaiming the burial site of King Arthur. Farther down in the ground was a coffin fashioned from a hollow log, and within the coffin were the bones of a tall man."

"A scholar of Arthur in addition to a mechanical genius," Gemma murmured, appreciative. "Such a variety of talents."

Catullus actually looked a little smug, which charmed her. "Monomania makes for a limited intellect."

She pressed her advantage. "Nothing more stimulating than a man of many passions."

"Miss Murphy, you are an inveterate flirt."

"Just with you, Mr. Graves. Something within me can't seem to resist."

They shared a smile, but briefly. Neither could pretend they were on a moonlight jaunt in a romantic ruin. As each minute passed, the sense of gathering energy grew, until Gemma felt it not only on the surface of her skin, but within herself as well.

She and Catullus surveyed the tree-fringed field. The only stirring came from the mist carpeting the ground.

"That mist . . ."

"I noted it. Fogs come in sometimes from the Bristol Channel, but not like this." Catullus swung down from his horse and lowered into a crouch.

Gemma was half afraid the mist might harm him somehow, swallow him like a living thing, yet when he ran his hand through the silvery vapor, nothing happened.

He rubbed his fingers together as if testing the texture of the mist. "I can feel it moving, being drawn toward something. Like a stream directed toward a cataract."

"But look." She pointed. "It isn't resting here. It's moving elsewhere. Somewhere to the east."

He got back into the saddle. "If Arthur is being summoned, the abbey isn't the place."

Astrid came riding up from the dark form of the church, Lesperance loping beside her. What should have been an odd pairing—the golden-haired woman and the dark wolf—seemed to Gemma to be precisely right. More linked the two than outward appearance. Each as fierce as the other, perfectly formed counterparts.

It made Gemma wonder about the pull of other opposites. About possibility.

But Astrid's clear, strong voice brought Gemma back into the present. "Not here. We searched the site of the tomb, but I can feel it."

Lesperance gave a *whuff* of agreement. He nosed at the mist and whined lowly.

"Follow the mist." Catullus tilted his chin in the direction toward which the gleaming vapor streamed.

As one, everyone turned to watch, and it became clear, with the moonlight burning down, where the mists were being drawn.

A high, narrow hill jutted to the east, taller than all the other hills clustered nearby. Slight terraces ridged the formation. At the very top stood a single ruined tower. A sentinel over the whole of the eerie landscape. Toward this tower the mists flowed, even climbing *up* the hill itself to collect and spin around its base. And as they spun, the mists increased their speed, roiling like a river over stones.

Gathering. Massing. The collective dreams of ruthless men, drawing magic toward a single point, with a single purpose.

Gemma pressed her palm against the back of her neck to keep the hairs there from rising.

"What is that place?" she breathed.

"Glastonbury Tor." Catullus's voice held a comforting authority. "The tower at the top is St. Michael's Church."

"Not the burial place of Arthur."

"No," said Astrid. "But his myth is bound up with the tor. It was said to be his stronghold. And—"

"And . . . ?" Gemma prompted, when Astrid gritted her teeth and fell silent. "What is it about that place that draws the mists?" She both did and did not want to know, fearful and eager for the answer.

"Legend holds that the tor marks the entrance to Annwn." Catullus turned to her, and the moonlight reflecting upon his spectacles transformed his eyes into ghostly silver mirrors. "The Otherworld."

Her father's tales of faerie realms beneath the earth echoed in Gemma's mind. Hollow hills. The Fair Folk. Stolen brides and changeling children. Beauty—and danger. Mortals who strayed past the boundary and never came back. Or, if they did, they were never the same, wasting away as they pined for the distant land.

And she rode straight toward its entrance.

It didn't escape her, either, that St. Michael the Archangel fought against the powers of hell and Satan. No coincidence that a church was built in his name. The monks must have known that Glastonbury Tor marked the portal between worlds, and sought to hold back its magic with their own fragile beliefs.

Old habit made Gemma furtively cross herself as she, Catullus, and the others raced toward the odd hill. She'd take any protection she could get.

Though she had an idea that Catullus would protect her far more than prayer. He was a living man, and capable. Gemma wasn't used to relying on anyone other than herself—but she couldn't deny a sense of relief, knowing she wasn't alone as magic collected to summon . . . she had no idea what it would summon, only that it would hold a power unlike anything anyone had ever seen before.

They sped toward the tor. The mists thickened, growing stronger. Dark fire scented the air. The horses began to struggle and shy as they neared. Lesperance leapt away as the animals lunged, dancing, their hooves nearly grazing him as he ran alongside. Astrid swore savagely, cursing her horse.

Gemma's horse reared up. She fought to control it, clenching her teeth, pulling hard on the reins. She struggled to keep her seat.

Catullus immediately rode toward her, hand outstretched to grab her horse's bridle. Then his mount, too, reared, tossing its head in fear. The horses grew more and more frenzied.

"No good," Catullus gritted. "Jump clear."

After gulping a breath, Gemma flung herself from her horse. She landed and rolled, arms covering her head from the stamping animals. A single blow from a hoof could split her head in two. Not how she wanted her English adventure to end, with her brains splattered at the base of Glastonbury Tor by a frightened horse.

She looked up to see all three horses charging away. The mounts ran off, thundering, until they fled into the night.

Two large, strong hands lifted her up until she stood, gazing up at Catullus's concerned face.

"Are you hurt?"

She shook her head. "Fairly soon, I'll be an expert at jumping off moving things."

"We can present our findings to the Royal Society together." He offered a brief smile, and brushed her hair back from her face.

Astrid appeared beside them, with the wolf Lesperance protectively at her side. She looked pained, but not by the jump from her horse. As the mists thickened, they seemed to pull on her, too, tugging on something deep within. She kept one hand on Lesperance's neck as she staggered. Lesperance rumbled, pushing himself against her for support.

The Englishwoman pointed up the hill. At the summit, the mists collected. They climbed up the tower like vines, and there was no way to know whether the moon made them shimmer or if they created their own glow. Didn't matter. Not when they started spinning and swirling until the top of the hill became a vortex.

Astrid rasped, "It's beginning."

Chapter 8

Rex Quondam, Rexque Futurus

Catullus's life in his workshop was a series of choices which he carefully studied, weighing the advantages and disadvantages, the potential outcomes, if the result merited the risk. He loved being presented with a problem or situation and then slowly, methodically analyzing it. As Astrid had said, the best part of invention was the process. Copper wiring, or gold alloy? Spring-driven, or hydraulic? All possibilities could be entertained, explored.

In the field, he didn't have that luxury. Decisions had to be made in an instant. Lives, including his own, could be lost if he hesitated. So, he acted, using instinct and experience to guide him. His companions in the field were other Blades, trained, fully aware of the inherent risks of their calling. They all gambled.

He enjoyed the dichotomy, the two halves of himself. He went into the field more often than any other member of the Graves family, for that very reason, because he relished the balance between deliberate thought and instinctive action.

Here now arose a problem he couldn't resolve.

Leave Gemma at the foot of Glastonbury Tor, away from

the danger at the summit. Or take her with him to the top. If he left her behind, she'd be alone and vulnerable. If he took her with him, he'd be leading her straight into the unknown—which was where danger usually dwelt. And the Heirs were still out there, somewhere, searching. Even now, the Heirs could be drawing closer in the darkness.

Torn. He didn't know what to do.

Then he realized he didn't have a choice. Astrid and Lesperance charged up the terraced hill. And Gemma was right behind them.

Damn that courageous woman.

At the least, he managed to keep his shotgun when he'd jumped from his horse, and he had one cartridge belt lined with ammunition. Everything else was lost when the animals ran off. With his gun slung across his back, he raced up the tor, his long legs making quick work of the slope.

He still wasn't entirely certain what any of them planned to *do* when they reached the top, but he'd think of that when he got there.

Overhead, the moon seemed to grow larger, its cold light burning down over the mist-shrouded hill. Halfway up the hill, what had been a slight breeze down in the abbey turned now into a squall, pulling on Catullus's coat and lashing the women's skirts around their legs. Lesperance snarled into the gale, supporting Astrid as she staggered on her feet. Gemma, too, swayed from the wind buffeting her.

Catullus was at her side instantly. He pulled her against him, shielding her from the gale that tore tears from eyes and stole breath. She held tight to him but didn't burrow or hide.

The mists disengaged from the tower. Serpentine, they shimmered into a tall column that stood level with the tower's high, arched doorway.

The mists formed a distinctly human shape.

"Bugger," said Catullus.

They were too late. It was happening.

He planted his feet then drew his shotgun, holding it with one hand and pointing toward the inchoate human form. At the same time, he thrust Gemma behind him.

"What do we do now?" Gemma cried above the frenzied wind. Her copper hair whipped around her face as she stared up the ridged hill.

Trouble was, there wasn't anything *to* do, but hold on and hope. Catullus loaded two shotgun shells and snapped the gun closed. A bit of firepower could prove useful where hope failed.

The mists rioted with colors never seen in the known world. A figure coalesced within them—huge, but human. Massive legs, enormous arms. Easily twelve feet tall. God, had the Heirs summoned a monster?

More and more the mist solidified, until the moonlight revealed a giant, bearded man. His eyes burned like super-heated iron, white and piercing. Atop his head he wore a golden crown the size of a wagon wheel. Around his colossal body, the mists formed into armor, a miscellany of chain mail, plate, and leather, all topped with a golden surcoat. As the moonlight struck the armor, it reflected back in dazzling beams that spread out from atop the hill like a beacon. Surely the Heirs would be drawn to such light.

Catullus squinted to shield his eyes from the glare. Astrid and Gemma did the same, holding their hands up against the blinding light, but none of them could look away.

"Oh, my God," Gemma whispered, pressing closer to him. Catullus held her tightly.

There could be no mistaking who stood at the summit of Glastonbury Tor.

Arthur. The once and future King of England. Summoned by the Heirs of Albion to lead the nation back to glory.

He glowed, the light of myth and legend blazing from within, as he surveyed the kingdom he had left behind. Confusion furrowed his vast brow. He seemed to be searching for something.

Catullus, who'd spent much of his childhood immersed in books and read tales of chivalric adventure late into the night until his mother admonished him to put out the light and go to bed, could hardly believe he was looking upon the face of King Arthur.

This moment was horrible, or wonderful. Catullus couldn't decide.

The mists dissipated, the moon dimmed, but Arthur remained.

Catullus turned to Gemma. "Stay with Astrid and Lesperance," he said lowly. Gently, he disengaged himself from her.

"Where are you going?"

"To talk to him." And he started up the hill.

He felt Gemma's hand gripping his arm, staying him.

"Genius or madman," she whispered. "You don't know what he might do." Her face was a pale oval, her eyes wide with apprehension as she took in the giant standing at the top of the hill.

"Only one way to find out."

Acting on impulse alone, Catullus leaned close and kissed her, hard and brief. Her lips opened beneath his, he tasted her sweetness, the fierce energy of her that sent bolts of heat and life through him. Her hands came up to rest on his shoulders.

Much as he wanted to continue the kiss, there was such a thing as time and place. So he pulled back. "Stay with Astrid."

Taking a breath, he strode up the slope, all the time watching Arthur, yet conscious of Gemma behind him. The king did not seem to notice him, his eyes focused on a distant point somewhere to the east. Catullus's heart kicked against his ribs. Not from the exertion of climbing a steep hill, but because he was walking toward *King Arthur*.

Catullus had experienced some exceptional moments in

his life as a Blade. Cutting free a feathered serpent from an enchanted net deep in the Central American jungle. Battling brigands and a golem in a Buddhist monastery high atop a mountain in the Gobi Desert. Yet nothing quite equaled climbing an ancient tor in order to speak with the most renowned, exalted figure in all of British lore.

The closer Catullus stepped to Arthur, the more he realized how unbelievably huge Arthur was. Twice Catullus's own over-six-foot height, proportioned on a gigantic scale. Which made sense, considering Arthur's enormity in the minds and imagination of England. Likewise, Arthur's diverse armor proved that he was not the historical man—if such a man ever existed—but the mythological construct created by over a millennium of legends.

What Catullus would give in order to study him in depth! Just as Gemma's mind rioted with possibility at hearing Arthur's stories, Catullus wanted to unlock the mysteries of the king's mind, to examine the various otherworldly metals of his armor. So much potential.

Suddenly, Arthur turned his forceful gaze on Catullus.

Catullus's steps froze, and all scholarly thoughts fled. Twenty feet separated him from Arthur.

The king's eyes blazed as he took Catullus's measure. From the toes of Catullus's admittedly less-than-pristine boots to the top of his head. Warlords crumbled beneath such scrutiny. Catullus made himself stand tall beneath this thorough perusal. He needed to show respect, but also his own strength. When Arthur's gaze snared on the shotgun, Catullus slowly, deliberately slung the weapon across his back, then held up his empty hands.

How did one address a legendary king?

Possibly, one should kneel. But, having had ancestors suffer the yoke of slavery, Catullus could not allow himself to kneel before anyone, even King Arthur.

Respectful speech, however, *that* he could do.

"Greetings, Your Majesty," Catullus said with a cautious bow. "You are welcomed back to a grateful nation."

Arthur stared at him for a long time, still frowning. He said nothing. His arm lifted. Trails of mist gathered, collecting in his open hand. They flowed and twined, beginning to take solid form. A strong scent of lake water. Light shone off a surface, even more brilliantly than the armor's reflection. A long, metallic shape—blade, hilt, pommel, guard. The blade itself was the length of a full-grown man.

A sword materializing. *The* sword. Excalibur. With which Arthur had forged a nation, slaying enemies and any who tried to undermine the glory of England.

Which meant—

Catullus whirled and sped down the hill. "Run!"

Gemma—looking very tiny and fragile compared to Arthur—stared for half a second, then turned to gather her skirts and flee. Astrid did the same. Everyone, including Lesperance in wolf form, bolted.

As he ran, taking the ground in long strides, a slash of heat grazed Catullus's back. He chanced a look behind him to see that Excalibur had not fully materialized, and Arthur swung the half-formed sword.

Catullus dove forward as the ground shook. Clods of dirt rained down on him. He struggled to his feet, then felt two small hands pulling him up. Gemma. She'd turned back to help him.

The angry words at her foolishness died as they both stared at the trench in the earth hewn by the partially manifested Excalibur.

Arthur, ferocious and scowling, raised the materializing sword again as he bore down on Gemma and Catullus.

Seizing hold of Gemma's wrist, Catullus ran as fast as he was able. Beside him, Gemma did not stumble, keeping up while they partly ran, partly slid down the rest of Glastonbury Tor. A mad plunge over the terraced slope.

Astrid and Lesperance dashed ahead. Her curses

about wearing skirts drifted back as Catullus and Gemma followed, racing over fields. The ground continued to shudder from Arthur's pursuit. He shook the earth with his tread.

Even as he ran, Catullus angrily felt the futility of their retreat. Between Arthur's enormous stride and the might of Excalibur, the king would destroy them utterly in moments. One couldn't hide from Arthur, not *this* Arthur, formed of legend and fable.

There had to be some way to safeguard Gemma. A dense stand of trees marked the edge of a field, and Catullus turned toward its shelter. "Get to the trees!" he bellowed at Astrid and Lesperance. The two veered off toward the woods.

He might be able to secure Gemma in the thick underbrush, then provide enough of a distraction to Arthur to lead him off. It wouldn't take long before Excalibur split Catullus into halves like a muffin, but it should give Gemma enough time to get herself to better shelter.

"Don't . . . think it." Gemma's words came out a gasp as she ran, but beneath her spine of steel didn't waiver.

Catullus scowled. "Don't . . . bloody . . . argue."

"So . . . you . . . can sacrifice . . . yourself?"

Almost at the edge of the trees. "Just—"

"Wait! He's stopping!"

They skidded to a halt just at the limit of the woods. Arthur had, indeed, stopped his pursuit. Instead, he swung around and tilted his head, as if trying to hear something.

He threw a glance over his shoulder, toward where Catullus and Gemma stood, then, after a brief hesitation, turned away. With ground-eating steps, he strode away to the east.

Holy God, that had been close. Terrifying, and incredible.

Catullus and Gemma watched Arthur go, both fighting

to regain their breath. Foliage behind them rustled, and Astrid and Lesperance emerged from the woods.

Gemma gasped quietly. Lesperance had shifted into his bear form—his most physically powerful—and made a huge dark shape beside Astrid. Gemma hadn't seen this form yet. Although she knew that Lesperance could transform into a grizzly bear, knowing and seeing were very different experiences.

Yet she quickly collected herself. "I'm not complaining, but why did he stop?" She glanced in the direction which Arthur marched.

"Seemed as though he was being summoned," Catullus mused.

"The Heirs," said Gemma.

"Very likely." Astrid looked grim. "Bloody hell . . . did you *see* him?"

"A myopic earthworm could see him," answered Catullus.

Lesperance grunted, causing Gemma to jump a little. Even Catullus found Lesperance in this permutation to be intimidating.

"He swung at you without cause." Gemma looked incensed at the idea. "Didn't even speak. Just—" She mimed Arthur waving his sword.

Catullus mulled over this. "That, too, must be the influence of the Heirs. If they perceive Blades as a threat to the prosperity of England, Arthur would feel the same way."

"And attack you," Gemma concluded, grim.

This was bad news for all Blades. None of them were safe with an armed, angry giant stomping across England.

Catullus turned to Lesperance. "I need you to get to Southampton, tell the Blades what's happening."

Another grunt; then Lesperance shifted quickly into a hawk and perched on Astrid's offered arm. Gemma stared in open fascination at the metamorphosis.

"One hell of a night," she murmured.

Catullus gave Lesperance directions to Southampton, since the Canadian had never been there before. As Catullus did so, he pulled a notepad from one of his many pockets and began scribbling a message. "The Blades might not trust you, but say to them, 'North is eternal, South is forever, West is endless, East is infinite.'" He tore the note from the pad. "And this should explain everything, just in case. Find a man called Bennett Day and give him the note." Catullus moved to secure the message to Lesperance's leg, but Astrid stopped him, taking the paper in her hand.

"Give us a moment."

Astrid's eyes shone, revealing the raw pain of separation. No one knew when or how she and Lesperance would see each other again. The last time they had been apart for more than a few hours, she had been abducted by the Heirs and barely escaped torture and death.

With a nod, Catullus turned away. He and Gemma walked several yards, and they both scrupulously tried not to eavesdrop when Lesperance, in human form, spoke to Astrid in a low, urgent voice that resonated with need. Nor did Catullus and Gemma listen to Astrid's impassioned response. Then there was silence, which Catullus concluded had to be Astrid and Lesperance kissing.

He refused to look and corroborate that theory. Instead, feeling the agony his old friend must be experiencing, he reached down and took hold of Gemma's hand as if to confirm that she stood next to him, and would not be leaving his side for some time. The feel of her skin against his sped his heart, heated his blood. Unable to stop himself, he raised her hand to his lips. She made a soft hum of pleasure.

The skin of her hand felt so soft, supple as a zephyr. He wondered what her skin would taste like.

Now was not the time to be entertaining such thoughts.

Reluctantly, he lowered her hand from his mouth, but kept her fingers interlaced with his, feeling her strength, her living self, whole and safe. The thought of her being hurt

shook him even more than the fact that he'd been chased
and nearly cleaved in two by King Arthur.

"That was an unwise thing to do," he said, careful to
keep his voice level, rather than growl, which was what he
felt like doing. "Coming back for me."

She looked both exasperated and affectionate. "But sac-
rificing yourself on my behalf was the height of brilliance."
When he started to object, she gripped his hand tighter.
"Who's to say what's wise and what's foolish, where the
heart's concerned?" She tilted her head toward where Astrid
and Lesperance were taking their farewells.

Catullus nodded, understanding, amazed that this forthright American woman possessed so great an insight. He
reckoned himself to be at least ten years older than her—
but she could lead him down paths he'd never ventured
before.

Together, they looked out at the dark, peaceful fields.
The moon shone down placidly, and faint sounds of life
began to stir farther beyond, in Glastonbury. Whatever
magic thrall had been cast during Arthur's summoning, it
was nearly gone now, a veil drawn back.

"I still cannot believe it." Catullus heard the amazement
in his own voice. "That was truly King Arthur. I never
thought to look upon him with my own eyes."

"Incredible," Gemma agreed. Wonder lit her face. "A
legend, made real."

"Glad it was you," he said before he could stop himself.

She looked at him, questioning.

"I'm glad that . . . of anyone . . . it was you . . . sharing it
with . . . with me." An awkward necklace of words strung
together, and he hated how fragmentary and ungainly he
became whenever he tried to express something meaningful to her.

Yet, she seemed to understand. Even in the moonlight,
she blushed rosily. Then lost her blush as she darkened.
"But, God, that sword. Swinging at you. That was the worst

sight I've ever seen." She scowled. "It made me so damned angry. I had to do something, had to help you."

Simple words from her, but they shook him deeply. Blades made friends with one another, and always watched each other's backs in the field. All too often, the dark news would reach headquarters that a Blade didn't survive their mission, and a heavy pall fell. But there was a certain fatalism to it. Each and every Blade knew that when they or their comrades set off on another mission, the odds were strong that they might not return. Astrid's grief over Michael's death hit her harder—he was her husband. Five years she'd hidden herself away. Only the force of Lesperance had been able to pry her from her self-imposed exile. Yet her devastating pain remained the exception to how Blades faced loss.

Gemma's unrestrained concern for him filled Catullus with a kind of agonizing warmth, like long-frozen limbs thawing before a fire. No one had ever felt that way about him before. He was awed, humbled, and, if he wanted to be honest with himself, pleased beyond measure. He didn't want to cause her any pain, but, by God, it felt good to have someone—especially Gemma—care about him.

He wanted to write sonnets. Instead, words struggled to form, and the best he could offer was a rasped, "Thank you." He grimaced at his own verbal ineptitude.

But Gemma stepped in front of him, placed one warm, slim hand on his face, and smiled, as if she understood exactly what he had wanted to say but could not verbalize. "You're most welcome."

They both turned at the sound of flapping wings. They saw Lesperance, back in his hawk form, take to the air. The note was secured to his leg. Astrid followed with her eyes, turning her body like a compass needle finding true north, as he wheeled overhead, then headed southeast. She watched him, her face a stone mask, for a long time. Until the night sky swallowed him.

Only when Astrid faced Catullus did he see the silver tracks of tears staining her face. Otherwise, stoicism hardened her to marble.

His heart ached for her. She'd held Michael as he had died, which had been terrible. But now she was forced to part from Lesperance—and the love she had for him was fierce, deeply rooted in the fibers of her soul. If anything happened to either of them, they would be far apart. The apprehension could devastate. And if the worst news ever came . . . Astrid might survive if Lesperance was hurt or, God forbid, killed, but she would be ruined beyond repair, only a shell.

And if anything happened to Astrid, Catullus had not a shred of doubt that Lesperance would hunt down and slaughter anyone remotely connected to her death. Including Catullus.

"You'll see him again." Gemma did not patronize, but spoke simply, and with conviction. For that alone, Catullus felt her penetrate further the protective mechanisms surrounding his heart.

Astrid dragged her sleeve across her face, wiping away the signs of her heartbreak. She straightened her shoulders.

"Let's go," she growled. "We've a king to catch."

Life had indeed returned to normal in Glastonbury. The dinner hour concluded. People walked the streets, men congregated in taprooms, and a stable was open to provide three horses for Catullus, Gemma, and Astrid.

"Though I don't know where you plan on going," the stablemaster noted, cinching a saddle. "The moon's out, but the hour is growing late."

"Going to see an old friend," Catullus answered. Which was something like the truth.

The stablemaster shrugged at the peculiar ways of strangers, but continued to get their horses ready, casting a wary glance at the short-muzzled shotgun slung over Catullus's shoulder. Yes, in civilized England, men didn't walk the streets armed. But civilized England no longer existed, whether its citizens knew it or not.

Catullus paced over to a sheltered spot in the stable yard, where Gemma and Astrid waited quietly.

"Shouldn't be much longer."

Astrid only nodded, nearly ossified from her separation from Lesperance.

As usual, Gemma overflowed with questions, a ready contrast to Astrid's taciturnity. "What are we planning on doing? Talking with Arthur nearly cost you your head. If we can't speak with him, how do we know what he or the Heirs mean to accomplish? Can Arthur be stopped from . . . whatever it is he plans on doing?"

Catullus held up his hands, but couldn't fight his smile. He adored her relentless pursuit of knowledge. "Slowly, Madame Query."

She pressed her lips together in an attempt to curb her barrage of questions. He struggled against the impulse to cover her mouth with his own, stopping her questions with a much more pleasant activity.

"We need to stay as near to Arthur as we can manage without him becoming aware of us." Catullus ran through scenarios and solutions in his mind, seeking answers. "He sees us as his enemies—doubtless he is influenced by the will of the Heirs. Whether the Heirs know that Arthur has been summoned, we do not know. Nor do we know where Arthur is headed. The best we can do is keep close to him, track his movements." A large trench already marred the base of Glastonbury Tor from a partially manifested Excalibur. The amount of destruction the completely embodied sword could accomplish chilled Catullus's blood.

"And then?" Gemma pressed.

"And then . . ." He stuffed his hands into his pockets to

keep from reaching for, and polishing, his spectacles. "We see what happens next."

Gemma frowned. "You Blades of the Rose are supposed to be prepared, to have plans."

Even Astrid chuckled at this, though it sounded more like a rusty hinge than a laugh.

"Plans," she snorted.

"My dearest lady," Catullus said, "Blades are reckless fools who traverse the globe seeking more and more exotic ways of killing ourselves. Surely you understood that by now?" When Gemma only scowled at him, he amended, "In truth, we can plan and strategize all we like, but experience in the field has taught us elasticity. Whatever we prepare for almost never comes to pass, and something entirely unexpected often arises."

"Couldn't you—"

A crash and shout cut off Gemma's suggestion.

They swung around to see the stablemaster yelling, waving his arms and pulling at his hair. At first glance, Catullus thought the man suffered some kind of fit. Looking closer Catullus saw tiny creatures resembling human children clinging to the stablemaster's clothes and gripping the man's hair and beard. The creatures had burnished bronze skin, and though some wore minuscule caps fashioned of leaves, almost all were naked. Their ears came to little points, their features sharp.

Pixies. Dozens of them.

They shrieked with glee, golden eyes glittering, as they pinched and tormented the stablemaster.

Horses' frightened whinnying drew Catullus's attention. More pixies, clambering through the horses' manes, swinging from their tails. The stable itself crawled with pixies as they cavorted amongst the tack and threw handfuls of dung at one another.

Yells and screeches in the streets. Catullus, with Gemma

and Astrid right behind him, dashed out of the stable yard and into the road to investigate.

"Someone please tell me I'm drunk," Gemma muttered.

"We are all, unfortunately, sober," Catullus said.

Glastonbury swarmed with pixies. Everywhere Catullus looked resembled bedlam. The tiny fairy creatures ran amok, torturing anyone unlucky enough to be out in the street. Just as they did with the stablemaster, the pixies pinched, pulled, and bedeviled whomever they could get their minuscule, tormenting hands on. They tugged on hair, compelling men to run up and down the streets like wild horses. They scratched faces and shredded clothes. Even dogs snapped at pixies clinging to their tails.

Those inside had no reprieve. Women and children fled their homes as pixies scrabbled up their clothes or chased them outside.

Pixies smashed lamps and windows, threw rocks, broke furniture. Some swung from shop signs, dropping onto anyone unfortunate enough to pass below. The constabulary offered no help, since they were suffering just as much as the civilians, and one poor constable was chased through the streets by pixies wielding his own club.

It was the worst scene of chaos Catullus had ever witnessed. And he'd been to university.

"Where did these things come from?" Gemma swatted at pixies trying to climb up her skirts.

"My guess? Arthur." Catullus flicked away pixies leaping onto the hem of his coat. He managed to grab one, but it slipped from his fist with a laughing squeal. The damned creatures were harder to hold than wet butter.

Gemma pried loose a pixie trying to wriggle between the buttons of her bodice. "Get out of there, little bastard!" Flinging the creature aside, she said, "When Arthur was summoned, he brought other magic with him?"

"Or it was roused by his appearance, and the Primal

Source." Astrid glared at a clot of pixies swarming toward her, and the fairies shrieked in fear before scampering off.

"You have to teach me how to do that," Catullus said. He plucked a pixie from Gemma's hair. "We must leave. Now."

Gemma stared. "Abandon everyone here to these . . . *things*?"

"Short of spraying the whole of Glastonbury with pixie repellant—which, alas, I don't happen to have on me—there isn't much we can do. And I've a suspicion that, wherever Arthur goes, more magical outbreaks like this will follow." He kicked out, sending pixies clinging to his boots flying in all directions, then strode toward the saddled horses. Methodically, he scoured each animal, finding and tossing away handfuls of the tiny fairies. The horrible creatures giggled as they flew through the air.

Gemma and Astrid assisted, though Gemma stopped her work for a moment to help the stablemaster rid himself of some of the more aggressive pixies. As soon as he could, the man sprinted off, abandoning his business.

Once the horses had been reasonably cleared, Catullus, Astrid, and Gemma mounted up. All three of them trotted out of the stable yard and surveyed the anarchic streets, where pixies had turned what had once been a perfectly respectable, rather pretty English town into a nightmarish scene out of a Brueghel painting.

The clang of a bell summoned the fire brigade to some part of town. Catullus wondered how long it would take before the pixies burnt the whole of Glastonbury to the ground.

"Laugh or scream, can't decide which," Gemma said, looking about at the literal pandemonium. Homes and businesses were being destroyed all around. Townsfolk crowded the street as they ran in fear, their shouts and screams echoing down the lanes. Incredible what the diminutive pixies could accomplish. Mayhem embodied in creatures no bigger than an apple.

Catullus tried to imagine what might happen if the totality of Britain was overrun with pixies. "Amusing, perhaps, for about fifteen minutes. And then"—he ducked as a heavy porcelain basin went flying overhead—"hellish."

He wheeled his horse around, pointing in the direction which Arthur had disappeared. At his signal, he, Gemma, and Astrid all kicked their horses into a run, weaving through the throngs as they sped out of town. And into the dark countryside.

"The damned Heirs of Albion," Astrid growled. "They had no idea that when they unlocked the Primal Source, they also released hell on Earth."

Chapter 9

The Silent Village

The madness of Glastonbury faded behind them, but Catullus could not forget what he'd seen. He wished there was something he might do to help the townspeople. Perhaps later—if there *was* a later—he could return and help rebuild. For now, his duty lay in tracking Arthur, and safeguarding Gemma.

He could only imagine what kind of story she'd write, if she'd expose the existence of the Blades in her pursuit of the truth. He discovered he didn't care. So long as she survived, she could write whatever she damn well pleased.

The thought shook him. Always, *always*, his loyalty to the Blades came first. He'd learned that when still mucking about with scraps of wire from his mother's workshop.

"Blades before all, Catullus," his mother often admonished him. "The Graves family has a great responsibility, and we cannot shirk it for our own selfish purposes."

In the whole of his twenty-three years of service to the Blades, he'd never chafed against this imperative, never had a reason to. Now his reason rode beside him, bent low over her horse's neck, eyes bright with amazement at the wonders she'd seen. She wore her spirit like a golden mantle. Across the width and breadth of this world he had traveled, and not once seen her equal.

God help him if he ever had to choose between her and the Blades.

But it hadn't come to that. Not yet, anyway.

As he, Gemma, and Astrid galloped into the night, Astrid stayed at the head of their group. Astrid's connection to the Primal Source, and by extension, to Arthur, still ran strong. She served as their compass, guiding them through fields and down roads in their pursuit. Wherever Arthur was heading, it lay somewhere to the east. Catullus wondered if the legendary monarch meant to stride across the English Channel and lead a one-king invasion of France—England's old enemy.

The road he, Gemma, and Astrid now followed took them through open country. Stone walls banded the road. All around rose the low backs of gently rounded hills, empty at this hour even of sheep.

A crossroads emerged ahead.

"This way," Astrid called over her shoulder. She took the road to the left, and Catullus and Gemma did the same.

"I hear something," Gemma said.

Catullus strained to listen above the pounding of the horses' hooves.

"Behind us." Her voice was flat, a reluctant admission.

He turned in the saddle. Then promptly grabbed his shotgun, swearing.

A pack of dogs ran after them. Not ordinary dogs, but beasts nearly as large as the horses they pursued. More magic brought forth by Arthur's summoning. Their black coats soaked up the moonlight, obliterating it, and their feet churned up the hard-packed road with thick, jet-colored claws. And their eyes . . .

Catullus prayed that the horses did not catch a glimpse of the hounds. Horses were skittish animals, and not inclined to react favorably to giant dogs with burning eyes and gaping mouths full of long, tearing, yellow teeth. Catullus himself wasn't feeling very sanguine about the fiery saliva dripping from the dogs' mouths. It hissed and smoked where it dripped.

"Not a local breed, then," Gemma said. She pulled her derringer.

"They go by many names in Britain." He checked, as he rode, to be sure that his shotgun was loaded. "Wisht hounds, yeth hounds, black dogs, padfoot. They follow and," he gritted, "devour travelers."

"Oh," said Gemma. "Wonderful."

"Though I've only read about them," he cautioned. "The truth may be altogether different."

"Let's not put it to the test."

The hounds snarled as they drew closer. A smell of sulfur clung to their huge bodies and gusted from their mouths. Growling, they snapped at the air.

"We can shoot them, though," Gemma offered.

"We can try."

Both he and Gemma aimed—no easy feat when facing backward on a galloping horse.

"On my count," said Catullus. "One . . . two . . . three . . . *now*."

"Wait!" Astrid shouted.

But he and Gemma had already fired. Her shot went a fraction too wide, ricocheting off a stone wall. His, however, hit. The shell slammed into the lead dog's chest, sending the monster tumbling to the ground. Its packmates simply ran around the toppling hound. Not much honor among demon dogs.

Catullus soon understood why they were so little concerned about their comrade. As the shot dog rolled on the ground, it split straight down the middle as neatly as a walnut. Both halves continued to tumble, and, as they did so, they reshaped in a blur of black fur and yellow teeth. Then regained their footing and continued to give chase.

"Sons of bitches."

Thanks to Catullus's shotgun, one hell dog was now two. And both of them had taken his gunfire personally. They growled, furious, as they stretched out their long legs, coming nearer.

"*That's* why you don't shoot those things!" Astrid yelled over her shoulder.

"I'll keep that under advisement." Catullus slung his shotgun again onto his back.

The horses finally became aware of the dogs. Catullus considered it a minor miracle that none of the mounts reared back in panic. They ran all the harder, but the hounds caught the scent of fear and lunged. The teeth of one dog grazed the pastern of Catullus's horse, and the monster received a kick in the face for its attempt. It yelped, but didn't fall back.

Damn, damn. No matter how frightened the horses were, they'd been going for hours, and would weary long before the dogs abandoned their pursuit. Catullus couldn't shoot the bloody beasts. And even if he'd kept his luggage, he had nothing in his arsenal of inventions that could be used against demonic canines. What the hell could he do?

"There!" Gemma pointed off to the right.

He squinted into the darkness, his night vision never particularly robust. Then he saw it.

A small stone bridge, about a half mile ahead, crossed a fast-moving river.

"Head for that," she shouted to both Catullus and Astrid.

But Catullus wasn't certain. He did not think the dogs would tire and give up their chase before they reached the bridge. And the bridge wasn't where he and the others were headed. They might lose valuable time with a detour.

Gemma, seeing him busily deliberating, yelled, "Stop thinking and just do it!" Seeing the stone wall give way to a low hedge, she turned her horse and jumped over.

Astrid followed immediately after.

Catullus glanced back at the nearing hounds, then over to where Gemma and Astrid sped over a field toward the bridge.

"Sod it," he muttered, and followed, as well.

Heavy, rasping breaths sawed behind him as he pushed his horse faster and faster. The choking smell of sulfur told him the demon hounds were closing fast.

Nearer to the bridge. Gemma galloped across, Astrid just after her. Alternately swearing at and encouraging his horse, Catullus urged the animal to the limits of its ability.

The bridge clattered beneath the horse's hooves. Catullus breached the other side.

Howls rent the air.

All three travelers wheeled their horses around in time to see the hounds erupt into flame as they crossed the bridge. Flares of noxious light burst. The dogs exploded into sticky ash. Flakes wafted down to the water, only to be carried away by the swift current. Nothing remained of the foul beasts but a lingering, sulfurous smell.

Catullus turned to Gemma. "How did you know?"

"Tales my granda told me. In Ireland, such creatures are called *coin iotair*, and can't cross running water." He didn't mind that she looked a little smug. In fact, she could go on gloating until *next* Michaelmas Term.

He forgot to be reserved.

Slowly, he brought his steaming horse nearer to hers. She watched him steadily. When he was alongside her, he leaned over, threaded his fingers into her hair, and brought her close for a potent, thorough kiss. She didn't resist, but met his passion with her own.

Soft. Silky wet. Delectable.

When they finally separated, she opened glazed eyes and said breathlessly, "Glad to see you don't mind."

"Mind what?" His own brain blurred at the edges from a combination of many things—a night full of danger, magic running unchecked through the countryside, but mostly her.

"That I knew something you didn't." She gave him a cheeky grin.

"On the contrary," he answered, "I look forward to furthering my education."

"There's a rampaging mythological monarch on the loose," Astrid's diamond-sharp voice announced. "Save the seduction for a less desperate time." Before either Catullus or Gemma could answer, Astrid brought her horse around and urged the tired animal into a trot.

Gemma gave Catullus a wry glance, then, looking slightly surly, guided her horse after Astrid.

For a moment, Catullus stared at the bridge, where a pack of demonic hounds had, moments ago, exploded into flame. But, to his mind, the *real* marvel of the evening was that he'd been seducing—and kissing—Gemma. Rather well, too.

Catullus Graves, acclaimed inventor, inveterate outsider, now successful wooer of women. If *that* didn't convince him that the world was about to end, nothing would.

Determination kept Gemma upright in the saddle. If she stopped focusing for even a second, she'd tumble right off and into a ditch. Dimly, she wondered when she'd been so exhausted, and nothing came to mind. But she wouldn't let her weariness win. Time meant everything. And she didn't want to get a face full of mud.

For hours, they'd followed in the wake of Arthur. They never caught another glimpse of him—amazing, considering that the king was a *giant*. Astrid's connection to the Primal Source served as their means of tracking.

After the incident with the demon dogs, everyone kept alert for more magical creatures. Yet, as the miles and night wore on, nothing with pointy teeth leapt out from the hedgerows, no enchanted music wove over the hillsides to ensnare the unwary. Gemma had no idea what time it was, but she felt certain that it was hours after midnight. She couldn't concentrate on anything but staying on her horse.

Her head snapped up. Hell. She'd been nodding off again.

Catullus, damned observant man, saw this, and frowned. Not with anger, but concern.

"At the next village," he said, "we stop and rest for a few hours."

"I'm not tired," she answered at once.

He sent her a glance that showed he was not at all gulled. "Perhaps *you* are not, but *I* am, and so is Astrid."

"I'm wide awake," Astrid said, rubbing her eyes with her fist.

Catullus rolled his eyes at having been burdened with not one but two obstinate females. "Forgive me, O Indefatigable Women. I meant that the *horses* are stumbling on their feet. If we don't give the poor beasts some rest, they'll drop from under us and we'll have three dead animals and no means of transport."

"Then we'll change horses at the next village," Astrid countered, "and continue on."

"Absolutely not." He turned to Astrid. "You, more than anyone, know how important it is to be at one's utmost capability in the field. If we push on without pause, our bodies and minds are useless."

"But—"

The look he gave Astrid stunned Gemma with its steel. Courteous and well spoken Catullus might be, but there was no denying that he possessed an autocratic streak. He commanded, and he was obeyed. With an internal shiver, Gemma remembered how, in the dark of their shared room at the inn, Catullus had touched her, urged her to rapture without compromise.

And the kisses he'd given her this very night—those had been downright dominant. And wonderful.

Yet she wasn't easily broken.

"A few hours," Gemma said. "Then we're back on Arthur's trail."

He gave a slight nod, almost as if he was angry with her compromise. But a minuscule smile revealed that he liked the fact that she wouldn't capitulate entirely. Despite the fact that her brain was cottony with fatigue, she knew with certainty that no other man she'd ever known would ever appreciate that quality in a woman.

In silence, they rode on until rounding a bend, where the unmistakable shapes of cottages rose up. She couldn't prevent a swell of happiness at the sight. Despite arguing for continuing on, Gemma really would appreciate a bit of sleep. There had to be an inn or maybe an accommodating townsperson with spare beds or even a hayloft somewhere around here.

The moon had set. Everything within the village was dark. As Gemma, Catullus, and Astrid plodded their weary horses down the central thoroughfare, they saw a few shuttered shops, a public house, a quaint little church. Some smaller avenues branched off the main street, revealing more houses and shops. A square marked the center of the village, bound by a postal office and saloon. In the middle of its space stood a stone cross surrounded by a low wall, a monument to an old battle. The village was smaller than Glastonbury, yet looked large enough to support a decent-sized community. A slight, predawn breeze blew down the lanes. Shingles squeaked on their hinges.

Something was wrong.

Every single window was dark. Not one candle or lamp burned anywhere. Gemma strained to hear some human sound, some movement. Nothing.

A chill plucked along her spine.

They halted in the square.

"This place is deserted." Even whispering, her voice sounded loud in the unnatural quiet.

"It may just be the lateness of the hour." But Catullus didn't sound convinced.

Astrid guided her horse toward the shingle announcing the village bakery fronting the square. The sound of her mount's hooves on the cobblestones echoed along the deserted street. "The baker would be up by now, lighting his ovens, getting ready to make the village's bread." She peered through the window, then frowned. "I see no one inside."

"Here's the taproom. Wait outside." Catullus swung down from his horse and, carefully easing his shotgun into position, edged inside.

Gemma held her breath, her hand on her pistol, as she waited for him to emerge. She glanced over at Astrid, yet the Englishwoman's face revealed nothing. Her own pistols appeared in her hands.

After what felt like an eternity, Catullus came out of the saloon. "Completely empty. Not even a dog by the fire."

The uneasiness along Gemma's spine spread through her body. "Where is everyone?" She lowered her voice even more. "Maybe Arthur came and . . ." The idea seemed too horrible to think about.

Catullus shook his head. "He wouldn't attack ordinary citizens. It's Blades he sees as his enemies. And there aren't any bodies."

"A hundred people can't simply vanish." Then, she added in a less certain voice, "Can they?" She glanced around, expecting to see some malevolent creature staring from the black shadows that painted the street and clung along the sides of buildings.

Catullus strode into a home whose door had been left ajar. He came back out moments later, his hands full of scraps of fabric. "Here's our answer."

"The town was attacked by rags?" Even this seemed a little strange to Gemma.

"Boggarts." He moved closer, showing her that what he

held was, in fact, clothing, torn into shreds. "Destructive little fiends. They sour milk, make animals lame. Hate things that belong to the home, especially, for some reason, garments. Perhaps clothes represent too much civilization for their liking."

"Must've chased everyone in this village away." Gemma imagined the scene of chaos as people fled their homes—not much different from what happened in Glastonbury. "Will they come back?"

Tossing the heap of ruined clothing aside, Catullus said, "Unlikely. It's an unfortunate trait of boggarts that they follow whomever they've decided to torment. Somewhere out there, a whole village's worth of people are being pursued by hordes of boggarts. Come." He held out a hand to her.

She stared down at the offered hand. "We can't mean to stay here."

"God only knows where the next village is, and it may be in just as sorry a state as this one, if not worse." He took hold of her hand and pried it loose from the reins. "At least we know there are plenty of empty beds."

Gemma tried to argue, but weariness overtook her, sinking heavy claws into her shoulders. Before she knew what happened, she found herself off of her horse and in Catullus's arms. He cradled her to him as if she weighed no more than a sheet of paper. Oh, Lord, he felt so warm and solid, his muscles firm beneath the fabric of his clothes. She wanted to lay her head upon his shoulder, clasp her arms around his neck, and breathe in his scent.

She tried to pull away, to stand on her own feet. He held her steady.

"None of that. You need to sleep." His voice rumbled, and she felt its vibrations through her body.

"But, the horses . . ."

He pushed open a door to a house with one boot. From the shelter of his arms, Gemma saw they were in a neat little house, snug as an embrace. Save for the heaps of tattered garments strewn about, everything within seemed entirely orderly. Catullus moved through the house, shouldering open doors, until he came to a bedroom just off the kitchen. A small bed with a plain quilt lay in the corner, and a family's framed photograph held pride of place beside a picture of Queen Victoria.

The bed looked so inviting to Gemma, she thought she might cry. Still, she struggled to sit up after Catullus gently lay her upon it. His large, strong hands tenderly clasped her shoulders, holding her down.

"No, I won't let you up. So enough with your struggling."

The room was quite dark, so she felt rather than saw his exasperated smile. The bed dipped slightly as he sat down on its edge. She reached for him. Yes, she was exhausted, but the idea of sharing a bed with him could banish all thoughts of sleep. Ever since . . . well . . . all day, she'd craved his touch. They'd shared danger, coming to each other's rescue. Having seen him in magnificent action, knowing the strength of his body and mind, and her own capability, her craving turned to fiery need.

Yet he captured her seeking hands with one of his own. "Rest now."

"Lie with me." She didn't care how bold or shocking her words must sound. Weariness and the vicissitudes of the day stripped away everything but immediate desire. "Even just to sleep." Feeling him next to her, laying his long body down alongside her own—at that moment she couldn't think of anything she wanted more.

"Have to keep watch." He hesitated, then brushed strands of hair from her forehead. His rueful laugh was a hoarse rasp in the darkness. "But, God, how you tempt a man."

She did not want him to retreat. Not now. Not when they were on the verge of something significant. "Catullus—"

"Sleep." He bent and brushed his lips across her forehead, his breath warm, feathering across her face.

Then, releasing her, he stood. He made a large, dark figure in the doorway—but not threatening to her. A guardian. She tried as long as she was able to look at him, but exhaustion refused to be denied, and the last thing she saw before sleep took her was his tall form, standing watch, protecting her.

When Gemma's breathing slowed, confirming she'd finally fallen asleep, Catullus quietly went out into the street. He spent a goodly amount of time patrolling the perimeter of the house, ensuring that he'd chosen the most safe dwelling in the village. He longed for his full complement of tools beyond the little case in his pocket. With his whole workshop at his disposal, he could fashion impervious locks that only Gemma's magic could breach.

Finally satisfied that there was no place safer, he went and found Astrid already tending to the horses in an empty stable off the square. A lantern on the ground softly illuminated the scene. Two horses had been stripped of their tack and put into stalls. The other, she now rubbed down.

"Not even a horse or mule stayed behind," she said without looking up from her work. "Boggarts must've scared them off, too."

Wordlessly, Catullus pumped water into a bucket and brought it over to the trough. "This is dark magic, Astrid. I've never seen its like."

"Nor I." She patted the horse's nose. Still looking into the animal's large, brown eyes, she murmured, "I don't know if we're going to survive this one."

"We will," he said immediately, reflexively. Yet even Catullus understood that the Blades' fatuous optimism could not withstand the threat they now faced.

Astrid glanced up, holding his gaze with a look that said

she believed him as much as he believed himself, which was to say: not at all. Under the scrutiny of his old friend, Catullus couldn't support the weight of illusions.

He removed his spectacles and wearily rubbed at his eyes. "Perhaps we won't survive," he allowed, "but we cannot fail in our mission to take back the Primal Source and stop whatever the Heirs plan on doing."

"Damned hard to do that, when none of us know how. Or even what it is we go up against. Hell," she muttered, "if this village and Glastonbury are any indicators, we're facing a magic that no one in the history of the Blades has ever confronted."

"All the more room for exploration and discovery. Where the map is blank, the world is open." Putting on his spectacles, he saw Astrid staring at him. "What?"

She shook her head. "Nothing. Just then, it seemed as though—never mind." After leading the final horse into a stall, she came out, dusting her hands. "So, shall we find ourselves a deck of cards and amuse ourselves until your American scribbler wakes?"

"Her name is Gemma, and *you* are going to find yourself a bed and get a little sleep."

Astrid folded her arms across her chest, mulish. "Absolutely not. I'm not leaving you on your own in this eerie place." Her words slurred with exhaustion.

"And you're barely coherent," he countered evenly. Seeing her flat refusal, he had no other option but negotiation. "We'll sleep in shifts. I shall take first watch."

Still, tired as Astrid was, she remained obstinately standing in the middle of the stable's yard. Short of bodily picking her up, as he'd done with Gemma, there did not seem to be any way to get Astrid to go to bed. And, as Catullus did not fancy receiving one of Astrid's feet in his groin or a punch to his nose, he needed another tactic.

"Do you remember Latimer?" he asked.

She blinked, trying to recall. "The beefy chap from Cornwall?"

"That's the one. You, Michael, Latimer, and I had to go to the Orkneys when the German cabal tried to capture some selkies."

"Right. Yes. The selkies." She suddenly realized where his story was headed, and scowled. "I am *not* going to fall asleep on my gun and accidentally shoot myself."

"Latimer refused to rest, even though we told him he had to. And almost lost a leg as a result."

"He was an idiot, trying to prove himself on his first mission."

"His *last* mission, too, as I recall. Went back to Cornwall and became a publican." Catullus's voice gentled. "If anything happens to you because you're too tired to react in time, Lesperance will waste no time disemboweling me. It's my own welfare I am considering."

At the mention of Lesperance, even in conjunction with the idea of him ripping out Catullus's entrails, Astrid's scowl faded, and tender affection softened her face. Finally, she tipped her head forward in minute acknowledgment. "Very well," she grumbled. "You can have first watch. But you'd better come and get me in an hour."

"Three hours," Catullus countered.

"Two," Astrid shot back.

"Done." In truth, he was pleased she consented to two hours, but wouldn't let his satisfaction show. That was the shortest route to having his teeth knocked out of his mouth. He consulted his pocket watch to mark the time. Sunrise was at least three hours away.

Carrying the lantern, he and Astrid left the stable and returned to the house where he'd installed Gemma. He peered in to make sure she was still asleep and sound, and his heart contracted sharply in his chest to see her face, smooth and lovely in repose, but not fragile. He allowed himself a moment to marvel at the things she'd seen this day, and the strength with which she faced them—and the gentle snoring she made now.

Satisfied that Gemma was well and safe, he closed the door and discovered Astrid behind him, staring at him again with a strange, speculative look.

"What?"

"I like this side of you, Catullus." A trace of a smile curved her mouth.

"It scares the hell out of me," he confessed.

"That's one of the reasons why I like it." With that, Astrid ventured off in search of the other bedroom in the house.

Catullus drifted to the kitchen. He busied himself there, making a pot of coffee and finding some slightly stale bread. The coffee was bolted down, the bread gnawed on. Thus fortified, he took a chair, and sat outside the front door, shotgun across his lap and pipe in mouth, to wait out the night.

She dreamt. Of clockwork castles and mechanical dragons. A storybook world powered by steam and gears. Empty streets that clicked as cogs and wheels turned. Yet in the middle of this mechanized kingdom beat a heart of glowing, pure magic, dazzling in its countless colors, its crystalline wonder. She reached out to touch it, and it was made of glass—the same glass in a man's spectacles. Behind that glass, she knew she would find the truest heart. All that remained was to reach it, without shattering its vitreous surface.

But how?

Men's voices filtered in to her, deep and masculine. They spoke in urgent tones, words coming quickly, and she strained to make them out. One voice she knew well—it was the rich, resonant sound she longed to hear. The other she didn't recognize. And that made her frown as she slept.

It wasn't right. No other man was here except *him*. Danger, then. A threat.

She pushed herself through the layers of sleep. Had to wake. He needed her.

Gemma felt a fleeting panic when her eyes opened. She lay in a strange bed, in a strange room. Where was she?

A moment, and she remembered. Arthur. The race across the English countryside. Demon dogs. The empty village.

Catullus.

She heard his voice in the other room. And another man, one she couldn't place. Hard to tell the nature of their conversation, only that it was low and pressing. One of the Heirs?

Quietly, Gemma slipped from the bed. She tread lightly across the floorboards, making sure nothing squeaked beneath her feet, then pressed herself against the door, listening.

". . . God *damn* it. . . ."

". . . rotten bastard . . ."

She eased the door open and peered out to the kitchen. A dark-haired man swung his fist at Catullus, who evaded the blow and threw one of his own. The unknown man nimbly leapt out of the way.

"Hands up," Gemma clipped. She stepped into the room, pistol drawn and trained on the dark-haired man.

His eyes went round—she faintly realized that his eyes were an astonishing shade of blue. She quickly took his measure: not as tall as Catullus, and younger, too. Lean, athletic body. Smartly dressed. And also, quite simply, the most handsome man she'd ever seen, and that included all the justifiably vain actors she had interviewed.

This unfamiliar man smiled at her. Surely women's underthings spontaneously dissolved when he smiled. Nothing compared for masculine beauty. For herself, she felt only removed interest in his appearance. He could be Adonis in the flesh, but if he threatened Catullus, then he'd better say farewell to his pretty face before she blew a hole in it with her derringer.

His hands remained at his sides. "You've got the wrong idea, love."

"What you've got in looks," she gritted, "you're missing in brains. My gun is loaded. So get your damned hands up."

He finally complied, raising his hands, but he didn't look concerned to be on the pain-inducing end of a pistol. "This must be her," he said to Catullus.

"Gemma," said Catullus, wry, "may I have the dubious honor of presenting you with Bennett Day, reprobate and only recently reformed scoundrel. Ben, you filthy sod, this is Miss Gemma Murphy of Chicago, Illinois, the United States."

Gemma glanced over at Catullus, who had his thumbs tucked into the pockets of his waistcoat. "A friend of yours?"

"'Friend' is a rather pleasant term for 'someone I barely tolerate,'" he answered.

"Come now, Cat," Day chided, "is that any way to speak of the fellow who has seen you drunk, wearing only a tea towel, and swearing that the next evolution in transportation was to be one-man hot air balloons?"

"Go ahead and shoot him," Catullus said to Gemma.

"Catullus!" a woman exclaimed, coming into the room. She was delicate and pretty, with honey-colored hair and a lively face, her clothes fashionable—in contrast to Gemma's threadbare, somewhat grimy traveling dress. "I would be *extremely* vexed if your friend shot my husband."

Gemma lowered her pistol, and Day let drop his hands. Clearly, neither of these newcomers were Heirs of Albion. The only threat Bennett Day presented was the fact that he annoyed Catullus.

"And this is London, Bennett's wife," Catullus said.

The stylish woman gave a refined curtsy, which Gemma returned. With a cultured voice, London said, "Always a pleasure to meet friends of Catullus, Miss Murphy."

Gemma looked at Catullus. "Drunk, in a tea towel?"

A flush darkened Catullus's cheeks. "A very uninteresting story."

"I'd like to hear it."

Day said cheerfully, "We were in Prague and there were these, well, I suppose one wouldn't call them *ladies* precisely—"

"Enough, Ben," growled Catullus.

"Yes," said Day's wife. "I think we would *all* appreciate not hearing that tale."

Day strode over to his wife and wrapped her in his arms, smiling down at her. "Merely practice, love. Preparing me for you."

"Naturally." Yet she allowed her husband to kiss her, boldly and thoroughly, in front of Gemma and Catullus.

Rather than watch Bennett effectively seduce his wife, Gemma busied herself by stashing her derringer in her pocket. She glanced up when Catullus drifted to her side.

"Thank you for coming to my aid," he murmured.

His voice was velvet along her skin, and she felt her cheeks warm. "When I heard him call you a rotten bastard, and I saw him swing at you . . ."

Catullus grimaced. "Ben's way of saying hello. He's the Blades' most expert cryptographer, but sometimes he has the behavior of a poorly socialized warthog."

"I am a very *nicely* socialized warthog," Day interjected.

Catullus ignored him. Still speaking softly to her, he asked, "Did you rest well?"

"Well enough, but," she added quietly, "it would've been better if you'd taken me up on my offer." She had to show him that her interest hadn't ebbed, and appearance of his old friends hadn't changed her feelings.

He looked pleased, then flushed again and cleared his throat. He plucked his spectacles from his face and carefully polished them—his habitual gesture when he found himself at a loss.

Then, as if pushing the words out, he rumbled, "That would . . . be nice."

Nice wasn't precisely how she wanted a future tryst described, but she knew that she flustered him, and so couldn't take offense at what words he was able to cobble together. He was letting her know, in his way, that he wanted her just as much. She took the victory for what it was, and so guided the conversation back to more stable ground.

"Did you get any sleep?"

He took the offered distraction. "Astrid spelled me, until Bennett arrived."

"How did your friends find us?" she asked.

"Lesperance. He flew to Southampton—"

"And caused quite a stir," interrupted Day. "We don't see many naked people showing up on our doorstep, and even less who can change into an animal."

"None, I think," added Mrs. Day. "Though I am fairly new to the Blades."

"After we found him a pair of pants, Lesperance told us everything." Day shook his head. "Watching King Arthur rise up from the great beyond? Must have been a hell of a sight."

"Nearly cost me my head," Catullus said, "but, yes, it was a sight." He grinned. "Like something from the old tales."

"I envy you, you bespectacled bastard."

Catullus drew himself up, smoothing a hand down the front of his waistcoat. "As well you should."

Gemma looked back and forth between the two men, marveling at the change Bennett Day's arrival wrought in Catullus. She knew he and Astrid had a close relationship, but it was clear that Day and Catullus held that unique bond only men could share with one another. Part brother, part tormentor. A friendship crafted of many years, many adventures. She wanted, just then, to take Catullus away and crawl into his mind, not only to hear the countless tales he surely had, but to know him as well as his friend did.

A strange jealousy, one she'd never experienced before. She had never felt the need to delve into a man's innermost self. Even as close as she'd thought herself to Richard, she didn't want to explore every part of him. But it was different with *this* man, as complex and intricate as a many-chambered nautilus. The going might be challenging, yet the rewards, she felt with utmost certainty, would be worth it.

If only the damned man wasn't so reserved!

Day said, "The hawk fellow guided us back here. Said he had some kind of bond with Astrid and could find her anywhere." His brilliant eyes gleamed with pleasure. "It's good to see her truly back. And it's clear that she and Lesperance are mad about each other."

"Where *is* Astrid?" Gemma asked, glancing around.

Mrs. Day said, "As soon as we arrived, after greeting us, she and Lesperance . . . ah . . . sequestered themselves." A dainty pink stained her cheeks, so very different from the violent red Gemma would turn whenever *she* blushed.

"Cat—" Day began.

"You know I hate that moniker," Catullus groused.

"Cat," Day said, "what happened in this village? Where is everyone, and why are there piles of torn clothes everywhere? That can't *all* be Astrid and Lesperance's doing."

Catullus's expression turned serious. "Boggarts. Overran the town."

Day looked shocked. "What? That kind of fey activity hasn't been seen in over a hundred years."

"And there's more." Quickly, Catullus outlined everything that had happened since Lesperance had left their company, including the pixie rampage in Gloucester and the demon dogs' pursuit. The more Catullus talked, the more Day's ready good humor ebbed. "Did you observe nothing like this en route from Southampton?"

"No magical activity," said Mrs. Day.

"Must be Arthur," Gemma offered. "He seems to call the magic up wherever he goes."

Soberly, Catullus said, "But I fear that the longer he is manifest, the more his power will grow. His influence will be felt farther afield, even places where he has not been." Turning to Day, he concluded, "We have to go after him. Find a way to curtail his growing power. If your horses are rested, we can set out at once."

Mrs. Day and her husband shared a concerned glance, sending apprehension glinting through Gemma.

"Leaving this place is going to be a problem," said Day. His handsome face grim, he pulled his wife close. "The village is entirely surrounded by Heirs."

Chapter 10

Mr. Graves Takes Control

A moment's shocked silence, then Catullus demanded: "Tell me everything."

Day gently disengaged from his wife and took down from a cupboard a jar of something dark and viscous. He went to the table in the middle of the kitchen and set to one side a coffeepot and mug. Opening the jar, he dabbed his finger into the sticky contents, then began to smear it across the table.

Gemma realized he was drawing a map of the village.

"This is where we are," he said, indicating the house's position just off the square. "The high street runs straight through the plaza, west to east. Two smaller lanes lead off the square." He drew those, as well. "But they both terminate in dead ends. Which means that there's only one way in and out of the village. The Heirs have positioned themselves about half a mile at either end of the road leading to town." He made large X's, denoting the location of the Heirs.

"Half a mile," Gemma mused. "Enough distance for us to sneak past them."

Yet Day shook his head. "They've enchanted a web that,

while it can't hold us inside the village, it *will* alert them if we try to breach it." He drew a large circle around the whole of the map. "Within a minute, they'd descend on us."

"How did you get in?" asked Gemma.

"It's a talent Bennett has." Mrs. Day looked proudly at her husband. "He can find the gaps where seemingly none exist, and slip through them."

"Then leading us past the Heirs and their web should be easy."

"It's only possible with two people." Day shrugged. "Any more than that, and they'll be all over us like cats on cream." He stuck his finger in his mouth and sucked away the sticky substance covering it. "Mm, treacle. I could lick this up by the gallon." Eyebrows raised, he glanced back and forth between the jar of treacle and his wife. "Perhaps you and I could . . ." A smile, devastating in its sensuality, played across his face.

"Later, my dear." But Mrs. Day sounded distinctly breathless, her cheeks staining pink.

Even though Gemma had only just met the couple, she could easily imagine that they lead a very active life in the bedroom. Bennett Day all but glowed with sexual energy. And his wife had the radiance of a well-satisfied woman. Considering the way that Astrid and Lesperance could not bear to go longer than a day without ravishing one another, it was a marvel any of the Blades could get any work done.

She cast a sidelong glance at Catullus, who was bent over the impromptu map and studying it intently. Would he be the same way, once he took a lover? Thorough and inexhaustible? Or would he time the whole endeavor, striving for efficiency?

It seemed she would never find out. If they could only find a moment where they weren't running for their lives. She felt him, through her careful give and take, edging closer, slowly breaking down the reserve that confined him. Freeing himself, trusting them both, would take time, though.

Time they did not have. None of them might survive the next few hours.

"When do the Heirs plan on attacking?" Catullus asked Day. "Or do they mean to wait us out?"

"They move in at dawn." Everyone looked up as Lesperance and Astrid, hand in hand, came into the room. Lesperance wore only a pair of trousers, and Astrid's clothes looked decidedly rumpled. Neither of them seemed a bit embarrassed by their appearance. "I heard their plans as I flew overhead," said Lesperance. "If we don't attempt to leave the village by sunrise, then they'll come for us. They're all well armed: shotguns, rifles, and pistols."

"How many men?" Catullus demanded.

"Eight on the eastern road, six on the west."

"And six of us," said Astrid. She hefted a rifle, which she must have taken from somewhere in the village. "We have firepower."

"That won't be enough," Day said. "Aside from the enchanted web, we have to assume they have some other magic at their disposal. Which we don't have."

"There's mine," offered Lesperance.

Day nodded in acknowledgment. "And we'll make use of your ability. But even a bear, hawk, or wolf can't withstand dark magic."

Tension descended over the room as everyone contemplated the circumstance. The Heirs hadn't been seen for over a day, their threat never forgotten, but now they loomed close. A small iron clock near the stove showed that dawn was only an hour away.

Gemma glanced around the kitchen, at each Blade of the Rose. They each seemed veterans of this kind of dire situation, and wore their years of adventuring like invisible armor. If anyone could figure out a solution, a means for them all to escape to safety, these men and women were the ideal candidates. Yet Catullus's words to her on the ship came back vividly. Blades knew full well that their lives were precarious things, lost in a moment. Success was never a guarantee.

Catullus braced his hands on the edges of the table, his wide shoulders straining the fabric of his clothing as he stared down at the map. His brain, Gemma knew, sped more rapidly than a steam engine, and it fascinated her to simply watch him think. An inundation of ideas and hypotheses that he both produced and organized.

After several silent moments, Catullus looked up.

Gemma found herself holding her breath as five pairs of intent eyes stared at Catullus, each of them instinctively turning to him for guidance.

"I have a plan," he said.

In unison, everyone exhaled. Catullus was no divine being, but he, more than anyone in the whole world, might create a clockwork miracle.

In groups of two, they combed the village, going from house to house, ducking into shops, taking whatever might be useful to repel a siege. Catullus gave each group a list of things he would need. So they spread out through the empty little town in what had to be the strangest scavenger hunt ever undertaken.

Catullus would have enjoyed himself, if the circumstances weren't so dire.

"Didn't think anyone could top my family for oddness," Gemma said as they made their way along the row of shops along the high street. "Those friends of yours would give them a run for their money, though. It'd be one hell of a poker night."

"Sometimes I think the Blades go out of their way to recruit eccentrics." He glanced up at the shingles, looking for one in particular. Hopefully, the village wasn't too small for what he had in mind.

Ah, this was the place!

"My kind of people." She grinned saucily at him, and, God, if he didn't want to press her against the shop door and kiss them both dizzy. She was a freckle-faced temptation with a sharp mind and lush body.

She might not outlive the day if he didn't focus on the task at hand. So he put thoughts of kisses and freckles and sumptuous breasts from his mind—a job more easily proposed than done.

He tried the door on the shop, but found it locked. "Miss Murphy, if you would do the honors." He stepped aside and presented the door to her with a flourish.

With an eager nod, she stepped forward and opened the door. He understood how much she needed to be useful—it had to be difficult when faced with a collection of dyed-in-the-wool adventurers who had spent years facing precisely this kind of danger. Yet Gemma was more than willing to meet the challenge.

The door swung open, and they went inside. Catullus held up a lantern. What he saw made him smile.

The shelves were lined with marked glass jars. *Spt: Vini:. Meth:. Pulv: Sapo: Cast:. Tinct: Fer: Perch:. Liq: Sennœ:.* There were dozens more. And small tinted bottles with labels, advertising their wondrous properties. Most of these held nothing but colored glycerin, but there was quite a lot to work with.

A chemist's shop. Paradise.

In two strides, he stood in front of the shelves, examining labels, plucking jars down, muttering to himself as he mulled chemical combinations.

Several minutes passed before he became aware of Gemma, leaning against a counter and watching him, her eyes sparkling. "You're like a child set loose in a toy shop."

"This is far better than any jackstraws or whirligig."

He held up a jar full of a crystalline substance in liquid. Removing the stopper from the bottle, he held it out to her.

She took a tentative sniff, then wrinkled her nose. "Smells like a satanic egg."

"Sulfur compound." He replaced the stopper. "This will definitely be coming with us."

"I take it you aren't making perfume."

"It won't *smell* pleasant, but what I have in mind should have pleasant *results*. For us, anyway. Not for the Heirs."

At his direction, he and Gemma collected several bottles and made their way back to the center of the village. Everyone awaited them, the fruits of their searches piled up on the ground. Hands on hips, Catullus surveyed the amassed goods.

A crate of iron scraps, taken from the blacksmith's. An empty barrel. Obtained from someone's carriage house, a metal canister of oil. Gunpowder.

"Will this do, Professor?" asked Bennett.

"It will," Catullus said. "Very well, indeed."

Heavy explosives were to be prepared by Catullus and Bennett. The task of creating blockades in the side lanes, using furniture and whatever could be gathered, fell to Astrid and Lesperance. They were also responsible for dragging heavy wooden horse troughs into position in the central square.

"And what about us?" Gemma asked, pointing at herself and London. "Don't tell me to stand around and look pretty, or I'll feed you your pocket watch."

"Had my breakfast, thank you." Catullus gingerly handed Gemma the canister of oil, but not before wiping the outside of it clean with a handkerchief. "And you'll look pretty no matter what you do." He flushed at his compliment, almost as much as she did to be its recipient.

She glanced down at the oil can now cradled in her arms.

"Typically, men give flowers." Then she looked up, holding his gaze with her own. "But you're definitely not typical."

"And that pleases you?" His voice was low, meant for them alone.

"Oh, yes. Nearly everything about you pleases me."

He smiled; then a furrow appeared between his brows. "*Nearly* everything?"

Before she could answer, Bennett said, "Sunrise is coming, and the Heirs right after."

Gemma stepped back from Catullus and hefted the canister. "I'll treasure this forever. Now, what am I supposed to do with it?"

He outlined his plan quickly, if still somewhat distracted by her earlier words. Once she and London received their instructions, they headed off toward the eastern entrance to the town. Catullus watched her go, noting her purposeful stride, but mesmerized by the movement of her succulent hips, the sway of her vivid hair down her back.

Turning around, he found Bennett grinning at him. Never a good sign.

"Let's put this thing together." Catullus strode toward the empty barrel. "Start handing me the sharpest pieces of iron scrap."

Bennett handed him bits of jagged metal. "Lovely girl, your Miss Murphy." He glanced in the direction which she and London had disappeared. "Fiery. Quick. And"—he double-checked to make sure he and Catullus were alone—"a hell of a figure. Don't mistake me. I'm happily enslaved to my wife's body." His eyes glazed over as if revisiting in his mind London's carnal charms, before he recollected himself. "But, dear God, temples have been built to honor breasts like Miss Murphy's. They're . . . the Platonic ideal of breasts. Except one wouldn't feel very platonic toward them. I'd say they were the erotic ideal, if such a concept exists. In fact—"

"Shut it," Catullus gritted. He arranged the iron pieces

within the barrel to keep himself from plowing his fist right into his friend's blathering mouth.

"So you *are* besotted with her," Bennett hooted. "About damned time. Here I was, thinking that cock of yours was only for show. Oh, and for occasionally poking that mercer's widow in Southampton."

Catullus straightened. "My cock is none of your sodding business. And you know about poking . . . I mean, my situation with Penelope?" He'd always been so careful about keeping his arrangement with her private.

Bennett looked affronted. "If I, the Blades' cryptographer, can't figure out who my best friend is plowing on a semi-regular basis, then I'd better turn in my Compass."

"You were bloody spying on me," Catullus growled.

Bennett just smiled, crossing his arms and leaning against the barrel. "Of course. But we're not talking about the widow. We're talking about that ripe peach of an American."

"No," said Catullus, getting back to work, "we're not."

"She likes you."

"I like her."

"I mean, she really *likes* you. More than that wrinkled brain or that antique body of yours. The person that you are. She likes you."

"So you keep saying," Catullus grumbled, while a small explosion of pleasure went off in his chest to hear this. Not just a flirtation for her, or an interest born out of necessity— he was the only single man she'd encountered in a while. Bennett's juvenile words were actually confirmation that Catullus's deep feelings for Gemma were—amazingly—not one-sided. But Catullus staunchly would say no more on the subject. He wasn't like Bennett, readily and easily discussing the most intimate of subjects. God knew how many times Catullus had been forced to listen to Bennett ramble on about this woman or that woman, one who could do the most *incredible* things while standing on her hands, and the noises this other made that resembled an aroused parrot. Although, Catullus realized, Bennett offered no such private details about his wife. A sign of respect, he supposed.

So, rather than voice any of this, Catullus remained silent, carefully arranging the pieces of iron.

"She has freckles," Bennett added. "I know how you like those."

Still, Catullus said nothing, but cursed his friend's excellent memory. Catullus had only mentioned his preference for freckled women *once* six years ago, after imbibing a little too much Trappist ale whilst in Ghent.

"Have you bedded her yet?"

Catullus sprang back up again, seething. "That is also *none of your goddamned business*."

"That would be 'no.'"

"Look, do you want me to beat you senseless?"

"What's the problem, then? Clearly, the woman is willing—though," Bennett added as an afterthought, "I don't know what it says about her that a lumbering oaf like you could attract her."

Briefly, Catullus considered taking the piece of metal in his hand and gutting his friend with it. Then an idea, quiet but sensible, whispered to him. Where women were—or had been—concerned, no one was better at understanding and seducing them than Bennett. Before Bennett met London, fidelity had not once enticed him, nor did it have reason to. Bennett's skill with women had been the stuff of legends. Whatever woman he wanted, he had, an endless banquet of sexual delight. And not only because Bennett had the face of a Renaissance prince. Something within him had an unerring instinct for what females wanted, what they needed.

Precisely the opposite of Catullus.

"I don't know," he said quietly. He gazed down into the barrel, seeing the serrated shapes of iron within. Words came from him, words just as jagged as the iron. "I want her so badly, I think I'll go mad from it. She's . . ." He searched for the right word to encapsulate and describe Gemma. Unsurprising that here, his vocabulary failed. Words seemed small and confining where she was concerned.

He spread his hands, not a shrug of dismissal, but a gesture of expansiveness. The world was a bigger place with Gemma in it.

Bennett gave a low whistle. "Damn, Cat. You're serious."

"I . . . am."

"What do her kisses taste like? This is assuming you've actually kissed her. You know how it's done, correct? I'd demonstrate for you, but your beard would chafe my delicate skin."

"No demonstrations. I know how it's done," gritted Catullus. "And I have kissed her. I'm not going to tell you what she tastes like," he added when Bennett started to speak.

"Once? An awkward peck?"

"A few times, and we *both* enjoyed it."

"More details," Bennett demanded. "It isn't fair, you know, hoarding this kind of fascinating information when I have been so generous sharing my own experiences."

"That generosity was never appreciated."

Bennett sighed in exasperation. "Give me a *little* more to work with, Cat. Clearly, you need my assistance."

"Usually I've kissed her after some threat or danger," Catullus finally admitted.

"When your blood's high and you don't have time or room to overthink your actions."

Catullus blinked at Bennett's perspicacity. "Yes, I suppose so."

"And you've said she's responded well to these kisses?"

Remembering the silken fire of Gemma in his arms, the feel of her lips against his, the furnace within his body blazed high. "Very well."

"Good, good." Bennett nodded, an encouraging uncle. "Have you done anything else with her besides kissing?"

"We . . . ah . . . exchanged some . . . intimacies."

"Intimacies," Bennett repeated. "Care to be more specific?"

"No," Catullus said through gritted teeth. He absolutely was *not* going to tell Bennett about the night with Gemma at the inn. About caressing her full breasts and satiny skin through the thin cotton of her nightgown. About finding her wet and slick for him, and stroking her until she moaned her release into his mouth. About her own hand on him, firm, demanding hands that gripped and slid until he, too, surrendered to bliss.

The furnace within his body roared, until he was fairly certain he'd burn his clothes right off.

"Whatever those 'intimacies' were," Bennett remarked, dry, "they must have been good."

Catullus rasped, "I think that's a safe assumption."

"But it was *her* initiative, I'd wager."

Again, Catullus found himself caught off guard by his friend's insight. "When did Bennett Day, rakehell and trickster, become such a sage of the human condition?"

Bennett grinned. "I'd say when he met a certain young woman with an aptitude for language and a hunger for adventure, then somehow managed to convince her to marry him. The lucky bastard." Then he shook his head. "Let's not get off the subject. If you only kiss Miss Murphy after something dangerous has happened, and if *she* was the one who instigated your 'intimacies,' then it's bloody well time you take charge of the situation. Next time you have a chance, kiss her giddy and then, for God's sake, make love to her. Be bold. Be commanding."

"Force her?" Catullus was appalled.

Bennett rolled his eyes. "Don't coerce her, but allow yourself to be aggressive."

"She's very forthright and independent. I don't think she'd appreciate that."

"Forthright and independent women are *exactly* the

type who enjoy an assertive man." He spoke with absolute assurance. "They don't want to be cowed into submission, but they find it gratifying to meet a man as strong-willed as they are, a man who shows how much he desires her, a man who's willing to take charge in bed. Trust me, it's very arousing for both parties." Some particularly potent memory flickered across his face, and he smiled.

Yet, still, Catullus felt unsure. Could he? Lead the dance, instead of follow dizzily in her steps? If he blundered, or said or did something wrong, and lost her, he'd hide himself off to some godforsaken tundra and wait for frozen death. "I'm just not certain."

Bennett knocked his fist into Catullus's shoulder. "Then *get* certain, idiot. A passionate woman like Miss Murphy won't wait around forever. She needs to know you want her. Here. Use this." He reached into his coat pocket, then pressed the produced metallic object into Catullus's hand.

A flask.

"And that's prime Scottish whiskey," added Bennett.

"I'm not going to get her drunk and take advantage of her," Catullus sputtered indignantly.

"It's not for *her*, Cat. It's for *you*."

While Catullus gaped, Bennett stood straight and rubbed his hands together. "Aren't we supposed to be building a bomb?"

Gemma finished sprinkling dirt over the now oil-slicked cobblestones. The sky stretched dark overhead. Sunrise would be coming presently. A faint sensation—an awareness—prickled along the back of her neck. She looked up from her work, straining for some glimpse, some sound. All she saw was the road leading east, out of the village, the boundary between dirt road and paved street, placid fields.

Nothing. No one out there. Soon, though.

She turned to Mrs. Day, who held the empty oil canister. Neither woman spoke a word, but their eyes met and held. An exchange of silent communication.

They both hurried back to the square. There, they found Catullus and Day carefully putting a lid onto the barrel. Mrs. Day immediately went to her husband, and they stood with their arms around each other.

"We've finished our task," Gemma said.

A flutter of wings, and Lesperance in his hawk form landed on the eave of a nearby roof. With a swirl of mist, he shifted into a human and nimbly leapt down onto the pavement. Gemma carefully avoided looking below his waist, particularly when Astrid appeared, a revolver in one hand, rifle in the other.

Catullus glanced at the sky, then at his pocket watch. "Sunrise in half an hour."

"And then battle," said Astrid.

Everyone looked at one another, surveying the people beside whom they would fight, each wondering privately who might be hurt or worse. And yet, there was a kind of wild excitement that danced between them, a gleaming readiness for whatever lay ahead.

"Let's trounce the bastards." Day smiled, ferocious, and he was no longer the lighthearted scoundrel but a warrior ready to do battle.

"With pleasure," said Astrid, her own smile savage.

Lesperance pulled Astrid close and kissed her, the act somewhere between primal claiming and tender devotion, and Gemma couldn't help but watch the private moment. At the same time, Day and his wife also came together in a searing kiss.

Gemma looked at the two embracing couples. A sudden longing beset her. What might that be like? To have one person who meant everything? Who stood beside you even in the most perilous circumstances? For, truly, she'd been alone most of her life. By choice, but still, alone.

Suddenly, Catullus stood in front of her, quick as shadow. His arms wrapped around her, strong and sure, and a kind of fierceness was in his face that sent a bolt of basic feminine need racing through her. He drew her against his long body. Her hands came up to grip his shoulders, broad shoulders that didn't falter, as he lowered his mouth to hers and proceeded to kiss her giddy.

Here it is, she thought. What she'd been missing. Here.

She tightened her hold, feeling the muscles beneath, breathing him in. He tasted of coffee, tobacco, intent.

With a growl, he pulled away, then took her hand. She could only follow as he led her to the house where she'd slept earlier.

Catullus paused in the doorway. "As soon as dawn breaks," he said to Day, "come get me. But until then . . ."

"You're not to be interrupted." Day grinned.

Gemma was far too aroused to be embarrassed. When Catullus ushered her inside, a possessive hand on the small of her back, she gladly acquiesced. Surrender never felt so good.

He led her to the bedroom at the back of the house. He shut the door firmly behind them, and they were enveloped in warm semidarkness. There wasn't much time. Gemma didn't know where to begin.

Fortunately, Catullus—inveterate planner—did.

With deliberate intent, his eyes never leaving hers, he removed his spectacles and placed them on a nightstand. He set his shotgun against the wall. Then, as she watched with her pulse in her throat, he closed the distance between them. His hands came up, and she half expected him to simply pull her against him and kiss her. Her eyes began to shut in anticipation.

Yet, he surprised her. Softly, he brushed his fingertips

across her forehead, over her cheekbones, down the bridge
of her nose. All the while, he stared with fascination.

His touch felt soothing, gentle, exploratory.

"Strange," he murmured. "I almost believed your freckles would be hot to the touch."

"They're just naturally tinted bits of my skin," she
said, wry.

"But they are burned into my mind." He leaned closer
and grazed his lips over her cheeks. "Each and every one."

She didn't mind her Irish complexion just then.

"You've even got some freckles here." He stroked a fingertip across the lobe of her right ear. Then, his breath warm
and soft, he dipped nearer and touched the tip of his tongue
to her earlobe.

Keeping her eyes open became almost impossible as he
lightly traced the outline of her ear with his tongue. She
never thought having a man lick her ear would have been at
all arousing, but the slight, warm and wet touch echoed in
other parts of her, made her think of his tongue elsewhere
on her body, and once *those* thoughts entered her mind, it
was all she could do to keep standing.

"They ought to taste sweet, as well," he breathed. "And
they do. They taste of you." He nipped at the very tip of her
earlobe, and she shivered.

Oh, God, if he was going to be *this* thorough, she might
not survive the next few minutes, let alone the battle that
loomed.

His fingers threaded into her hair, his large hands easily
encompassing the back of her head, which he tilted so he
could have access to her mouth. "Gemma," he whispered.
Their lips joined.

Finding precise and defined words to describe events
and situations was Gemma's business. She long ago learned
how to reduce the chaos of an experience into sharply delineated, concise language so that a reader could know exactly what transpired. Occasionally, she even caught herself

mentally describing events taking place around her—*the man walked up the short flight of three stairs to deliver a bottle of milk to a girl in a striped apron*—which kept her engaged, if not a little removed from everything around her.

That skill, that habit, evaporated with this kiss. She knew only the feel of his mouth, his tongue rubbing and stroking hers. Sleek, warm wetness as they drank each other in. A mutual exploration. Yes, they had kissed before, but there was something open and unrestrained now. Something tender and desperate.

But even these precise thoughts and words had no place, because all she could do was feel and taste and touch, her mind abandoning her entirely to sensation.

Her hands craved the texture of him. She let them roam where they wanted: over his wide shoulders, down the length of his long body, across his chest, where she could feel through the layers of his clothing the hard beating of his heart. Her hands dipped beneath the fabric of his heavy coat; she touched the broad expanse of his back, then let her hands go lower. When she cupped the tight muscles of his buttocks and gave them an appreciative squeeze, he laughed, low, into her mouth. His laugh turned to a groan as she stroked and kneaded him. Who knew a man could have such an incredible backside?

One of his hands moved to stroke her neck.

"Accelerated pulse," he rasped. "Shallow breathing. Definitive signs of arousal."

"Keep touching me," she said with what breath remained in her, "and you'll find more."

"Here." His hand drifted from her throat, along the line of her collarbone, and then he cupped her breast. They groaned together. Yet it wasn't quite enough.

"Lie down," he rumbled.

Gemma pulled off her boots and then stretched out on the bed. Catullus had already shucked his coat and jacket and tore at the buttons of his waistcoat. She watched the knot and play of his muscles beneath the fabric of his fine, white shirt, the exposure of his throat as his neckcloth sailed off to drape over a straight-backed chair. His boots thudded onto the floor. As he stood above her, shirt open, pushing his braces down, she'd never seen him look so fierce, as if he'd been chipped away to the sharpest point.

Then he stretched alongside her, surrounding her with his arms and his need. They clung to one another, kissing with exposed hunger. Without the barrier of so many clothes, she let her hands roam all over him. So much strength here, so much energy and potency, a shifting land-scape of sinew and bone that pulsed with unleashed desire.

He urged her up on her elbows as he pulled at the but-tons down the front of her dress. Some awkwardness as she pushed the top of the dress down her arms, the fabric pulling tight, then loosening as, at last, it came down to col-lect at her waist, until all she wore was her chemise. She hadn't put her corset back on, and was grateful she'd waste no time undoing all the hooks and laces.

For a moment, she felt a spur of embarrassment that Catullus would see her in so shabby a garment—reporters, especially female reporters, didn't make them-selves rich through writing, and she hadn't the budget for silk underwear—but he barely saw it.

He pulled the frayed ribbon that gathered the neck of her chemise. This, too, was thrown aside, and she watched it flutter to earth like a wish granted. The top of the chemise gaped, and he all but pushed it down until it also gathered at her waist. She felt like an exposed and ripe piece of fruit once the protective blossom had fallen away.

Lord knew Catullus looked at her as if he'd devour her in one gulp.

He stared at her bare breasts.

There was no denying it: her breasts were sizable. She'd developed them at an early age, and had to deal with the un-fortunate consequence of unwanted male attention, even before she knew what the attention meant. Sometimes, she resented her breasts. They were often the part of her that garnered the most notice, the first thing people—especially men—saw when she entered a room. As a woman in a man's profession, she didn't need further reminders for her colleagues that she wasn't like them. She'd even tried to bind her breasts, but all she received for her troubles was a sore chest and even more pointed looks at her chest from the boys in the newsroom, as if to ask, *Where did they go?*

I'm up here, she'd wanted to shout.

She knew that Catullus was unlike any man she'd known. But, when he gazed down at her breasts, then up at her, what she saw in his eyes went beyond animal male lust. Something else shone in his gaze, something much more profound.

"You are so beautiful," he rasped. And rather than paw or squeeze her breasts, his hands came up to hold her face and kiss her tenderly.

She knew, then. She knew what he'd come to mean to her. And she kissed him back, blinking away a sudden sheen of moisture in her own eyes, swallowing the burn in her throat.

The gentle kiss shifted, becoming passionate, deeper and demanding.

She covered his hands with her own, then pulled them down slowly, so slowly, until his palms cupped her breasts. They sighed. For a moment, neither of them moved, simply letting the sensation of his bare hands upon her flesh soak into them both. Faintly, almost too faint for her to perceive, he trembled. This, too, sent a bolt of purest emotion to her innermost self.

His hands were big, so that, instead of her uncomfortably spilling over, he encompassed her. With infinite tenderness, he began to stroke her breasts, tracing her, gathering her up. A slight abrading from the calluses on his skin, evidence that he worked with his hands, and the rasping against her own, softer flesh was delicious. His fingertips circled her nipples, bringing them to tight beads.

Then he bent his head and licked them, one, the other.

She gasped. Arched her back, up, into his touch.

He was thorough, as she knew he would be, licking and sucking her, lightly taking each nipple between his teeth, soothing and inflaming her with strokes of his tongue. She writhed beneath him, holding him to her.

She'd known she could gain pleasure from her breasts. But she'd never experienced *this* kind of pleasure, so acute and all-encompassing that she barely heard the moans that rolled from her.

Cool air touched her legs as he gathered up her skirts. He stroked up her legs, over the rather coarse knit of her stockings. Her drawers were removed so quickly, she barely felt them sliding down her legs. Once she was divested of her drawers, his touch returned to her legs. Past her garters, to the bare skin of her thighs. His breath came hot against her chest as he caressed her. When he stroked between her legs, where she was fevered and slick and ready for him, she moaned again and was matched by his growl.

Her hands possessed their own instinct. Along the broad contours of his chest, his tight belly that heaved in and out as he fought for breath, and then lower, to grasp him through trousers. The heat of his cock burned her, even with the barrier of fine wool. This wasn't enough. She undid his trouser buttons and took him in her hand. He sucked in air, a hiss, and, even though time was in short supply, they let themselves explore for a few indulgent moments—her soaked folds, the aching pearl of her clit, the silken steel of his cock, its round, smooth head. A big man. He was a big man, all of a proportion, but she wasn't afraid, because if anything was right, it was this. Them. Together.

"I think . . ." he rumbled, "you *will* drive me mad."

"Like this?" She dragged a hand down his cock, then up. "Or this?" Her fingernails lightly scored his shaft.

He tightened and growled, growing hotter, harder.

She loved this power she had over him. And, as he dipped his fingers into her clinging heat, putting exactly the right amount of pressure exactly where she needed it, he had power over her. They ruled each other and reveled in both their sovereignty and servitude.

She did have a good imagination, and there were scores, no, *hundreds* of things she wanted to do to him and with him. But there wasn't time, and she was careening in a free fall of desire.

Her legs widened, and she urged him closer, between her thighs. "Now, Catullus." She could barely get the words out, her need all but choked her. "I can't . . . wait any longer."

A blaze of triumph flared in his eyes. Then, in a movement too fast for her to fully understand, he suddenly rolled on his back and positioned her so she straddled him. She braced herself above him, hands upon his chest. He gripped her thighs in a hold almost painfully strong. With subtle adjustments, she brought him to her entrance. The first touch of flesh to flesh, only the head of his cock at her opening. She felt her moisture coating him, proving she was more than ready. Their gazes locked.

A silent agreement without gesture or word. She slid down, taking him inside her.

"My God." For a few heartbeats, all she could do was feel him within her, his size and heat that filled more than just her pussy, but everything of herself.

He panted beneath her, head thrown back, fighting for control and allowing her whatever she needed, but it cost him. And when, experimentally, she rose up and then sank down, his teeth clenched. If, for him, this felt even a fraction as delicious as it did for her, no wonder sweat gleamed on his throat and chest.

She began to rock on him, an exquisite slide and drag. Pleasure concentrated where they joined and radiated out in solar waves.

"So good," she gasped. "Need more."

"Yes."

Faster she moved, her gentle rocking giving way to a harder, more urgent rhythm. He met her hips with his own, drawing them back and then surging forward. Each thrust tore a gasp from her, as if she could hardly believe the ecstasy she was feeling.

"Touch yourself," he growled, a tender command. "Ride me and touch yourself. I want you to have pleasure. So much pleasure."

She readily obeyed. As Catullus gripped her waist, guiding her up and down, she let one hand rise up to caress her breast; the other circled and stroked her clit. Her fingers brushed his cock plunging in and out of her, driving into her.

This was too much. Her climax refused denial. It crashed over her as she exploded outward.

No sooner had one wave ebbed, than another took its place. And another. An unending deluge of pleasure.

Wrung out, she finally draped herself over him in a boneless heap. Then she was on her back, his hands beneath her hips, as he thrust into her. His face was almost grim, his lips compressed into a line. His speed increased, and she bent up, into him, wrapping her legs around his slim hips. Yes.

He froze, arms rigid, and groaned out his release. More than a release. A surrender. She felt him within her, pulsing in time with her heart.

They were immobile, trapped in the amber of deepest intimacy. Forever they would stay like this, two lovers eternally bound, the object of future study and envy.

Slowly, carefully, he lowered himself down. Yet he was careful not to crush her, rolling them both so they lay on their sides, facing one another, yet still intimately locked. Their breathing rasped in and out, trying to regain normalcy, as if such a thing could ever happen after what they'd just shared.

She pressed kisses over his face, rubbed her cheek against his, and then tilted her head back so she could see him more fully.

He brushed damp strands of hair from her forehead, and, for a while, they looked into each other's eyes in the silence of the room.

He gathered one of her hands in his, then slid her fingers into his mouth and licked. She felt a renewed blush—not of embarrassment, but desire—when she realized he licked the fingers she had used to touch herself. She could hardly believe the diffident and reticent man from only a few days ago was the same one who commanded her to stroke herself as she rode him.

"Gemma," he murmured, when he removed her fingers from his mouth. His eyes shone with warmth as he looked at her. "I waited. I waited so long."

She smiled and kissed him, knowing he meant more than waiting for the opportune moment to make love. A lifetime, he'd waited, a stranger in his homeland, eternally alone.

No longer. For the time they had, they had each other.

A tap sounded on the bedroom door.

"Sunrise," said Day.

Time to fight.

Chapter 11

Of Scarabs and Sulfuric Acid

Gemma had never been in a battle before. She didn't know if they had definitive starts; maybe someone walked out onto a field and dropped a handkerchief, signaling the onset of combat. Or did they trickle into being, one shot becoming another, and then another, until gradually gunfire and smoke were everywhere? They might be as individual as fingerprints or the same from one to the other.

All she knew now was that one moment, the village was quiet, preternaturally still, with her and the Blades taking up positions within buildings at each entrance to the small town. Gemma stood in readiness at the eastern entrance, inside a house, with Astrid crouched within another house across the street, the nose of her rifle poking out of an open window. Gemma pointed a pistol out another open window, her loaded derringer in her pocket. She'd never deliberately shot at a man with intent to kill. But Catullus had been clear. No bullet was to be wasted on just wounding. The Heirs would kill her, and every Blade, if given the chance. She was not to give them the chance.

If it meant protecting Catullus, she was ready to do what was necessary.

Oh, God, Catullus. Her body still glowed in the aftermath of his lovemaking. The experience had been . . . extraordinary. She wondered that her skin didn't gleam like a pearl, because he made love to her as if no one and nothing were more precious.

Would she experience that ecstasy, that adulation again? There was a distinct possibility she would not.

These thoughts spun through her mind. Then—chaos.

Men charged toward the village. Armed men, faces hard with purpose. They weren't there, and then they were, and Gemma realized they weren't trying to be quiet. It didn't matter to them whether or not the Blades knew about their attack, because they believed there was nothing the Blades could do to stop it.

The group of men barreled down the road, keeping in an orderly group. Until one stumbled, slipped. And then another. They struggled for balance, but their feet slipped underneath them. In tangled knots they fell, swearing. The Heirs at the rear of the charge found their assault blocked by the struggling men on the ground.

Gemma caught Astrid's eye through the windows across the street, and they shared a brief smile. Per Catullus's instructions, the cobblestones had received a generous coating of oil, with a dusting of dirt on top to hide the telltale slick.

Taking advantage of the confusion, Astrid aimed and fired into the lurching group. One of the men yelled, catching a bullet in the foot; then his comrades shot back.

Bits of wood and glass exploded above Astrid as the Heirs returned fire. She did not let up, shooting and reloading so quickly her actions blurred.

But Gemma didn't want only Astrid to bear the responsibility of holding the Heirs back. Gemma peered up over the window frame and squeezed the trigger of her pistol. The gun kicked in her hand, yet she fought to keep herself steady. She crouched for cover when the Heirs, learning her position, began firing in her direction. The window above her shattered, and she covered herself from the broken glass.

Though the slick had slowed the Heirs' advance, they were already gaining their feet. Two limped, but pushed forward with anger blazing in their eyes.

If she stayed inside the house, she would be trapped.

"Fall back," Astrid called across the street to Gemma. "We'll lead them to Catullus."

Gemma nodded, then scrambled out of the house into a run. As she raced toward the center of the village, she heard Heirs' shouting behind her, felt the hot trails of bullets as they sped past. She couldn't waste time in being afraid. There was only the need to move ahead.

She and Astrid ran, dodging gunfire. Then Catullus appeared, standing in the middle of the street, brandishing his shotgun. If she wasn't hell-bent on running for her life, Gemma would have admired the sight he made—fierce and lethal, a man capable of anything, the weapon held easily and comfortably in his big hands.

The wooden barrel lay on its side in front of him. Heat radiated out from the barrel, though it didn't appear to be on fire. She didn't have time to consider how or why this could be. As Gemma neared, Catullus's face hardened, jaw tight, gaze dark and angry.

"Get behind me," he commanded.

She did so at once. He kicked the barrel, sending it rolling down the street, straight toward the advancing Heirs.

Catullus blasted two shots at the Heirs before grabbing Gemma by her arm and hauling her toward the shelter of a doorway. Astrid, too, dove for a doorway, pressing herself against the jamb.

Once in their doorway, Catullus braced his arms on either side of Gemma, shielding her. She peered around him, needing to see what was coming.

The barrel continued to roll toward the Heirs. The men looked perplexed, seemingly wondering what an ordinary barrel was doing rolling in their direction, but didn't stop their advance. They charged up the street, and, as the barrel came toward them, stepped aside to let it pass. One of their number—a bulky brute of a man—made to kick the barrel to one side. As he did, he suddenly yelped in pain. The leg of his trousers began to char and smoke.

"Stay down, damn it," Catullus growled, shoving Gemma against the unyielding mass of his body. For a moment, all she knew was the heat and press of him, shielding her.

A detonation rocked the ground, and Gemma would have stumbled if Catullus wasn't there, holding her up. She heard the explosion, followed by the screams of men.

When Catullus stepped back from the doorway, allowing her freedom to move, Gemma looked down the street to where the Heirs had been advancing. She gaped at the scene.

Three of the men lay on the ground, unmoving. They were bloody and torn. Two others staggered on their feet, covered in cuts large and small. The remaining three sported lesser injuries, but they shook their heads and struggled to regain clarity.

"The barrel exploded," Gemma murmured, stunned.

Grimly, Catullus surveyed his handiwork. "It was packed with gunpowder and iron scrap."

"I didn't see it burning."

"I soaked the wood in very pure, distilled alcohol from the chemist. Burns invisibly."

"So the Heirs wouldn't know to get out of the way."

He gave Gemma a clipped nod; then they and Astrid turned at the sound of an enraged animal bellow coming across the village, from the western entrance.

"Nathan." Astrid sprinted toward the sound, a look of angry fear tightening her face.

Catullus and Gemma moved to follow, but a sudden, loud clicking filled the air. The lightening sky dimmed. The whirring, clicking grew even louder as the sky darkened. A strange, shifting cloud of shadows. Spinning around, Gemma saw one of the slightly less wounded Heirs chanting while gripping something metal in his hand, something that was not a gun. Looking harder, she saw it was an ankh, an Egyptian cruciform that symbolized eternity.

"He's got—" she began, but then the cloud descended.

Everything became a swirling, seething mass. The noise deafened. She and Catullus found themselves pelted by thousands upon thousands of enraged, sharp bodies. Pincers and serrations scored her face, her hands. She had just enough presence of mind to slip her pistol into her pocket. Gemma batted uselessly at the tempest, her hands contacting untold numbers of flying, biting creatures. Squinting, she tried to make out what the things were, but there were too many, their numbers too thick and their attacks relentless.

Something wriggled in her hair. She reached up and plucked it from her head. When she examined what it was she held, she fought down a gag. A copper-colored beetle, the size of her palm, legs and antennae waving, mouth snapping. The air was thick with them, coming at her from every direction. She felt the insects trying to wriggle down her collar and climb up her legs.

The only thing that kept her from screaming was the fear the beetles would climb into her mouth.

All her exposed skin burned as a thousand mouths bit her. Mandibles gouged at her face. She tried to pluck the insects from her, but no sooner had she flung one aside than two took its place.

Reaching out, her eyes screwed shut against the onslaught, she searched for Catullus. Blindly, she waved her arms, contacting only more flying creatures. They came so thick and fast that she staggered against their bombardment. Maybe she could take shelter inside one of the shops or houses along the road.

She heard glass breaking—the insects crashing through windows. No shelter, then.

A heavy mass slammed into her, and she fell backward to the ground. Under her back, she felt the crunching of dozens of beetles, their bodies releasing sticky ooze. But she paid this no mind. Instead, she focused on the bulky body crushing her. A man. Pinning her to the ground, robbing her of breath.

She opened her eyes to slits. An unknown man's face snarled down at her. His thin lips were twisted, his eyes cold. Vaguely, she noticed that a pocket of air surrounded him, free of beetles. Some protection insulated him against the insects. Gemma struggled furiously beneath him, clawing at him.

"Blade bitch," he spat.

One of his hands came up and cuffed her across the cheek. A constellation of pain sparked, dimming her sight, yet she struggled against unconsciousness.

When she felt the cold press of a gun barrel under her chin, she went very still.

"That's better," the man hissed, shoving his face closer. "Treat me nice, and I won't have to kill you."

Gemma allowed her body to soften even more, compliant. "I'll be good."

The Heir smirked, slightly lowering the gun.

Her hands shot up between them. With one hand, she pushed his gun away from her. And with the other, she dug her thumb into the man's eye. He howled, and she pushed all the harder, until something wet ran down her hand.

Gemma used his distraction to shove herself away. As she did, she left the small shelter provided by the Heir's nearness. Beetles surged around her as she rolled to one side, then crouched low. With one hand clapped over his ruined eye, the Heir struggled to his knees. He still held his pistol, and Gemma threw herself back down to the ground as he fired wildly.

A loud blast punctured the roar of swarming beetles. The Heir toppled over, gurgling, a red stain spreading across his torso. Insects immediately covered him. With his death, the protection around him vanished.

Then Gemma was being pulled to her feet. In the thick, stinging cloud, she found herself cradled in the shelter of Catullus's chest.

"Hurt?" he breathed close.

She shook her head, then reached up and touched his face. Like her, he was covered with bites and scratches, but he was alive, and so was she, and, even in the middle of this hell, she allowed herself a moment of relief.

It was short-lived. Somewhere, the Heir's chanting grew louder, sending the beetles into a frenzy.

Catullus pressed them both down to the ground. He covered her as the insects surged, and the darkness was everywhere, without end.

Catullus sheltered Gemma with his larger body. Beneath him she felt tiny, delicate. Yet not a moment ago he'd seen her effectively cripple an Heir with nothing more than her thumb. That did not mean she was bulletproof. When Catullus had gotten his opening, he took his shot. Now the Heir was nothing but rotting meat in the road. She was safe from that son of a bitch's threat.

But the damned scarabs kept coming. Catullus didn't know if the insects were flesh-eating or just extremely maddening. Now was not the time for entomological studies. With the swarming beetles everywhere, and the Heirs insulated against them, Catullus, Gemma, and the rest of the Blades were hobbled. Vulnerable.

As long as the Heirs had the Ankh of Khepera, the scarabs were theirs to command. And the Blades were defenseless.

Not entirely defenseless.

He lowered his mouth close to Gemma's ear. "Move with me." He felt her slight nod.

Slowly, like a crab, they crawled along the ground, he forming a protective shield around her. His sense of direction never failed him, and after long moments, they pressed against a wall. He guided her to turn into it. "Now, stay here," he murmured. With a quick movement, he stood, throwing off his long cashmere coat and using it to cover her.

Scarabs swarmed everywhere, all over him, burrowing between the gaps in his clothing. Their eager mandibles bit and pinched, their legs scrabbling everywhere. He was glad to see, however, that the wall and his coat effectively shielded Gemma from the worst of it.

No time was wasted as he turned and plowed through the living storm. He remembered exactly the position of the Heir—some sod named Baslow, as Catullus recalled—who held the Ankh.

Even though the Ankh's magic buffered the Heirs from the scarabs, their visibility was still hindered by the swarm. The hazy shape of Baslow stood in the middle of the street, searching. Catullus contemplated firing his shotgun at him—but he'd give away his position if he missed, which, at this distance, and with the confusing barrage of scarabs, was not likely.

No guns, then. Not yet. Using the beetles to hide his approach, Catullus eased around Baslow, then tackled him from behind. The Heir's gun flew from his hand, but he held tight to the Ankh.

They grappled and rolled over the cobbled ground, wrestling for the Ankh. Catullus gritted his teeth when the Heir threw a solid punch to his ribs, then countered with his own to Baslow's jaw.

Still, the Heir managed to spit, "You can't stop it, Graves. The Blades will be destroyed. England *will* rise again."

"Not at this cost."

They struggled together on the ground. Catullus knotted his fist in Baslow's thin hair and pounded the Heir's head against the paving stones. Baslow's eyes grew hazy. Seizing his advantage, Catullus reared up and drove an elbow into the Heir's wrist. A spasm forced Baslow's grip on the Ankh to loosen. Catullus grabbed the Ankh.

At that moment, the scarabs dropped from the sky. In thick waves they fell, and as soon as their bodies hit the ground, they burst into clouds of desert-scented sand. An inch-deep coating of sand covered all surfaces. The village, cottages, and shops were thickly smothered in grit and were of a fashion culturally midway between Egypt and England. Catullus tucked the Ankh into a hidden pocket in his jacket.

Baslow regained his wits, and writhed as he fumbled for something on his leg. He brought his hand up, clutching a knife. Catullus dodged the intended blows, holding the stabbing arm away, but Baslow's loss of the Ankh gave the Heir a surge of strength. His knife burned a slash down Catullus's shoulder.

Heavy black fabric suddenly covered Baslow's face. Gemma, her teeth bared in a fierce snarl, wrapped the cashmere coat over the Heir's head and wrested it closed.

Baslow struggled to dislodge her, but she held tight. The Heir began to flop like a fish washed ashore.

In a single, swift motion, Catullus pried the knife from Baslow's hand and shoved it between his ribs, right into his heart.

Baslow jerked, then went still.

Catullus leapt up, ready to take on the remaining Heirs. But, aside from those already lying dead in the street, the others were gone.

He turned his gaze back to Gemma. For a moment, all either could do was stare at each other, panting, over the Heir's body. She glanced down at the corpse, then back up

at Catullus, her eyes wide. Even as they drifted away from
Baslow's unmoving form, Catullus returned her gaze levelly.

This was him, as well. Not only an inventor, an adventurer. But, when it was necessary, a killer. He didn't enjoy
killing—it bothered the hell out of him at the beginning—
yet he learned that sometimes there wasn't a choice. End
one life to protect many more. So he did it when he had to,
clean and fast, without apology.

That did not mean his heart didn't pound in his chest as
he watched Gemma learn this aspect of him, her eyes straying to the knife sticking from Baslow's chest. She also
glanced behind her, where the Heir that had attacked her
now sprawled in the street, dark with blood.

She turned her bright gaze back to Catullus. Swallowed.
And then nodded. A small nod, but one that showed she understood.

When he reached for her, to brush sand from her hair,
she didn't flinch or edge away. She smiled, and performed
the same service for him, sweeping her hands along his
sand-covered shoulders. He reclaimed his coat from the
body, shook it out, then donned the garment.

The sounds of nearby combat reached them—guns
firing, men cursing, a large animal roaring.

Taking hold of Gemma's wrist, Catullus sprinted toward
the noise. The battle was not over.

In the small square at the center of the village, the Blades
and remaining Heirs fought. Heirs positioned themselves in
doorways and behind flower boxes at the far end of the
square. Catullus recognized some of the men from their
eastern assault. Felt a fierce satisfaction to see that some
bled from injuries inflicted by the barrel bomb.

Bennett and London had taken up positions behind the
wall surrounding the stone monument, firing on the Heirs.
In another recessed doorway, closer to the Heirs, Astrid had

her rifle blazing. And . . . hell . . . Lesperance in human form lay propped against the doorjamb, clutching at a wound in his arm. Blood dripped from his elbow to splatter on the ground.

Dodging bullets, Catullus and Gemma sprinted across the square to crouch beside Bennett and London.

Bennett looked relieved to see them, but grim. "Thanks for stopping that damned scarab infestation." He nodded toward the gritty sand carpeting the square.

"Status?"

"Took out two of theirs, but we can't hold out against them for too much longer."

"And the troughs?" Catullus asked. He glanced over to the three horse troughs that were arranged in front of the village postal office. In order for Catullus's plan to work, the Heirs would have to advance.

"We need to flush the Heirs out and corral them into place. Don't know how. They're dug in, won't budge. Tried to fake a retreat so they'd follow. But they didn't."

"What happened to Lesperance?" asked Gemma.

Bennett's face hardened with rage. "When we attempted the retreat, an Heir made a grab for London. Seems that she's something of a prize, being the sister of the Heirs' leader."

Gemma started in astonishment from this revelation, but Bennett continued. "I was pinned down, couldn't do anything. Lesperance turned wolf and ripped the bastard's throat out." He nodded toward a splayed body in the square. "Not before catching a bullet."

"This ends, now," Catullus growled. He glanced at Gemma. "Pistols loaded?"

She held up two guns—her derringer and a revolver—and looked keen to use them.

"Good lass. I'll need cover."

"It's yours."

His heart swelled at her quick courage. A magic-and-gun

battle with Heirs had to be a far cry from anything she'd ever experienced, yet she held firm to her valor.

"On my count," he said, readying himself. "One . . . two . . . *three.*"

Under Gemma's covering gunfire, he ran across the square.

Gemma used the stone wall surrounding the cross to help keep her aim steady. Among her, Day, and his wife, they lay down enough bullets to distract the Heirs from Catullus.

Blessedly, he made it uninjured to the doorway in which Astrid and Lesperance hunkered. Gemma finally released the breath she had been holding.

Catullus examined the wound in Lesperance's arm, and, even though Gemma couldn't hear what they were saying over the noise, she saw Lesperance's assurance that his injury wasn't serious. The two men conferred about something. Astrid tried to object to whatever it was they discussed, but Lesperance seemed adamant.

Finally, with an angry nod, Astrid consented. But looked downright surly.

Lesperance transformed, shimmering, into a hawk. He immediately launched himself up into the air. A tenuous moment as he struggled aloft, hampered by his wound, and then he gathered himself and soared high. He outpaced the Heirs' bullets in seconds, disappearing into the hazy dawn.

Gemma wondered if he meant to go find help, but she didn't think anyone could arrive in time. What, then?

The Blades and the Heirs continued to trade gunfire, smoke filling the square. Gemma noted that the Heirs had lost several men, but they still outnumbered the Blades almost two to one. She didn't know anything about combat, yet surely there had to be some way, some advantage the Blades could take to tip the balance.

A terrifying roar echoed through the square. Only the
threat of being shot kept Gemma from leaping to her feet.
Men screaming in panic replaced the sound of gunfire. The
Heirs all bolted from their positions, looks of blank terror
on their well-born faces. Within a moment, Gemma realized
what caused such fear.

Lumbering after the Heirs with surprising speed, an
enormous grizzly bear pursued. Lesperance. Gemma had
not fully grasped how gigantic he truly was in his bear
form—the darkness had hidden his size—but now seeing
him, easily the largest animal she'd ever encountered, his
lips peeled back to reveal a set of huge white teeth, it was
all she could do to tamp down the primitive instinct to flee.
She'd seen one bear, a female, when in Canada, and at a
goodly distance. This one, however, made the grizzly she'd
spotted seem like a miniature suitable for a nursery. She had
to remind herself that *this* fearsome bear was actually Lesperance, an ally.

In a group, the Heirs ran, with Lesperance close behind
them. When one of the men tried to break away, a growl and
swipe of Lesperance's paws kept them together. That's when
Gemma saw what Lesperance was doing. He herded the
Heirs straight toward the post office—and the positioned
horse troughs.

As soon as the Heirs had been maneuvered into the
proper place, Catullus leapt from his cover. He lobbed three
bottles in rapid succession. Each one splashed into the
water-filled troughs. The troughs exploded in a rain of fire
and steam. A rattling boom, and then water splattered down
on the Heirs.

Only it wasn't water anymore. Whatever had been in the
bottles Catullus threw, it had transformed the water into a
different substance. It made the Heirs scream, shrill, ago-
nized sounds. Their clothing sizzled and dropped from their
bodies, the flesh beneath also blistering. The weapons they
held were flung away as the metal corroded within seconds.

Clawing at their faces, shrieking in pain, the Heirs reeled around the square. One ran right into Lesperance's path. A swipe of the bear's paw had the man slumping to the ground, his torso ripped open. Gemma winced at the sight. She'd heard of bear attacks when out in the Canadian wilderness, and seen animal carcasses left behind by grizzlies, but she'd been fortunate to have never witnessed a bear killing anything except salmon.

Astrid dropped another Heir with a single shot.

"Fall back!" one of Heirs yelled.

The remaining men fled the square. Some limped. Others ran full-out.

Bennett, Astrid, and Catullus gave chase, using what remained of their ammunition to ensure there were no stragglers. Gemma and London followed, but by the time Gemma reached Catullus's side, all of the Heirs either had abandoned the village or lay in the road.

The Blades, and Gemma, stood in the empty street. Sand covered everything. The walls lining the main street bore countless bullet holes. Broken windows threw back partial reflections, silvery and black.

After the chaos of the last half hour, the silence that fell deafened in its nullity. Then, incongruously, a bird began to sing.

Morning.

Gathered in the empty saloon, the Blades silently considered the man propped up in a chair. A stout rope tied him down, binding his arms. Cuts and abrasions marked his face. His clothes were torn.

He glared at them with a mixture of hatred and fear. "You going to torture me?"

"Blades don't torture," Astrid said. From one corner of the saloon, she finished bandaging a partially clad Lesperance's injury. The wound had already begun to heal—perhaps another of Lesperance's magical abilities. "Unlike Heirs."

Gemma, standing behind the bar, watched Catullus stride toward the prisoner. The captive Heir blanched as Catullus towered over him.

"Tell us what you know about the Primal Source."

But the Heir sneered. "You Blades are a lot of misguided fools—trying to stop what needs to be done." He glanced over at Mrs. Day, seated nearby. Disgust twisted his features. "Never would have believed it if I hadn't seen it with my own eyes. Joseph Edgeworth's daughter is now the Blades' whore." He spat.

Day's fist smashed into the Heir's face, and the man slumped in his seat, out cold. Blood and teeth spattered down the Heir's dirty shirtfront. Only Catullus's restraining hand on Day's arm kept him from punching the Heir again. Catullus's arm shook with the force it took to hold his friend in check.

"Let go of me, Cat," Day snarled.

"We're better than this," Catullus answered with enforced calm.

Day bared his teeth. "I'm not. Hands off, or I take you down, too."

A smaller hand rested on Day's tense forearm. "Don't," Mrs. Day said softly. "I understand languages better than anyone. His words mean nothing. And you mean everything."

Jaw tight, Day slowly lowered his arm and stepped back, though clearly he wanted nothing more than to beat the Heir into a paste. Instead, he gathered his wife into a protective embrace and moved them both toward the cold fireplace at one end of the saloon, as if standing next to the Heir would prove too much of a temptation for violence.

Catullus set his hands on his hips, staring down at the unconscious prisoner. Without turning around, he asked, "Astrid, are you sure Arthur is drawn to the Primal Source?"

"Not a doubt in my mind," she answered immediately. "I can feel it now. The Primal Source called him into being, and he's following it, like a beacon."

"So, wherever the Primal Source is now, that's where Arthur is headed." Catullus frowned at the captive Heirs. "Trouble is, there are numerous properties belonging to the Heirs. The Primal Source could be in any of them."

"This jackass has to know which one," Gemma said, drifting closer.

Catullus rubbed his jaw, mulling over their options. "Getting him to talk is going to be difficult."

"I could cross-examine him," Lesperance offered.

"Doubt he'll respond to questioning," Catullus answered.

Lesperance's grin was feral. "On the stand, I've made defendants cry and soil themselves."

"Sounds . . . untidy," said Catullus.

"Let me persuade him." His blue eyes sharp, Day took a step forward, but his wife maintained a surprisingly strong grip on him.

"There has to be another way," she said, quiet but firm.

Gemma looked at Catullus and the other Blades. "There is."

"First, I need something to drink." No sooner had the words left her mouth than Catullus handed her a full pewter mug. She smiled her thanks, and, as she sipped at the malty beer, their gazes held, fraught with promise of more. He looked at her with undisguised heat and need. No reticence. No uncertainty. And this sent a profound ache through her, an ache of wanting. Making love with him before the battle was just a taste. They had barely begun to map the new land of their shared desire, and she burned with the need to explore it.

Yet it must wait. The siege had been survived, but more

had to be done before any of her or Catullus's wants could be satisfied.

Gemma took a drink of the beer. Then splashed the remainder of the mug's contents in the Heir's face.

He sputtered awake. Through the liquid dripping down his face, he glared at Gemma standing above him. "You're that Yankee strumpet."

Catullus tensed, his hands coiling into fists, but Gemma held him back. He muttered something, then relaxed his hands.

The prisoner would never know just how often and how close he came to being walloped into oblivion.

She shook her head at the prisoner. "What is it with you Heirs? Seems any woman who has a mind of her own suddenly becomes a slut."

"Because you Blades trollops don't know your proper place," the Heir shot back. "Women are fragile, delicate creatures, meant to strengthen their country by offering their men the comforts and solace of home. Anything else is unnatural, disgusting. Whorish."

Gemma glanced at Mrs. Day. "You had to listen to this claptrap?"

The Englishwoman's mouth curled, wry. "All the time."

"I *like* being a slut," said Gemma. "How about you?"

"Oh," said Mrs. Day with a smile, "I like it, too. Very much."

"Can't keep my legs together," added Astrid.

"We're all whores, and happy to be so." Gemma crossed her arms over her chest as she turned back to the bound Heir. "Now that that's settled, let's get down to business. Where is the Primal Source being kept?"

The Heir only glowered at her.

She stared back at him, urging her magic to draw the answer from him. But she felt herself batter against a will trained in resistance. He would not give easily.

Gemma stilled, closing her eyes and reaching into herself

to call upon the magic that dwelled within her. It did not take much, just a slight tug upon an invisible, yet glowing, thread, and she felt it unfold—the power that bound her to generations and generations of her family, far back into houses of weathered stone, the gold and green hills of Tuscany. Vineyards and fountains. This was the gift of her kinsmen, and she needed it, now more than ever.

When she opened her eyes, the Heir recoiled with a hiss. He tried to look away, but the strength in her gaze wouldn't let him.

"Where is the Primal Source being kept?" Gemma repeated.

The Heir shook, fighting her magic. She did not relent, prying open the locked chambers of his mind. He had a remarkably simple mind, but it had been reinforced with a sense of privilege and prerogative. A lifetime of believing he, and the cause he supported, were right. Gemma shoved at this bulwark, strengthened by her magic.

The Heir began to sweat as he trembled.

"In London," he yelped. "In the Heirs' headquarters in London." Shocked at himself, his eyes went round.

Loud swearing behind her broke Gemma's concentration. She turned from the Heir to see all of the Blades grim-faced, especially Astrid, who continued to swear in the most explicit and elaborate curses Gemma had ever heard.

"London," Catullus growled, pacing. "God *damn* it. I cannot begin to imagine what variety of chaos Arthur could cause in London."

"Just picture what we saw in Glastonbury," said Astrid, "and then multiply that by a million."

Gemma felt cold dread numb her body as she looked at Catullus, hoping for reassurance that this nightmare wouldn't come to pass. But his furious scowl as he paced back and forth across the floor of the saloon only proved that she had good reason to worry. She half expected smoke to trail him, his mind worked so feverishly.

Then Astrid gasped and went pale, tottering a little where she stood. Lesperance immediately wrapped supporting arms around her.

"What is it, love?" he demanded.

She looked up at him, and then at the assembled Blades. "I felt it, just now. I didn't just feel it, I *saw* it."

"What did you see?" asked Bennett.

"Arthur and the Primal Source, together. In London. Not what *has* happened, but what *might* happen. If Arthur should physically touch the Primal Source." Astrid paled.

Worried glances were shared across the pub. Whatever Astrid saw, it wasn't pleasant.

"Let me help you, love," Lesperance said as Astrid sagged in his arms. "Tell me what you need."

"What we need is to keep Arthur from touching the Primal Source." Her eyes were silver ice, chilled by what she foresaw. "If he contacts the Primal Source whilst he's under the sway of the Heirs' dreams . . ." She fought a shudder. "I saw it. The loss of the world's freedom. Britain's magic belonging entirely to the Heirs, and everything they want coming to pass. *Everything.*"

Silence worked through the room as cancerous understanding spread. The Blades stared at one another, immobilized. Thousands of scenarios flew through Gemma's mind—as they must with everyone else—and none of them were less than disastrous. Nations would fall in radiating circles, like an earthquake might trigger floods and devastation, as the power of Arthur and thousands of years of English magic served the Heirs' cause of complete British domination. Even Britons—those that were able to survive the onslaught of unleashed magic—might find themselves trampled underfoot by this new tyranny.

Harsh laughter tore into the silence.

Everyone whirled to face the bound Heir, who sat, captive but exultant. "You're fighting something that can't be fought," he laughed. "There's not a damn thing you can do to stop us.

King Arthur will lead England on to its greatest triumph, and every last Blade will be carrion." Jubilant, the Heir roared with laughter until tears ran down his reddened face.

His laughter suddenly turned to choked wheezing. He struggled for breath, fighting to draw in air. The Heir's face began to turn even more red. His eyes bulged.

The Blades clustered around him, voices blending together.

"What's happening?"

"Is he having a fit?"

"Give him something to drink."

Catullus tipped a mug of water to the Heir's mouth, but the liquid just splashed down his chin. Horrible gurgling sounds tore from the captive's throat. He struggled against an invisible force, his tongue protruding, his face going purple.

The Heir pitched in his chair. Only Catullus's steadying hand kept him from crashing to the ground. Whitely, the Heir's eyes rolled back as the sounds grew worse, more tortured.

And then, abruptly, he went slack. His mouth gaped open, tongue hanging out. Wide, staring eyes gazed sightlessly at the timbered ceiling.

Catullus bent and pressed his ear to the Heir's chest. Slowly, he stood, then drew the Heir's eyelids closed.

"He's been strangled to death," Catullus said.

Chapter 12

The King and the Heir

Morning light barely penetrated the gloomy dell. Instead, the bright glow licking along tree trunks came from a hastily constructed fire. Men's shadows grew and shrank as the flames flickered. They formed a ragged ring around the fire—most of their numbers were dead, and those that lived bore wounds. A far different gathering than the one that had assembled before dawn. Then, victory over the Blades of the Rose had been all but assured.

Now, angry, hurt, exhausted, the surviving Heirs watched their leader exact a pitiless retaliation against the comrade who'd been unfortunate enough to be captured.

Jonas Edgeworth's scarred hands formed a choking hold on what appeared to be only air. But the chant that droned from his mouth proved he was, in truth, working a dark magic. His already-disfigured face twisted into even greater contortion, shaped by rage.

The chanting reached a crescendo, then stopped. Edgeworth dropped his hands.

"Treyford's gibbering has been silenced." He speared each of his men with a glare. "Unless any of you lot want to go blathering to the Blades."

A muted chorus of "No, sirs" rose from the assembled Heirs.

None of them would look at Edgeworth directly. Once, this bothered him. He'd been the handsome son of Joseph Edgeworth, and his father's status as a pillar of the Heirs of Albion ensured that Jonas Edgeworth would be met with smiles and welcome wherever he went. Daughters of other high-ranking Heirs were paraded before him, each eager to cement alliances through marriage. Jonas even had a bride already selected, a perfect candidate for both families' ambitions. Eventually, he would succeed his father and take over the venerable Edgeworth tradition of leadership within the Heirs of Albion.

Then, everything collapsed.

Jonas, on a mission to acquire a Source in Mongolia, tangled with the damned Blades of the Rose. Thanks to those Blades, the mission failed, and Jonas had been forced to retreat using the Transportive Fire. No one ever used the Fire for anything but sending paper communications. Men did not travel well through its flame—and Jonas was living proof.

When he emerged in Heirs' headquarters, the fire left him a twisted hulk of flesh, burned so badly, no one, not even his mother, recognized him. It took months to recover from his wounds, but the scarring remained after the skin healed. His fiancée ended their engagement. People could not look at him without wincing in horror. Jonas refused to leave his family's Mayfair home, skulking about its corridors and prone to violent rages. He would never have left his house, if it hadn't been for those son of a bitch Blades.

His father undertook a rare field mission to Greece, bringing his widowed daughter, Jonas's sister, London, with him. She had been the only person with enough linguistic knowledge to decipher some ruins that would lead to a Source. Everyone had believed Joseph Edgeworth was making a terrible mistake, involving a woman with a mission. Women were fickle bitches—Jonas knew this more than anyone.

Turned out that everyone was right. London fell under the seductive allure of Bennett Day, who beguiled her into joining the Blades. Her betrayal cost the Heirs not only a powerful Source, but the life of Joseph Edgeworth.

Scarred, fatherless, his sister a betraying whore, Jonas's anger knew no bounds. He all but leveled the Mayfair home. And then, in the smoking ruin of his life, cold understanding grew. A void in the Heirs had been left by Joseph Edgeworth's death. The Primal Source belonged to the Heirs, its power theirs to use. The time was ripe for Jonas to ascend to his rightful place as leader of the Heirs of Albion.

He would accomplish his father's dream for a global English empire. He'd crush anyone who crossed his path. And he vowed by his dead father's soul that the Blades of the Rose would be obliterated. Each and every one of them would face an excruciating death, especially his slut sister.

He wielded his disfigurement like a weapon. Intimidation came so much easier when one wore the face of a monster. No one disobeyed him, fearful of what he might unleash. And it wasn't only his appearance that had been changed by the Transportive Fire.

The element of fire was his to command. He could travel through it at will. One fire to another—distance didn't matter. He'd even traveled all the way to the Canadian wilderness to rescue that miserable failure of a mage, Bracebridge. And now, this morning, his men had been so abysmally routed by the Blades. In retreat, needing guidance, they built a fire and summoned him.

First order of business was silencing Treyford.

"Doesn't matter that the Blades know the location of the Primal Source," he said to his assembled men, once that had been accomplished. "They'll never be able to reach it."

"What if they do, sir?" asked Lilley. A makeshift bandage was wrapped around his head. Graves had built some kind of shrapnel-filled bomb, the clever bastard, and now the surviving Heirs looked like the walls of a besieged town. God, if only the Heirs had the mechanical genius for their own. But the color of Graves's skin blighted what could have been a fruitful partnership.

"Even if they make it to London," said Edgeworth, "headquarters is protected by firepower and spells. They couldn't breach the outer walls. And," he added with a glower, "if they get through *those*, they'll be dead long before they reach the chamber holding the Primal Source."

"But the Blades—"

"Enough," snapped Edgeworth. "Follow me."

The men trooped after Edgeworth, trailing him as he led them out of the dell, and up to the summit of a hill. The hilltop provided an excellent view of the village the Heirs had fled. Empty streets at this hour of the morning attested to the fact that the town had been abandoned by its citizens. Seeing it, such a humble little town, renewed Edgeworth's disgust that his men couldn't take it, couldn't rout a handful of Blades. Such an easy task.

"Do we have to go back?" whined Watton.

"Watch, idiot."

The men fell silent, but then gulped when a towering figure appeared on the horizon. It looked to be as tall as a farmhouse. A giant man. In the light of day, he gave off a dazzling radiance, glowing like a beacon of true Englishness. With each step he took, the ground trembled. Golden light shone from the crown encircling his head, and silver fire flared from the enormous sword he brandished.

He dwarfed the landscape. In a matter of moments, he reached the village, and his regal face gathered into a dreadful scowl. He raised his sword.

"Arthur will do what you fools could not," Edgeworth said.

As the Heirs watched, Arthur swung Excalibur at one of the stone houses lining the high street. The sword smashed into the wall. Bolts of bright energy shot from the blade. The heavy stone walls crumbled to dust, and shock waves from the blow radiated outward, leveling other homes and shops along the street. With each step he took, Arthur swung Excalibur, and each swing demolished more and more buildings.

The village fast evolved into a smoking ruin.

"Oh, my God," rasped Watton.

"Spyglass," Edgeworth demanded. Someone pressed one into his hand, and he trained its lens on the village.

What he saw made him cackle with glee.

The Blades were running from the devastation. Someone—it looked like Graves and that American bitch—actually sped to free the horses from where they were stabled. As the animals ran off, Arthur approached, and Graves and the Yankee leapt aside to dodge a blow. The sword slammed into a stone wall, and the structure turned to powder as rocks and debris rained down on Graves and the woman.

Graves shielded her from the wreckage. Sadly, neither of them seemed to be hurt. Then Graves grabbed her hand—the sight of a black man *touching* a white woman made Edgeworth ill—and the two of them ran in the direction of the other Blades.

"They're fleeing like ants! Look at 'em!" Edgeworth snickered.

The Blades sprinted toward a nearby wood, until Edgeworth lost sight of them. Even for a force such as Arthur, it would take days to root them out of the dense wood. Arthur moved to give chase.

"Hold, King," Edgeworth said.

Though he spoke in a normal voice, and though what remained of the village was a half-mile distant, Arthur seemed to hear Edgeworth. He stopped his pursuit and lowered his sword. Slowly, the king pivoted until he faced the hill. With burning eyes, he stared at Edgeworth and the gathered Heirs. Then began to stride toward them.

"Wh . . . what's he doing?" squeaked Lilley.

"Heeding me." Triumphant, Edgeworth handed the spyglass to a trembling Watton. "England's greatest king is ours to command."

Breath a hard burn in his lungs, Catullus tore across a field. He held Gemma's wrist in an iron grip as she ran beside him. Just ahead sped Bennett and London, followed by Astrid and Lesperance in wolf form.

None dared chance a look over their shoulders to see if Arthur gained on them. The devastation of the village glared too brightly in their minds. Only animal instinct for preservation got them out in time—any hesitation would have them buried in rubble or cleaved to pieces. Catullus refused to imagine Gemma or any of his friends cut down by a misguided king. Move forward, think only of the next step, and the next.

The dark fringe of a late-autumn wood rose up on the right as they ran. Shelter, of a kind. As though thinking with the same mind, the Blades turned and ran toward it.

They plunged into the forest, ignoring the bare branches that slapped at their bodies and faces. No one spoke. There was only survival.

Until Bennett slowed slightly to glance behind him. He stopped abruptly, and London wheeled around.

"He isn't chasing us anymore."

Everyone halted and followed Bennett's gaze. Sure enough, Arthur had left off his pursuit. The forest obscured where Arthur might have gone—though where a giant mythological monarch might disappear to remained a mystery.

Panting, London asked, "Why?"

"The Heirs," Catullus answered. His heart continued to hammer inside his chest. At least Gemma was safe, though winded. She braced her hands on her knees, gulping in air, yet her face was ashen with shock. "They must be able to command him, since it's their dreams that brought him to life."

"Why didn't they command him to pursue us?" asked London.

"We don't matter anymore," said Catullus. "They have Arthur. The sooner he is joined with the Primal Source, the sooner they fulfill their wishes. Including our extermination."

"Hell, Cat," Bennett said with a shake of his head. "He razed that village to the ground. And us, too, nearly."

"Once he reaches London," said Astrid darkly, "he'll inadvertently kill tens of thousands."

Gemma recovered her breath. "He's supposed to be the greatest king England has ever known. If he knew that what he was doing was wrong, he'd stop."

Lesperance shifted back into human form, and it was a measure of how distracted everyone was that not even London and Gemma blushed at his nakedness. "We need to communicate with him," he said. "Convince him."

"Whilst he's under the Heirs' influence," Catullus pointed out, "there is no way to communicate with him. I tried to talk to Arthur, and he attempted to dig a trench in my skull."

"Perhaps it's a matter of language," London offered. "He mightn't speak modern English. Using the language of his time, I could try and talk with him."

"You're not getting anywhere near that royal lunatic," Bennett growled.

London narrowed her eyes at her husband. "I had enough of being told what to do by my first husband."

"He was an overbearing jackass," Bennett said. "I'm being protective of my beloved wife."

She softened, but only slightly. "Yet, if there's a chance—"

"It isn't a matter of language," said Catullus, hoping to forestall an argument. "This King Arthur isn't the real Arthur, if such a man existed. He's the *idea* of him, embodied in the minds of contemporary England."

"So he'd speak modern English," concluded Gemma. She frowned in concentration. "There has to be *some* way of getting through to him. If we don't, Arthur is just the Heirs' pawn, and anybody or anything the Heirs don't like . . ." She slapped her hands flat together.

"He won't listen to any of us," Astrid grumbled. "Nor any Blade."

"Is he deaf to anyone but the Heirs?" asked London.

"Very likely," Bennett said.

As this was being debated, Catullus found himself pacing, hardly hearing the crunch of dead leaves beneath his feet or the sounds of his friends' voices. An answer lay buried within all this, somewhere. If only he had the means of unearthing it. He set his brain to unraveling the tangled mystery.

Arthur could not be stopped by force. And, even if the Blades did have access to magic, it wouldn't stand up against the strength of Arthur, shored by the Primal Source. There had to be a means of communicating with the king. If he would not hear the Blades, surely there had to be someone, besides the Heirs, to whom he would attend.

"Someone he trusts," Catullus muttered to himself.

Gemma turned to him, breaking away from the ongoing discussion "What's that?"

Glancing up at her, Catullus said, "It has to be someone Arthur trusts, someone whose words and advice he heeds unconditionally. *That* is who he would hear." He resumed his pacing, unable to stop the movement of his body as his mind worked.

"All kings have advisers, don't they?" Gemma asked. "A person in whom they can confide. Who can give them guidance."

"Guinevere?" London suggested.

Bennett looked dubious. "She and Arthur didn't turn out very well. Rogering your husband's most trusted knight has a tendency to dim that husband's opinion."

"Unless said husband wasn't satisfying his wife's needs," London noted.

Raising an eyebrow, Bennett asked, "Registering a complaint, *kardia mou*?"

"Absolutely not, *agapi mou*." She blushed prettily.

"Not Lancelot, but one of his other knights, then," Lesperance offered.

Catullus halted, mid-stride. He felt the bolts of his mind slide open. Sudden, precise insight came to him, as if waiting to be liberated from dark confinement. With this understanding, a crystalline rapture shot through him. Until he'd felt Gemma's touch, this had been his only true sense of pleasure.

He would have the ecstasy of her touch again. But, sadly, it would have to wait. Now, he'd uncovered the only means of reaching Arthur, staying the legendary king's destructive hand.

"I know who Arthur will listen to," he said.

All conversation stopped as five pairs of eyes stared at him. "Merlin."

Never before had Edgeworth the privilege of speaking with a monarch. The Heirs dealt solely with ministers and shadowy members of the government—the Queen herself meant little compared to these forceful, influential men.

But even Disraeli himself was nothing more than a mewling milksop compared to the powerful majesty of England's most revered king: Arthur.

Edgeworth bowed, a hand pressed to his chest, as Arthur approached the hilltop where he and the other Heirs stood. Excitement the likes of which Edgeworth had never known hummed through him, in time with the ground that shook with each step Arthur took. At last! A true ruler for the glorious English Empire! The Heirs had summoned King Arthur when his kingdom needed him most, just as it had been prophesied. Edgeworth could barely begin to imagine what glories lay in store for his homeland, and felt a savage surge of pride that it was *him*, Jonas Edgeworth, who had allowed it to happen.

None of the Heirs, himself included, knew precisely what the Primal Source might do once it had been unlocked. Mages toiled at all hours, pouring through dusty tomes, chanting spells in dark mirrors. The one who knew the Primal Source best, Astrid Bramfield, had hidden herself away in the mountains of Canada, and the attempt to abduct and torture the information from her failed. But that didn't stop the Primal Source from working its power.

Arthur's resurrection had sent a beacon of purest magical energy straight to the Heirs' scrying mirrors. Everyone gathered around the mirrors to watch not only the coming of the king, but the genesis of the England each Heir had dreamt of since the organization had been founded, hundreds of years ago. An England who was master of the globe. Cheers and celebration, even some tears.

Yet now, as the giant advanced, the Heirs were too awed to do much beside stare.

"Bow, you fools," Edgeworth hissed.

As expected, the Heirs obeyed him at once, each bowing low. They all looked pale beneath their makeshift bandages and bruises, but Edgeworth flushed with glee. Within moments, *he* would speak to *King Arthur*. If only his father were alive to see this!

Memory of his slain father wrapped cold rage around Edgeworth's throat. He would soon have his vengeance against the Blades, especially Bennett Day. As he waited for Arthur, he amused himself by replaying thousands of painful scenarios, all of them agonizing, and all of them ending with Edgeworth forcing his traitorous sister to watch Day's torture and murder, before Edgeworth reclaimed his family's reputation by killing her.

"What darkness shadows your heart, knight?" thundered Arthur.

Edgeworth peered up to see that Arthur stood two dozen

feet away. The Primal Source must allow Arthur access to the Heirs' thoughts and feelings. Edgeworth would have to remember that, to guard himself. "Forgive me, Your Highness." He bowed lower. "I seek only to restore honor to my family and enforce those noble virtues which Your Highness upheld in the splendor of Camelot."

Evidently, this response pleased Arthur. He rumbled his approval. "You and your retainers may rise."

Slowly, Edgeworth obeyed. His gaze traveled up the length of the king, seeing the golden surcoat, the armor, Excalibur, the gleaming crown atop a regal head. The embodiment and image of English nobility. Exactly as he'd imagined Arthur to look.

He had done this! *He* had brought King Arthur back to England!

"My liege and king, words cannot express—"

Arthur's eyes burned down at him. "You have summoned me for a reason, have you not?" His voice boomed like ancient cannon. "Else why tear me from the silence of Avalon and deathless slumber?"

Not used to being interrupted by anyone, even a legendary king, Edgeworth found himself fighting his irritation. "Indeed, yes, Your Highness." He glanced back at his assembled men, who naturally looked to him to speak for them all. Turning back to Arthur, he said with deliberate reverence, "You know from our dreams that we seek the restoration of your kingdom."

"Since my waking, I have sensed your desires. Your hearts reveal that there are those who seek to obstruct these ambitions."

"They are the enemies of England, Your Highness. They undermine all that is good and great in our nation." Rancor ground his voice to an edge.

Arthur shifted, gazing stonily at the village he had leveled. "The next time I encounter those villains, my hand will not stay my sword."

Edgeworth hoped he would be witness to the destruction of the Blades by Arthur. But even their deaths were secondary to the Heirs' true purpose. The mages had divined shortly after Arthur's resurrection that when the king was united with the Primal Source, all magic within England would belong to the Heirs. And this was but a stepping stone to the conquering of every nation. Every dream of the Heirs would come to pass, once Arthur touched the Primal Source.

It was too risky to take the Primal Source from its security in the Heirs' headquarters. They must get Arthur to London.

"Your Highness's presence is urgently required in the capital."

"I have felt the call," answered Arthur.

"If you would but follow me." Edgeworth gestured down the hill, toward the dell where the fire still burned. "I can transport us there immediately."

"Transport? How?"

Edgeworth roiled with impatience. He had already taken Bracebridge from Canada via the fire. It might task his command of the element to bring Arthur through the fire to London, but Edgeworth was willing to chance it.

"A simple and harmless form of magic," Edgeworth answered.

Arthur frowned. "I like not such uses of enchantment. It has the sinister glamour of my treacherous sister, Morgan."

Didn't Edgeworth know all about treacherous sisters? He gritted his teeth with a combination of frustration and fury, renewed by thoughts of London. "Truly, Your Highness, there is nothing sinister about what I propose."

"Dare you to challenge me?" Arthur rumbled.

Temper, the same that had been Edgeworth's lifelong blessing and burden, flared. The Heirs behind Edgeworth stirred anxiously, knowing that Edgeworth never responded well to being opposed. Had Arthur been anyone other than who he was, Edgeworth would have given him the beating of a lifetime—and had done so, many times. But this was

King Arthur, the mythical king, and a hulking giant of a man, to boot.

Biting down his anger, Edgeworth bowed. "Of course not, Your Highness."

"I shall march on the capital," Arthur declared.

Edgeworth smiled coldly. This could work to his advantage, especially if Arthur crossed paths with any Blades along the way. And if Arthur ever somehow broke away from the will of the Heirs, Edgeworth had something that ensured the king's disobedience wouldn't last long.

"Once there," he vowed now, "you shall be welcomed as king and savior." With Arthur as king, the Heirs controlling Arthur, and Edgeworth in command of the Heirs, dominion over the globe would be his. First order of business would be the extermination of the Blades. Finally, he would have everything he ever wanted: power and vengeance.

Stunned silence greeted Catullus's revelation. Until—

"That's bloody *perfect*," Bennett breathed.

Everyone began talking at once. Everyone, except Gemma, whose quiet caught Catullus's attention much more than anyone shouting. In the midst of the general chatter, she stood, still and separate, a pensive line between her brows.

Catullus strode toward her and took her slim hands in his own. "Something troubles you."

She looked up at him, so serious and lovely, her eyes blue as daydreams, yet the awareness within them showed she was no dream, but a woman fully in and of the world. Interestingly, a flare of ruefulness gleamed there.

"This is where I prove I'm just an ignorant American." Her mouth curled, wry. "I know Merlin was a magician in Camelot, but not much more."

Ah. She wanted knowledge, just as he did. "Like everything about Arthur, there are countless myths and stories about Merlin. He's thought to be a wizard, a prophet, an adviser. Of everyone within the legends, Merlin is believed to be the one Arthur trusted most."

"If Arthur can live again, then we can find Merlin," she said decisively.

He savored her spirit, which was as integral to her as breath and blood. "It shan't be easy."

"Never thought it would be otherwise." Her brash smile stirred within him a potent combination of respect and desire.

"Yes," broke in Bennett, "it's all well and good to say, 'Let's go fetch Merlin.' Quite another pot of stew to actually *locate* the bugger."

Trust Bennett to phrase this dilemma so eloquently.

"So, what do we know about Merlin?" asked Lesperance. "What was his fate in the legends?"

"He fell in love with a sorceress, Vivien," Astrid recalled.

"But she only wanted his magic," added Catullus, gently releasing Gemma's hands. "Sealed him up within a tree. Merlin knew it was going to happen, that she'd beguile and betray him, but he couldn't help himself. He wanted what he wanted, and damned the consequences."

"Love does that, I've heard," murmured Gemma. She didn't look at him, but one of her blushes turned her cheeks vividly pink.

Catullus's heart abruptly began to pound. He pointedly ignored Bennett's meaningful grin. "Yes, well, to the best of anyone's knowledge, he's still in that tree. Not dead, but not entirely alive, either."

"Where is this tree found?" asked London.

"An enchanted forest," said Astrid.

"There can't be too many of those." Gemma glanced around. "Anybody have a map of enchanted forests in England?"

"Indeed, no." Catullus prowled the archives of his memory, searching through shelves and stacks to find precisely what he needed. Turning to Bennett, he asked, "Do you remember Bryn Enfys?"

"The pixie who sometimes delivers reports to headquarters?"

London's face lit up. "I know him, too! Or, at least," she amended, "I did, long ago."

"Don't mention pixies," Gemma said with a shudder. "I can still hear their awful giggling and feel their pinching little fingers."

"There are dozens of varieties of pixies," said Catullus. "Some more benevolent than others. Bryn has been helping Blades for centuries. He occasionally visits my workshop to see what I'm tinkering with. Rather fascinates him, actually. Calls it my 'human magic-making.' One night, I asked him where he goes when he isn't amongst us mortals. He said that the realm of magic exists, not so much beneath this world as it does *parallel* to it. Otherworld."

A communal shiver ran through the group, but not from fear—it was a recognition rising up from the innermost reaches of collective imagination.

"You spoke of it before," said Gemma. "At Glastonbury Tor."

"That's one entrance of many to Otherworld."

"And that's where we'd find the enchanted forest that holds Merlin," Gemma deduced.

"In all of the Blades' history," continued Catullus, "none have ever been to Otherworld. But, if that's where Merlin is, we need to find a way there."

Bennett, who never heard of a quest he didn't like, beamed, as did London. The pair of them seemed to thrive on adventure. For most of her life, London had lived under the controlling thumb of her father, and then her late husband, who both firmly believed that virtuous English ladies were decorative, empty-brained vessels. London was anything but that. And Bennett . . . well . . . there wasn't an experience on this earth that Bennett didn't want to have.

Catullus thought it was a fortunate day indeed when the two of them found each other. Likely, they would drive anyone else mad with all their capering about.

"When do we start?" asked London eagerly. "I've always wanted to see the realm of faerie."

Catullus gave her a rueful smile. "I'm sorry, London, but we cannot spare so many of us on this task."

She looked crestfallen, yet dutifully nodded. "Of course." Then she brightened. "Bennett and I can go to London, gather information, and cause a spot of trouble. It used to be *my* city," she added with a saucy wink.

"Someone needs to let the Blades know that Arthur is headed for London," said Astrid. She and Lesperance held each other's gazes in a silent communication. At his subtle nod, she announced, "Nathan and I will travel to Southampton, reconnoiter with the other Blades."

Before Catullus could speak, Gemma turned to him, determination shining in her gem-bright eyes. "And I'll go wherever you go."

"You and I will be searching for Merlin. If we are to open a door to another world, who better to have with me than a woman who can defeat any lock." He was surprised he sounded so calm, so level, when inside he rioted with fierce pleasure at the thought of not only seeking the mysterious Otherworld but having Gemma, and only Gemma, with him on this voyage of discovery.

Leave-taking was muted. The knowledge of what was at stake weighed heavily upon everyone, so that, when it came time for the group to disband, they did so without the usual high spirits that characterized so much of the Blades' various comings and goings.

In the wood, good-byes and well wishes were exchanged like small silver coins passed from hand to hand, quietly given, tucked away.

As the women said their farewells to one another, Catullus faced his old friend and irritant, Bennett. "What are your plans, Ben?"

"London's going to try and talk to some of the ladies she knew when she was part of that world, see if she can't rally them to our cause."

"These would be the Heirs' women."

Bennett nodded thoughtfully. "Most of 'em don't know much about what their husbands, sons, and brothers do. It's how the Heirs operate—keep their females ignorant." He gave a disgusted snort. "Could anything be more repulsive? Even London, the cleverest woman I know, even *she* was kept in the dark until she was taken to Greece, right up until she met me." His grin flashed quickly. "She was hungry for knowledge, and I was happy to provide it."

"Let's leave that aspect of her education out of it," said Catullus.

Sobering somewhat, Bennett continued. "Suffice it to say, when she learned the true nature of her family and dead husband's work, she wanted nothing to do with it. Joined the cause of the Blades without regret. Now she's hoping to enlighten the Heirs' other women. We could use all the allies we can muster."

"And what will you do whilst your wife plants the seeds of revolution?"

Bennett tucked his thumbs into his waistcoat pockets, and Catullus had to sigh. All of Catullus's fresh clothing had been lost, including two gorgeous silk waistcoats he'd purchased in New York. Being in the field often meant forgoing his own exacting standards of dress. A burden for him to bear, but more so because he wanted to look his best for Gemma. At the moment, he resembled a crumpled, street-grimed advertisement for a gentleman's emporium.

"Oh, the usual," Bennett said, unaware of Catullus's acute case of clean-waistcoat envy. "Gather information exercising my talents as a second-story man."

"A fortunate set of circumstances that led you to being a Blade and not England's most notorious thief."

"Who says I'm not both?"

"You'd have better taste in boots."

Bennett glanced down at the footwear in question. His boots were appallingly scuffed and, if Catullus wasn't mistaken, stained with saltwater. The haberdasher within Catullus shuddered in horror.

"Badges of honor," Bennett said. He looked over at Catullus's boots. "Isn't that a scratch on your own bespoke Jermyn Street boots?"

"I don't want to discuss it," Catullus said darkly.

They bantered, but an undercurrent of tension made each attempt at levity feel that much more false. Eventually, their words drifted away like dried weeds.

"It's going to get brutal out there," Catullus finally said. "Be careful, Ben."

"Where London's concerned," Bennett answered, serious, "I'm always careful. You, too, Cat. None of us has ever gone to the realm of magic. Stay sharp. And take care of your Yankee."

"I won't let anything happen to her." He'd never meant any words more.

"Glad you took my advice," Bennett said, looking like a proud uncle.

Catullus said nothing. Bennett was his friend, but like hell would Catullus describe the wonder that had been making love with her. Still . . . "My gratitude, Ben."

Bennett nodded, approving. "Godspeed to you."

The two men shook hands, then broke apart.

Catullus turned, to see Astrid staring at him with her wise, clear eyes. Her expression bordered on cool, but he knew that, after the trials she'd endured and survived, she kept her innermost self well guarded. She still felt as deeply, only with less openness.

Yet, when she stepped closer to him, there was no hiding the bittersweet warmth in her gaze.

"We've not truly been apart since you came to Canada," she murmured, "to protect me against the Heirs." Before that, she'd hidden herself deep within the mountains for four years, four years of silence that had strained their friendship terribly. "I still don't know why you came all that way, just for me."

"I wonder that, myself." But they both knew the bonds of friendship endured beyond distance and time.

They shared a small smile, and he could not help thinking how utterly Astrid had changed from the eager young girl arriving with an equally young new husband at the Blades' front door so many years ago. Catullus wouldn't wish Astrid's sufferings on anyone, yet she'd emerged from them as tempered steel, and with the love of a man as strong and fierce as she.

Suddenly, Astrid wrapped her arms around Catullus in a hard, quick embrace. "Thank you," she said, her voice low and urgent. "I don't know if I said it before, but . . . thank you."

Catullus clasped her close, feeling the tough leanness of her body, this dagger of a woman he loved as he would love any member of his family. "We'll see each other again."

"Not a doubt." She stepped back, and cast a quick look over her shoulder, where Gemma was shaking hands with Bennett and London as now-dressed Lesperance looked on. "She's a good one, Catullus." Astrid's voice turned gruff. "Got a spine, and a brain. Worthy of you."

Catullus tried but could not stop himself from staring at Astrid. Her words absurdly touched him, given, as they were, almost against her will.

Yet Astrid still had a prickliness about her, and she wouldn't care for excessive shows of sentiment, so he only nodded and said, "Thank you." The two of them, standing there and thanking one another as if for small acts of politeness, and not earth-shifting alterations in the way they saw the world and lived their lives.

Then Astrid abruptly turned and strode over to where Gemma and the others had gathered. For a moment, Astrid and Gemma just stared at each other, two formidable women who had clashed and fought—each other, and side by side—and Lesperance, Bennett, and London watched them with a wary awe, wondering what might happen. No one really knew.

Astrid suddenly stuck out her hand, and Gemma took it and gave it a shake, with a respectful nod that was returned.

Everyone let out the collective breath they hadn't known they held.

And then it was time to go. So much needed to be done, and in so short a time, there could be no more lingering. With final waves, the Blades parted, three pairs diverging from a briefly shared path.

Gemma and Catullus stopped at the edge of the forest to watch Bennett, London, Astrid, and Lesperance disappear.

"Going to miss them?" she asked.

"I always do," he answered. "But, then, I also like working alone."

"Oh." Her vibrant face clouded a little, and he saw what she thought, that he might prefer this mission to be a solo one.

Only a day ago, he might have fumbled for words, awkward and embarrassed as he strove and failed for understanding. Yet a whole day contained many lifetimes, and he was not the same man he'd been even a dozen hours earlier. He knew her intimately, now, and he knew himself.

"I've never truly had a partner before." He picked up her hand and pressed a kiss to its back, and she smiled, her azure eyes warm. "I think I'll like the experience."

Chapter 13

A Hunger Not Sated

Seeking an entrance to the magical Otherworld was all well
and good, but Catullus was starving. He'd only had a bit of
stale bread and some coffee—and that paltry meal had been
burned up in the furnace of lovemaking and battle. Though
she hadn't complained, Catullus knew Gemma had to be
hungry, as well. She'd had no breakfast. Come to think of
it, neither of them had eaten much of anything since yester-
day. He had to do something about that.

The desire to provide for her reached into the most prim-
itively male part of him. He found, after years of scrupulously cerebral existence, that he rather liked indulging that
aspect of himself. It felt like stretching a long-unused
muscle.

He wanted to hunt. With knife and arrow. Cook the
animal he killed over an open fire and give her only the
choicest morsels. But this was modern England, not the pri-
mordial steppes. He'd have to settle for something a little
more civilized.

Soon after parting company with the other Blades, he
pounded on the door of an isolated farmhouse. A woman in

an apron came to the door, peering around it timorously, with a knife held unsteadily in her grip.

Catullus immediately put himself between Gemma and the woman. "Come now, madam," he soothed, taking a step back and holding up his hands. "No need for that. We're only travelers in search of a meal."

The woman visibly relaxed and tucked the knife into her apron pocket. "You near scared the wits out of me," she laughed, but her laugh was strained and breathless.

"Is anything amiss, madam?" Catullus asked.

"Strange doings, sir. Strange indeed." The woman, a sturdy country lady, as evidenced by her work-roughened hands, smoothed her apron after taking in the quality—if not the condition—of Catullus's clothing. "Tom Cole said he went to sell apples in Crowden this morn, and weren't nothing left of the whole village but rubble and ruin. And not a soul in the place, neither."

Catullus and Gemma scrupulously avoided looking at one another. "That's terrible," Gemma murmured.

The farmwife's eyes widened with surprise. "Bless me, are you a Yankee?"

"Chicagoan," Gemma replied.

"That another country?"

"Yes," said Gemma.

"Well, you're welcome to this corner of England, miss. But you've come at a bad time. All the cows' milk has spoilt, and folks is afraid to walk the streets at night, what with all the odd beasties roaming up and down. 'Struth, when I heard you hammering at my door, I thought for certain the gwyllion had come for me."

"Gwyllion?" asked Catullus.

"The hill faeries, sir," the woman whispered after first casting a fearful glance over his shoulder. "Frightful creatures my old Welsh mam warned me about. I used to think they were just stories, but after John Deever and Peg Goode got set upon last night and barely made it home alive, and

Susan Paley near had her babe stolen from its crib, I didn't think they're just stories anymore. With my son gone to Dover for the week, and me alone here, I brought this to the door." She patted the pocket that held the knife. "The gwyllion don't like knives, and I wasn't taking chances. You'd be wise to do the same."

Catullus had, hidden beneath his coat, a horn-handled hunting knife, but he thought it prudent, with the farmwife agitated as she was, not to go brandishing it about. "We're well prepared for whatever we meet."

The woman looked dubious, but did not argue. A maternal expression crossed her weathered face as she studied them. "The two of you look fair worn to dust."

Catullus glanced at Gemma, whose freckles stood out on her pale, weary cheeks. She needed sustenance and rest. A couple of hours of sleep barely compensated for everything she'd undergone these past days. Rest wasn't possible at the moment, but a meal must help.

"All we need is some food to take with us, if you've any to spare. You'll be well paid."

The farmwife opened the door farther. "I'll take your coin," she said brusquely, "for it's a hard living out here, but, sure as I love sunrise, you'll eat at my table and not crouching in the dust somewhere like a pair of vagrants."

"Many thanks, madam." Catullus ushered Gemma ahead, and they both entered the small farmhouse. Following the woman and Gemma, he had to bend down to keep from knocking his head against the low, timbered ceiling, and soon found himself in the kitchen. A pot of something savory, smelling like the gates of heaven, simmered on the hearth, and a large orange tabby cat regarded them with disinterest from his place in front of the fire.

"Now, sit yourselves down," the woman said, gesturing to the table and chairs, "and I'll have some good food ready for you. Killed the old cockerel this morning, and he's been stewing half the day."

Both Catullus and Gemma could only murmur their thanks as the woman bustled about, fetching bowls and bread. Two mugs of cold cider appeared, and Catullus felt himself on the verge of inarticulate growls of joy. He downed the cider in a single gulp, then smiled when Gemma did the same.

"They brew that in town," the farmwife said proudly. She refilled the mugs.

"If the Church of England believed in saints," Catullus said, "surely you'd be canonized."

"And you haven't even tasted my cooking." She set down two battered tin bowls filled with a rich-scented stew, then brought a wedge of cheese and loaf of coarse brown bread to the table, wrapped in a clean cloth.

"Go on, then," she urged, when Catullus and Gemma only looked at her. "I've had my midday meal. No need to stand on useless ceremony."

Like ill-mannered badgers, both Catullus and Gemma attacked their food. The only sounds either made came from their spoons scraping the bowls or the soft tearing as they pulled pieces of bread to stuff into their mouths. Doubtless, Catullus's grandmother Honoria would suffer apoplexy to see him comport himself thusly, but he couldn't bring himself to care. He was too busy cramming food into his gullet.

"Forget sainthood," Gemma said around a mouthful of bread, "you'll be made *goddess*."

The farmwife chuckled, taking pleasure in the enjoyment of her guests. "A goddess of plenty, for there's more."

Ultimately, Gemma ate two bowls of stew and Catullus three, and not the tiniest crumb remained of the bread. From one of his many pockets, Catullus produced a stack of coins that made the woman's eyes widen.

"Sir, that's too much."

"Consider it payment for the food and the company. Besides," he added, "we may return under more impecunious circumstances, and it always helps to have a good reputation with the house."

Slowly, as if afraid the money might jump off the table, the farmwife reached out and scooped the coins into her palm. She dropped the lot into her apron pocket, and smiled at the jingling sound they made.

From her seat, Gemma sighed and stretched, her arms reaching overhead as she interlaced her fingers. The unconsciously seductive movement caused her breasts to press against the lightweight fabric of her dress and jacket, her body arched with innate sensuality. The sight stirred in Catullus a hunger that had not been sated. If anything, his need for her grew exponentially by the minute. It felt like far too long since he'd tasted her mouth, touched the silken curves of her body. Made love to her. Now that he knew precisely how she felt, the noises she made in the throes of pleasure, every moment not spent caressing her bare skin, sinking himself into her body, became an ordeal.

A sudden image flared: sweeping the bowls and mugs off of the table, laying Gemma across it, dragging up her skirts, and then, as he knelt, feasting on her between her legs with lips and tongue. He hadn't tasted her yet. Would she be sweet, or spicy? He would find out as he made her come, again and again, her thighs draped over his shoulders.

"Catullus?" Gemma asked, lowering her arms. "Feeling all right? You look . . . feverish." She peered at him curiously.

"Splendid," he rasped. Thank God he'd forgone etiquette and kept on his long coat. As it was, he'd have to sit at this table for the next dozen years whilst waiting for his massive erection to subside to a chimney from a smokestack.

Gemma suddenly smiled with wicked understanding. She glanced at the part of the table that mercifully shielded Catullus's lap, and then, *Good God*, licked her lips. Catullus expected the heavy table to simply flip over from the force of his rearing cock. To keep himself from making good and then elaborating on his vivid imagination's scenario, he gripped the table's edge, his knuckles paling with the force he exerted.

He actually began to sweat, and his spectacles fogged.

"Is there anything else you'd like?" asked the farmwife, unaware of the carnal battle raging within him. "Tea? Muffins?"

"We're satisfied," Gemma said, smiling at the woman politely. Then Gemma turned her eyes to his as her smile evolved into something much less polite and altogether arousing. "For now."

He almost groaned.

"I'll fix you a hamper for the road, then." The farmwife fussed about, getting provisions together.

Catullus used the time constructively, casting his eyes up at the ceiling and mentally reviewing theory and debate surrounding Euclid's Fifth Postulate. By the time he reached Beltrami's essays on hyperbolic geometry, he felt himself under enough control to get to his feet.

"If you'd like to freshen yourselves before setting off, there's a basin and ewer for the lady." The farmwife pointed toward a bedroom. "And, if you don't mind the roughness, sir, we've a pump outside in the back, just next to the rabbit hutch."

"Obliged, madam."

Gemma disappeared into the bedroom, shutting the door behind her. As Catullus strode outside, he tried not to picture what she must look like, semi-dressed, running a damp cloth over her face, down her slim neck, and, if she'd removed the top of her dress, in the satiny valley between her breasts. . . .

More roughly than he intended, he threw off his coat and jacket, tossing them to hang from the bare branches of a nearby hawthorn tree. Rabbits within the hutch scampered into the corners as he also tugged off and pitched away his neckcloth, his waistcoat, and finally, pushing down his braces, his shirt. The hawthorn tree looked as though the top half of a man had exploded all over it, leaving only garments. And it wasn't entirely proper, either, stripping himself to the waist in a stranger's yard.

Catullus couldn't care. He needed to cool down, and he needed to do it thoroughly.

He tucked his spectacles into his trouser pocket, then stuck his head under the spout and pumped the lever. After a few good pumps, frigid water came pouring out, splashing in his hair and running in cold rivulets over his shoulders and down his torso. Bracing, tonic. Yet he did not quite feel the cold—the engine of his desire burned too hot. Their lovemaking had been far too brief. He needed more—but God knew when they would have the time.

He took handfuls of water and splashed them across his chest and under his arms. When he felt that he'd reached a reasonable level of cleanliness, he straightened and rubbed his hands over his face. Taking his hands from his face, he saw a familiar cream-and-copper figure standing nearby. He fumbled with his spectacles. The figure coalesced into Gemma, a few feet away and staring at him as if she planned on turning cannibal.

Being eaten never sounded so stimulating.

She held out a small cloth, but her eyes didn't leave his bare chest. "Mrs. Strathmore thought you could use this." This Gemma said in a voice both breathless and throaty.

Catullus took the cloth and used it to dry himself. He wasn't above a bit of preening, and took his time running the toweling over himself slowly, across the width of his chest and down the ridges of his abdomen. Everywhere the cloth went, her eyes followed avidly. He remembered now that he had unbuttoned but not removed his shirt when they'd made love. He had seen her bare chest, but she hadn't seen him fully.

He might have been forty-one years old, inventor and man of science, but he kept himself in prime condition. His

work as a Blade demanded it, and he firmly believed in the
Athenian balance between mind and body. At the moment,
given the way Gemma watched him, his body was most definitely firm. She stared at the thick ridge his cock made
along the front of his trousers.

Once dry, but not at all cooled down, Catullus dressed
himself. Gemma watched this, as well, blushing but not
turning away. Masculine pride energized him to see Gemma
so very admiring of his body, and he also exulted that she
wasn't ashamed to show her desire.

She'd put up her hair, and he saw damp tendrils clinging
to the smooth column of her neck. He wanted to run his
tongue there, bite her a little, and feel her pulse with his
mouth.

For a moment, after he'd dressed, they just stared at one
another. He knew with absolute clarity that if either of them
took a step toward the other, they'd wind up tangled together, rolling in the dust, tearing at clothing. A hard animal
coupling. And, sweet heaven, how he wanted that.

"You two heading off, then?" asked Mrs. Strathmore,
coming to the back door.

Both Catullus and Gemma blinked, and the tight spell of
need wasn't broken, but delayed. "Yes, we've an urgent
errand we have to undertake," he said, ripping his gaze from
Gemma.

"Mind you take care on the road," the farmwife cautioned. "There's danger afoot."

"We will," he promised, but when it came to his desire
for Gemma, he could not promise caution. In that, he gladly
consigned himself to reckless abandon.

As Gemma and Catullus headed away from the farmhouse, following a bridle path over rolling fields, she
sensed the waves of purpose and resolve emanating from
him like a kind of low, barely audible music, the sort one

felt rather than heard. Purpose about their mission, but also about her. For he still wanted her, and they both knew it, just as they both knew she still wanted him. Making love once most definitely had not been enough. And only time and circumstance stood in the way of them taking more of what they needed.

When that time might be, the saints only knew. She'd touched and felt his body in the darkness of a small bedroom. She had been gifted with the magnificent sight of Catullus Graves in the daylight—bare to the waist, broad shoulders, the expanse of his chest and smooth knots of muscle of his flat stomach, narrow waist, the shadowy lines of sinew disappearing under the waistband of his trousers—all of this delicious skin, beaded with water, and the thick outline of his cock demonstrating how very much he continued to desire her. He'd been diffident and shy before. Long before. That was gone now. He returned her stare and even deliberately teased her, running a cloth over his body with calculated, tempting slowness.

She wanted to take it further. But they didn't. Catullus dressed, and they now carried a basket packed with some sandwiches, walking on a little path, discussing the mysterious place known as Otherworld.

She just wanted to drag him off to a secret, mossy place and there ravish him until he forgot how to add two plus two, let alone perform the complex mathematical equations she knew he was capable of calculating. She also knew that her own body's demands had to wait when the fate of millions hung in the balance.

They needed to find Merlin in order to communicate with Arthur. Merlin was somewhere within the Otherworld. But how to *get* to the Otherworld . . . that was a conundrum neither Gemma nor Catullus had yet solved.

They walked now without specific direction, only knowing that they had to keep moving, for definitely this enigmatic place would not seek them out.

"Glastonbury Tor has been called the entrance to the realm of faerie," Catullus mused. He took the land in long strides, which, through force of will, she *just* managed to match.

"Can't go back there. It's too far for our purposes—and the place is probably still crawling with pixies." She hoped she would never have to encounter one of those little monsters again.

"There must be other ways of entering Otherworld. Hollow hills, or other portals."

"Maps don't exactly show such places."

"Not maps, but . . ." He glanced around, then, seeing something that she could not, strode off the bridle path. She jogged to follow.

Gemma trailed behind him until he reached a cluster of birch trees. Pushing back the undergrowth, he uncovered a tiny puddle of water, then crouched down beside it. She watched with open curiosity as he plucked from one of his pockets a single brown-and-cream bird feather and held it over the water.

"There has to be some explanation for what you're doing."

He shot her a grin so full of boyish exuberance, she thought a brass band would pop out of the bushes to play a rousing tune, celebratory fireworks would pinwheel with color, and any of a dozen foolish but wonderful things to happen. His happiness made *her* happy purely for its own sake.

After the disenchantment of Richard, Gemma had taken lovers, with varying degrees of duration. She expected nothing from them, only distraction and temporary assuaging of her body's needs. Not a one of them ever made her feel as she did now with Catullus, as though his sorrows cut her deeply, his joy feeding her own. She hadn't felt that, even with Richard. Now, with Catullus, she did. It was terrifying and wonderful.

"Birds are exceptionally sensitive to magic," he explained, bracing his forearms on his knees and twirling the feather between his fingertips. "Blades often use them to help identify Sources, since they react strongly to its presence. For years, now, I have been trying to create a device that utilizes this sensitivity in order to locate magic. So we can be more precise instead of, as we sometimes are wont to do, blundering around using a haphazard mixture of scholarship and conjecture."

He held up the feather. "I keep one of these handy, just waiting for the proper opportunity to use it. The device that I have in mind would work along similar lines as a compass." With surprising delicacy, given the size of his hands, Catullus set the feather onto the puddle. The feather immediately glided across the water's surface, coming to rest on the edge to Catullus and Gemma's left. He picked the feather up and repeated the experiment twice. Both times had the exact same results.

"That's where we'll find magic," said Gemma. She pointed in the direction which the feather moved.

Yet he shook his head. "It's a negative reaction. The closer a bird comes to magic, the more it becomes agitated."

"Which means that we go in the opposite direction from where the feather is aiming."

"You're a quick study, Miss Murphy."

"I've got a good teacher, Mr. Graves."

Their gazes held, a wordless communion. They drew closer. Their mouths met in an open, consuming kiss.

Heat washed over and through her, and she clung to him as if by instinct, her body knowing without her conscious understanding that she had to hold tight to him, drink in his kisses, because this, he, nourished her.

The kiss turned hungry as he met her with his own demands, and her breasts grew sensitive, heavy. A slick warmth gathered between her legs with each sweep of his tongue against her own. She would have pulled him down on top of her, but he broke away with a growl.

"Can't," he rasped. "I shouldn't have . . . not when we can't take this to where it needs to go."

"Insanity's starting to look mighty appealing." But she knew he was right. They had important business to undertake. Everything else was, unfortunately, a distraction.

So Catullus marked the opposite direction from which the feather pointed, put the feather back into his coat, and they both rose up on limbs grown clumsy with unfulfilled desire. Gemma wondered if she'd ever before lived in such a state of frustrated need. She thought she wanted him greatly before they'd made love. Now that she knew the pleasure of his body, that desire increased a hundredfold.

When they might have the time and security to give in to that desire . . . she did not know.

"I keep picturing it," Gemma said as they wended their way down into a tree-lined vale. "The entrance to the realm of magic."

"And what do you see in that fertile writer's imagination of yours?"

"A moss-covered stone arch, the surface of the stone covered in arcane carvings." She plucked a tall grass and began to chew on it thoughtfully.

"Reasonable assumption." Catullus wore his thoughtfulness with the comfort of a man who was happiest when thinking, a born scholar. "So, in this conceptualization, does one simply walk under the arch to be transported to Otherworld?"

"Seems too easy. All the fairy tales my granda told me made it seem a bit more complicated than that. It wouldn't be right to have humans just waltzing in and out of fairyland whenever they feel like it."

"Get a bit crowded."

"And drive up the prices of real estate."

"Or lower them—humans can be awfully annoying."

"*All* of them?" she asked.

"Others are quite . . . pleasant. And by 'pleasant,' I mean one human in particular drives me mad with desire."

His words heated her, but she felt compelled to note, "You were crazy *before* you met this certain human."

"She took me from the boundaries of merely being eccentric into being verifiably insane."

"Don't worry," she assured him. "We'll keep each other company in the sanitarium."

"Then I will be a happy man in my straitjacket."

They smiled, and she didn't realize until that moment that she had been just a little worried. She'd given him her body, and he had come to mean a great deal to her, but the truth was that she hadn't been quite sure whether or not she and Catullus actually . . . *liked* one another.

As she and Catullus smiled at one another, walking comfortably side by side, she saw that this most extraordinary man suited her, and she him. She was pretty damned content just to be in his company.

A friend, she realized. He was her friend. They were hard to come by, especially given the choices she'd made over the course of her life. Richard had not been her friend. Nor had the men who'd come after him. And she knew few women, still fewer who liked and respected Gemma and her line of work. Now that she had that which she'd lacked for so long, nothing would be taken for granted.

Chill insight pierced the warmth this understanding brought her. They had nearly been killed that very morning, and the risks that lay ahead were even more hazardous. Everything was tenuous. Everything could be lost. Not just her own life, but his. In the span of several days, he had come to mean so much to her. Losing him terrified her.

He saw her expression darken, and, with his usual quick comprehension, he grasped its cause.

Sobering, he returned to the topic they'd been discussing. Within the riddle of the Otherworld lay the slim possibility of victory over the Heirs. "So, it shan't be easy to cross into the realm of magic. Perhaps it will require some variety of incantation. Or an offering."

With her spirits lowered, Gemma shrugged. "We won't know until we get there. Right now, all of this is conjecture."

He wouldn't let her sink, so he said, almost cheerfully, "I happen to *enjoy* conjecture. Just as I like postulation, theory, and speculation. If life was reduced to simply dealing with what we conclusively know, it would be a dull business indeed."

She nodded her agreement, but felt herself torn between her enjoyment of his company and the real possibility that it wouldn't, couldn't, last.

They crested a small rise, and their steps slowed. All speculation on the portal to Otherworld soon ended abruptly and, actually, a bit disappointingly.

"This isn't what I was expecting," Gemma said. "Are we sure this is what we're looking for?"

"No ruins, no arches, nothing but this . . . this . . ."

"Old well."

For that's what it was. In the shelter of trees and bracken stood an old stone well, nothing more than a low circle of rough stones forming its walls. It had no roof, not even a cranked windlass for raising and lowering a bucket. A rusty metal eyebolt gouged into the top of the wall held the tattered remains of rope. No inscriptions. No fanciful carvings or altars. As far as Gemma could see, this was a perfectly ordinary, entirely uninteresting well that hadn't seen use in decades.

"There's an old, old book in the Blades' library," he said as they approached the well. "Must have read it a score of times. All about faerie lore. *Blaiklock's Faerie Miscellany.* In it, I saw that, over and over again, the entrances to the faerie realm often lie within the circle of toadstools, or within the stones surrounding a well."

It wasn't a small well—its diameter roughly five feet across—and the wall that encircled it came to her waist. Weeds poked up through the stones, nodding in the faint breeze.

They peered over the wall, looking down into the shaft of the well. It was very dark.

He picked up a pebble and dropped it down the well. After what felt like a long, long time, a faint splash echoed up the shaft. "It's not dry."

Not precisely a comfort. Someone might drown at the bottom of the well, instead of having their neck broken.

"This doesn't look much like the entryway to the realm of magic," she said doubtfully. "Maybe the feather misled us."

"Don't be too hasty." He braced his hands on the wall and continued to gaze down into the well, as if answers could be drawn up from its dark waters. "Bodies of water often served as boundaries between the mortal and enchanted worlds."

"And we just jump into this?" If she had to, she'd do it, but the prospect of leaping into an old well, with no real way to get *out* of the well, didn't strike her as very appealing.

"Not precisely." He snapped his fingers. "Remember how we were thinking one might have to make an incantation or something similar to open the portal?" When she nodded, he continued, his voice growing animated as he reasoned out the conundrum, "One thing that remains consistent in faerie legend is the love and importance of music. In the tales that mention toadstools and wells, to get to the land of faerie, you've got to sing and dance around the circle. That opens the door."

"Widdershins," Gemma said suddenly.

"Pardon?" He blinked at her.

"That's what my granda said. To get to the other realm,

you had to walk or dance widdershins. Backward, or counterclockwise," she explained, twirling her finger.

"Against the movement of the sun. Which makes sense, since many legends of faerie involve its existence as a complement or opposite to the mortal world."

"Contrary little buggers, those faerie folk."

He straightened, then held out his hands. "Shall we?"

It was her turn to blink. "Now?"

"Might as well get to it."

Gemma didn't believe herself to be a coward—she *had* leapt off a moving train, been in battle only that morning, and acquitted herself pretty well, if she did say so, herself. But she wasn't entirely eager to plunge down into some crumbling, dank well. A deep, dark well. With no way out.

Chapter 14

Crossing the Boundary

Catullus watched Gemma stare down into the well. Trepidation left its tight mark upon her face, yet, despite the fact that she was frightened, she would do what she must to complete the mission. Courage meant doing something in the midst of fear, and she had courage in abundance.

He wanted to crawl inside her mind. He wanted to learn every part of her, from her earliest memories to the secret joys of her heart and even the most mundane thoughts she might have. Charles Dickens or Jane Austen? Or perhaps she favored some American authors—though he couldn't think of a single one. Did she prefer raspberry jam or orange marmalade? Everything of hers was wonderful to him, all of her precious.

He couldn't believe he was waxing rhapsodic over what type of jam a woman preferred, but that's what he'd come to. Making love with Gemma had been one of the most magnificent experiences of his life, if not *the* most magnificent. She was giving and responsive and passionate and aggressive, and all of this, all of her, enabled him to become more fully himself. He'd never let go with any other lover the way he'd been able to with her.

Touch yourself, he had said. *Ride me*. And she had. The sight of her on him, finding and giving pleasure, filled him to repletion. Not once had he ever spoken thusly to a woman. He had not trusted any of them enough to allow this kind of exposure.

But he didn't want to think of anyone else. He allowed the slate of his sexual history to be wiped clean. Everything before had been mere biology, two components fitting into one another until a desired result was achieved. With Gemma, it was not simply carnal, corporeal—although, God knew, that aspect had been wonderful—but something much more profound. This woman knew him, intimately, deeply, as he knew her. She alone allowed him to venture into the unknown, without fear, giving him room to learn not only her, but himself. She was the only woman to see him as more than an intellect, more than a maker of machines. A man of flesh and life.

They had found one another, but perhaps too late. Danger, the prospect of disaster surrounded them. He had so much more to lose, now.

They had to reach Merlin, stop Arthur. And the only way to get to the sorcerer was through a gate to the Otherworld. Down the well.

They stared down into the well's depths. Somehow, at the bottom, they might find an entrance to Otherworld.

"You'll need to open the portal," Catullus said.

"Maybe I can open it from here," Gemma mused. She closed her eyes, deep concentration knitting her brow together. After some time, she opened her eyes. "I can't feel anything."

"Perhaps because nothing yet *exists* down there."

"Can't open something that isn't there."

"So we make a door." Catullus sounded a good deal more confident than he felt. "Call it into being."

"And we do that, how?"

"Dance counterclockwise around the well, singing."

He held out his hand, as if asking her to waltz. The irony of the gesture was not lost on him. They would have never met in a ballroom. "Shall we?"

She did not want to jump into the well, yet she put her hand in his easily, comfortably, as if that's exactly where it belonged. It surely felt that way.

"What should we sing?" she asked.

"How about 'Au fond du temple saint'?" he suggested.

She stared at him blankly.

"From Bizet's *Les pêcheurs de perles*," he explained. "Granted, it's for a tenor and baritone, but I think your contralto should work."

Gemma continued to look at him.

"All right. Let's try 'Bei Männern, welche Liebe fühlen,' from *Die Zauberflöte*."

"I had to review operas," she said dryly, "not memorize the librettos. Do you know 'My Grandfather's Clock'?"

"Not familiar with it."

"It's popular in all the music halls."

"Of which I am not a habitué."

"How about 'The Little Brown Jug'? *Everyone* knows that."

"Except me."

"Damn it." She frowned, frustrated by the impediment. "We're from such different worlds."

Now that he had found her, Catullus refused to surrender. "Not so different that we cannot learn from one another. Teach me the words to one of your songs."

Her brows raised. "Really?"

"Yes, really."

A smile slowly blossomed. "All right." And then she began to sing. Her voice was, as he'd suspected, a lovely contralto, warm and low, untrained, but clear. So pleased was he by the sound of her singing, he did not pay full attention to the lyrics, until . . .

Wait, she couldn't *actually* be singing about a—

"'That's why we call her Susie, the Seventh Street whore,'" Gemma warbled as the song drew to a close.

"Gemma!" Even to his own ears, he sounded like an outraged vicar.

She blinked at him, a look of pure innocence. "Yes?"

For a moment, he simply looked at her. Such a lovely face, those crystalline blue eyes, the sweet, soft mouth, and, of course, the dainty freckles stippling her nose and across her high cheekbones. No one would ever suspect that such beauty hid a wicked soul.

Surprises could be quite wonderful.

He asked, "Was the second line, 'She threw her skirts in the air,' or 'She threw her drawers in the air'?"

Her mouth quirked. "Skirts."

"Ah. Very good." He sang the song back to her, putting extra emphasis on the words *thrust* and *bang*. "Think I've got it."

She tugged on his hand, and he allowed her to pull him close, wherein she promptly, thoroughly kissed him within an inch of his sanity using her delightfully vulgar mouth. "Hearing you say things like *pump* with your gorgeous accent," she breathed, "makes me want to throw you to the ground and bite your clothes off."

He couldn't stifle a groan. She may very well destroy him. And he would be happy in his destruction.

"You've only yourself to blame," he rasped. "Where on earth did you learn such a crude song?"

"Chicago slaughterhouses aren't hotbeds of propriety."

He shook his head. "The company you keep."

"My taste is improving."

Drawing a deep breath to steady himself, he yet again cursed time and circumstance, because everything within him wanted her again, and again, however he could have her, and everything outside of him—with the notable exception of Gemma, herself—demanded otherwise.

She understood this. They both drew apart, reluctantly. Then, at his nod, they began to dance counterclockwise around the well, holding hands and singing Gemma's extraordinarily obscene song. Hopefully, the magical realm enjoyed lewd tunes just as much as the mortal one. He felt mildly ridiculous, capering around a crumbling old well like some confused, depraved Morris dancer, but there was also something rather freeing about singing a dirty song whilst skipping about. Having a beautiful woman holding his hand and doing exactly the same thing made it even more enjoyable.

What would the sober, reserved members of the Graves family think of him, the current Graves scion working with the Blades of the Rose, acting like a complete and absolute madman? He honestly didn't care.

When the song concluded, they stopped and looked down into the well. It looked just as dark and clammy as before.

"Has anything happened?" Gemma asked. "I don't know if I can sense a door."

"Difficult to tell. Let's give it another go."

They had just begun the second verse when a gunshot split the air. An overhead branch cracked and tumbled to earth.

Catullus pulled Gemma down to the ground behind the well, shielding her. He had no awareness of even drawing his shotgun, but it was in his hands and ready. Gemma drew her pistol. They both peered over the stone wall encircling the well, and they both swore when they caught sight of four armed men heading toward them, running through the woods. Catullus recognized two of them as Heirs. The others had to be newer recruits. But even in the dusk, there was no mistaking their posture, their appearance and attitude of privilege. The excellent quality of their firearms purchased from the finest St. James' gunsmiths. Guns aimed at Catullus and Gemma.

Catullus returned fire, as did Gemma, but the Heirs didn't stop their advance. Within a minute, or less, the Heirs would be on top of them.

"Two choices," he gritted over the gunfire. "Stay and fight the Heirs."

"Who outnumber us," she said as she reloaded.

He took aim and shot, but the Heirs dodged for cover. "Or hazard leaping into the well."

"Hoping a door to the Otherworld waits at the bottom."

He and Gemma shared a glance. And then a nod, followed by a brief, but significant, kiss.

They took hold of each other's hands. Drew a breath. Then rose up, perched on the edge of the well, and jumped.

Cold, moist air swallowed Gemma. One moment, she crouched on a narrow stone wall, bullets flying around her, Heirs' shouts cracking like whips, and the next, she and Catullus plunged down into absolute darkness. Her stomach flew up to lodge somewhere in her throat. She held tight to Catullus's hands, the only sure and solid thing in this pitch-black drop.

She expected them to splash into the water at the bottom. Waited for it. Perhaps the water wouldn't be very deep, and they'd smash into a pile of broken bones while the Heirs above watched and laughed.

Yet she and Catullus fell. And fell. An endless descent. She glanced up to see the heads of the Heirs peering down into the well, growing smaller, farther away. She barely heard their angry yells.

"How deep *is* this thing?" she cried to Catullus.

He sounded much calmer than she felt. "As long as it needs to be."

She did not appreciate his cryptic response. Not when

they were falling down and down a bottomless well shaft. If they had created a portal to Otherworld, it kept itself damned scarce.

Then— "I feel it! The door!" A presence below. Not physical. A nexus of energy, quick and bright. Beyond the door, she sensed limitless space, unbound by wall or constraint, free from the confining hold of mortality.

"Perhaps now would be a good time to open it," Catullus murmured, wind whistling around them.

But it wasn't like an ordinary door that could simply swing open at a touch. Without a physical object, she did not know exactly *how* to open it. It didn't help that she was falling, her skirts billowing up around her. Focusing on the opening of an intangible door wasn't the easiest task on which to concentrate.

If she *didn't* focus, then either she and Catullus would be falling down this well forever, or they'd hit bottom— eventually—and either be killed or have to find a way to scale a well shaft hundreds of feet deep while being shot at from above.

The door to Otherworld is a mind, she thought. It works just as someone's mind worked, not as a material object but as a state of consciousness, of being. She had to access it as she did the thoughts of people. Tap into its essence, and allow herself to unlock its core.

She pictured it, no easy task in the middle of a free fall. Gave it shape and definition, coalescing energy into the shape of an actual door, with wood and hinges and a handle. Upon its handle, she placed her hand. Then, with an indrawn breath, she pushed against the door—not with force, but gently, because Otherworld was not her realm, and one must use caution and respect when venturing into someone else's home.

Nothing.

Her heart fell with her.

No—she couldn't fail. Not for herself, and not for Catullus. The door *must* open.

She tried again, with greater command. Waited. And then . . .

It swung open.

She and Catullus crossed the boundary. It sizzled across her skin, a fiery membrane, and from the darkness of the well, light engulfed her. Dazzling light so brilliant she saw nothing, knew only heat and brightness, both outside her and within, as if she had been flung into a star.

Catullus's hands were tugged from hers. She reached out for him, scrabbling to keep hold. He disappeared. She tried to call out to him. Her voice dissolved.

All around her was light, and in her ears rang a kind of music she'd never heard before, notes from an instrument unknown to mortals, sung with inhuman voices. This, too, enveloped her. She lost herself in the light and sound, and, without Catullus to anchor her, she spun off into measure-less time and place. She fought for consciousness. The brightness became too much, and she surrendered to oblivion.

Voices. A host of voices, hovering around her like a cloud of gnats. Gemma couldn't tell what language they spoke—nothing she'd ever heard before, though it sounded similar to the Gaelic old Granda sometimes spoke when he grew wistful for the old country. But these voices didn't have Granda's rusty pipe sound. No, if anything, they sounded small, silvery, halfway between a child and a flute.

What were they *saying*?

She couldn't understand the words, but she might be able to figure out the intent. She let herself into their minds, an easier task now, and a throng of images assailed her, impossible images of spun-glass castles, beasts of all shapes and sizes, vast revels lit by starlight. Wading

through these visions, she found the gleaming thread of
thought, and, the moment she touched it with her own
mind, the voices suddenly cleared, becoming comprehen-
sible, even if the words themselves were not.

Where did they come from? one asked.

Brightworld, another answered. *Knocked the door down
and tumbled in.*

They didn't!

Saw it, myself. Through a waterdoor. Down down.

I like the color of that one's skin, like darkest walnut.

This one is cream and fire. Bright hair, Brightworld.

*I should like a nibble. Bet they taste good. Good and
mortal. Fleeting flesh. Tasty tasty.*

Gemma's eyes flew open.

She found herself looking up at a dozen tiny faces, faces
that were both childlike and wizened. Large black eyes,
canted, black from corner to corner. Wide mouths full of
sharp teeth, upturned noses, pointed ears. Skin the hue of
river stones.

She's awake!

"Anyone who tries to eat me or my friend will get a
punch in the face," Gemma warned.

Shrieking, the creatures disappeared.

Forcing herself to sit upright, Gemma's head spun for a
moment. The world wobbled, then settled into . . . nothing
normal.

She sat upon the ground, on a bed of moss, which
seemed ordinary enough, if one imagined moss to be made
of crushed sapphire velvet, adorned with jeweled mush-
rooms. The moss covered a hollow in the roots of a massive, twisting tree. Its branches shifted and sighed, yet
there was no breeze. The tree was *moving*, of its own volition. And in its branches glittered miniature human-shaped
creatures of every color, gold and blue and violet, their
wings droning.

For a moment, Gemma could only marvel at the tree, at

the beings within it. What would Catullus think of such wonders?

Oh, God. Catullus.

Gemma shot to her feet, ignoring her dizziness, and looked around frantically. She was in some kind of forest, whose boundaries seemed to stretch on, infinite. Dark green shadows unfolded everywhere. The forest pulsed with life. But, to the massive flowers and silver streams tumbling down gemstones, she paid no attention. She needed to find Catullus. Now.

He had to be nearby. But where?

She clambered out of the hollow at the base of the tree, and stood upon one of its giant roots. She saw nothing, only more and more forest expanding out on every side.

Fear gripped her. Not for herself, but for him. What if those awful little cannibals took him? He could be injured, could be lost. Of course, she had no idea where *she* was, but maybe he'd hit his head when they crossed the boundary, and wandered around, dazed and hurt. If anyone, if any *thing*, so much as harmed a single whisker of his beard, she'd tear them into mattress stuffing.

She cupped her hands around her mouth. "Catullus!" Her voice echoed through the woods, sending a flock of . . . something . . . bursting from the trees and into the golden air. "Catullus!"

A very human-sounding groan came from someplace to her right. Heart knocking, she jumped down from the roots and scrambled over grassy hillocks and through a rivulet, toward the source of the groan.

There. In a small clearing. Catullus lay sprawled on his back, his arms flung out. Close by lay his shotgun. His eyes were closed. She ran toward him.

Gemma fell to her knees beside him, and exhaled only when she saw his own chest rising and falling. Gently, so gently, she plucked off his spectacles, set them aside, then touched her shaking fingers to his face.

"Catullus?"

His eyes blinked open. They seemed clear, but this did not quite ease her fear. Carefully, she ran her fingers along his head, searching for any cuts. He winced slightly when she touched a growing bump on the back of his head.

"I'm sorry," she said quickly. "So sorry." But no blood dampened her fingers, so she was grateful for that. "Are you . . . all right? Can you move your fingers and toes?"

Gingerly, he did both. That, at least, was a relief.

"Can you speak?"

He rasped, "We're forever making leaps, you and I."

A laugh, slightly frayed, burst from her. "As long as you're beside me, I don't mind the jump."

He smiled at that.

"Jumping later," she said. "Let's try sitting up now."

At his nod, she slipped her hands beneath him and helped him to sitting. He was bigger, and heavier, than her, and she served mostly as guidance rather than actually lifting him up. All she truly wanted to do was touch him, assure herself that he wasn't badly hurt. Lightly, he touched the bruise on the back of his head, grimacing, then glanced over at her, concern in his eyes.

"And you? Are you hurt?"

She shook her head. "Chased off some kind of pixies or elves or something that wanted to have us for supper, but fine."

His eyebrows raised. "Carnivorous fey. That's new."

"All of this"—she waved to the forest around them—"is new."

He squinted, then muttered, "Damn, I lost my spectacles. My spare pair, too."

"Here they are." She handed the spectacles to him.

Catullus rose to his feet, nimble and swift, and helped her to stand. Their hands clasped and held as they looked around, taking in the spectacle of the magical forest.

"We did it," he said, low and amazed. "We traversed the boundary between the mortal and magical worlds." He turned to her, admiration in his gaze. "Because of you. You opened the door."

"But we both called it into being." Still, she savored his praise, the genuine respect when he looked at her. "And now, here we are."

The forest stretched on around them, trees of massive size forming overhead canopies of glittering leaves, their trunks netted with twisting vines older than memory. Light from an unseen sun pierced the canopy—yet the light was not merely gold, but shifted into dozens of colors, green and blue and rose. Flowers, wide across as Gemma's outstretched arms, chimed. Some yards distant—a dozen or a hundred, she could not tell—a waterfall cascaded into an emerald pond, and there drank animals that resembled small gray cats. When the sound of a branch snapping startled the cats, they all dissolved into a vaporous mist and wafted away.

"We've fallen right into a fairy tale," murmured Gemma.

"What I wouldn't give for a microscope," Catullus breathed.

"Can't quantify or analyze everything." She stared up as a slim creature of indeterminate gender and lavender skin sailed by on a dandelion the size of a parasol. "Including this whole place." She smiled. "Wouldn't my granda love to see this? All his old stories come true."

Catullus bent to study flowers that looked like oversized cowslips. He started when an entirely naked, golden-fleshed girl popped out suddenly from one of the yellow blossoms. She angrily jabbered at Catullus before disappearing in a puff of floral-scented dust.

"Cannibal elves, rude cowslip fairies." He shook his head. "An appalling lack of manners in Otherworld."

"That'll be our contribution to this place. Etiquette lessons." She hardly believed that what she saw—this immense forest and all the beings that dwelled within it—could be real, and yet she knew it was. As much as Catullus longed for a microscope, she wanted to sit with her notebook and write down everything she observed, every texture she felt and sound she heard. Yet that, too, felt wrong, as though attempting to capture something that would wither and die once confined in immobile words.

At the least, she was here now, experiencing it with Catullus. She loved to see the wonderment on his face as he beheld Otherworld as much, if not more than, seeing the place itself.

"I could spend years exploring here," she said.

"An eternity," he agreed; then a shadow fell over him. "Yet we haven't that kind of time. Arthur's on his way to London as we speak. We need to find Merlin, and quickly."

Staring at the seemingly limitless forest, Gemma said, "Find him? We can't even find ourselves."

He drew his Compass from one of his pockets and looked down at its face, frowning. The needle spun, first in one direction, then another, never still. "One thing we did *not* take into account was navigating Otherworld. This will do us no good here." He shut the lid with a decisive snap and slipped it back into a pocket.

"Maybe we can ask directions," Gemma said, only partly joking. She figured that the native populace would either try and devour her and Catullus, or else lead them into some perilous swamp full of man-eating boggarts.

But, ridiculous as she thought her suggestion, Catullus actually looked as though he was considering it.

"Only teasing," she said quickly. "I don't want us to wind up trapped in some faerie equivalent of the zoo. These creatures here don't seem particularly welcoming or friendly."

"Not to strangers, no. Yet there may be one who might be willing to help."

"But we'd have to find them first, which, in this place, could take decades."

"There possibly could be another way to reach him." He patted down his pockets, searching for something.

"Him? Who?"

"Ah, this will do." In his broad hand he gripped a flask.

"After everything we've been through today, a drink sounds damned good." She reached for the flask, but he held it away from her.

"Not for us," he said with a wry smile. Unscrewing the cap, he added, "A little inducement for our friend."

The aroma of fine Scotch whiskey made Gemma's mouth water. "Couldn't we have a sip, ourselves?"

"Don't think Bryn would appreciate getting someone's leftovers." He poured some whiskey into the cap and held it out. "Bryn! Bryn Enfys!" Two more times, Catullus called the name into the woods.

"Faerie must have good hearing," Gemma mused.

"Names are powerful things. Especially when summoning."

"And especially when twenty-year whiskey is being offered," added a small voice behind Gemma.

She spun around to face a man, no bigger than her hand, hovering in midair. He wore a miniature frock coat and knee breeches, the kind worn by country folk in the last century. A pair of dragonfly wings sprouted from his back, keeping him aloft. In lieu of a shirt, a bib of leaves covered his chest, and a wee tall hat perched atop his head. His oak-brown eyes glinted at her with a mixture of amusement and curiosity.

"Have you brought me a lass, too, Catullus?" the little man asked. "It can get powerful lonely in Otherworld, and I've gone too many centuries without a wife."

Gemma opened her mouth to protest, but Catullus spoke before she did. "The whiskey's yours, Bryn." He held out the flask's cap, but wrapped one protective arm around Gemma's shoulders. "The woman is mine."

She bristled to be spoken of like a disputed hound bitch ready for breeding. "The woman belongs to herself," she said.

The little man chuckled, the sound like water lapping at

the sides of a boat. "Fire and cream, just like the goblins said." He reached for the cap of whiskey, which Catullus handed to him. In one gulp, Bryn downed the cap's contents, and wordlessly held it out for a refill. Catullus topped off the cap three more times before the pixie spoke again.

"In all my years knowing the Blades," he piped, "not a one has ever come across." Bryn fixed them with a pointed look. "'Tis a dangerous and bold undertaking, Catullus. Few mortals who make the journey ever come back. Why, in the Grey People's court, there are dozens and dozens of mortals held in thrall, serving their Faerie Queen. Some have been there since the reign of your King James."

Gemma fought down the swell of fear that she and Catullus might get trapped in this other world. Beautiful and fascinating it might be, but her home was not here.

"Only the most dire of circumstances has brought us to Otherworld," Catullus said.

Bryn nodded as he held out the cap for another drink. "It's the talk of Otherworld. The summoning of Arthur. Fey beings crossing back and forth as bold as you please." He bolted down his drink, then looked skyward with a frown. "All the courts are worried. Seelie. Tylwyth Teg. Tuatha Dé Danann. We are to be enslaved, should the Risen King touch the Primal Source. Our magic would belong to the hard, cold men of Brightworld."

"That's why we've come," Gemma said. "To stop that from happening."

"Two mortals holding back all the magic of Otherworld?" Bryn's frown deepened. "Can't be done."

"There's one here who can help," said Catullus. "One who can reach Arthur and keep the worlds apart."

"Not a creature I do not know in this forest," Bryn answered. "From the tiniest sprite to the biggest Fomorian."

"Then you can help us find who it is we're looking for," said Gemma.

Bryn doffed his miniature hat and scratched his head. "Mayhap."

"His name is Merlin," said Catullus.

The pixie only shrugged. "Names are not often given. Or, if they are, they're false names."

"Why?" asked Gemma.

"To know someone's true name gives you power over them." Bryn smiled, but it was a feral little grin, and not particularly friendly. "And now I know the name of who you seek, whoever this Merlin may be."

"He is a sorcerer of great power," said Catullus. "Or he once had power and hasn't it any longer."

"You just described near half of the sorcerers wandering around here."

Catullus strongly hoped they didn't meet one of these roving enchanters. Doubtless they were mercurial creatures, and Catullus had no desire to be turned into a bespectacled toadstool should he inadvertently cross one of these sorcerers. "This one is special."

"They all say that." Bryn snickered.

"This sorcerer truly is," Gemma insisted.

"And he wouldn't be doing any wandering," Catullus added. "Given that he's trapped within an oak tree."

The pixie grew alarmed. "You mean the Man in the Oak!"

Catullus and Gemma shared another glance, the thrill of discovery.

"That's the one," said Gemma. "Can you take us to him?"

"Oh, no." Bryn's wings fluttered in agitation, and his tiny face paled. "No, no, no. I'll not go near him."

"Why ever not?" Catullus demanded.

Bryn looked appalled at the idea of seeking out Merlin. "Because I want to keep my wings, that's why!" He lowered his voice to a piping whisper. "The Man in the Oak is mad. He was mad when he came to Otherworld, and he's grown even more mad since he's been trapped in the tree. He plucks the wings from pixies for sport. He turns fey into slugs and takes their tongues."

The more he spoke, the more distressed Bryn became, until he quivered in fear.

"We'll protect you." Catullus tried to soothe the pixie. This only made Bryn more upset.

"You can't! You're only two mortals with just a scrap of magic between you! I'll lose my wings, and you two will be turned into beetles. No. No, no, no!"

Sending them one final glare, Bryn flew away as fast as his wings could carry him.

Gemma and Catullus stood by themselves in the middle of the huge forest. They turned in slow circles, gazing at the seemingly endless woods.

The enormity of their situation hit them at the same time. Otherworld stretched all around them, an infinite place neither of them knew. The task of locating one sorcerer within this vast world felt almost impossible.

"I don't know how we're supposed to find Merlin," Gemma said. She struggled to keep herself from acknowledging hopelessness. "Or if we should. He sounds dangerous."

Catullus gazed around, determined. "Dangerous or not, he's the lynchpin in our strategy. We have to locate him."

A boom of thunder nearly smothered Catullus's words. Moments after the thunderclap, the skies opened up. Torrential rain soaked both Gemma and Catullus in seconds.

"This day isn't going very well," she said above the noise of the downpour.

He peered through the rain, searching for what, Gemma did not know. Seeing something, his face suddenly brightened. "It already has gotten better." Taking her hand in his, he led her, sprinting, through the now-marshy forest. They found themselves laughing, laughing like lunatics, as they ran.

It was strange to laugh, considering the circumstances: lost, wet, a quest of infinite scope looming before them. The task daunted. But she and Catullus would explore this world. Face its dangers and strive toward their goal. Together.

Chapter 15

Shelter

A cottage nestled at the base of a tree. Either the house was exceptionally small, or the tree was huge, or perhaps a mix of both.

"It doesn't look like much," Catullus called above the rain. "But its roof appears intact, and that's all we need." He felt oddly giddy. Getting caught in torrential rain happened more often than he cared for, yet there was something thrilling and stimulating about sprinting through the rain with a laughing Gemma. Regardless of the situation.

"As long as it isn't an outhouse, I'm happy." She squeezed his hand as they ran.

They neared the cottage. Closer, Catullus saw that it was, indeed, tiny, resembling a child's playhouse more than somewhere an adult might actually live, its steep shingled roof like a book lying open upon a set of walls. No smoke came from the chimney. He cupped his hands around his eyes and peered in the dark, plate-sized window.

"Anyone home?" Gemma asked.

"I cannot see much in there, but it seems unoccupied. I'll go in first and make sure it's safe."

He tried the door. Unlocked. In order to get himself

through the minuscule doorway, he bent almost double. When he crossed the threshold, he slowly uncurled, fully expecting to slam his head against the low ceiling. Yet he straightened, and straightened, until he stood at his full height.

"Blimey." He couldn't understand it. From the outside, the cottage appeared diminutive. Inside told another story.

The cottage was a single room, but substantial in its size. It contained a hearth, a table and chairs, several cupboards, a bookshelf, and, incredibly, a large four-poster bed that looked as though it was fashioned of living trees, one for each post. A wooden bathing tub sat in front of the hearth. Everything was full-sized, proportioned for adult mortals.

"Is everything all right?" Gemma asked from outside. "Is it too small for us both?"

He poked his head through the doorway, holding out a hand. "I think we should find this more than comfortable."

She looked puzzled but took his hand. He led her inside, both ducking to keep from knocking their heads against the lintel. Once she'd crossed the threshold, she, too, rose up slowly to stare at the interior of the cottage.

"How . . . ?"

He spread his hands. "Otherworld has its own logic, I am discovering. Physics do not seem to apply."

A small smile curved her mouth as she walked through the cottage, running her fingers over objects scattered throughout. She held up a fingertip. "Everything's clean. Someone must live here." She strode toward the cupboards and pulled them open. "Damn. There's plenty of dishes and cups, but nothing to eat. Maybe no one *has* been here for a while."

Catullus pulled off his sodden coat and draped it over the back of a chair. Several logs nestled in a basket next to the hearth, so he piled them high and set them ablaze with a spark from his flint. "Whomever they are, I fully intend to take advantage of their hospitality. At least until the rain stops. Sit here and dry off." He pulled out another chair, setting it near the hearth, and waved her toward it.

With a grateful sigh, Gemma sank down into the chair. She stretched her legs in front of her and pulled her skirts up to her knees, warming herself. Beneath lowered lashes, her eyes were fire-kissed sapphires. "I like the way you're staring at my legs."

"Am I staring?" He was transfixed by the sight. Yes, he'd touched her legs, and been between them, but never fully saw them, not until now. Long and slim, but, beneath the dark knit of her stockings, the curves of muscles formed elegant shapes. A small hole in her stocking revealed a cameo of pale flesh. He wanted to run his hands up her legs, looking at them in the firelight as he did so. He wanted to touch his tongue to that oval of exposed skin.

"Come here." Her voice stroked him like velvet. "You can do more than stare." To demonstrate, she ran a caressing hand from the top of her ankle-high boot up to her knee.

It took supreme effort to resist this siren call. "Best not. Once I get started, I won't be able to stop." God, his voice sounded deeper than a canyon.

"And time is of the essence."

"Once the rain stops, we have to find Merlin."

Dropping her hand, she sighed again, this time with disappointment. "Damned timing. The Blades better be grateful. We're making a hell of a sacrifice."

He pulled another chair toward the fire, yet kept a safe distance between himself and Gemma. Lowering himself down to sit, he told himself to focus on the cheerful fire and not on the large, soft bed beckoning in the corner. *Don't think about scooping her up in your arms and tossing her onto the bed. Don't think about peeling off her stockings and her wet clothing. Don't think about her nude body beneath the covers, and laying your own naked body atop hers, and kissing her until her legs opened, and pinning her wrists down onto the mattress, and . . .*

"You haven't heard anything I just said."

His attention snapped back. "What's that?"

She smiled, wry and knowing. "I can't stop thinking about it either." Her eyes, full of meaning, strayed toward the bed.

He pulled off his spectacles and scrubbed at his face. "You aren't helping," he gritted. He fought the need to adjust his painfully aching cock straining within his trousers.

"Fine. What should we talk about while we wait? Something dull and chaste. What's that boring English game called? Cricket? You can explain the rules of cricket to me."

"Some people happen to find cricket very exciting."

"Are you one of them?"

He replaced his spectacles. "More of a rugby man, myself. Though I make a point to learn about and play different sports—helps keep the mind sharp as well as the body."

"If you don't want me dragging you to that bed, then don't talk about bodies, especially your own."

Her words and heated gaze did not help tame his rampant erection. He shifted uncomfortably in his chair.

"I'll . . . avoid that topic."

She cleared her throat. "So, in cricket, a man swings at a ball with a paddle in order to do . . . something."

"It's called a bat. And the striker is attempting to score a run by hitting the ball with the bat and running between the popping creases."

"I am definitely not aroused by that," she said. "Tell me more."

The next twenty minutes were spent in as dry a discussion of cricket as Catullus could make it. Which, he discovered, wasn't much of a challenge. Assuming his most professorial air, he talked at length about the history, rules, and strategies of the game. So successful was he in eviscerating any excitement from the sport, Gemma almost nodded off. Twice.

Midway in his analysis of pace bowlers and swing bowlers, he glanced up at the roof.

"Rain's stopped," he noted.

Yawning, Gemma stood and stretched. He pointedly focused on dousing the fire rather than watching her. Once the fire had been fully extinguished, he also rose and donned his coat. The garment was marginally drier than before, but decidedly worse for all the rigors it had endured.

"I doubt anyone in Otherworld will be willing to lead us to Merlin," he said, checking to ensure his shotgun was in working order, "if he's as volatile as Bryn claims."

Gemma shook out her skirts, the hems of which now boasted a goodly bit of mud. Adventuring was not for the overly fastidious. "Merlin's very powerful. There should be some strong energy around him," she mused. "A kind of imprint."

"All we need to do is keep ourselves as receptive as possible to change in the atmosphere. Then follow it."

"Guide or no guide, we'll find Merlin."

"Of that, I have no doubt." He buoyed himself up on their shared optimism. Bryn's abandonment was merely a temporary setback. Blades faced far steeper odds. Catullus, himself, had thought himself utterly lost more times than he cared to recall, yet he'd persevered and prevailed. As he and Gemma would now. He strode toward the door and opened it. "Madam," he said with a sweep of his arm, "shall we?"

"Indeed, let's," Gemma said in a rather ridiculous English accent that made him smile.

With a regal tip of her head, she ducked to go through the door. Then stopped midway through and clutched either side of the doorframe. "Uh, Catullus? We might want to consider an alternate plan." She backed up until she was fully back inside the house. "Take a look."

Puzzled, Catullus bent over so he could look through the doorway. "Bloody hell," he breathed.

The cottage no longer sat at the base of a tree. It was now up *in* a tree. Somehow, the little house found its way off the ground and into the branches of an extremely tall tree. They must be at least a hundred feet up.

Had this been their only impediment, Catullus would have devised some means for him and Gemma to climb down the tree and continue on their search for Merlin. Yet their sudden height was only a fragment of a much bigger problem.

The tree in which they now found themselves wasn't in the Otherworld forest. It was, in fact, the only tree for miles. The tree stood alone. In the middle of water. Not a puddle, or even a lake. But a sea. As far as Catullus could see stretched an infinite ocean, sunlight glinting off its endless waves until he was dazzled.

Even if Catullus and Gemma could find a way down, there was no place to go. He might attempt to fashion a boat, but, if he did, he had no idea in which direction to sail or what they might find, if anything. This sea could truly be endless. Otherworld defied all reason, all geography.

"I think we're trapped," Gemma said.

Catullus crouched inside the doorway, staring at the limitless sea. His mind turned and worked, seeking a solution, for surely there had to be one. They couldn't be trapped. Not truly. They had journeyed so far, and so much hung in the balance, that he refused to believe there was no way out. Failure was impossible. The Blades needed him and Gemma. Countless lives relied on them.

With his forearms braced across his knees, he dropped his head into his hands. He simply did not know what to do, and this shook and angered him.

The Graves family always knew what to do. They always found an answer.

"Catullus." Gemma's hand lay softly against the back of his neck, her slim fingers gently stroking him. "We'll figure something out. A way out."

He rasped a mirthless laugh. "There is no way out. Or, if there is, my goddamn brilliant brain cannot think of a single solution." He backed away from the door to stand inside the room. "My foolish choice led us to this cottage, and now everything's going to hell."

"No—"

But the anger had him now, a lifetime of expectations dashed. "I prided myself on the fact that if I had anything, it was a sterling history of service to the Blades. And a momentary decision threw it all away."

Her own anger blazed, indignant. "We *both* made the choice to come in here. This isn't your yoke to bear."

"I—"

She marched up to him and placed her clenched fist in the center of his chest. "No. Enough. If we *are* trapped here, it's because of a decision we made together. You and I. There's no blame. No fault. A place like Otherworld takes away cause and effect. And," she continued, her voice gentling, "if it means being here with you forever, then I can't regret our choice." Her fist uncurled so that her palm spread over his heart.

Anger dissolved as he stared down at her.

What made her so beautiful to him? More than the loveliness of her face, with her soft, clever mouth and gemstone eyes and scores of freckles. She had been pretty when he first saw her in that rough Canadian trading post. Now her beauty surpassed everything. Not simply for the attractiveness of her exterior, but who she was within. Her spirit. Her courage. Her audacity.

"Gemma." He cupped the back of her head with his

hands, weaving his fingers into her damp hair. "I wanted more than this for you."

"And I don't want more," she answered immediately. Her expression changed, becoming heavy-lidded, alluring. "We're trapped in a cottage with a very large bed. There are better things we can do besides assign blame and argue."

There was logic, and then there were truths too significant and substantial to ignore. And the truth was that he wanted her. More than the pleasure of her body. All of her. Within and without. Everything else burned away—or, more accurately, was washed away in the waters of an endless sea. Leaving him with a need so great, it became its own force.

He pulled her closer. Whipped off his spectacles, stowing them God knew where. Then kissed her. A fever overtook them as they consumed each other, the slick and hot contours of their mouths, the slide and stroke of tongues. And with each taste and touch, desire ripened further, until they panted into one another, hands roaming over backs, shoulders, bodies pressed tightly.

His coat slid to the ground. They worked at their clothing—frenzied, clumsy movements that frustrated as much as aroused. An energy pulsed between them, rising up from the movement of muscles and limbs and hunger.

She broke the kiss with a gasp. "Catullus, look." She directed his gaze toward the hearth, where the banked fire blazed again. "We did that."

"And that." He nodded at the bathing tub, filled now with steaming water.

"Seems we have our own magic."

Catullus stepped back. Before she could protest, he began carefully, methodically undressing her. Each garment, piece by piece. Revealing silky flesh. Her bare arms. Lush, gorgeous breasts tipped in coral. The soft curvature of her belly. Red-gold at the juncture of her slender legs. Down to her bare feet, which were not a lady's dainty, pampered feet, but revealed that she carried herself and moved and had her own momentum propelling her forward.

By the time Gemma was fully nude, Catullus could not control his shaking.

"Frightened?" she asked him.

He shook his head, but he felt awkward and tight in his movements. "I want you so damned much."

"Have me." When he stepped forward to touch her, she held him back with an outstretched hand. "First, there's something I need."

"Anything," he rumbled.

She smiled, wicked. Walked her fingers up the buttons of his waistcoat and then began with agonizing slowness, to undo them. "I get the same privilege."

He submitted himself to the torture, willingly. In a distant corner of his mind, growing more distant by the second, he wondered if all women had an instinct for sensual torment, because Gemma seemed to delight in bedeviling him. Each layer of his garments came off, slowly peeled away by her caressing hands. When she'd bared his torso, she stood behind him, pressing her breasts into his back, running her hands down his twitching thighs.

Button after button, she unfastened his trousers. Reached into them once they were open to take his cock in her hand. He hissed with pleasure as she trilled her approval. "Can't wait to have this inside of me," she murmured.

"God, Gemma." His hips bucked, pushing into her hand.

Maddeningly, she took her hand away. "Not yet. Take off your boots."

He doubted boots had ever been removed faster. As soon as he was free of his boots, he shoved down his trousers and kicked them away.

Both of them stood naked before each other. Without his spectacles, the edges around her softened, yet only slightly. He could still see her, every dip and curve, could see her hair fanned over her shoulders, and the desire etched in her face.

"You're magnificent, Catullus," she breathed.

Reflexively, he glanced down at himself. He'd seen his own body before—with its archive of scars revealing a history spent in battle—in all states, all conditions. Even aroused. But, under her gaze, his excitement built to dizzying heights. He's never seen his cock so upright, so thick and demanding.

He looked back up at her. The tips of her breasts were tight points, and a flush covered her skin.

"Get in the tub," he growled.

She hurried to comply. As she slid into the water, she sighed. "The temperature's perfect." Once she settled herself, she leaned back against the side of the tub, flicking her fingertips through the water. She smiled invitingly. "Now you."

God, how he wanted to. But . . . "Don't think there's room."

"I'll make room." She scooted forward, bringing her knees up closer to her chest. With a temptress's voice, she said, "Not going to ask twice."

And he didn't need to be asked again. Telling himself that logistics could go hang, he eased into the tub, fitting his long body behind hers. Once more, he found himself astonished when he should have been inured to the whys and wherefores of Otherworld. Both he and Gemma fit effortlessly in the bathing tub despite its appearance. There was room enough for him to stretch his legs, and for her to lie back against him, resting her head on his shoulder.

They twined their arms and fingers, sliding together, adjusting, until they were perfectly situated.

He closed his eyes to allow himself to feel the brilliance of her sleek, wet body against his own. The curves of her buttocks nestled against his upright cock.

A growl rumbled deep in his throat.

His eyes opened. He needed to see. Positioned as he was, he had a faultless view of Gemma's body, its secrets and pleasures. The water made her shimmer—or perhaps she shimmered with her own light. This would not surprise him.

"Time for the mermaid's bath," he whispered. He scooped up a handful of water and poured it between her breasts. She purred and arched up. The curve of her back thrust her generous breasts upward, like an offering.

His heart pounded as he filled his hands with her breasts. They were silken, full, flawless. Each caress turned her liquid and supple, and when he circled and rubbed her nipples, her sighs lowered to moans. She turned her head so that he felt her quickening breath against his throat.

"I love your . . . hands," she gasped. "I love to see them on me."

As he continued to worship her breasts with his hands, their mouths came together in a long, thorough kiss. He loved the taste of her—could live on this alone.

One of his hands moved from her breast to glide down her abdomen. He traced circles on her flesh just below her navel before dipping lower. When he slid his fingers between her folds, discovering them to be flushed and full, he swallowed her moan. Even in the water, she was slick for him, and he stroked her intimately, committing her flesh to memory through touch. He learned more of her secrets.

This is how she liked to be touched. *Here*, in this way, he found what she needed, where to be gentle, where to be commanding and firm. He stroked the bud of her clit. She writhed atop him, her arms draped over the edges of the tub, her legs wide. Entirely open.

"Oh, that's . . . that's . . . yes," she rasped, tearing her mouth from him. "Catullus."

He lightly pinched her nipple as he continued to stroke between her legs. Her movements grew more frenzied, and the sensation of his cock rubbing against her buttocks pushed him to the very edge. He held tight to his release like a man clinging to salvation, for he refused to give in.

On a keening cry, she came. She bowed upward and water churned around them, spilling onto the floor. The sight of her glistening nude body was too much. He squeezed his eyes shut, for if he looked at her, at the firelight over her wet skin, he was done for.

Gradually, in waves, she relaxed. She sank against him as his hands gentled to touch her soothingly. He ached all over with the force of suppressing his own release.

Eyes languid, she turned to partially face him. "Such a talented man." She trailed her fingers along his neck, down his chest, and lower.

His hand on her wrist stopped her before she could reach his cock.

"Why not?" She made a playful pout.

"I'm not like other men, sweetheart." He chuckled, rueful. "Once I achieve my climax, my mind focuses elsewhere. On a new invention. Or a hypothesis that's been proposed in the latest technological publication. Not very romantic, but it's the way I am fashioned."

"You're a man of science," she murmured. "You like experiments. We could try an experiment, see how many times we can get you to come and keep your focus."

Her words alone would push him past his endurance. Knowing he could not last much longer, he stood, pulling her up with him. Water sloshed from the sudden movement.

"I've a better idea," he said. "Let's see how many times I can make *you* come before I fuck you."

The bright color in her cheeks revealed how much she liked his crude words. He stepped from the tub and helped her out.

"I like the sound of that experiment," she said.

"Thought you might." What he did not say to her was that he needed to give her as much pleasure as she could bear—more, if possible. Everything around them had fallen apart. They were trapped in this cottage whilst somewhere in the mortal world, devastation and disaster moved inexorably forward. All he could provide for Gemma was pleasure, and he vowed in this he would succeed.

He led her toward the bed, but instead of throwing back the covers and getting in, he lay her atop the blanket, her bottom just at the edge of the bed.

Her breath came in quick swells as he knelt on the ground, between her legs. She propped herself up on her elbows to watch him.

He ran his hands up and down her thighs, feeling the knot and release of muscles beneath his palms. Catullus took a moment to look at her, ready like a feast, the glisten of her pussy an irresistible lure.

"I've been theorizing what you would taste like," he rasped. "And the surest way to prove a theory is to test it." Caressing her thighs, he lowered his mouth to her.

At the first touch of his tongue to her, she arced up with a soft scream. He licked and stroked, discovering anew the flesh he'd learned with his fingers.

"You taste of honey and spice." His voice was a low rumble. "Delicious."

This was an act he enjoyed for its very intimacy, and now, with Gemma, he could at last allow it to be the adulation for which it was meant. To have his lips and tongue worship her most secret, responsive self, to consume her, take her into him—he knew bliss.

She splayed back onto the bed and her hands came up to cup his head. His name rose and fell from her in moans, sighs, pleas, and demands.

A climax burst from her, full-throated. She dug her heels into his back. And he did not pause or grant her any mercy. He tasted and stroked, insatiable. Orgasm after orgasm wracked her, but he would not yield, not until she stretched limp across the bed, her hands falling away from him.

Finally, allowing her leniency, he lifted his head. She

stared up at the leafy canopy over the bed with glazed, dreamy eyes.

"How many was that, do you think?" he asked. "Two? Three? More?"

"Lost count." Her voice was gratifyingly slurred.

"But we're not done," he said. "There's a methodology to scientific inquiry. Must explore all variables." Rising to his feet, he gently drew her also up to standing. He led her as they moved to the foot of the bed, next to one of the trees that formed a post for the canopy.

Positioning her so that she faced the post, he brought her hands up to wrap around it. "Hold tight," he whispered in her ear.

"What, why—?"

He stood behind her, planting his feet wide. "Shh. There will be a time for questions after the experiment concludes."

"No such thing as too many questions," she tossed over her shoulder.

"Sometimes," he said, taking hold of her hips, "it's better to"—he arranged himself so that the head of his cock was positioned at her opening—"experience something"—he thrust forward, sheathing himself fully within her—"to . . . Good God . . . truly understand it."

"I see what you . . . yes . . . mean. Ah." She moaned as he slowly, slowly withdrew and then plunged forward.

Her hands clutched the post with each thrust, and she pushed her hips back to take him. The neat compartments of his brain and structure of the world as he knew it all burst apart, because this—the slide and cling of her all around him, hot and soft and tight—decimated everything. All he knew, all he wanted to know, was her, taking him into her innermost self.

Before his own demands took over, he slid one hand from her hip, around her middle, then lower, until he touched her swollen clit. He knew it now, this small bit of sensitive flesh, and with exhilarating knowledge he stroked her, understanding through instinct and experience what was needed.

He stroked as he thrust, and her grip upon the post became tighter, the movement of her hips more frenzied. Sometimes he teased, sometimes he demanded. And when she came, the force of her climax made her scream and shudder.

His own control broke. Clutching her hips hard, his rhythm quickened. He lost himself to the fierce demands of his body, to the pleasure that obliterated identity. Catullus drove into her until he could no longer withstand his release. It pounded through him with such strength he thought surely this was how gods came to be, created in the fire and forge of sensual communion.

Not merely two bodies coupling, for that was simple biology. This was so much more than that.

Once he felt confident that his own legs would not buckle beneath him, Catullus swept Gemma up in his arms and tucked her into the bed. She mumbled a sleepy demand, which he obeyed without complaint, sliding between cool sheets and gathering her damp body against his own.

Gemma wrapped her arms around him, nuzzling against his steaming flesh. He stroked her hair and felt a peace settle over him he knew, given the circumstances, he had no right to feel. It had him, just the same, and he gratefully yielded to oblivion.

Catullus awoke from a doze to find Gemma kneeling between his legs, his astonishingly hard cock in her hands. He couldn't believe it at first—he thought perhaps he dreamt—but no, the feel of her wrapped around him, stroking his thick erection and drawing desire in widening waves, this was real. She was real. And when he made a strangled sound of pleasure, she looked up at him with siren's eyes.

"Now it's *my* experiment," she murmured. "Let's test

your focus." Her breath feathered across the glistening head of his cock. She leaned forward, presenting the most incredible view of her breasts pressed against each other, and then—

"Holy God!"

She took him in her mouth.

In a helpless wonder, he bid good-bye to his sanity. The inside of her mouth was silken, wet paradise. She licked and sucked, sometimes slowly, sometimes with control-decimating speed. To watch her, to see her taste him with pleasure written on her face . . . he'd never witnessed anything so arousing. And to be the recipient of her attention, her deft tongue and clever mouth, truly he was blessed beyond all men.

As she worked him with her mouth, she also stroked with her hands, pumping him in time. His chest swelled as he dragged in air. Of their own volition, his hips rose up from the mattress. He was utterly in her power and happy to consign himself to a life of servitude, if it meant this overwhelming ecstasy. When he threaded his fingers into her hair, gently guiding her, she glanced up and their gazes locked. Her own arousal gleamed in her eyes, and something more.

Trust, he realized. He trusted her as he did no other. Just as she trusted him, for they were both vulnerable, open, and also unafraid.

His climax gathered, yet he held it off.

"Not yet," he growled. In half a second, he had her on her back. He held her wrists above her head as he settled himself between her legs.

"Seems I made a monster." She squirmed beneath him, the satiny press of her breasts pushing him beyond endurance. "A very focused monster."

"Face the consequences." Maddened, he drove into her.

She bucked, moaning. "I'm not . . . sorry."

"Unrepentant . . . minx." Already roused to a fever, he

could not be gentle. His thrusts came quick and deep, raking him with pleasure.

Her ankles hooked just above his buttocks, clasping him to her. She was as mad as he, thrashing and writhing, meeting him thrust for thrust. He did not recognize himself. He didn't know her. They had both transformed completely into creatures ruled by sensation and demand. And it was good. So damned good. This wild woman who made him wild, too.

He had enough rational thought to shift his body so that, with each surge into her, he rubbed her clit. This turned her into a demon, and she broke her wrists from his grasp to score her nails down his back. The hot trails of pain shifted to fiery pleasure.

"The claws come out," he rumbled.

She was past hearing. "Catullus . . . yes . . . *please.*"

He gave her what she asked for, letting slip all control and thrusting with every ounce of his strength. The bed shook, its branches quaking as if in the middle of a storm.

Her legs locked around him as she came with a cry, her head thrown back, mouth open.

His orgasm hit him with the force of a gale. It rolled on and on, draining him, lifting him. Each time he came inside her, he believed he'd reached the pinnacle of pleasure, and each time he gained still greater heights. Now he soared above mountains. His release was endless, and yet over too soon.

He lowered himself down and then rolled to his side, cradling her against him. For some time, they simply looked at one another, running hands over sweat-dampened skin, languidly kissing, making incoherent murmurs that they still managed to understand.

"Have to follow procedure," she said, languid. "Post-experiment interview."

He groaned. "Can't talk. Lost power to speak."

She admonished, "Mr. Graves, you have to respect the methodology. How can we learn and advance our understanding without sticking to the rules?"

"Hang the rules." He nuzzled the base of her throat.

"Subject is being unruly. But he doesn't seem to be losing focus. Do you feel like inventing something, Mr. Graves? Reading a technological publication?"

"God, no." His body and mind both felt utterly satiated, incapable of anything but lying in bed with her supple, warm body pressed to his.

"Your initial hypothesis has been disproved," she continued in a precise, practical tone. "And since the variable has been altered, we can thus conclude that you do *not* become distracted after orgasm." Her smile turned self-satisfied. "Not when you're with the right woman."

He saw this was so. And it amazed him. He had no desire to get up and busy himself. His mind didn't whirl with a thousand ideas, all demanding his attention. Peace. She'd given him peace.

"I've never been so happy to be wrong." He pulled her tight against him, wrapping her in his arms. A flame of a woman who blazed without burning.

They were quiet, breathing in and out together. Sharing flesh and heartbeats and stillness.

"I could be like this forever," she whispered.

An unwelcome edge of reality cut along his contentment. "You may have to."

She smoothed the tip of one finger across his furrowed brow. "No, none of that. This is our moment. Our island and shelter."

Her touch soothed, and lassitude stole over him. When his eyelids drooped, he fought to keep them open.

"Rest now," Gemma murmured. "The time for worry is later."

Time, he thought, sinking into sleep. That was all he wanted with her. And now they had time in abundance—the sweetest punishment he would ever know.

Chapter 16

The Hazards and Habits of Otherworld

"Wake up! Eyes open!"

Catullus started awake to see Bryn hovering over his face. The pixie fluttered his wings anxiously, stirring minute currents of air across Catullus.

"How the hell—?" Catullus's groggy mind, roused from an uncharacteristic deep slumber, struggled to make sense of what he saw.

"We must go!" Bryn piped. He zigzagged back and forth across the bed. "Now, now!"

True to form, Gemma continued to sleep, entirely unaware of the pixie's shrill demands.

Sitting up so that the blankets pooled at his waist, Catullus ground the heel of his hand into his eyes, rubbing them alert. "How did you get here?"

The pixie looked at him blankly. "I flew."

"I mean," Catullus gritted, growing irritable, "how did you find this cottage? We're up a tree in the middle of an ocean." To demonstrate, he rose from the bed, stalked to the door and threw it open. As before, an endless sea stretched all around.

"That's if you leave by the door," Bryn explained as if talking to a slow child. "Try opening the window."

Catullus frowned, glancing at the small windows. The view out of them was the same as what the door revealed: limitless ocean. Figuring that he had nothing to lose by proving the pixie wrong, he strode to one window and, after unfastening its catch, swung it fully open.

An astonishing view. Forest. The selfsame forest in which he and Gemma had arrived.

Mystified, Catullus walked back to the open front door. The ocean continued to glitter, uninterrupted. Several times, he went back and forth between door and window. Each time demonstrated that what he saw was not illusion. Somehow, if one exited the cottage via the door, one would tumble down into an immeasurable sea. Yet one would stand on a forest floor if leaving the cottage through the window.

"Goddamn Otherworld logic," he muttered.

"This is the Sea of Lovers," Bryn explained at his shoulder. "When you and the woman entered the cottage together, you created an enchantment."

"I don't have any magic, and hers isn't strong enough to do something like this."

"Everything is made of magic in Otherworld. Even cottages. After you both entered this place, you fashioned a spell. To give you what you desired most: time and solitude."

"So we were transported to this . . ." Catullus waved at the ocean out the window. "Sea of Lovers."

"And when you were ready to leave, you could."

"Through the window." He chuckled ruefully. Seeing Bryn staring at him, Catullus realized he was naked. He gathered up his clothing and began dressing. "What are you doing here?"

The pixie perched on the lip of the tub, which was now empty. "I went to Brightworld. Had to see for myself." He shivered. "Bad, bad. The giant king moves ever closer to the Primal Source. Chaos. Terror. And if he reaches the Primal

Source . . ." His wings trembled, but he managed to collect himself. "You say the Man in the Oak can speak with the giant king, make him stop?"

"Yes," Catullus answered, though this had yet to be proven.

"Then I will take you to him." Bryn tried to imbue his words with bravado, only partially succeeding.

Catullus would not ask Bryn if he was sure, lest he talk the pixie out of his decision. Knowing that time grew scarce, he padded over to the bed to wake Gemma. It took him saying her name three times, and then giving her a rather ungentle shake before she finally stirred.

Seeing him sitting on the edge of the bed, she smiled drowsily and stretched. "More experimenting?" Her voice, husky with sleep, sent dark currents of need shimmering through him. She scooted up to sitting. The blankets fell from her, revealing her breasts, and she reached for him.

Catullus quickly drew the blankets back up to cover her, which pained him, not unlike drawing a curtain over a magnificent stained-glass window. "Experimentation later. We have a guest." He glanced over at Bryn, who sat at the foot of the bed, eyes the size of pennies.

Clutching the blankets to her, Gemma blushed. "Turn around, pixie," she ordered.

Bryn obliged, though he looked quite disappointed. Catullus wondered if it was bad luck to crush a pixie in one's fist.

As Bryn stared at a wall, Catullus brought Gemma her clothing. She stood and, after looking gloomily at her decidedly grubby dress, began to clothe herself. For Catullus, watching her dress was another exercise in self-restraint.

"You look almost as unhappy as I do to be putting these things on again," she noted, fastening the buttons on the front of her bodice.

"A shame," he sighed, "putting clothing on that goddess's body of yours."

She smiled wickedly. "I'm looking forward to more

worship." With the last button done and fully dressed, she gathered focus. "Tell me what's going on."

Succinctly, Catullus explained everything that Bryn had told him, and why it was imperative that they leave immediately to locate Merlin. As he spoke, Gemma grew serious and attentive.

"We've tried thinking it through," she said. "Between the two of us, we couldn't find a way out of here. We're still trapped in this cottage, in the middle of the ocean."

"Go out the window, of course," Catullus answered.

Some aspects of a person's character were so deeply ingrained, nothing short of death could alter them. For Catullus, the desire to build and create and understand the mechanics of everything around him remained a constant presence, from his earliest memories. Even as an infant, he couldn't be left alone in his bassinet, lest he disassemble the whole thing with his stubby, curious fingers. More than once his mother had come into the nursery to find his cradle in pieces, or a wind-up toy reduced to its smallest parts, with him in the middle of the chaos, quietly and happily sifting through the debris.

He had no recollection of this, being rather small at the time, but family lore held sway over individual memory. It didn't surprise him, though. He continued to take apart and reassemble anything that wasn't welded together. Most likely, he'd try to dismantle his coffin as it was being lowered into the ground.

For Gemma, her curiosity and need to know wove into the fabric of her essence. She could not stop being a reporter in search of information. He loved this intrinsic quality of hers, revealing a mind fully aware, a searching, questing nature that called to the exact attribute in himself. In all his life, he'd never met anyone, male or female, with the same driven mind as his own.

Still, he was glad that he wasn't on the receiving end of Gemma's queries now. Bryn Enfys had that privilege.

As they journeyed through the endless forest of Otherworld, through sheltered vales, along creek beds, passing scores of creatures straight from a child's book, Gemma peppered the pixie with a nonstop deluge of questions. Fortunately, Bryn's vanity enjoyed being the center of so much attention, and from so lovely a woman.

"Is all of Otherworld like this?" She waved at the arching canopy of branches overhead. "A vast, hyperbolic English wood?"

The pixie, buzzing just ahead, chuckled despite his continuing apprehension. "Otherworld has many forms, many guises. Immeasurable sapphire seas, as you've seen. Gold and green fields that roll to infinity. Cities of crystal, of fire, of ice. One could never map Otherworld. For as many minds and souls there are in Brightworld, so Otherworld grows and shifts."

"How are Otherworld and Brightworld connected?" She picked her way along the edge of a pond, where curious water faerie watched. When one of the tiny female creatures swam close to Catullus, eyeing him with interest, Gemma scowled and swatted at the faerie. It drifted away, giggling.

Catullus hid his own smile, but felt a rush of gratification. He never thought he'd inspire jealousy in a woman.

"Otherworld is made by Brightworld," Bryn explained. "Just as Brightworld needs Otherworld. They each shape and create the other, existing side by side. We fey beings need the mortal imagination—it feeds us, gives us the breath of our lungs and flesh of our bodies. Builds our homes and causes the trees to grow."

"And how does Brightworld need Otherworld?" asked Catullus, whose own curiosity was mighty and ravenous.

"The mortal mind and soul must have magic, else they shrivel and becomes dead things. There had been a time when magic flowed freely between the two worlds, sustaining each other." Bryn looked somber. "That time is long past, and every day more and more mortals wither inside, trapped in their world of smokestacks and steel. Soon, they will be nothing but barren desert within."

"And if that does happen," pressed Gemma with a frown, "what then? Will Otherworld disappear?"

The pixie smiled wryly. "Otherworld will go on, but it will not grow, will not flourish. And there will always be some mortals of Brightworld who have magic within them, even when encased in prisons of brick and commerce."

For some time, Gemma was pensive, quietly slipping into her own thoughts as they continued to trek through the forest. There was much to ponder, and, as much as he took pleasure in her curiosity, he respected the depth of her mind, too; that she not only asked questions, but truly contemplated what she learned. Yet she did not live exclusively within her head, as evidenced by her voyaging alone to the Canadian wilderness in pursuit of story and experience. And she handled a derringer damn well. And made love like a pagan.

Impulsively, he took hold of her hand and kissed it.

She glowed with surprised delight. "My gallant knight."

"My lady warrior."

"I'm no fighter," she laughed. "Merely a journalist."

"Nothing 'merely' about you." He stopped and tugged her close. They stood, chest to chest, hands interlaced, gazing at one another. He felt the rise and fall of her breath, saw the life and energy of her shining in her azure eyes, the humor curving her lush mouth. The mouth he had to kiss.

He bent his head, and she tilted back to meet him. It had been only hours, and yet far too long had passed since he kissed her, touched her bare flesh. Made love to her. And he needed all of these things, as much as he needed water or food to sustain him, if not more.

The thought of food roused his stomach, and a loud

growl issued from his belly. Gemma gave an uncharacteristic giggle.

He sighed and stepped back slightly. So much for romance. He glanced up at the sky, but time functioned differently in Otherworld, and golden light seemed to speckle the ground regardless of the hour. They had been walking and walking for what had to be hours, but no change was reflected in the light and shadow. His pocket watch wasn't working, either. No way to judge the time.

"We'll stop for a moment and have something to eat," he said. "I believe Mrs. Strathmore packed us some sandwiches."

Gemma frowned, but not at him. Her anger was for herself. "I dropped the basket when the Heirs started shooting at us. Damn it."

"Don't castigate yourself. I would've done the same." He pressed a kiss on the tip of her nose. "We can forage. I've done plenty of that." He turned and looked around for some promising bushes and trees. Something had to produce edible fruit, and they could try fishing in one of the ponds or creeks.

"No need," chirped Bryn, fluttering close. "You've but to speak, and I can have any food you desire. What do mortals like? Beefsteak?" A platter with a sizzling, red steak appeared, hovering in front of Catullus and smelling like paradise. "Or . . . what is that dreadful thing called? Pudding?" The steak vanished, and a flaming plum pudding took its place. The spicy scent immediately transported Catullus to New Year's dinners with his family.

His mouth watered. "I'd love a good mutton pie."

"Done!" The pudding disappeared, and the most gorgeous, golden brown mutton pie materialized. Gravy bubbled up from the vents cut into the top crust.

An unseen knife sliced into the pie, and a perfect wedge hovered up and into Catullus's open hand. He allowed himself the moment's pleasure of simply staring at and smelling the culinary wonder, little caring that it had been summoned through magic. Then he brought it up to his mouth, ready to take a bite.

"Catullus, no!"

Gemma slapped the mutton pie out of his hand. The wedge flew through the air to land in some nearby mud. He stared at it, stunned, as his empty stomach rumbled in complaint.

"Why—?"

"The stories my granda told. About traveling to the land of the Fair Folk." Her eyes widened in alarm. "I just remembered. You're never, never supposed to eat *anything* in faerie land. Not a crumb, not a bite."

"Why the devil not?" He eyed the wedge of spoilt mutton pie with dismay.

"Because it will trap you here. Forever."

His attention snagged, he turned back to her. "If either of us eat anything in Otherworld, we will be unable to leave?"

"Stuck here eternally."

"Like Persephone and the pomegranate seeds." He whirled on Bryn, and, while the remainder of the mutton pie vanished, the pixie did not. "You knew," Catullus gritted.

The pixie smiled without a hint of regret.

"Not much of a friend," Gemma said tartly.

Bryn only shrugged. "The ways of Otherworld outweigh such mortal ephemera as friendship. We always seek to add more mortals to our realm. We like their light," he added by way of explanation.

Frowning, Catullus said, "Foolish. If you trap Gemma and I here, who will go back to Brightworld and stop Arthur from reaching the Primal Source? For you know that once he touches it, the magic of Otherworld will be enslaved."

Bryn looked abashed. "I hadn't thought of that."

"Even pixies can be thick in the head," Gemma snorted.

Catullus pressed a hand to his still-growling stomach.

Now the journey was all the more troublesome, since neither he nor Gemma were to have anything to eat or drink for as long as they were in Otherworld. He'd gone without food before—a long siege against a band of Heirs in the Sud Tyrol came immediately to mind—and he didn't care for it, but he was more concerned about Gemma.

"Will you be all right?" he asked her. "I don't know how long we will be here, with nothing to eat."

Her mouth twisted ruefully. "My mistake for dropping our provisions. But I'll manage. With a family as big as mine, every meal became a fight for food. I went to bed hungry more than once. Until," she added with a grin, "I learned how to use my fork as a weapon. Stabbed my brother Patrick right in the hand when he made a grab for the last biscuit."

"I promise I will always give you the last biscuit," Catullus said, solemn.

"Ensuring the safety of your hands."

"As well as the health of one freckle-faced reporter."

He sent one final glance toward the piece of mutton pie, lying in the mud. A hedgehog-like creature wearing a waistcoat sniffed at it, and then dragged the food off to its burrow.

"Back to our quest," Catullus said. "The sooner we can reach Merlin, the sooner we can return to our world."

"And eat," added Gemma. She sighed wistfully. "I really do like biscuits."

They pushed onward, Bryn at the lead, the two mortals trailing behind. The trees grew together densely, forming thick boundaries of twisting wood, their branches interwoven into a dense overhead canopy. Otherworld's constant golden light pierced the canopy infrequently. It scattered like thrown coins upon the forest floor. Beams of light stretched down, motes of pollen dancing within, yet some of these particles were sentient—tiny creatures no bigger than a dandelion seed. They circled and spun along the rays of sunlight.

Everything else was obscure green shade, a tangle of bracken and flora, and from the deepest reaches of the forest came the sounds of voices, faint music, the rustle of leaf and wing.

Catullus found himself torn between observing this remarkable landscape and watching Gemma as she, too, marveled at the scenes around her. Both fascinated him. Watching the play of interest and emotion across her expressive face sent sweet, sharp arrows into his heart, a welcome pain.

"What are you grinning about?" she asked him.

"This magical place suits you." He saw her—a vision of fiery hair tumbling over her shoulders, creamy skin, luscious curves—amidst the verdant wilds. "You could be a lost faerie princess."

She made a face. "I never wanted life in a tower. That's why I left home, to slay my own dragons."

"That's one of the reasons why I love you." The words popped out of his mouth before he could stop himself.

They froze, staring at one another. She looked utterly shocked, probably just as shocked as he felt. In the whole of his life, he'd never uttered those words to anyone, never thought he would. And now, they had leapt from him as if he was speaking a foregone conclusion, as if they were entirely natural and right.

He wasn't like Bennett, who fell in and out of love as often as most men changed socks. This had altered once Bennett met London. Theirs was a deep and abiding love, carnal, sacred. Enviable. Now, Bennett had eyes and love for only one woman: his wife. Yet, until London appeared in Bennett's life, he gave his heart as freely as his body, and God above knew what an almighty slut Bennett had been.

As for himself, Catullus very seldom shared a bed with

a lover. And not once did he share his heart. He had shared a bed with Gemma, and now offered her his heart. He did not know how the recipient felt about this.

A flush stained Gemma's cheeks, hectic and burning. She stood as one ensorcelled, staring. His heart stopped. Then started up again in a hard pound within the circumscription of his chest. Sweat beaded down his back.

God—he'd made more than his share of leaps in his life: down cliffs, across ravines, from the back of a racing horse. This was, by far, the most terrifying.

"Catullus—" Her voice was low, but her *tone* . . . he couldn't tell if it was reproach, uncertainty, joy. *Please let it be joy.*

"Here! Here!" Bryn whizzed by, through the space between Catullus and Gemma. The pixie darted in quick, abrupt angles, revealing his agitation. "The sorcerer in the tree! Just over this ridge."

Deciding he'd rather take his chances with a legendary and mad enchanter entombed in a tree than the doubt of his own heart, Catullus said, "I'll take the lead." If the sorcerer was as dangerous as Bryn claimed, Catullus had to protect Gemma.

Thoughts of love, reciprocated or denied, dwindled when they entered a clearing. In the center of the glade stood the largest oak tree Catullus had ever seen. Six grown men could not encircle the trunk—wider than most sitting rooms. Huge gnarled branches spread out over what had to be at least an acre, twisting in all directions as if feeding on the energy of life itself. A mosaic of serrated leaves shifted in the breeze, and they sounded like the hands of time applauding.

The size of this oak held only part of Catullus's amazement. Within the tree—no, *part* of the tree—was a man.

Slowly, on cautious feet, Catullus approached, with Gemma behind him.

The man's face bore lines and crags of age, deep runnels

from years too numerous to count. Silvery hair covered his cheeks and chin, growing out into a sage's beard, and what hair topped his head also shone silver in the clearing's light. His eyes remained closed, even as Catullus and Gemma neared. He wore a robe, embroidered knotwork along the collar and at the cuffs of his long, hanging sleeves. Could this man be alive? Catullus could not understand if this was so, for the lower half of the old man's body was entirely encased in bark, was, in fact, enmeshed within the tree, and what had initially appeared to be the folds and pleats of his robe were actually tree roots spreading out into the ground as thickly as the branches above.

Ashen, Bryn pointed to the ground close to the tree. Light reflected off of at least a dozen pairs of faerie wings. And there did seem to be an inordinate amount of slugs clinging to one of the tree's roots.

"I'll wait over there," he whispered, glancing toward the edge of the clearing. The pixie zipped away to huddle in green shadow.

"Holy hell," whispered Gemma, turning back to the man in the tree. "Is that—"

The man's eyes opened. Catullus felt himself drawn in, through the darkest and most arcane pathways of history, of myth. The blackness of the man's eyes was absolute. Within, they contained the whole of experience, mortal and immortal, and one could not help feeling very small when presented with such immensity.

Within those eyes also glowed the forge of madness, the blaze of a mind and power too old and too long confined.

Instinctively, Catullus and Gemma sought and then took each other's hands. Their touch grounded them.

"A river of mercury!" the man shouted. "The rose devours the serpent!" His deranged, wise eyes fixed on the two mortals standing before him. "Bright sparks in the tinder. Douse the flame."

He raised his hands. Gemma gasped and Catullus

grunted as invisible bindings trapped them where they stood. Catullus fought to move, but his arms were pinned to his sides.

"Cannot have a fire in the forest," the old man muttered. "Choke it, choke it out."

The bonds around Catullus and Gemma tightened. She squeaked. Catullus felt his ribs compress as an unseen hand slowly crushed him.

Catullus summoned his thinning breath. "Merlin, wait!"

The sorcerer held up a hand. Though the invisible vise halted in its slow, agonizing crush, neither did it release its captives.

"Merlin, Merlin," the old man muttered. His gaze sharpened, losing some of its madness. "Have not heard that name in centuries."

"But you *are* Merlin," Gemma gasped. "Aren't you?"

"I have been. I have been many names, many faces. I am the oak and the wind. The darkness in the diamond." He shook his head, as if scattering a momentary lucidity. "No more. The flames feed the blaze. Choke it out." With a wave of his hand, the unseen binds resumed their agonizing crush.

Good God—had he and Gemma come all this way, fought Heirs and immense magic and devastating odds, only to be choked to death by a mad sorcerer?

Chapter 17

Courage

Blackness swam in Catullus's vision. "It's Arthur," he managed to rasp. "He's . . . been summoned. He needs . . . you."

Clarity returned to the sorcerer's gaze. With another gesture, he stopped the grip. He cocked his head to one side, catching a familiar name. "Arthur?"

"Magic. Brought him back. He marches now. To London. Devastation." Catullus fought to keep conscious. He saw Gemma struggle to do the same. Pain lanced through him, not only from the chokehold around him, but also because she was being gradually strangled right in front of him, and he couldn't do a damned thing to stop it.

"He has been summoned, has he?" Merlin asked abruptly.

"Men. Called the Heirs. Stolen magic."

The sorcerer's eyes grew more alert. "I shall see," answered Merlin, "here." He lifted his arms and gave a small wave of his hands.

A metallic gleam appeared before the sorcerer. It hovered in the air, a small flash of light; then, as Catullus and Gemma watched, it spun and grew. From the size of a ha'penny, it unfolded outward, growing, turning the atmosphere alive. When it was as big as a wagon wheel, Merlin waved again, and the light stopped its expansion. The sorcerer muttered something. The light coalesced, becoming liquid, reflective.

"What . . . is it?" Gemma asked, battling for consciousness.

"My eyes," came the answer. "And now they must focus."

As everyone watched, the surface of the circle clouded, becoming hazy. Shapes began to coalesce within it. Catullus saw the greenish, low forms sharpen, until they became the familiar figures of hills. Several houses dotted the hills, bound together by a ribbon of road. Night covered the landscape, but moonlight revealed enough details for Catullus to recognize the placid English countryside.

"Where?" Gemma whispered to Catullus.

"Anywhere. From Salisbury. To Epsom."

It seemed a quiet enough scene, but then the ground shook and Arthur strode into view. Merlin gave an opaque mutter to see his old protégé again. The king looked just as determined as before, advancing eastward toward the capital, while a contingent of Heirs followed behind on horseback. Neither Arthur nor the Heirs paid any mind to the isolated village they passed. Frightened villagers watched the procession from the shelter of their homes.

Catullus expected at any moment for Arthur to strike out with Excalibur and level this village as he had done in the past. These fears went unfounded. Catullus exhaled as Arthur and his disciples-cum-masters left the village behind, moving onward, out of the range of Merlin's vision.

Suddenly, thick roots exploded up from the ground surrounding the houses. They shot into the air, fast as snakes, as if with the minds of serpents, too. The vines engulfed the houses, choking windows, winding over rooftops. People inside the homes tried to open their doors, but the vines grew too impenetrably over the doorframes. The windows offered no escape, either. From the distance of Merlin's scrying disk, the people appeared tiny and pitiful as they fought to free themselves from the leafy prisons growing rampant over their homes.

Within minutes, nothing could be seen of any of the houses, not a candle flicker, not a stone. Only dense, thorny vines. Sleeping Beauty's castle could not have been more impassable.

"Help them," Gemma urged. "They'll starve. Or worse."

There wasn't much Catullus could do, trapped as he was, and fighting unconsciousness. Had he been free, he would have tried to mix up a corrosive or herbicide. Yet he wasn't free, and, even if he was, didn't know *where* he might find the necessary chemicals, but he, too, needed to help the trapped villagers.

"See." She tipped her head toward the vision. "Someone has . . . an ax."

From the inside out, a man chopped away his front door, then hacked at the vines blocking his way. It took some time, but at last he cut his way free. He ran toward the snare of vines choking another nearby house, and set about chopping into them. He was a rough country fellow, strong of arm and shoulder, and freed an elderly man and woman from their prison. A goodly while later, all of the villagers were at liberty, and they took flight, some on horseback and cart, some on foot. They took a few possessions. But their homes were lost to them.

Merlin waved his hands, and the scrying surface vanished.

With another movement, the bindings around Catullus and Gemma released. They both fell to the ground, sucking in shuddering gulps of air.

"Bitter root," the sorcerer muttered, frowning.

"Things like that have been happening ever since Arthur was summoned," rasped Catullus on his hands and knees.

"So I have seen."

"Then you know," Catullus continued, getting to his feet

and helping Gemma to stand, "what will happen if he should reach London, if he touches the Primal Source."

"Disaster," said Merlin, weary. He seemed to have fully regained his sanity, only to emerge as a tired old man.

"You have to speak with Arthur," Catullus urged. "Let him know that he is being misled by the Heirs of Albion. He believes he is to be England's savior, but he will doom not only this nation, but all nations, all people." Purpose shored Catullus's words. "There is only one voice, besides the Heirs, that Arthur will heed, and that is yours."

Merlin spread his hands. "Little I can do, whilst I am like this."

"We can break the spell," said Gemma. The color was at last returning to normal in her face. "Get you free and take you to Arthur."

The sorcerer's smile held only traces of humor. "My enchantress bound me here using my own magic. Powerful magic, I must admit. To extricate me from this oaken prison is beyond your mortal capabilities. Not even," he said to Gemma, "using what little magic you *do* possess."

"This *must* be done," said Catullus with resolve. "If we haven't magic of our own to liberate you, tell us where it can be found."

"Wherever it is," Gemma added, "we'll grab it for you."

Merlin contemplated Catullus and Gemma for some time, his infinitely dark, unblinking eyes searching their faces, their souls. It felt like an exploratory root reaching, testing, within Catullus. The profoundest appraisal, which saw its way into Catullus's core, wherein lay his wishes and desires, fears and strengths, thoughts and feelings he shared with no one, not even himself. What would the sorcerer find there? Catullus could not know, but he held himself motionless under Merlin's study.

Gemma, too, felt the same scrutiny. The tight set of her lips showed it unsettled her as much as it did Catullus. Yet, like him, she forced herself still, submitting to this scouring of the soul.

Then it was done. Merlin blinked, and the subtle pressure receded.

"One way," the sorcerer intoned. "One chance. A hazardous path."

"Naturally." For the over two decades Catullus served the Blades, no journey or quest ever came easily. Anyone who expected a mission to be straightforward and safe either quickly learned otherwise or wound up dead. He'd seen it happen—reckless, overconfident Blades falling because of their own hubris. Those that survived, including himself, bore scars on their bodies and minds, emerging stronger, tempering their strength with wisdom.

At least, Catullus *hoped* he was wise. In some ways, he believed he was. In others . . . He cast a glance at Gemma, who watched the sorcerer with avid interest.

No—it was the wisest thing he'd ever done, and could not regret it. He loved her. The words, once spoken aloud, resounded within him with their truth. And if she could not reciprocate his feelings . . . it would hurt like hell. He'd be blasted and torn. But a better man, for all that.

"Any hazard, we'll gladly face," Catullus said.

Merlin gave another enigmatic smile. "We shall see."

"Give us our marching orders," said Gemma.

The sorcerer tipped his head. "At your own peril." His eyes focused on a point beyond their sight. "It is water that I require."

An abundance of water was nearby—en route to Merlin, they had passed countless streams, creeks, ponds, and rills—but it would not be so easy.

"From where should we get this water?" Catullus asked.

"Mab's Cauldron," replied Merlin.

From his hiding spot just outside the clearing, Bryn gasped.

"I take it Mab's Cauldron isn't an ice-cream parlor," said Gemma.

The pixie flew tentatively forward, his wings fluttering in agitation. He glanced warily at Merlin. "The Faerie Queen's cauldron lies in the Night Forest."

"Is it far?" asked Catullus.

"No," Bryn answered as he twisted his tiny hands. "But its name tells you what you need to know: In the Night Forest, it is eternally night. No sun ever lights the sky."

"I'm not afraid of the dark," said Gemma.

"Oh, but you should be." A forbidding note frosted Merlin's voice. "The Night Forest is home to Otherworld's most dangerous creatures. The sort that journey to your mortal world in the depths of night to lurk in shadow and bring terror. It is the native soil for the creatures of your nightmares."

"Lovely," muttered Catullus. Being a Blade meant traveling through and combating danger, but *just once* he wouldn't mind if a quest took him someplace innocuous and pleasant. Perhaps the Land of Feather Mattresses and Endless Almond Tarts.

"You know that I see well at night," said Gemma.

"Good—don't want us both stumbling heedlessly into the dark."

Gemma could take her liquor. Scotch. Whiskey. Bourbon and rye. Her strong stomach came from years in the newsroom. When starting out, at the end of her very first day at the *Trib*, her male colleagues pulled bottles from their desks, along with battered tin cups, and drank straight shots of liquor. They snickered and offered her a dainty raspberry cordial. She had poured herself a cupful of Tennessee whiskey and bolted the whole thing down. Took everything she had not to bend over and breathe fire, her eyes streaming tears, but she didn't. They respected her a little more, after that, and she grew to actually like the taste—the smoke and burn.

She didn't drink often, but it had its social and medicinal uses. Right now, she'd take on a ring full of bare-knuckle brawlers to have a single shot of whiskey. Bryn, the little lush, had polished off the contents of the flask. She never would have guessed that so tiny a creature could put away so much alcohol, and without a slurred word or tipsy loop in his flying.

She was going to have to face the Night Forest entirely sober.

And what she had to say to Catullus—that demanded a little fermented courage, too.

They made their way silently through the forest of Otherworld, following Bryn through woods that grew increasingly more dense, the path tangled. Vines and brambles. Thick stands of trees nearly impassable. Surly brownies throwing rocks and insults. Bits of sod that were actually faerie creatures with grass growing on their backs, who'd snap and snarl if you accidentally stepped on them. Rough going.

"Is it a lot farther?" she asked Bryn.

The pixie had not yet recovered from his encounter with Merlin. This was made worse by his anxiety growing by the minute, if minutes existed in Otherworld. Bryn fluttered closer. "Not too much. So eager are you to face the banshees and fachans?" He shuddered.

She didn't know what a fachan was, and had even less desire to meet one, judging by Bryn's reaction. "I want to get started on this search," she answered. Journalism required patience, and she had that by the barrel, but the edgier she got about the Night Forest, the more she wanted to just *be there* already and face whatever it was she would have to face.

"I'll get you there," the pixie said, "by and by." He zipped away, though with a little less vim than usual.

Catullus sent her an unreadable glance, but continued to stride ahead of her, his eyebrows drawn down in intense contemplation as he threaded through the overgrown forest. She allowed herself a brief indulgence to admire him. He did move magnificently. Surprising, given how much time he spent in his mind, and yet it shouldn't be such a surprise—he'd made love to her with a fierce beauty that made her head light and body liquid, even now.

It had been more than his body he'd shared. His heart, his love—those he gave to her, too.

He wanted something from her—acceptance, reciprocation, rejection. He liked exploration and learning, but he liked definitives even more, and her silence had to grate.

Catullus nimbly vaulted over a huge tree root nearly as tall as Gemma. She tried to leap over with the same dexterity. Skirts, and lack of experience, had her scrabbling for a grip. She floundered, slipping, then felt his firm grasp around her wrists holding her steady. Gently, he pulled her up and over, until she stood on the other side of the root with his hands clasping her arms just beneath her elbows, less than a few inches separating them.

Warmth at his nearness enveloped her, the potency of his active body, his scholar's face.

The moment grew fraught as they stared at one another. He hadn't spoken much since they had left Merlin, and even those few words were subdued, pensive. Now his onyx eyes moved over her face, searching and guarded and yearning, all at once.

"Words are my business, Catullus." She chose them now, very carefully, as one might search for flakes of gold amongst the silt. "I know their value. Their significance and weight. I can't just toss them out there."

"And I take what *I* say very seriously, as well." He released his hold on her arms. An echo of warmth remained, but he held himself at a remove. He bowed to her—actually *bowed*—and turned away to resume their journey.

Oh, hell, now he'd retreated behind genteel politeness,

his spine perfectly straight, his demeanor irreproachable and unreachable.

"Damn it." She grabbed his arm before he could move away. She pulled him around to face her, though she suspected he *allowed* her to turn him. He was bigger than her, and stronger, so very strong. "I'm trying to say that I—"

A whistling overhead caused them both to look up. Then spring apart. A thick, pointed icicle slammed into the ground, narrowly missing them. Sprawled on her back, Gemma raised herself up on her elbows to stare at the icicle—a lance of ice as long as her outstretched arms, sharper than an iron spike. Catullus, crouched on the other side, also gaped. If either she or Catullus had been a little bit slower, they would've been impaled.

They looked at each other, shock widening their eyes, before glancing up again. Branches stretched overhead, only instead of leaves hanging from the boughs, now wicked spears of ice hung down and shuddered in the wind. All of the trees surrounding them were suddenly encrusted with rime, their bark hidden behind coatings of frost. Moments earlier, the trees appeared at the height of summer abundance. Now harpoonlike icicles shivered, ready to drop down and skewer Gemma and Catullus.

Another hard gust of wind shook the trees. The icicles shook ominously, rattling like bones. Gemma scrambled to her feet as Catullus appeared beside her, gripping her wrist and helping her to stand. Neither spoke. There was only time to flee. They ran, more shrill whistling sounding overhead.

Icicles rained down all around them, shrieking through the air before ramming into the ground. Gemma and Catullus ran serpentine as heavy, sharp spears of ice plunged down, blocking any direct path. The atmosphere chilled. Everywhere around them became a forest of ice, blue and white and slick. She felt the frigid air as icicles continued to fall from the branches, barely missing her and Catullus.

"What kind of Otherworld magic is this?" she shouted above the din.

"Bryn!" Catullus bellowed.

The pixie appeared beside them, fluttering to dodge shards of ice.

"You led us into a goddamned ice forest," Catullus growled.

Bryn shook his head. "'Tisn't the way of this place. There are other woods, eternally winter, but not here! I do not know why—" He darted to one side as an ice barb nearly took off one of his wings.

Gemma chanced a look over her shoulder, seeking answers. "There," she said grimly.

Following her lead, Catullus also glanced behind him. "Son of a buggering bitch."

A group of men pursued. They all held firearms, but one gestured intricate patterns in the air, gelid blue light forming between his hands whilst he chanted. None of the icicles were falling around the men, and Gemma realized that the man wielding the magic controlled where and when the ice dropped. She and Catullus were the targets.

Gemma recognized the men as the Heirs that had shot at them just before jumping into the well. Clearly, they'd followed, though she had no idea how the Heirs had opened the portal. Likely using some of their stolen magic.

A loud bang punctuated the falling icicles, followed by another and another. Ice exploded around Gemma and Catullus.

"Goddamn it," Catullus growled. "They're shooting at us. Can't stop to return fire. We'll be skewered before we fire a single round." A spear of ice plowed into the ground inches away, punctuating his words.

"Those bastards won't give up," she muttered. She glanced at a skittish Bryn. "Do something!"

"Such as what?" the pixie shrieked.

"You say you know everyone in this sodding forest." Catullus glared at Bryn. *"Call them."*

"Who?" Bryn cried.

"Anyone," snapped Gemma.

The pixie looked momentarily mystified; then epiphany lit his tiny face. He grinned, and suddenly winked out like an extinguished lamp.

"Little deserter," she muttered. But she couldn't blame Bryn. If she had the power to simply vanish herself and Catullus out of the path of danger, she'd do it without a please and thank you.

Catullus kept his steel grip on her wrist, and when a particularly large icicle plummeted down, he threw himself at Gemma. She felt herself pushed aside moments before the icicle would have gutted her. She and Catullus tumbled on the ground until he stopped their roll, blocking her with his body. His arms came up to cradle her to him as smaller spikes of ice clattered down. They bounced off his shoulders and back. She felt the hiss of his indrawn breath and knew that some of the spikes had broken through his heavy coat, wounding him.

He'd tear himself to tatters to protect her.

Shoving at his shoulders, Gemma pushed him back and leapt to her feet. She hauled him up with her, staggering a little at his weight, and pulled at him to keep running. Something wet gleamed in spots on his coat. His eyes glinted. He fought a grimace of pain, but did not slow in his step. They ducked and dodged. Bullets and ice, everywhere they turned.

She grit her teeth, moving onward, one arm wrapped around Catullus. They hadn't even reached the dangers of the Night Forest yet! And they might not reach it, not without some kind of help.

Yells of outraged shock sounded behind them. Gemma threw another fast glance over her shoulder. A tiny smile inched up the corners of her mouth.

Heirs scattered beneath an onslaught of wickedly sharp icicles. Huge spears of ice broke from their boughs, hurtling to earth and sending the pursuers running for cover.

"I thought you controlled the bloody ice!" one Heir shouted.

"This isn't me," yelped the magic-wielding Heir. He frantically waved his hands. "I can't make it stop!"

The other Heir's angry retort was lost beneath the crash of more falling ice. Thoughts of pursuit vanished as Heirs sought only to save their hides from impaling.

A strange quiet, though, descended where Catullus and Gemma continued to run. She glanced around. "It's stopped."

Catullus, jaw tight, also took stock. Though ice, and icicles, still covered the surrounding trees, none of it was falling down around Gemma and Catullus. The ice cast an eerie hush around them, punctuated by the distant sounds of crashing icicles and cursing Heirs.

Bryn winked back into existence. He hovered in front of Gemma and Catullus, wearing a smug grin. "This way."

They followed the pixie for some time, until they reached a secluded dell. Satisfied that they were safe, everyone stopped to catch their breath.

"The ice falling on the Heirs was your doing?" Gemma asked.

"Me, and my friends," the pixie answered.

Catullus frowned. "Don't see anybody."

"All around us." Bryn waved his minuscule hands.

"The trees," said Gemma.

Again, the pixie looked pleased with himself. "*Everything* is alive in Otherworld." He sent a scornful sneer back toward where the Heirs were presumably shielding themselves from the ice storm. "Their mage thinks he controls magic, but not here. Feeble little mortal." The idea of a creature as tiny as a pixie calling a human man "little" seemed ridiculous, but it only showed how appearances belied truth in this contrary, magic-imbued world.

"Thank you," said Catullus.

Bryn looked at Catullus sharply, hearing the note of suppressed pain in his voice. He fluttered around to inspect Catullus's injuries and made a sound of displeasure. Gemma made an even louder sound when she finally got a good look at the damage, peeling away the coat and jacket to reveal Catullus's bloodstained waistcoat. Several wounds dotted his back in a red constellation.

"Goddamn it, Catullus." Anger at the Heirs heated her face. She hoped those bastards were all skewered like suckling pigs. "We have to bind these wounds."

"'Sfine," but the slur in his words revealed that it *wasn't* fine. "No time for doctoring. Have to get to the Night Forest whilst the Heirs are distracted." He shrugged on his jacket and coat, sucking in his breath at the painful movement.

A hurried glance showed that the Heirs still fought to avoid the falling icicles, but the men hadn't stopped their advance. The closer the Heirs got, the greater likelihood that they'd start shooting again, and bring the falling ice spears—and the possibility that Gemma and Catullus would be impaled by the icicles—with them.

Catullus was right. He and Gemma *did* have to keep moving. And it infuriated her. She wanted to tend to him, care for him as he had protected her.

"Give me your flask," said Bryn.

"It's empty," Gemma bit out. She didn't have patience for the pixie's fondness for spirits. "You drank everything."

"Give it to me."

Muttering about tippling faeries, Gemma pulled the flask from one of Catullus's pockets. She handed it to Bryn, and felt an uncharitable glee when the pixie staggered under its weight. Bryn held the flask in his arms, shutting his eyes. He didn't attempt to take a drink. After a moment, he opened his eyes. "Doff your waistcoat and shirt."

Gemma hurried to help Catullus remove the garments. Under normal circumstances, she would have appreciated the sight of Catullus's bare torso, the planes and ridges of muscle shifting as he moved, but all she could see were the wounds scattered across his flesh. Each had a depth of about half an inch, and dark blood pooled and ran down the length of Catullus's back. She ground her teeth together to keep from crying out at the sight.

Though the injuries weren't of themselves life-threatening, they had to hurt like the devil, and the possibility of infection loomed, especially so far from mortal civilization and medicine.

Bryn offered the flask to Gemma.

She opened the flask and was surprised to find liquid inside. She sniffed it, frowning. "What is this?" Worry tightened her voice.

"Something he needs," came the answer.

"Neither of us can eat or drink anything in Otherworld," she objected.

"Not to drink," corrected Bryn. "Pour this over his wounds."

Still, she hesitated. "I don't want to hurt you."

"It's all right, Gemma," Catullus said.

Drawing a deep breath, Gemma poured the liquid green contents of the flask across Catullus's back. It smelled of musty cabbage. As the liquid hit his skin, sizzling and hissing around the wounds, he gave an involuntary grunt of pain. She immediately stopped pouring.

"It *is* hurting you."

"No, no. Keep going."

Reluctantly, she did, continuing to douse his flesh. Acrid bubbles foamed over the wounds. The smell was punitive.

She gasped. The punctures along his back . . .

"Catullus," she breathed.

He tried to look at his back and only succeeded in turning in circles.

As he spun around, Gemma *did* see his back, and gasped again. "The wounds . . . they're closing." Minuscule bits of fabric, embedded in the wounds, came bubbling up before dissolving. The injuries shrunk to pinpricks, then smaller, until nothing but smooth, unbroken skin covered his back. "How do you feel?"

"Fine. Good. Marvelous, actually. My thanks," he said to Bryn. "You're help has been invaluable. All the Blades will hear of your generosity."

"I can't thank you enough," added Gemma.

The pixie looked bashful. "'Tis only a bit of magic. And your cause is just."

Catullus smiled, a sight that blossomed inside Gemma. He picked up his coat and stuck a finger through one of the holes torn in the fabric. "But I'm afraid this Ulster is now truly a lost cause."

"I don't care about the damned coat." She threw her arms around him, feeling him whole and solid and perfect. "It's *you* I care about. It's *you* I love."

He jolted, dropping the coat, and she realized that the words had jumped from her mouth without any preamble.

"That's what I was trying to say," Gemma confessed, leaning back a little so she could look into his handsome, shocked face, "before the Heirs and their ice showed up. I'm a writer, so I have to pick my words carefully."

He watched her, eyes dark and bright, saying nothing.

"I wanted," she pressed on, "I really wanted, to say exactly the right thing at exactly the right time." Her laugh was rueful. "Guess I didn't get that chance. Just blabbed it out, and at a not very convenient moment." She shook her head. "So much for getting it right."

Catullus continued to stare at her, his expression so surprised as to be almost funny, if it didn't mean everything. Astonishment slowly left his face, replaced by cautious wonder. "Do you really mean that? That you . . . you . . ."

"Love you," she finished. "Yes. I love you, Catullus Graves." The words made her giddy, buoyant. It amazed her that a simple combination of consonants and vowels could contain the whole of human happiness. She cupped the back of his head, feeling the sleek muscles along his neck. The words she had been carefully piecing together at last emerged.

"I've never met anyone like you," she said, "and I never will again. I love your brain and your body. I love that you're just as strange as I am, that you accept me as *I* am. Just as I accept you as *you* are. All of our idiosyncrasies. Our quest to discover the world's secrets and stories."

She drew a breath, now finding words to be hollow substitutes for what she felt. After Richard, there had been other men in her life, in her bed. She thrived on excitement and enjoyed sex. Some of the men were a night's enjoyment and nothing more. They sneered at her afterward, calling her a whore for having their same desires. Gemma sat and smoked and gazed at them with boredom until they left.

Richard had said "I love you," but he had meant, "I want to own you."

She wanted to love and be loved, but the cost had been too high. She refused compromise. And that is what Richard had wanted: to stay the same while changing her to suit his definition of who he wanted her to be.

Catullus—he made Richard and the men she knew after resemble wind-up toys, repetitive in their actions, shrilling nonsense. Catullus saw her as she was. Not a tabula rasa to be molded and possessed. Not a prodigal to redeem. A woman. Complete and whole. He gave her room to use her own mind, her own will. And with every ounce of that will, she loved him. This bespectacled eccentric who thought like a scholar, fought like a warrior, and made love like a pagan.

"It makes a strange sense, to say this here." She waved at the ice-encrusted forest, the crystalline glade where they sheltered now. "A place of magic. You and I, we made our own magic." She let heat and intent steal into her eyes. "If there wasn't a passel of Heirs on our behinds, I'd show you *exactly* how much I love you."

Ferocious exultation sharpened him to gleaming brilliance. His eyes darkened, his arms enfolding her as his long, strapping body pressed close. God, she loved the feel of him. Vitally male. Solid and fit. Yet with the mind of a towering intellect.

Nothing intellectual in his look now. "Gemma," he rasped, lowering his head. She closed her eyes, waiting, wanting his kiss, his claim.

Something tugged him backward.

"Not *now*," Bryn piped, gripping Catullus's ear. "Must leave, must flee. Before the trees grow tired of their game."

Indeed, from within their sheltered glade, they could distantly hear the fall of icicles slowing. The tree branches began to quiet. The pursuers would gather themselves.

Catullus snarled something that would have been entirely unprintable in the *Trib*. He stepped away from Gemma and quickly threw on his shirt, waistcoat, jacket, and coat, all of the garments grimy and stained. But he did not seem to notice the condition of his clothes, which startled her. He was a changed man from the one who had been so fastidious in his wardrobe.

Once he dressed, he interlaced their hands. Their palms pressed together—the only flesh-on-flesh contact it seemed they would get for a while. A torment and solace.

"Lead on," he growled to Bryn. When the pixie flitted ahead, Catullus turned to Gemma. "Some time, some day," he said, low and fierce, "you and I are going to have a proper declaration of love. Hours and *hours* in bed."

"Hours?" Gemma repeated, an eyebrow raised. If what they had done in the cottage's bed was any indicator, those would be unforgettable hours.

"Days," he amended. "Weeks. I won't let either one of us leave that room, wherever it is, until we've both nearly perished from exhaustion and starvation."

"I'm starving right now." She pressed a hand to her empty stomach.

"So am I, love." His eyes gleamed wickedly. "And only you will sate me. I cannot wait to taste all of you again."

She flushed to hear her elegant scholar say such things to her, and flushed even deeper to realize how much she loved hearing him speak this way. And making good on his plans . . . that would be even better.

"Come *on*," Bryn shrilled.

At that moment, a bullet whizzed past Gemma and Catullus. Out of time.

Hand in hand, they ran deeper into the forest.

They left behind the Heirs, the ice-encrusted forest, heading deeper into the woods. The atmosphere shifted. Instead of lush summer, an autumnal cast descended, the trees growing thicker, more twisted, as gusts of chill air tossed dead leaves in eddies. Whispering sounded from darkened crevices. Creatures scuttled in the underbrush and overhead. A permanent dusk lengthened shadows, deepened by the close-set trees.

Gemma shivered, more from the sinister undercurrent than the cold. She stuck close to Catullus as they pushed onward, and even Bryn kept nearby instead of flying on ahead.

"This place could use some brightening up," she whispered. "A cheerful lamp, maybe a few colorful rugs."

"A box of lucifer matches." Catullus remained vigilant, attentive to everything around him, but his hand was warm and steady.

Bryn pulled up short, hovering. "There, ahead. The Night Forest."

All quips died as Gemma and Catullus had their first glimpse of eternal night.

Darkness formed a wall separating the Otherworld forest from the Night Forest. The transition was abrupt—on one side, feeble sunlight shone, and on the other, deepest night cloaked the woods. The faintest traces of moonlight gleamed on barren branches. Shapes of unidentified plants—or creatures—loomed. A low, keening wind rattled boughs and scrub.

Slowly, they approached the boundary. Catullus peered at it, moving his free hand back and forth between the two forests to watch the shift from light to darkness on his skin. "Extraordinary," he murmured.

"Mab's Cauldron is in *there*?" Gemma asked Bryn.

"I have heard that to find it, you must follow the Deathless River to the Lake of Shadows, cross the lake, and on the farthest bank, you will find the cauldron."

"Haven't you been there, yourself?" she asked.

The pixie's eyes widened in alarm. "None of my kind ever venture into the Night Forest. It is sure death."

Not the most reassuring words Gemma had ever heard.

"We're on our own, then," Catullus said.

"I will wait for your return." Bryn did not appear particularly happy with even this prospect, but he settled himself atop a large toadstool.

Catullus gave the pixie a bow. "Again, you've my thanks, and the gratitude of all of the Blades for your assistance. Our debt to you—"

Bryn waved this away. "What I did was freely given. No obligation or debt exists between us."

"Come to headquarters, once this is all over. I think we've a surplus of excellent Scotch that needs depleting."

The promise of future whiskey brightened Bryn a great deal. He smothered his glee to nod regally. "I shall consider it."

Unspoken, but present in everyone's minds, was the very real possibility that neither Catullus nor Gemma would make it out of the Night Forest alive.

Bryn stuck out his hand, and Catullus offered him a forefinger to shake. Gemma likewise held out a finger, but instead of shaking the tip, as he'd done with Catullus,

Bryn swept off his hat and, with a flourish worthy of an old-fashioned courtier, kissed her finger.

"I'm immortal, you know," he piped. "Never grow old, unlike *him*."

"Thanks," she answered, "but I'll stay with my aging mortal."

Catullus scowled. "I'm not *aging*."

"We're both getting older," Gemma said. She cast a glance toward the thick gloom of the Night Forest. "Though I think this next adventure might take a few decades off my life."

Catullus brushed a strand of hair off her cheek, his eyes warm. "Together, we'll face it."

Knowing he would be with her every step of the way, she felt her courage return. What was an old dark forest, when the man she loved walked beside her? Yet that small, doubting voice whispered again, try as she did to ignore it. *Even love*, it murmured, *is no guarantee of protection*. Astrid Bramfield had loved her first husband, and he'd died in her arms. Would she or Catullus have to face the torment of watching the other die?

No—she pushed aside doubt and apprehension. They had a duty, and nothing must stop them. Too much lay in the balance. Fear had to be conquered. For herself. For Catullus. And the fate of all nations.

With a final parting, she and Catullus left Bryn, stepping over the boundary into eternal night.

Chapter 18

Perilous Crossings

Profound cold enveloped her. It was not simply a matter of less light or its absence, but a vacuum, utter and complete. This part of Otherworld had never felt the touch or warmth of the sun. Back in the mortal world, even in the depths of night an echo of heat remained in the ground. No trace of warmth here in the Night Forest. And with its absence came palpable dread.

It was all Gemma could do to keep from climbing onto Catullus's back, trying to borrow some of his heat and vitality. Instead, she crept beside him as they slowly delved into the vast, bitter reaches of the Night Forest.

"Can't see anything," she whispered. Something plucked at her skirt, and she whirled with her fists ready, only to discover the offending creature was, in fact, a tree branch.

"I had a device to see in the darkness." Catullus moved some undergrowth aside, giving them both room to pass. "Sadly, I had to leave it behind in Canada. And all of my illumination tubes were used up."

She didn't know what an illumination tube was, but she had no doubt it would be useful right now. "Anything else in those numerous pockets of yours? A lantern? Torch?"

"My screwdrivers are handy," he murmured, "but they won't allow us to see in the dark. As for making a lantern or torch . . . a peculiar thing about light in dark places—it acts as a lure."

"No torch, then," she said quickly.

"We'll just have to let our eyes grow adjusted."

He was right, of course. Gemma hadn't boasted when she said she had excellent night vision. In minutes, she could see. Not as well as if it were day, but well enough to know that she didn't like what lay before her.

From within, the Night Forest was a nightmare landscape. As in the other part of the Otherworld forest, huge trees dominated the surroundings, only here, all life had been stripped from the trees. Their branches stretched toward the inky sky like misshapen limbs, once broken, improperly set. Thickets of thorns covered the ground, scratching at any exposed flesh. Looking up at the boughs overhead, Gemma saw silver-eyed creatures scuttling along, clicking their claws and watching the progression of the two mortals foolish enough to enter their home.

Gemma started when she realized many of the trees weren't trees at all, but bark-covered beings, half crone, half tree. Pale, hanging moss served as their hair. Knots in their trunks formed their numerous eyes. They reached out with long, twiggy fingers to pick at Gemma's hair and Catullus's coat, and when Gemma slapped their hands away, they cackled, the sound like splintering wood.

Catullus kept his shotgun ready, and she took some comfort from this and the derringer in her pocket, but she had no idea whether bullets could harm, let alone kill, anything in this forest. She hoped it wouldn't come to that.

Catullus spoke, his voice a welcome comfort in the darkness. "Bryn said we're to follow the Deathless River to the Lake of Shadows." He smiled, wry. "Charming names."

"Think of the bragging rights they'll get you. Sitting by

the fire, smoking your pipe, talking about that one time you and the American scribbler—"

"*My* American scribbler," he corrected.

She liked the sound of that. "The two of you faced some of the worst, most horrible monsters imaginable along the banks of the Deathless River."

"Fighting side by side—" He drew closer.

"Fearlessly defeating whatever foul beast crossed your path—" She, too, stepped nearer.

"Until you came to Mab's Cauldron, and there confronted the Witch Queen herself—"

"Who saw that she was no match for your might and intellect—"

"And, after vowing her eternal protection—"

"And generously giving bags full of gold and jewels—"

"Presented a goblet full of water, which was used to free Merlin—"

"Stop Arthur, defeat the Heirs—"

"And save the world—"

"After which, a huge meal of mutton pie and biscuits was devoured—"

"Followed by weeks in bed."

She slid her hands up his sleek chest. "Kiss me."

He did. Awareness of everything fell away. There was only him, his mouth exploring, demanding. She felt it in the communion of their mouths, the difference a few words had, imbuing each stroke of their tongues, each taste with greater depth and meaning. Bound. They had bound themselves to each other, willingly, finding in each other their perfect counterpart.

A rattle in the nearby bushes broke them reluctantly apart. They both panted with frustrated desire. It did not seem to matter that they were in the middle of a sinister, perilous forest. She wanted him. And she knew from the rasp of his breathing that he wanted her. Not here, though, not now.

"The river," he grated. "Have to find the river."

"Yes. Right." She stepped back and pressed her palms to her cheeks. He'd dispelled the chill that had settled in her from their first steps into the Night Forest. "We don't have a guide."

"Don't need one. Most places Blades tread aren't on the map."

"Blades have never been to a parallel world of magic," she noted.

"True," he acknowledged. "Though the setting has changed, being a Blade hasn't."

"Meaning?"

"We both have all we need to find our way. Here"—he pointed to his eyes—"and here"—he indicated his ears.

"What about taste?"

"Rather not lick anything—except you, of course—if I can help it."

Catullus . . . *licking* her. She shook her head to gather her scattered wits. For a few moments, they stood quietly, listening. Then—

"I hear something," she said.

At the same time, Catullus said, "There."

Distantly, the sound of rushing water. A river.

With careful, deliberate steps, they followed the sound. Boggy ground made the going even slower, not to mention a nest of hissing, luminescent snakes in their path. Gemma and Catullus cautiously made their way, the noise of running water growing louder and closer. Until, finally, they found themselves standing on the bank of a river.

It wasn't a wide river, but Gemma had no desire to get close to it. The water gave off an evil, sulfurous stench. Ordinarily, rivers flowed fresh and clear, but the Deathless River ran a sludgy, murky course. Sharp-tipped reeds scraped like rusty knives along the banks, and jagged rocks slick with moss and fungus rose up from the riverbed.

Gemma thought she saw some yellow-eyed creature slither into the water.

"Our senses proved themselves," Catullus said, surveying the river. "Here's our path."

"I'm not swimming in that." There was brave, and then there was brainless.

He looked appalled by the very idea. "Good God, no. We'll just follow it until we come to the Lake of Shadows."

He made it sound so easy. But if Gemma had learned, almost nothing came easily. If it did, it wasn't worth having.

The Deathless River held nothing *but* death, a constantly shifting course of water that reeked of decay and served as home for dozens of repulsive, disturbing creatures. Even the Thames in the summer couldn't compete for sheer noxiousness.

Catullus did not mind. He was almost content to follow the river's path—though the fumes around it *did* make his eyes burn—holding close to his heart the knowledge that Gemma loved him

She loves me.

He'd known he was lonely, and envious of his friends for finding their own companions, but it wasn't until he'd gained Gemma's love that he realized how much he needed it, needed her.

All the more reason for him to stay sharply alert as they trekked beside the Deathless River. He never regarded himself as extraordinarily protective. He trusted the Blades, male and female, to look out for themselves, just as they trusted him to do the same. They watched each others' backs. And while he did have faith in Gemma's spirit and intelligence, the fierce, irrational need to shelter and protect her overrode all other instincts. It burned, this need, like a fire that consumed him from the inside out.

They carefully picked their way beside the river. Catullus

positioned himself so that he stood between Gemma and the water. Whatever threatened her would have to go through him.

And creatures were certainly trying.

"Buggering bastard!" Catullus kicked at a tentacle that slithered up the riverbank, toward him and Gemma. The tentacle recoiled, but didn't retreat. He swung his shotgun overhead and slammed the butt down. The end of the tentacle broke off with a wet squish. Dark, sticky blood squirted out, spattering on Catullus's boots.

Sullen, the tentacle slunk back into the river.

"I'd suggest we walk through the woods and not on the bank," Gemma said, "but that looks even worse."

Catullus glanced over toward the forest, though he knew what he would see. Darting from tree to tree, gape-mouthed trolls followed the mortals' progress. The trolls panted and drooled.

"I think we're supposed to be breakfast," she added.

"Just keep moving." Catullus growled at the trolls, and was rewarded with the beasts scuffling away, gibbering to one another.

The past hour had held more of the same—an unending barrage of Otherworld's most nasty, malicious beings. Between Gemma and Catullus, they had fended off carnivorous will-o'-the-wisps, goblins with poisoned teeth and an appetite for human flesh, and a pack of the same huge, lantern-eyed black dogs they'd had the misfortune of meeting in the mortal world.

"Our mortal energy seems to be an attractant," Catullus mused. He eyed a twisted hobgoblin-like creature crouched on the opposite bank. The creature watched them pass, clutching a sharp pike that looked well used. On its head it wore a bright red cap, and Catullus had a very good idea what served as the cap's dye. He increased the length of his strides, careful to ensure Gemma kept up.

She said, "There's got to be some way to conceal or cover our energy."

"Short of using magic ourselves, I cannot fathom how. Perhaps there's some way to use your own magic."

She stopped and closed her eyes. As she concentrated, Catullus kept watch for anything that might try to attack. After some time, she opened her eyes and growled in frustration. "I can open doors, mental and physical, but hiding our mortal energy isn't part of the package."

"We'll stay on guard. And not slow down."

Pushing onward, they continued to follow the river. Heavy, oppressive darkness pressed down on them—it was nigh impossible to keep one's spirits up amidst such gloom. Gemma's footsteps began to slow, her head drooping lower and lower, until she seemed to drag herself along the riverbank.

"Keep going," he said, when she suddenly halted.

She heaved a deep sigh. "I don't know why we're bothering. Even if we somehow survive this slog, Mab's Cauldron might not even be where Bryn said it was. He's never seen it. The whole thing could be a complete waste of time." Her eyes dulled with hopelessness as she sat down heavily. "And if it *does* exist, we have to bring water all the way back to free Merlin. The return journey could be fatal. Plus, the Heirs are still out there. If the Night Forest doesn't kill us, the Heirs certainly will. Merlin's out of his mind, so we don't know if we can rely on him. Then there's Arthur—"

Catullus strode to Gemma and crouched in front of her. "Stop it. This isn't you."

"But—"

"*No*, Gemma. It's this place." He gripped Gemma's shoulders, forcing her to look at him. "It sucks out the life and spirit, makes one want to give up. We can't. We won't." Seeing that she was about to object, he pressed on. "Yes, the odds are great, but that's what makes the adventure worth having. We have to fight, and keep on fighting. Use my strength if you have to, but you've enough of your own to make it through, to triumph."

"You really think so?" Finally, hope began to shine in her gaze.

"I know it to be true." He spoke with firm conviction. "You and I, we're the strangers, the outsiders, which means we're the best people for this quest. In all the fairy tales, it's the misfit who saves the day. Just as you and I will prevail."

Her shoulders straightened, and she lifted her chin. The Gemma that he knew, and loved, emerged, burning brightly with her vivacity and determination. "We'll take no prisoners."

"And have the Heirs weeping for mercy."

She smiled. He allowed himself relief to see her nihilism cast aside. "Thank you," she whispered, leaning close to press her mouth to his. "Don't know what came over me."

"In this place, anyone would be hard-pressed not to curl into a ball and weep."

"Not you," she noted.

"I have you to lift my spirits up." He nuzzled the juncture of her jaw and neck. "And lift up other things, as well."

She chuckled in appreciation.

A sound caught his attention. He lifted his head to hear it better. It was soft, almost too soft to hear, tantalizing with its very faintness. He strained to listen. A woman's voice? Or music? Or both?

"Catullus?"

He rose, barely hearing Gemma. Instead, he felt powerfully drawn to discover the source of the sound. Hardly aware of himself, he drifted away from Gemma, toward those faint, but fascinating, notes. He felt dazed, removed. The part of his brain that thought and analyzed—the majority of his thoughts—simply went dark, like a deserted building.

He shouldered into the forest, away from the river. Dimly, he heard Gemma calling his name, but he paid no attention, just as he disregarded the thorns that cut his face and hands as he delved into the woods. The music enthralled him as he went farther into the woods. It held a plaintive tone, sweetly persuasive, unlike any music he'd ever heard. All he knew was that he *had* to reach its origin.

In a clearing, he stopped. And stared. A woman stood there, beautiful and young. She smiled at him as she sang. She wore a long green gown, her golden hair loose about her shoulders. He did not know the language of her song, but, as she opened her arms to him, he was compelled to go to her.

As he drew nearer, he could not look away from her face. It shone like polished ivory, without a line, utterly smooth. Her lips were deeply red, as if flushed from wine, and her eyes were solid black.

"Dance with me," she sang, or, at least, he *thought* that is what she said. He couldn't be sure. She beckoned with slim hands topped by long fingernails.

Something, some buried voice told him this wasn't right. He wanted no woman but Gemma. Yet he could not stop himself, could not break away from this unknown siren.

Wordlessly, he stepped into her arms. She stopped singing, yet the music continued, weaving down from the surrounding trees and further muddling his brain.

Her hands curled around his, her grip strong and cold. They turned in the steps of a dance. Her black gaze held his—he could not look away, even when he felt the woman's nails rake down his face and throat.

"Catullus!"

He continued to dance with the woman, staring at her impossibly perfect face. Something behind him caught the woman's attention, and she snarled at it over his shoulder. If he had been in possession of his faculties, he would have seen how the woman's lovely features twisted like an angry animal's, but all he could do was gaze into her eyes and keep dancing.

"You want a bullet in your brain, lady?"

Gemma. He wanted to turn to her, tear himself from this woman, but could not. His limbs did not belong to him, and his mind went wandering amidst the labyrinthine turns of the unearthly music.

The woman laughed, and the sound was arctic, soulless. "Mortals and their harmless toys. But your lover can bleed."

He felt himself pulled closer to the woman, as if she used his body to block her own. Again, her nails scored him, and warm liquid trickled down his face. She leaned close and licked his cheek, making an appreciative sound. "Your blood is delicious, mortal. Full of light. I cannot wait to drain you of it."

Gemma cursed.

The woman began to lap at his skin again, but she hissed when Gemma shoved between them. He staggered back from the force of Gemma's shove.

"Maybe bullets won't work," Gemma gritted. "Let's try a blade, instead." She brandished Catullus's horn-handled hunting knife.

The woman shrieked as Gemma swung the knife toward her. Shivering in fear, the woman slunk back toward the shelter of the forest. She held her long-nailed hands out for protection. The music abruptly stopped.

Gemma advanced, holding the knife. "I don't cotton to uncanny whores trying to drink my man's blood." Her gaze was steely as she stared down at the woman huddling at her feet. "Get the hell out of my sight, or I'll cut off your claws—starting at the wrist."

Trembling, the woman turned and scuttled away. As she ran, the hem of her gown caught on a low-lying branch, revealing not a pair of human feet, but cloven hooves. With a snarl and tug, the creature—for she was no woman—freed herself and disappeared into the woods.

Catullus felt his mind, his will, come back into himself. He shook his head, trying to clear his thoughts, to find

Gemma standing in front of him, dabbing at the scrapes on his face and throat.

"Gemma . . ."

Gruff, Gemma said, "You all right? She didn't drink too much of your blood?"

"I'm fine. You stopped her before she could do more." He held himself still beneath her ministrations, which weren't precisely gentle.

"I didn't like seeing that." Gemma's voice was tight, faintly angry. "Seeing her touching and *licking* you. I almost wish she did put up a fight so I could've taught her a lesson."

"She learned, unquestionably." He stopped her hand rubbing at his face. "I'm sorry. I didn't want to go to her."

"You had no choice. That thing used powerful magic." Her eyes were sharp blue knives, yet she kept her hand within his. "This is new—jealousy. I've never felt it."

"I only want you, Gemma."

"Good." She pulled his head down into a possessive kiss.

He did not enjoy making her jealous, but he liked this, her heat and boldness. And, he admitted to himself, there was something darkly, erotically thrilling about her jealousy, having her want him all for her own. No one had ever felt that way about him before.

Yet the kiss ended too quickly. Threats loomed in the darkness. They had to keep going.

The Lake of Shadows was a black mirror reflecting back more darkness, an expanse of liquid night ringed by skeletal trees. Their branches reached up into the inky sky like worshippers invoking a god of calamity. Periodic shapes rose up from the lake's surface—the low humps of some creature's back breaking the water, then dipping back down into the depths with a heavy slide. Winged beasts flapped low over the water.

Somewhere, on the far bank of the lake, was Mab's Cauldron. The key to averting disaster.

As if expecting Gemma and Catullus, a small boat perched on the shore where they emerged from the forest. Gingerly, they stepped forward to examine the vessel.

"Looks like a perfectly ordinary rowboat," Catullus murmured, studying it. Oars waited in the oarlocks, and, while the hull wasn't in pristine condition, Catullus could not find any holes or anything else that might compromise the boat's buoyancy or integrity.

"Seems awfully convenient." Gemma eyed the water.

"Such boats and devices are often found in fairy tales. If any place would follow those guidelines, it must be Otherworld."

"Maybe we're being led into a trap. We could walk around the perimeter of the lake."

"You see there?" He pointed to the edges of the lake, where dark jagged shapes rose. "Rock formations. Or creatures that look like rocks. Climbing them will take as much time, and be equally, if not more, dangerous. And Bryn said that we must cross the Lake of Shadows, not go around it."

"Fairy tales are also very specific about directions. There's always a reason why someone must go a certain direction." She blew out an exasperated breath. "Looks like we're taking a little water jaunt."

"I'll row." He tested the oars and found they moved fairly smoothly in their locks. If only he could go to his workshop and get some oil! But then, if he had access to his workshop, he could build something a hell of a lot more sturdy and safe than a undersized wooden rowboat.

"I can't just sit back and twirl my parasol while you serenade me."

"No singing on this excursion. You stay alert for any signs of danger."

She glanced at the lake, and the dark forms that broke its surface and flew over its waters. "Guess I'll be busy."

* * *

"I can't remember the last time I was in a rowboat. Must have been years ago." Catullus moved forward and back as he rowed, adjusting to the slightly unfamiliar movement. It took a try or two, but he quickly gained his rhythm. The boat glided smoothly through the still water.

"Courting a sweetheart?" Gemma sat in the prow, her back to him, as she kept watch for threats.

"Courting fish is more probable. Bennett and I used to go on fishing trips in Devon. Never caught much. He hates to get up early and won't stop talking."

"I'm surprised you two are such good friends. You're so different from each other."

He truly hadn't thought of that. "Perhaps that's why we are good chums. Balance."

"Is it different, now that he's married?"

Catullus chuckled, rueful. "Wouldn't know. We haven't been in the same place for more than a few days in months. And I cannot begrudge him his happiness. He's needed the right woman in his life for a long while."

Gemma cast a wry look over her shoulder. "Seems like he had plenty of female company."

"Not the *right* kind."

"You sound downright moral."

He grunted. "I pass no judgment on Bennett—or anyone, I hope. But the needs of one's body and the needs of one's heart aren't always the same thing."

"Speaking from experience."

"It would have been grim, indeed, if I'd been a virgin at forty-one." He cleared his throat, wondering how to broach a topic that had been in his mind for some time. "And with you, when did you . . . have you had many . . . ?" Just the thought of another man touching Gemma sent bolts of unfettered fury through him. And if he so much as considered someone else kissing her, let alone . . . God help him. He

Zoë Archer

discovered . . . he was a jealous man. It wasn't Gemma he mistrusted, it was everyone else.

Was time travel truly possible? He might seriously consider developing a device that enabled him to travel back and beat each man who ever kissed her.

She turned to face him. "Let's give each other the same benefit. You've had other lovers. So have I. None of them matter now." The truth of this shone in her eyes.

The tightness around his heart eased. "You're correct. It doesn't matter." He would not change a thing about her, because everything, including the lovers that had come before him, made her who she was now, and to him, she was exactly right.

She smiled, and began to speak, but the boat suddenly rocked from side to side. Something heavy knocked into the hull.

Gemma braced her hand on the side of the boat as it pitched, and Catullus held tight to the oars. They held themselves still, waiting to see if the bump to the hull had been mere happenstance—possibly a bit of wood or other flotsam knocking into the vessel.

Thump.

The boat rocked harder.

"Maybe your knife will ward it off," Gemma whispered.

Balancing one oar across his knees, he unsheathed and brandished his blade, holding it over the water.

Thump. Violently, the boat pitched as the creature—whatever it was—struck the hull again. Catullus sheathed his knife, since it did not seem to have the ability to ward off this new threat.

"Can you swim?" he demanded.

"Yes, but"—she cast a wary look toward the water—"I'd sooner not."

"Trust me, love." He gritted as the boat received another battering. "If there is anything I do not want, it is for the boat to capsize and us to take a dip." At the least, neither of them would drown, but that was only assuming they were left alone. Given the fact that something kept ramming the boat, that was unlikely.

Catullus whirled, shotgun in hand, at a rasping snarl off the portside. Gemma spun to face the sound, as well, and gasped.

It was, quite simply, one of the most disgusting creatures Catullus had ever seen. The beast that rose up from the water resembled a large horse with only one eye and a gaping mouth. From its back a man's torso emerged, almost as if its rider had somehow been fused to the flesh of the animal. The human-shaped portion of the creature had long, long arms tipped with claws, and an oversized head that swayed back and forth as if too heavy to be supported by its neck.

Disturbing as all this was, the most alarming aspect of the beast was the fact that it had no skin. All the muscles were exposed, twitching and shifting as it moved. Veins throbbing with blood covered its body in a grisly network. Through the sinews and veins, a few pulsing organs could be seen.

In the darkness, the creature was the embodiment of nightmare. And it wanted the mortals within the boat. It charged.

Catullus fired two blasts from his shotgun. The beast jerked and slowed from the impact to its body, but didn't go down. Snarling from both its human and horse mouths, it charged again. Shots from Gemma's pistol had even less effect than Catullus's shotgun. The creature kept coming.

"How do we stop this thing?" Gemma shouted.

"Damned if I know." But he'd try.

The creature drew up right beside the boat. It was even more nauseating up close as it shied, waving legs that were partly flipper. Sensing Gemma was the easier prey, its humanoid arms reached out for her.

Catullus attacked. He swung his shotgun by its barrel, slamming the stock into the beast's horse head.

It shrieked. The boat rocked harder. Gemma clung to the sides, crouching low to keep from falling out.

Catullus braced his legs wide and lashed out with his shotgun. Every time the creature lunged, he dug the gun's butt into the creature's unprotected flesh.

With an outraged scream, the beast pounded one leg against the hull. The boat pitched, and Catullus suddenly lost his balance. His shotgun fell to the bottom of the boat as he tumbled into the lake. He heard Gemma shout his name. Dark, chill water closed over his head.

He pushed his way back to the surface, hampered by his long coat. As he broke the surface, gasping for air, something grabbed him, then pulled him back down.

The water all around was black. He could see nothing, but he felt the creature's slippery flesh and net of veins as it swam around him. It clawed at him, its horse's mouth also snapping. He managed to dodge the creature's flailing legs and landed a series of punches along its body. It was impossible to know where the creature was, or predict its movements. He fought to keep what breath he had when one of its humanoid hands clutched his throat.

The creature dragged him forward, and he grasped its wrist with both hands, trying to break its hold. Its human face swam into view as he was pulled closer. The thing resembled an opium-addicted anatomist's drawing, red flesh and white ligaments stretched over its monstrous head. Muscles twitching, it opened its mouth to reveal long, cutting teeth.

Catullus's lungs burned, his vision dimmed, and he definitively did *not* want this creature to bite him. He pulled his knife and slashed at the arm that held him, cutting deeply into the ropy muscles until black blood swirled.

The beast screamed in pain. Its hold suddenly lessened. With a shove, Catullus broke free and pushed his way up.

He broke the water's surface, gasping. Gemma was a dark shape balanced in the other dark form of the boat.

She cried out to him, "Catullus! Thank God! Swim back and I'll pull you in."

Gladly. He swam toward her, narrowing the distance between them. He had only a few feet to go when the creature shot up from the water. It blocked him from reaching the boat, shrieking.

"Bugger," muttered Catullus.

The beast reared up, readying to strike with its feet and long arms. Its horse's neck stretched toward him. Catullus prepared himself for the attack.

There was a loud thump, and the creature shrieked again. It abruptly halted its charge. Another bang sounded. The beast threw up its arms to shield itself from this new assault. Catullus peered into the darkness to see what attacked the monster.

Gemma. She clutched an oar and swung it down onto the creature's human head. The blow made a wet, thick smack. When the beast tried to swipe at her, she slammed the oar onto its cut arm, then across its back. It screamed in pain.

"That's for you, you piece of beef! Straight from the Chicago slaughterhouse!"

Catullus seized the distraction. He positioned himself in front of the horse's head, then plunged his knife into the monster's single eye.

The creature's bellow reverberated across the lake.

It pulled away, blood pouring down its horse's head. Flailing, the creature bolted. It swam off before sinking into the water.

Catullus did not wait to see if it would reappear. He swam to the side of the boat. Gemma dropped the oar— the heavy piece of wood thudding as it hit the bottom of the vessel—and reached down to haul him up. They both strained, him pushing, her pulling, until he dragged himself over the side to lie, sodden and exhausted, alongside the discarded oar and, he was pleased to discover, his shotgun. At least that hadn't taken the dive overboard with him. He still wore his spectacles, too.

Crouching at his side, her hands flew over him, testing for injuries.

"I'm fine," he said, though his voice came out a little hoarser than he expected.

She let out an unsteady breath. "At least you don't smell anymore."

"I do not smell." He sat upright and began fitting the oars back into the locks.

"Anymore." At his outraged expression, she laughed softly. "We had a bath, but our clothes are long past their prime. Trust me, we *both* have grown a little ripe."

"If there's anyone with whom I want to reek," he said, chuckling, "I want to reek with you."

"That's one of the nicest and most bizarre things anyone's ever said to me."

He tested the oars. They moved smoothly in their locks. "I made no claims to being ordinary."

"And neither did I."

He took up his position at the oars. No choice but to move forward.

Chapter 19

Conundrums

Catullus deemed it a minor miracle that he and Gemma crossed the remainder of the lake without incident. After the retreat of the monster, he fully anticipated it returning, along with several dozen of its closest friends, seeking retribution. Either the monster was less popular than Catullus had assumed, or all the denizens of the lake took its fate as a warning and stayed away.

He didn't care why the voyage was uneventful. All that mattered was reaching the far shore safely. When the prow of the boat touched the gravel-strewn bank, he practically threw Gemma out onto dry land, then followed.

"I'll take you boating in Regent's Park," he said as they stared at the unctuous surface of the lake. It appeared deceptively calm, yet he knew from experience what lived beneath the surface. "Much more pleasant."

"Less exciting."

"At this point, I'm willing to endure a little tedium."

More dense forest ran up to the lake's edge. After checking to make sure his shotgun was loaded and his knife ready, Catullus led Gemma into the woods.

They pushed through branches and brambles, unremitting

darkness on all sides. The cries of animals and other beings shrilled. Fighting weariness, Catullus wondered what god-awful beast or creature he'd have to battle next. The Night Forest held more than its share. If he ever did get a full night's sleep, doubtless he'd have bad dreams about this place. He was so willing to find a nice, quiet, soft bed for himself and Gemma—without the prospect of being trapped—he'd endure whatever nightmares visited.

The forest opened to a dell. Both he and Gemma started, sensing the potent air of magic surging through the clearing.

They spotted it at the same time. A three-legged pot, large and heavy, stood above cold ashes. A domed lid covered it. The pot looked precisely like the kind of vessel a witch used for brewing potions and poisons, yet surprisingly ordinary. As they drew closer, Catullus saw that the pot had no inscriptions, no decoration. It was homely and plain. Yet its unprepossessing appearance belied the power it radiated. Surely such magic would hold the key to freeing Merlin.

"This is it," Gemma whispered.

"Mab's Cauldron."

Catullus carefully set his hand on the handle of the lid. He waited to see if any charm or protective spell might come into play. More than one Blade lost a digit or eyebrow to a charm.

Nothing happened. Still, he wouldn't leave much to chance.

"Stand back," he cautioned Gemma.

She took a step backward. Not quite far enough for his liking.

"Farther," he said.

"I can't see anything if I'm too far away."

"And you'll be safer, too."

"I'm a *journalist*. You'll have to knock me unconscious

to keep me back." She scowled at him. "Are you thinking about it?"

"I do not hit women. Though I am contemplating how quickly I can concoct a sedative."

Her gaze narrowed. Then, to his relief, she took another step backward. "If I miss anything," she warned, "I'll turn your waistcoat collection into ribbons."

"You'll see everything. But when I lift the lid, you have to cover your eyes."

"Catullus—"

"To protect your eyes. If I have to part with my waistcoat collection to keep you from going blind, I'll do it."

This admission startled her, knowing as she did how precious his waistcoats were to him. Not the one he was wearing, of course, which was now utterly filthy and ruined. He started collecting waistcoats soon after his eighteenth birthday, and while his body had changed since then—he'd grown still taller, filled out, and added muscle—his love of a beautiful waistcoat had not altered. By his calculations, he owned approximately two hundred and twenty-five of the garments. They represented years of travel, since he loved to buy new waistcoats in exotic locations, and an investment of nearly a thousand pounds.

He'd give them all up without thought if it meant keeping Gemma whole and safe.

"I'll cover my eyes," she said.

He nodded. "At my count. One . . . two . . . three. Now!"

Gemma clapped a hand over her eyes as Catullus lifted the cauldron's lid. He, too, shielded his eyes, using his forearm to cover them.

He braced himself for whatever protective spell had been woven around the cauldron.

A minute passed. And then another.

"Can I look now?" Gemma asked.

Taking his arm from his eyes, Catullus peered carefully

at the cauldron. Water filled it, yet the water remained still and calm.

"Go ahead," he said.

She took her hands from her eyes and stood on tiptoe to get a better view. "Anything?"

"No, just some water."

"After all that hullabaloo, this is a bit of a letdown."

He sent her a quelling look. "Better you be disappointed than hurt, or worse."

"Yes, Preacher Graves."

Catullus resisted the urge to growl. Loving Gemma meant he had to embrace every aspect of her, including her cheekiness. He'd rather she be full of fire and impudence than meek and malleable.

Setting the lid on the ground, he studied the cauldron and its contents. Experimentally, he took a twig from the ground and stuck it into the water. Nothing happened. He tossed the twig aside, then dipped the tip of his finger in the water. Again, nothing.

"This seems suspiciously easy," said Gemma, edging closer.

"I have to agree. No magic yields without difficulty. Yet"—he glanced around—"no creatures or faerie are guarding the cauldron, no spells of defense have been cast, and the water itself appears to be simply that: water."

"Maybe we've finally caught a break."

He made a noncommittal sound. If it truly *was* to be this easy, he would not complain. They still had to cross the Lake of Shadows again, and make their way through the rest of the Night Forest. More of the forest's inhabitants would surely try to make a meal or capture him and Gemma. He'd not question any gifts.

From a pocket, he pulled his empty flask. He pushed up his sleeve before dipping the flask into the water. The small container filled.

He lifted the flask from the water and quickly screwed

the cap back on. "Water for Merlin. Now, all we have to do is take it to him."

"Good. I won't be very sorry to see the last of this forest. Can't wait to feel the sun again."

They both turned to retrace their steps. Catullus shifted the flask from one hand to the other. As he did this, something peculiar caught his attention. He held the flask up to his ear and shook it.

"I cannot hear anything."

"We both saw you fill it just a minute ago." She studied the flask. "Maybe it's too full to make a sloshing sound."

Seeking to allay his concerns, Catullus unscrewed the cap and tried to peer inside the flask. The opening was too small for him to see the contents. Figuring that he could always get more water from the cauldron, he tipped the flask to pour some of the liquid onto the ground.

Nothing came out of the flask.

He shook it, inverting it completely. Not a drop came out.

Catullus and Gemma shared a look. "Is there a hole in the flask?" she asked.

He rapped it with his knuckles. "This is solid silver. Having made it myself as a gift to Bennett, I can state with absolute authority that it doesn't leak. The flask was also in my hand the whole time, and I never saw or felt anything trickling out."

"Try filling it again," she urged.

He did. This time, he did not replace the cap. As he held up the flask, both he and Gemma stared intently at it. No drips or leaks. He tipped the flask. Nothing came out.

"Maybe we should try filling something else," suggested Gemma.

Catullus glanced around the clearing. After spotting a thick fallen branch, he broke it apart into smaller pieces. He used his hunting knife—now darkened with blood from the lake creature—to whittle the wood into a small cup.

The hard wood made for a watertight vessel, so Catullus's confidence was high.

The cup was dipped into the cauldron and filled. The moment Catullus lifted it out of the water, the cup's contents vanished. He tried this two more times, and each time had the same result, even after he placed his hand over the top of the cup. As soon as the cup left the cauldron, the water within the cup disappeared.

Catullus dropped the wooden container onto the ground. Truly frustrated, he cupped his hands together and plunged them into the water. Yet it made no difference whether the vessel holding the water was a solid flask, a wooden cup, or his hands. The water simply dematerialized when it was taken from the cauldron.

"Son of a bitch," Catullus gritted. He grasped the cauldron's handle. "I'll just have to carry the damned thing back to Merlin." With a grunt, he attempted to pick up the cauldron. It refused to budge. He tried once more. It did not move.

He stared at the cauldron, mystified. It would be heavy, especially made of solid metal and filled with water, but Catullus worked very hard to ensure his physical strength. It meant life or death in the field. Lifting this cauldron would be difficult, but possible.

"Let me help." Gemma stood, shoulder to shoulder with him, and also gripped the handle. At her nod, both she and Catullus strained with all their might to lift the cauldron.

After several minutes, they both stopped lifting, huffing from their exertions.

"This damned thing isn't going anywhere," Gemma panted.

"I should have known." Catullus ran the back of one hand across his damp forehead. "A Blade should always remember: If something looks too easy to be true, it is."

Gemma displayed her aptitude for cursing. The swearing that came from her pretty mouth would have made even the most battle-hardened sailor proud. Catullus was impressed. When she was done, she also pushed up her sleeves.

"All right," she announced, "I refuse to be beaten by some hunk of metal. Enough playing, cauldron." She glared at the offending hunk of metal. "Now it's time to do this the hard way."

Gemma studied the cauldron. It looked as ordinary as a large metal pot could, but as she'd just witnessed, its appearance deceived. Clearly, this was a test, one she fully intended to pass.

"It's a riddle," said Catullus, also studying the cauldron. He crossed his arms over his chest and stared down at the pot as if it were a mathematical equation that needed to be reasoned out. "Can't tell you how many times Blades have faced similar conundrums." He quirked an eyebrow. "Something about magic seems to feed on these puzzles. A direct proportion between the amount of power and the complexity of the riddle. That, and I think magic just likes to frustrate the hell out of people."

"If magic thinks its going to beat us today," she said, walking around the cauldron, "then it's mistaken. Hear that, hunk of metal?" She rapped her knuckles against the pot's side. "You won't get the better of us."

Bluster only went so far, though. She and Catullus had to figure out exactly how they could bring water from Mab's Cauldron to Merlin.

"Putting the water into a vessel is out," she mused. "We know that." ·

"The cauldron can't be lifted or transported, either. How, then, to move the water from one place to the other?" Unsurprisingly, Catullus began to pace.

She let herself have a moment to simply watch him move and think. It didn't seem quite fair that such a brilliant mind was housed within a long, athletic body. The two qualities didn't often coexist in the same person. Catullus, as he so often did, defied expectation.

She worked hard for the accomplishments in her life, which meant that she didn't allow herself complacency. With every achievement, she set her bar still higher, knowing she could do better, had more for which to strive. Watching Catullus as he paced the clearing, his mind deeply engaged, she allowed a brief bit of self-congratulation. She had thought herself in love only once before. She knew better now.

The true recipient of her love was, at that moment, trying to solve the enigma of Mab's Cauldron. There was no question in her mind that Catullus's scientific intellect far outpaced her own. But she didn't become one of the only female reporters in Chicago by flaunting her breasts and lifting up her skirts. She had a mind, too. A good one.

"What if we froze the water?" she theorized. "Maybe by trapping it in a solid state, we could move it."

"Theoretically, that might work. If I had access to my workshop, I might be able to engineer a device to chill the water to the proper temperature." He curled his hands into fists, still pacing. "But my workshop is literally in another world, and this place"—he gestured to the dark forest surrounding them—"hasn't got what I need to fabricate anything but the most rudimentary tools." He growled in frustration.

There was a solution in his words. She knew it. But she had to dig further. "Like what kind of tools?"

"A lever. Perhaps a wheel. A torch." He smiled ironically. "Fire. Man's first great discovery. Doesn't get more primitive than that."

"Prometheus brought fire to Man, and was punished for it. Nobody can refute how important fire is. America runs on cups of coffee—I know *I* do—and that wouldn't have been possible without a coffeepot and fire."

He abruptly stopped in the middle of his pacing, his expression sharp. "What did you say?" he demanded.

"Coffee wouldn't be possible without a pot and fire," Gemma repeated.

For a few seconds, he was perfectly still, except for the movement of his eyes, moving back and forth as if reading an invisible book.

"Bloody hell—that could be it." A moment later, he was all motion and intent. He strode around the clearing, gathering up fallen branches. "Collect kindling," he clipped. "The driest you can find."

She knew better than to demand explanations, not when his mind was in the process of piecing together a solution. Following his lead, she gathered armfuls of dry, brittle wood.

"Put that under the cauldron," he directed.

They both set bundles of kindling beneath the pot and he pulled up several handfuls of withered grass, which he tucked between the assembled branches. He crouched down, taking a flint from one of his pockets and using it to create a spark. Carefully, he coaxed the tinder beneath the kettle to burning.

Golden firelight carved out the glade. The trees surrounding them became both more solid and also more menacing, as light cast shadows over their knotted trunks. Yet there was a reason why Prometheus's gift of fire cost him so dearly. The gods feared that fire might embolden man too much, give them too much strength and hope. In a way, the gods were right. She felt her own strength and spirit revive to see the flames, to watch Catullus's gratification as he created fire. He pushed back the darkness and bestowed power to himself and her.

Satisfied that the fire blazed appropriately, Catullus rose and replaced the lid on the cauldron.

He might be in the depths of solving a riddle, but Gemma couldn't stop the questions bustling in her mind. "Are we cooking something?"

"No, but we do want the water to boil." He pulled his knife and turned to her. "I need your petticoat."

It wasn't exactly balmy here in the Night Forest, even with a fire going. Her petticoat had seen better days, yet it did provide some extra warmth. Still, Gemma complied, wriggling out of her underskirt. As she gathered up the yards of white muslin, she caught Catullus staring at her with a tight expression.

"Could you . . ." His voice rasped, and he cleared his throat. "I want you to do that move for me later."

Pleasure heated her cheeks. "I'll shimmy out of *all* my clothes, if you want."

"Oh," he growled, "I want." He took the proffered petticoat, then groaned. "God, it's still warm from your legs." A new thought occurred to him. "Damn, I'm sorry you have to lose a layer of protection from the elements. I'd give you this coat, but it's damp as a basement and less cheerful."

"If I can survive a Chicago winter on a writer's budget, a few hours in the Night Forest are nothing."

He gave her an encouraging smile. Right before taking his knife to her petticoat and tearing it into large squares. "I would've used my handkerchief, but it's too small. And wet, besides. Just like my shirt and trousers and . . . everything else I've got on."

"Hell, how can I complain about a little breeze up my skirt when you might catch pneumonia?"

"Pneumonia is number thirty-two on my list of concerns at the moment." He removed the lid from the pot. "First, let's try something."

He took one small square of cut muslin and tried to dip it into the water. The water's surface grew tacky, impenetrable, every time he tried, leaving the fabric completely dry.

"So much for soaking the muslin in water," he said. "I've another option." He stretched a larger square of fabric over the top of the cauldron. The muslin was bigger than the top, so that when Catullus replaced the lid, the muslin formed a ruffle around the lid's perimeter. "The seal is secure, so this ought to work. We need to get the fire burning as hotly as possible. More wood."

They both resumed the task of collecting tinder. "Can I ask you what you hope to accomplish?"

He gave an enigmatic smile. "It will be much more satisfying if you simply watch."

"And not ask questions?" She snorted. "Can't do it."

"Oh, you can ask as many questions as you like. That does not mean I will answer them."

More pieces of wood were fed into the fire until it blazed high, licking the sides of the pot. Catullus lifted the lid to peer underneath the square of fabric. "Good. The water's boiling. We have to keep it at a steady, strong boil." He replaced the fabric and lid.

"And now?"

"Now we wait. This could take some time, given the size of the cauldron." He glanced around the clearing, frowning. "Blast. I don't have anything clean or dry for you to sit on."

She found his solicitousness touching, but unnecessary. "I'm not a hothouse flower, Catullus. More of a scrappy weed."

"Don't demean yourself." He scowled.

"I'm not. Weeds are hardy, tough to kill. They can grow anywhere. Maybe they aren't the most beautiful plant—"

"You are to me," he said immediately.

How he'd changed from the tongue-tied scholar! "All right, some weeds are almost pretty," she allowed. "The most important thing about them, though, is that it takes a lot to keep them from enduring. They don't mind a little dirt. After everything we've both been through, sitting on the ground is unimportant." To demonstrate, she sat indecorously cross-legged. When he just looked down at her, hands on his hips and shaking his head, she patted the ground beside her. "Come on. Grab some dirt. It's comfortable," she added in a singsong tone. "Soft, cushiony dust. Mm."

He heaved an exasperated sigh before settling down

beside her. He folded his long legs as he sat, resting his shotgun across his lap. One hand hovered close to the knife at his belt. The fire gleamed on the glass of his spectacles, turning them into circles of light as he remained vigilant, continually looking around and assessing possible danger.

For a while, they watched the fire beneath the kettle in companionable, comfortable silence. Or as companionable and comfortable as one could be in the middle of the Night Forest, in eternal darkness, surrounded by dangerous, magical creatures on every side. Safe. She felt safe with Catullus, knowing that no matter what situation they found themselves in, he was the most capable, confident man she knew. Survival wasn't a guarantee, but she sure as hell felt better knowing that Catullus had not just her back, but her front and every other side.

She fought a yawn. God, she was tired. Her sleep in the cottage felt like days ago—and it might have been. If there ever was a place to take a nap, the Night Forest was not it. And she would not force Catullus to keep watch as she blithely slept.

Talking. They needed to talk to keep her awake.

"Watching this pot over a fire makes me think of food," she murmured.

He groaned. "Bloody hell, I'm hungry. Can't wait to get back to our own world and have Bakewell pudding."

"What's that?"

"A kind of tart—a butter crust with fruit preserves along the bottom and an almond custard on top." He smacked his lips. "Our cook at headquarters makes the best Bakewell pudding for tea. I've been known to bolt from my workshop in the middle of a project when Cook says she's made some."

"I detect a sweet tooth." It charmed her to think of Catullus like an eager boy racing down a hallway for a treat.

"On occasion. Too many Bakewell puddings makes for a Blade with a belly."

She gave him a poke in his very flat, very hard stomach.

"Yes, you're really going to seed. Didn't want to be obnoxious and point it out, though."

"Yankee jade," he said affably. "I'm not a young man anymore. I can't eat like one."

"Don't tell that to my mother," Gemma said. "Anyone who refuses seconds she treats like a challenge. She'll bombard you with food until not a single waistcoat will fit."

"Is she a good cook, your mother?"

Now it was her turn to smack her lips. "No one can top Lucia Murphy for cooking. Corned beef and cabbage for my father. Featherlight *gnocchi*. *Panettone* at Christmas. That's a sweet bread with raisins and candied orange."

"Sounds delicious."

"I could eat a whole loaf of *panettone* all by myself, but she always gives it away as gifts. If you come home with me, maybe she'll give you your very own loaf. But you have to promise to share."

He smiled warmly. "I'm looking forward to it. But, Gemma," he asked gently, "would she welcome me into her home?"

The question surprised her. "Why would you ask that?"

"I've been to your country. It isn't precisely the most progressive where colored people are concerned."

She bit back a retort. It wasn't *her* Catullus questioned, or even her family. And he had a point. In Chicago, parts of the city were white, parts were Irish, or Italian, or Polish. And black. Some of the neighborhoods mixed. Others . . . didn't.

What if she did walk into her family's parlor on Catullus's arm? Even if her family accepted him, the neighborhood wouldn't. Mixed marriages had been legalized in Illinois only the year before, but that did not mean they were applauded and endorsed. Some states wouldn't recognize marriages between different races, or outlawed them. In the newsroom, she'd heard stories of black families being forced out of white neighborhoods, violence, and the few mixed-race couples had a difficult time finding anyplace where they could make a home. The *Trib* boys laughed and said crude things about these families and couples, while Gemma sat silently, her face burning in shame. Shame because she did not speak out. Shame because she was surrounded by intolerance.

Her mood, which had been buoyed by Catullus's presence and the cheer of the fire, sank. Too much had been happening for her to stop and think about what lay ahead for her and him. It didn't matter what she felt in her heart. To her homeland, she and Catullus should not be together.

"Is that cauldron done boiling?" she asked, rather than voice any of her worries.

He rose to check the pot. As he moved, his spectacles lost their reflective gleam, so she could see his eyes again. A sadness there. They both knew that, if they did manage to survive this mission for the Blades and avert the Heirs' intended disaster, Gemma and Catullus had another battle to fight. A battle with no clear villains, no single evil to defeat. Neverending and amorphous. The hardest kind of battle to win.

His unexpected cry of triumph had her on her feet and at his side. "What is it?"

He held up the square of muslin. As he did so, steam rose up from the boiling water, misting his spectacles. "It's done."

Gemma peered at the fabric. Steam had soaked it until it became almost transparent. Lightly, she touched the muslin. "Wet."

"With water from the cauldron." He moved the damp fabric away from the cauldron, farther than the flask that had held water, and the muslin remained heavy with liquid.

She looked back and forth between the fabric and Catullus, truly awestruck at his inventive mind. "You are a marvel, Mr. Graves."

"Basic science, Miss Murphy." Yet he beamed at her

praise. Then sobered. "We cannot congratulate ourselves just yet. We have to take it back to Merlin before the water evaporates."

Gemma groaned, thinking of the long voyage back across the Lake of Shadows and along the Deathless River. No doubt more awful creatures would try to stop or hurt them, making progress painfully slow.

A feminine soft chuckle caused her and Catullus to spin around. At the edge of the firelight stood a woman, her skin the color of a starless night, hair like silver cobwebs waving in an unseen current. She wore a circlet, studded with black stones, and her eyes glowed whitely. A shadow-hued gown draped over her ageless body. As she floated toward Gemma and Catullus, her approving gaze lingered on him.

"Oh, God," Gemma muttered under her breath. "Not another magical tramp."

"No 'tramp,' mortal." The woman neared, becoming, upon closer inspection, even more uncanny, her proportions more elongated than a human's, as though she were an odd reflection of beauty. "A queen."

"Queen Mab," said Catullus.

Gemma gulped. It wasn't a smart idea to call faerie queens names as she inadvertently had. "Sorry, Your Highness. We had a little trouble on our way here."

"With a Baobhan Sidhe," Mab said, her voice cool as mist. "'Tis no wonder they tried to drink from your companion, mortal. With a light as strong as his, who could stay away?" She turned her gleaming eyes to Catullus and trailed her fingers across his jaw. "You even tempt one as ancient as I."

Catullus blushed. "Ah . . . thank you, Your Majesty."

Hell, Gemma thought. Was she going to have to fight this immortal queen for him? Well, Gemma knew a few dirty tricks, and she'd use them if it came to that.

"None have yet solved this riddle," Mab continued, turning

to the cauldron. "Until now. And I do so appreciate a clever, devious mind. For your cunning, I grant you two boons."

A small metal box appeared at the faerie queen's hem. "Place the fabric within this coffer, and it shall keep the water from returning to the air. You have but a few hours," she cautioned, "and then the coffer shall disappear, and with it whatever was inside. Take it."

Gemma quickly picked up the box, surprised at its heaviness. Catullus opened the box and carefully set the damp fabric inside before securing the lid.

"You are very generous, Your Highness," he said, bowing.

"My generosity continues, clever mortal. Within the coffer is a piece of iron."

Catullus's brow knit as he tried to understand the significance of this.

"In the old stories," Gemma explained, remembering, "iron is used to ward off faeries and faerie magic."

"So long as the coffer is in your possession," Mab continued regally, "you shall pass through the Night Forest unharmed."

Though Gemma knew next to nothing about being in the presence of royalty, she attempted a curtsy. "Thanks again, Your Highness."

The faerie queen inclined her head. "'Tis a trifle. You have amused me, mortals, and in my long, long life, I find it increasingly difficult to be amused. Now go," she said, voice cooling, "for my temper is a mercurial thing, and I may decide to punish rather than reward you."

Gemma and Catullus immediately began backing away from Mab. As they reached the edge of the clearing, the queen added, "And give my compliments to that madman in the oak. By sending you to me, he has supplied a moment's respite from the weariness of my existence."

"We are grateful—" Catullus began.

"Leave now!" Mab snapped. The air chilled, and barren trees rattled like bones at her words.

Not needing further encouragement, the two mortals hurried away, with Mab's brittle, uncanny laughter ringing through the trees.

The journey back through the Night Forest passed much more quickly than before. None of the inhabitants of the Lake of Shadows or the forest troubled Gemma and Catullus, though creatures did watch from the depths of the darkness with malevolent, baleful stares. Gemma had no doubt that if they didn't have the iron's protection, the return voyage would have been a messy, ugly business.

"Think we're not the most well-liked people in the Night Forest," she murmured as they passed a pack of growling demon dogs.

"Not here to nurture friendships," Catullus answered. He carried the box under one arm and had his shotgun ready in the other.

"You seem popular with the females, though," she pointed out.

He made a noise of disgust. "I don't want to be anyone's plaything . . . or meal. Besides," he added, "it's *you* I love, so the matter is closed."

There it was—that happy leap her heart gave when he said such things to her. She doubted she'd grow used to hearing him say that he loved her. Even in this damned dark forest, she couldn't stop herself from smiling. What the future held, no one knew, but for now, she had this, she had him, and she told herself it was enough.

"I think I see Bryn up ahead," she said.

The edge of the Night Forest grew nearer, the boundary between light and darkness still sharply delineated. Only when Gemma and Catullus crossed over into the dusky light did she allow herself to sigh with relief. Her eyes ached as they adjusted to the brightness.

Bryn hopped down from a nearby branch, clearly surprised.

"I never thought to see you alive," he piped. "Did you get the water from Mab's Cauldron?"

"We did," said Catullus.

Bryn danced in the air, gleeful. "You've done it! The Man in the Oak tested you, and you prevailed! 'Tis marvelous!"

Catullus wrapped an arm around Gemma's shoulder, and she clasped his waist, both grinning at the jigging pixie. It *was* marvelous. They'd faced some of the most dangerous, horrible creatures ever known, and solved the riddle of Mab's Cauldron. The experience had been awful and terrible and thrilling. Not only did she and Catullus survive, but they had succeeded in their quest.

"Even got Mab's protection for the journey back," Gemma said.

Hefting the box, Catullus said, "Have it here."

Bryn reared back. "'Tis iron! Keep it away from me!"

Catullus shifted the box away. "Apologies, Bryn."

The mood of triumph evaporated. Gemma realized that their quest wasn't over, only that they had accomplished only one small part of it.

Catullus must have realized the same thing. All levity gone, he said, "You must take us back to Merlin, at once." He glanced at the box. "We've but one chance to free the sorcerer."

"Will you truly free him?" the pixie asked anxiously. "Though he spoke sensibly, he is still quite out of his senses."

"In or out of his senses," Catullus said, grim, "he is our sole hope for survival."

The pixie gulped, but nodded. He fluttered away, marking the path for Gemma and Catullus's journey back to the mad sorcerer. There was still a long way to go.

Chapter 20

The Silver Wheel

Merlin remained as he had been for untold centuries, partially entombed within the oak tree. As Catullus, Gemma, and Bryn entered the clearing, the sorcerer was amusing himself by conjuring phantasms in the air. Figures of light and shadow danced to curious, hectic music, whirling together in dizzying reels.

Watching the shadow play, Catullus wondered if the figures reflected the spinning mind of the sorcerer. Hopefully, Merlin retained enough sense to remember who Catullus and Gemma were and on what errand the sorcerer had sent them.

Catullus and Gemma neared, with Bryn cautiously following. The sorcerer paid them no notice, absorbed in the spectacle dancing before him. Fascinating as it was, there wasn't time to indulge in amusements, and Catullus reluctantly cleared his throat to gain Merlin's attention.

"I know you are there, mortal." The sorcerer kept his eyes focused on the swirl of color and movement. "This must play out."

Catullus could not stifle his impatience. "But we haven't any time—"

Merlin's gaze darted to and from Catullus. In a distracted voice, he said, "And that is all I have. Time. An abundance of it. My mind is crowded with time."

The metal box in Catullus's hands, and its precious contents, could vanish at any moment. "We brought what you have asked for: water from Mab's Cauldron."

"We can set you free," added Gemma, hopeful.

"Free," Merlin repeated. He barked words in an ancient tongue, and the phantasms blew away like leaves. "The sun is free, and who shall reap his grain?"

A wary glance passed between Catullus and Gemma. They both wondered the same thing—if they *could* free Merlin, would the madman be of any use?

"Tell us what to do with the water," Catullus prompted.

Merlin shifted, and the trunk of the tree moved with him as though its bark were a long robe. The sorcerer bent at the waist, partially disengaging himself from the trunk and placed his hand in the earth at the base of the oak. Though the soil was firm, when Merlin rose up again, his hand left a distinct impression within it.

"Pour the water into that," the sorcerer directed.

From the metal box, Catullus removed the fabric. Thank God—or Mab—none of the water had evaporated. The box vanished the moment he took the fabric from it.

"Guess there's no going back," Gemma murmured.

Catullus knew they had the one chance to get this right. Crouching down next to the handprint, he grasped the wet muslin and wrung it out carefully.

"Clever." Merlin chuckled. "I believed the only way to take water from Mab's Cauldron was to use magic."

"I used the magic of converting liquid to its vapor state through the application of heat." Blades could not use magic that wasn't theirs by right or gift, and none of his family nor ancestors possessed any magic. In the course of his work with the Blades, Catullus had witnessed and felt the power of magic, but never wielded it. The scientist in

Catullus longed to experience it, even if only once. Sadly, he'd never been gifted with any magical power, and so could only speculate.

He focused now on the power he *did* command: the laws of science. Droplets of water dribbled from the fabric. It wasn't much, but Catullus hoped it would be enough. He watched, and scarcely believed what he saw. Once again, his notions of science dissolved in the logic-defying principles of Otherworld.

The water did not absorb immediately into the earth. Nor did it fill the hand-shaped imprint. Instead, the water beaded and moved like liquid metal, forming itself into a circle in the middle of Merlin's handprint. Spokes bisected the circle. The water solidified, turning not into ice, but silver.

"Take it," said Merlin.

Gingerly, Catullus picked up the tiny wheel. It exuded subtle warmth in the center of his palm. Peering closely, he saw that it appeared to be entirely solid, the metal an unbroken ring. He held it up between his fingers and it gleamed in the sunlight.

Gemma cautiously touched the circle and smiled faintly at the marvel of it. "Wonderful enchantment."

"It is the Wheel," said Merlin, solemn. "The Round Table. The circular World." He fixed Catullus with this fathomless gaze. "The Compass."

Catullus's hand unconsciously drifted to the pocket that held his Compass. No surprise that this essential symbol of the Blades meant so much. And it could not astonish Catullus that Merlin knew not only about the Blades of the Rose, but also about their use of the Compass as their symbol and unifying principle. Energy prickled along the back of Catullus's neck as he truly began to fathom the breadth of the sorcerer's power and knowledge.

"The circularity of Magic," Merlin continued. "No beginning, no end. Hold it sacred and safe, for the bearer of the Silver Wheel shall have the means to speak to and be heard by Arthur."

The wheel suddenly felt much heavier and more precious. "Meaning, that *we* are the ones who will communicate with Arthur and break his connection to the Heirs."

Gemma glanced back and forth between the silver wheel and Merlin. "Can't this free you from your prison? Wasn't that the reason we went into the Night Forest?"

"My liberation was never the purpose. The Wheel has not that power."

"We can't just leave you here," she objected.

"'Tis not your quest to undertake. Now your object is to reach Arthur before he reaches the Primal Source."

Catullus slipped the wheel into an inside pocket in his coat. The wheel's warmth radiated like a second heart. "On behalf of the Blades, I thank you. I am only sorry that we cannot help you."

"Presumptuous mortal," scoffed Merlin. "To assume I need or want your aid."

"I meant no insult." Negotiating the sorcerer's unbalanced mind proved a constant challenge.

Quick as lightning, Merlin's temper shifted again. Deep wrinkles of humor fanned at the corners of his eyes as he looked Catullus and Gemma up and down. "Fine knightly heroes you make in your tattered garb. In Camelot, you would've been sent straight to the kitchens. Or stables. No," he tutted, shaking his head, "this shall not do."

The sorcerer sang out a quick spell. The words left his mouth in a cloud of bright moths, fluttering around and then alighting upon Catullus and Gemma.

"Hey!" She tried to shoo the moths away. "They're *eating* my clothes."

"No great loss," Merlin chuckled.

The moths were, in fact, devouring both Catullus and Gemma's garments, faster than any moth in the ordinary world might. The insects ate everything. From Catullus's heavy coat to Gemma's drawers, nothing was safe. Not even their boots. The moths nibbled through the leather. The sensation was peculiar—not painful, more like an aggressive tickling.

As the moths moved over her, Gemma giggled, then scowled in consternation. Catullus, too, was forced to keep his mouth pressed tight to prevent a very unmanly giggle from escaping.

Within a minute, both mortals found themselves entirely naked. All the contents of Catullus's countless pockets had mysteriously vanished, including the wheel. His firearms also disappeared. At the least, the greedy insects hadn't chewed off his spectacles. But the wheel was most important.

Her arms crossed over her breasts, Gemma muttered, "I'm *not* ambling all over creation naked as a cat."

Much as Catullus loved to see her nude, he had to agree. "Can't fight very well without a scrap to cover oneself. And where are the wheel and my Compass?" Of all his material possessions, they were the most precious.

"The impatience of mortals," sighed Merlin. "Bide a moment."

Catullus again fought the urge to giggle as the moths fluttered over his body. He bit back a startled gasp as the insects worked the garment-devouring process *in reverse*. From their tiny mouths, scraps of fabric appeared on his body, as well as leather around his feet. More and more, until he and Gemma were both fully dressed.

Not with their original clothing. Nor in current fashion.

"Now you are truly worthy of your quest," said Merlin with approval as the moths flitted away.

Both Catullus and Gemma gaped at their new clothes. "We're straight out of a tapestry," she breathed.

Merlin had dressed them in garments from the pages of a courtly medieval ballad. Catullus wore a knight's white tunic and leggings, with soft leather boots laced to the knee.

Over this, he wore a blue sleeveless surcoat embellished by a silver embroidered Compass—an apt standard. In true chivalric fashion, a silver belt was slung around Catullus's hips, and heavy gauntlets protected his hands. The boy within Catullus delighted: He was a knight! Exactly as he'd dreamt of being so many years ago.

And Gemma was his lady. "Always knew you'd look stunning in green and gold," he said, husky.

She colored with pleasure at his compliment, and gave a spin to show off her new clothing. Merlin's magic had provided her with a dress worthy of a pre-Raphaelite faerie queen: a long gown of emerald silk, with long, trailing sleeves and a wide neckline that almost bared her shoulders. Intricate golden embroidery adorned the sleeves, neck, and hem, and a golden belt embellished with cabochon emeralds encircled her hips. As she spun, she revealed a tissue-thin underskirt of gold, and dainty slippers.

Catullus's eyes and heart filled near to bursting with the sight of her, so impossibly lovely, a vision of femininity worth any price. He didn't care what Gemma wore—he loved her regardless—but to see her in what could truly be described as raiment, it almost brought him to his knees.

"I never wanted to be a princess," she said, smoothing a hand along the embroidery at her neck, "but I might change my mind if I could dress like this every day. And you." She stepped nearer and, eyes glowing, stroked his chest. "Doubt any princess had so gorgeous a champion."

"For my lady, anything." His words were the forged steel of his vow. Turning to Merlin, he said, "Your gifts are generous, but I must have the silver wheel and my Compass."

"And I'd like my derringer back," Gemma added.

The sorcerer nodded toward them, and a satchel of soft hide appeared on Catullus's shoulder. Opening the bag, Catullus found that it held not only the wheel and his Compass, but his tools, the flask, his pocket watch, knife, and every one of the dozens of items he'd stowed in the pockets of his Ulster overcoat. Yet the satchel was surprisingly light, hardly hinting at the vast number of things Catullus had been carrying.

Catullus's shotgun appeared on his other shoulder, and he breathed a little easier. It might spoil the overall effect of a romantic knight, but he'd rather be prepared and anachronistic than authentic and ill-equipped.

As for Gemma, a small damask purse materialized on her belt. She grinned as she pulled out her pistol and checked to see if it was loaded. It was: "This princess won't be captured by any dragon. Not without a fight." Something else in her purse made her smile: her notebook. She held up the writing pad. "I can serve as scribe, too."

Catullus realized they hadn't discussed her writing in a long while. If they survived the upcoming battle, would she tell the world about the Heirs, the Blades, and Sources? To do so would compromise everyone's safety.

He cleared the thought from his mind. Too much lay between now and that distant future. Survival could not be relied upon. Better to face the impending battle with one objective: victory.

Though Catullus and Gemma were satisfied with their weapons, Merlin was not. He glowered at the shotgun and pistol. "Ill-fitting armaments for magic's champions." He mumbled words in a guttural tongue.

Warm metal materialized in Catullus's right hand. He stared as light took shape, forming, solidifying. A sword. Not an officer's sword—as he'd seen on numerous soldiers and Samuel Reed's mantle—but a knight's double-edged sword. It fit perfectly in his hand, balanced flawlessly, and he stepped back to give an experimental swing. Part of his training regimen included swordplay, but never in his life had he held such a wonder, moving as a natural extension of his arm.

Any doubts as to whether the sword was meant for him vanished when he saw the Compass motif wrought in its pommel, as well as the embossed gears adorning the leather scabbard on his belt. Catullus glanced at Merlin, and the sorcerer's eyes glittered at his own metallurgical wit.

"The lady shall not go defenseless," Merlin said. He stared at Gemma's right hand, and a dagger took shape within her grasp. Like Catullus's sword, the dagger was a marvel of craftsmanship as it gleamed in the sunlight.

"Pretty little thing," Gemma murmured, approving. She tested the edge of the blade with her thumb before hefting it with purpose. She held the knife out for Catullus's inspection. "It has a writer's quill worked into the grip."

"The pen and the sword," murmured Catullus, "mighty together."

"Are these weapons magic?" Gemma asked Merlin.

"No magic but the skill of who wields them," came the answer.

After a last flourish, Catullus sheathed his sword. He made sure the silver wheel was secure within the satchel. "The task ahead of us is a great one, and you have dressed and armed us as the heroes we hope to be."

"As the heroes you *must* be." Merlin stared hard at them both. "Arthur advances on London, and you must stop him." His eyes began to cloud, losing sharpness.

Catullus knew they hadn't much time before Merlin was mired once more in madness. He bowed respectfully to the sorcerer. "The world's magic owes you a debt, Merlin."

"Debt? There are no debts," the sorcerer answered, distracted. "Not when the walls collapse and the flame is loosed. The moon in the water. The metal heart is forged."

Gemma and Catullus shared a look. Already Merlin was slipping away into the labyrinth of his insanity. They began to back away, with an anxious Bryn hovering behind them. Making their way backward through the clearing, Catullus observed the sorcerer alternating between mumbling and shouts.

Yet Merlin was anything but a sad, mad man. He contained so much power, it was a wonder the whole of the

Otherworld forest wasn't ablaze. Catullus thought perhaps keeping Merlin contained within the oak was the wiser choice. Power such as the sorcerer possessed could level the world if unchecked.

As Catullus, Gemma, and Bryn reached the farthest edge of the clearing, Merlin shouted, "Fire. Air. One must have the other. Smother the beast."

Silence fell. Catullus waited, but Merlin did not speak again. The sorcerer turned inward, shutting out everything around him. Seeing that Merlin was entirely lost, his visitors withdrew into the woods.

"Poor guy," Gemma said sadly as they walked. "To be trapped in that tree, in that unbalanced brain forever. Do you think his ranting meant anything?"

"Sounded like alchemy," mused Catullus. He turned Merlin's words over and over in his mind. Some accounts of Merlin described him as not only a sorcerer, but a seer, as well. Was Merlin prophesying? If so, what was he trying to tell them?

"I like your new clothes." Gemma eyed him. "Gives me some wicked ideas about tempting the virtuous knight."

"The knight isn't so virtuous. He's thinking about ravishing the pure maiden."

"Not very pure, this maiden."

"Thank God for that. Still," he added, slightly melancholy, "I'm sorry to see that Ulster coat gone."

"It was a grimy disaster full of holes."

"Sentimental value." His thoughts drifted back. "I remember you standing on the deck of the steamship as we neared Liverpool, wearing that coat. How lovely and determined you looked—the kind of woman I never thought to call my own. I didn't know it then, but when I saw you"—he gazed warmly at Gemma—"I saw my soul. Wrapped in black cashmere."

* * *

Bryn flew ahead, darting between massive trees. The pixie barely waited to see if the mortals kept up, which they did, but barely. Human legs proved less speedy than wings. Perhaps that might be another project for Catullus, should he ever return to his workshop. He'd built glider wings—which Bennett had put to very good use in Greece—but a self-contained flying machine . . . his mind whirled with the possibilities and mechanics.

"A door between worlds is near," Bryn called back.

"Where will it take us?" asked Gemma.

"Where you need to be," came the opaque answer.

Catullus hadn't the patience for ambiguity. With time in such short supply, he needed to know where he and Gemma would emerge and how long it would take them to reconnect with the other Blades before moving on to London. "Care to be more specific?"

Naturally, the pixie would not answer. He zipped onward, with Catullus and Gemma all but running to keep pace.

Bryn suddenly darted back. "Not that way! We have to find another path."

"What?" Gemma asked, but the pixie shook his head.

"No time! Head back . . . it's coming!"

Bryn flitted off, leaving his mortal charges to hurry after him. Catullus threw a look over his shoulder to see what, exactly, they were trying to avoid.

It turned out to be a hunched-over, wheat-skinned creature, its form crudely human. A thick patch of tangled dark hair obscured most of its face, but did not quite hide its wide-jawed mouth. It shuffled with ungainly motion, dragging a heavy club, periodically stopping to sniff at the air. Catullus thought that perhaps Bryn overreacted to the creature, since it moved so clumsily and didn't seem to see very well. But as soon as the thing caught a scent, it leapt, quick as gunfire, and slammed its club down onto the ground.

With a large, yellow-nailed hand, it picked something up from the dirt. The smashed form of some forest animal dangled from between its fingers before the creature crammed the dead animal into its mouth.

"Troll," Bryn whispered, coming up beside Catullus. "Hungry and ill-tempered."

They ran on, careful to keep downwind. The troll smelled horrible, but better to smell its stench than have it catch their scent.

Yet they had not gotten far when sounds just ahead caused Catullus to skid to a halt. He pressed himself up against a tree, pulling Gemma with him. She knew better than to demand an explanation. They both held still, listening.

Human voices. Men's voices.

"God Almighty," one of them groaned. "When are we getting out of this accursed place? I hate it here."

"Did you see what happened to Coleby?" another said, horror in his voice. "Took one bite of that apple and then those . . . things . . . came. Dragged him right off. Staithes, you're our mage. Why couldn't we stop 'em?"

"Because," growled someone else, presumably Staithes, "that kind of faerie magic cannot be combated, even by a mage. Anyway, if Coleby was so stupid, serves him right."

"I still hear him screaming," the first voice said, horror chilling his words. "Let's just go, before that happens to someone else."

"Shut it," a fourth voice snapped. "We can't leave until we find and kill Graves and that Yank woman. Otherwise Edgeworth will burn us to cinders."

Catullus inwardly seethed. The very last thing he had time or tolerance for was a pack of Heirs. Ammunition for his shotgun was running low, and he didn't fancy getting into a sword fight, not when the Heirs had him and Gemma outnumbered and outgunned.

Retreat in the other direction was not possible, not with the troll making its slow, steady way toward them.

The troll . . .

"Wait here," Catullus whispered to Gemma.

Before she could speak, he sprinted away. Directly toward the troll.

Catullus's soft leather boots made almost no sound as he sped over bracken and grass, weaving a path toward the advancing troll. He spotted the creature long before it became aware of him, lumbering as it was with its nose high in the air.

The troll grunted in surprise when Catullus jumped in front of it—far enough to be out of range of its bloodstained club.

"Hey, Porridge-Brains." Catullus waved his arms to be sure the troll saw him. "I'm a tasty morsel. Yes, I am."

Growling, the troll raised its club, but Catullus turned and ran before the crude weapon could crash down on his skull. He dashed ahead of the troll, yet not so fast that the beast lost sight of him. A tough balance, for the troll could not run quickly, yet had the leaping speed of a grasshopper. Several times, the whoosh of acrid air announced the troll's presence moments before its club came swinging down. Each time, Catullus dodged the blow, though only barely.

With a burst of speed, he raced back toward the Heirs. He thought himself clear of the troll.

It leapt out from behind a tree, cutting him off.

Catullus tried to sprint around the hulking beast, attempting to lead it toward the Heirs. Its swinging club kept pushing him back.

"Son of a ruddy bitch," Catullus growled. His plan wasn't going to work.

"Hey!"

Gemma's voice.

"Hey!" she shouted again. "Limey bastards! With the bad teeth and waxy skin! Yes—I'm talking to you!"

What the hell was she doing?

A flash of russet hair up ahead. He spied her, standing not a dozen yards from the Heirs. When the men also spotted her, they stood, momentarily stunned that their intended prey stood nearby, literally waving her arms overhead so they could see her.

"The Yankee bitch," one spat.

"Come over here and call me that," she said. She turned, gathering her trailing skirts, and ran.

The Heirs started for her, all but the mage, who shouted warnings for the men to stop, that it was a trap. His admonitions went unheeded, and so even the mage was forced to join the pursuit.

Catullus, still dodging the troll's club, caught glimpses of Gemma as she sped toward him. Toward the troll. With the Heirs in pursuit.

He grinned, despite the angry troll trying to brain him. Gemma knew without being told exactly what Catullus had planned, and when that plan had faltered, she knew how to fix the situation.

Gemma skidded to a stop ten feet from the troll. The Heirs were closing in quickly. She picked up a rock and hurled it at the troll's back.

"Behind you, Ugly!" she yelled.

The troll spun around, arcs of saliva flying from its slavering mouth. It charged her.

Catullus lifted his shotgun, preparing to shoot the beast, but Gemma dove aside as the troll ran at her.

The troll, full of unstoppable momentum, barreled on and straight toward the Heirs. Shouts and guttural growls clashed with gunfire and crushing club.

Catullus ran to Gemma and pulled her up from where she lay upon the ground. He held her tightly. "Damn reckless woman!"

"Making sure your scheme worked," she countered. "And it did, didn't it?" A rhetorical question, since both Catullus and Gemma plainly saw the Heirs and the troll battling one another in a frenzy of modern technology, magic, and brute force.

"Like iron and carbon," he murmured, gazing at her. "Combined, they create steel."

She smiled up at him. "The steel of a blade."

They turned away. With the sounds of battle at their backs, Catullus, Gemma, and Bryn raced toward the portal.

"There it is," said Bryn.

The gateway between the mortal world and Otherworld appeared to be nothing at all. Only more forest.

Catullus's brow furrowed. "I don't see anything."

"Between those two trees," the pixie answered, exasperated.

Catullus studied the trees in question. They seemed ordinary—if gigantic, knotted trees could be considered ordinary, but definitions of what was and wasn't remarkable grew indistinct in Otherworld. He looked beyond where the trees stood, yet all he saw were farther stretches of the woods, deepening into gold and green shadow.

"It shimmers," Gemma said, "like liquid glass. I see it with my magic. The doorway."

This satisfied him, even though he wished he had her gift, something that allowed him to penetrate the realm of the visible using his own ability. "As long as one of us can see the door, that's all that matters."

She pressed her lips together, and seemed to come to a decision. Taking his hands in hers, she said, "There is something I've wanted to give you. It's been on my mind for a while. And now is the right time."

He tried to think of what she might have to give him. Her notebook? Her derringer? She didn't have much, and he was quite certain that a journalist, especially one from a large family, wasn't wealthy. The Graves family's coffers were more than full.

"You've given me your heart," he answered, "and that is all I want."

"There's more."

He meant to object, but she closed her eyes and an expression of deep concentration sharpened her features. She seemed to retreat deep within herself, drawing upon something unseen. He felt it then—a growing, gathering energy that hummed and pulsed through her. Her hands warmed quickly, almost fever-hot. The heat and energy radiated from her into him, first in his hands, and then unfolding up his arms, through his chest, until his whole body resonated with them.

The sensation was . . . not disagreeable. Quite pleasurable, actually. A connection between himself and Gemma, living energy that gleamed like silver threads both hot and cool. It wove into the fabric of himself, all throughout his mind and body: arms, chest, legs.

He knew of no scientific process to explain what was happening.

Something lodged itself into his will—not an object, but the pattern of a thing. His eyes closed to concentrate on this new presence, feeling it with his mind. It took shape there, in his thoughts and shadow-self. What was it? He did not deal with intangibles; this was new.

Concentrating. Bringing himself to narrow focus, as he did with mechanics and mathematics, yet this process focused within to the realm of subtleties. He had it now. It formed and solidified into—

A key.

His eyes flew open just as Gemma released his hands. She fluttered her lashes and looked at him speculatively.

"Is it there?" she asked. "Can you feel it?"

"Gemma," murmured Catullus, "what have you done?"

She demanded, "Can you feel it? The Key?"

"I can," he answered, scarcely believing what just happened. "It's there, inside me."

"Look." She turned him so he faced the trees that marked the portal. "What do you see?"

He started. Stretching between the two trees was a shining membrane gleaming with visible magic. Moments earlier, all Catullus had seen were the trees and the forest beyond them. Now, it was as though the lenses of his spectacles had been replaced with glass that revealed magical energy. To be certain, he removed his spectacles. The vision of the portal remained—though slightly blurred due to his nearsightedness.

He replaced his spectacles, then glanced back and forth between the portal and Gemma. "I see it. The doorway. I can see it now."

She smiled. "I did it. Wasn't sure it could be done, but it can."

"You gave me your magic." Amazement edged his words. "*All* of it?" If she'd sacrificed her family's legacy to him, he would find a way to return it. Immediately. It was too much. He could never accept her gift.

His heart eased when she said, "Half I kept for myself, but ever since the Primal Source was activated, it's been stronger than ever, so I barely feel a difference."

Even so, he shook his head at the enormity of what she had done. Something akin to awe roughened his voice. "I've never been given such a gift." He looked back to the portal that, even at his glance, moved to open for him. "No door is closed to me now."

She blushed with pleasure. He pulled her to him and kissed her, marveling at this fearless woman with a heart of steel, yet a generosity of spirit that seared his very core.

Bryn had less patience with the enormity of Gemma's gift. "Cross between the trees," he said tersely, "and you shall find yourself in Brightworld."

Catullus and Gemma broke apart to ready themselves for the passage. Now that their time in Otherworld had come to an end, Catullus found himself oddly sentimental for the maddening, dangerous place. Gemma seemed possessed by the same nostalgia, and they both looked around the forest with suspiciously bright eyes.

"I think I might miss it here," she murmured. "Even though we almost died half a dozen times. And I'm starving. And it seemed like every female we met tried to steal my man."

Catullus corrected, "One female wanted my *blood*, not *me*. Yet I must agree," he added. "Treacherous and confusing Otherworld may be, but I'll miss it, too."

He would always remember that in these enchanted woods, he and Gemma first declared their love for each other—and for that, Otherworld would forever be a place of profound magic. The magic within its forests and oceans became strengthened through the love of two mortals. She felt this, too. He saw it in the warmth of her gaze, the tiny smile in the corners of her mouth, a hint of wistfulness in her face.

Catullus moved to stand in front of a hovering Bryn. He offered an index finger, which the pixie took in his own little hand and shook.

"You're a good man, Bryn Enfys," Catullus said. "Couldn't have done this without you."

"It isn't done yet. Save the worlds." Bryn couldn't contain the pride in his expression. "And when you do, have your bards sing of me."

Multitalented though the Blades were—cryptographers, linguists, tacticians, inventors—they had a shortage of bards. Still, Catullus answered, "They will sing to make the ladies weep and the men envious."

The pixie beamed, then forced his glee behind a mask of brave stoicism. His impassivity did not last, however, when Gemma neared. She offered her finger to shake, and Bryn, reddening, turned her finger over and pressed a kiss to her knuckle.

"Should you ever weary of Brightworld and its narrowness," he said, shaking a little, "come find me here."

"I will," Gemma answered solemnly. She gave his cheek a light kiss, and the pixie nearly collapsed from joy.

He managed to regain a fragment of composure as Catullus and Gemma turned and walked toward the two trees. They stopped just at the threshold, looking back to Bryn. The pixie doffed his hat and waved it overhead. Both mortals waved in return before turning to the portal.

They each took a steadying breath, knowing that, once they crossed the boundary, the speeding train of fortune would not stop. Only one destination awaited them: all-out war with the Heirs. Perilous though Otherworld had been, Catullus and Gemma had stolen moments of peace for themselves. Such peace would not come again for a long while—if at all.

Hand in hand, they stepped over the threshold.

Directly into battle.

Chapter 21

The Blades of the Rose

Men and fog surrounded them. Artillery deafened. The acrid smell and smoke of gunpowder stung. Shouting hammered on all sides.

Gemma spun around, striving to make sense of the chaos around her. Catullus did the same.

She had thought, once they'd left the anarchic Other-world, they would return to the relative logic and stability of the mortal realm. Had even looked forward to some moment of comparative safety—no skinless monstrosities, no blood-drinking sirens. Normalcy. Order.

Clearly, she wasn't going to get her wish.

They now seemed to be in a large mist-shrouded . . . garden. Gemma made out the form of a greenhouse gleaming dully in the watery light. There were pathways and orderly box hedges, everything tidy and trim. A contrast to the noise of battle all around.

No one around seemed to have spotted them yet. Everything was a frenzied swirl of action as the men aimed and fired at an unknown enemy. But who the men were, and who the enemy was, Gemma didn't know.

"Where are we?" she shouted to him above the din.

"Don't know." Catullus drew his sword at the same time as he reached for his shotgun—movement that should have been awkward, but he managed it with fluid grace. "The portal has either a terrible sense of placement or a wicked sense of humor." He took a fighting stance.

Before Gemma could ask what Catullus meant by this, one of the men close by finally noticed them. His face twisted into a sneer; then he raised his pistol and aimed it at Catullus's head. Gemma grabbed for her derringer. She hadn't even gotten the gun cocked when, sword upraised, Catullus charged. The man stumbled back, surprised. He hadn't been anticipating a medieval weapon.

Catullus cut him across his chest before the man recovered his wits enough to shoot. The man grimaced in pain and took aim, but Catullus knocked the gun from his hand and, with the pommel of the sword, struck him square in the center of his face. Blood shot from the man's nose as he crumpled, unconscious, to the ground.

It all happened so quickly, Gemma could only stare.

"Heirs," Catullus growled, spinning around. "The portal stuck us right in the middle of a bunch of sodding Heirs."

The moment he said this, two men stopped in their tracks to see their fallen comrade. They glanced between the unconscious man and Catullus, a look of almost comic disbelief on their faces.

"What the hell? How'd Graves break the line? And why's he dressed like that?"

"Who cares? He's dead."

The men rushed Catullus. He kept them back with the blade of his sword. It swung in arcs, tearing across their arms and legs, and the Heirs yelped at the attack. Yet they were faster in recovering than their immobile friend had been, gathering themselves to charge Catullus. Gemma winced at the collision of fists and elbows, the savage, quick struggle between Catullus's sword and the Heirs' muscle.

"Two against one?" she demanded. "Not fair." She leapt forward, joining the fray with her derringer in one hand and her new knife in the other.

If the Heirs hadn't been expecting Catullus with his knight's sword, they anticipated Gemma and her dagger even less. She took a vicious glee in their wide eyes and hasty curses as she swung out with her blade. Her movements weren't as practiced and agile as Catullus, but she didn't really care when she stuck one Heir in the shoulder—just before he could fire his revolver in her face.

The man howled, then turned and ran. Gemma whirled around to see Catullus standing over the body of the other Heir, staring down dispassionately at the spreading crimson on the Heir's shirtfront.

"Sword-fighting is a messy business," he said grimly.

"I'd rather see *his* blood than yours," she answered.

He gave a clipped nod before gazing around. Disorder still raged on all sides as a battle was being fought. A dull red glow flared close by, penetrating the mist. It flashed, disappeared, then flashed again, sizzling as it did so. Voices cried out distantly.

"What is that?" Gemma asked. "Some kind of weapon?"

Frowning, Catullus strode toward the red flares, with Gemma half a step behind him.

She muttered a curse when she saw the source of the light. Not a weapon, but a man. A dark, thick beard shadowed his cheeks, and he had only one sighted eye. The other was a sunken hollow crossed with a thick scar. His hands were engulfed in red light. He chanted words in an obscure language, and the light surrounding his hands coalesced into spheres. At his command, the light leapt from his hands and shot off into the fog—toward an unknown opponent. A thunderous boom sounded remotely, followed by screams, indicating the balls of energy reached their target.

If these men were Heirs, that likely meant that they were fighting . . . Blades.

"We have to stop him," Gemma said urgently.

Catullus didn't answer. Instead, he brandished his sword and, sleek and silent as a hunter, stalked the magic-wielding Heir. The man did not seem to be aware of Catullus drawing nearer, but when Catullus raised his sword to strike, the Heir spun toward him. The light around the magic-user's hands spread, forming a shield. Catullus's sword glanced off the shield, and though the Heir staggered from the strength of the blow, he was unhurt.

The Heir smirked at Catullus. "Graves. We still have a debt to settle, you and I."

"Thank you for reminding me, Bracebridge," Catullus answered. "Lesperance isn't here, so I'll have to take your other eye."

The Heir snarled. The energy around his hands shifted, forming a gleaming ax. Bracebridge swung his weapon at Catullus, who sidestepped the attack and countered with a blow of his own. Gemma watched, horribly fascinated, as Catullus and the Heir fought, the air hot and bright from arcs made by Bracebridge's ax, Catullus moving with a warrior's fluidity.

Someone ran past her, breaking her concentration. She whirled, knife ready, as more men sped by. Either the fog was too thick, or they simply didn't care about her presence, because they shouted back and forth to each other without giving her any attention.

"Bracebridge isn't holding them back anymore," one man yelled to another.

"Doesn't matter," someone answered. "We took some of 'em out."

The first man wavered. "But they keep coming!"

"So let those fools come. They'll won't get far into the city, and even if they make it all the way to headquarters, they won't make it past the front door."

This thought cheered the group of men. "Imagine what

a mess they'll make—staining our stairs with their blood. Keep the housemaids busy for a month."

They chuckled, but their chuckles stopped when a figure silently leapt from the mist. The rifle seemed an extension of his hands, and he put the bayonet at the end of the barrel to good use—striking out at the Heirs, felling them as readily as one might harvest wheat. Gemma had never seen this fair-haired man before, yet he moved with the confidence and bearing of a soldier. She couldn't help but be impressed.

Gemma's attention was drawn by another person appearing from the mist. At first, she thought this person was another soldier, moving as efficiently and lethally as the fair-haired man. Peering harder, Gemma saw that this slim other man carried a heavy gun, and wore a peculiar long, belted tunic, and trousers tucked into embroidered boots. Maybe this man came from a distant shore—how else to explain the tied-back long, dark hair?

"Gabriel, behind you!"

Gemma started when she realized this second figure was, in fact, a woman. The fog thinned to reveal that she was a tall, striking woman. When she spoke, her unique accent sounded something between English and Russian. At her warning, the soldierly man neatly deflected an attacking Heir, then sent his assailant sprawling with a perfect punch to the jaw.

"Thanks, love," the man answered, and he had a gruff voice marked by his own unusual English accent, a working man's dialect, very different from Catullus's cultured tones. "One to your left."

The woman spun and drove the butt of her rifle into the belly of a charging Heir. When he bent to cradle his bruised stomach, she slammed the rifle stock into his forehead. He dropped like an anchor.

Gemma had never seen two more adept fighters in her life—male or female.

The woman became aware of Gemma and stalked toward her, rifle directed at Gemma. "Who are you?" she demanded.

"Who are *you*?" Gemma snapped back.

"Thalia," the soldierly man called. "Graves is here."

Both the tall woman and Gemma spun to see Catullus locked in battle with the magic-using Heir. Bracebridge, as Catullus had called him, noticed the newcomers at the same time that he saw his fellow Heirs speeding away.

"The battle line's been compromised," he muttered to himself. Then, to Catullus, he snarled, "This isn't a retreat. No use wasting my energy here." He turned and ran. He disappeared into the fog, with the rest of the Heirs following.

Abandoned by his foe, Catullus sheathed his sword before drawing his sleeve over his gleaming forehead. He started toward Gemma and the woman.

"Thalia?"

"Catullus!"

The tall woman made to embrace, but she stopped herself when she caught sight of Gemma's fierce scowl. "Made a friend, Catullus?"

They gathered together, Catullus, Gemma, the woman known as Thalia, and the man called Gabriel.

"It's been a year and a continent, Huntley," Catullus said to the man, offering a hand.

The soldierly man shook Catullus's hand. Up close, Gemma saw that this Gabriel Huntley possessed a rugged masculinity that contrasted with the touch of humor in his golden eyes. He draped an arm across Thalia's shoulders and pulled her close to his side. "Wish the circumstances for a reunion were better."

"We were called back from Mongolia by Athena Galanos," Thalia added. "It's been nothing but battles ever since we disembarked." She smiled warmly at Catullus. "It's good to see you again, regardless. And," she added, sliding a glance toward Gemma, "not alone."

Catullus made introductions as if they were in someone's parlor, and not standing on a mist-shrouded field with the bodies of both dead and unconscious Heirs around them. "Gemma, these are my friends Thalia and Gabriel Huntley. Huntleys, this is Gemma Murphy."

"The American scribbler?" asked Thalia.

"Just don't call me a hack," Gemma replied, sheathing her dagger.

Thalia's laugh was husky like her voice, belying her slim physique. "I think you'll suit us well. Clearly, you suit Catullus." She sent the man in question a playful, approving glance.

Gemma shook the hands of the Huntleys in turn, eyeing them with speculation. She could only imagine how the soldier met the Asian-dressed Amazon. A good story—one she'd want to learn later. However that had come to pass, there was no doubt they were remarkable fighters, tailor-made for one another.

"Where are we?" asked Gemma.

"Don't you know?" Thalia asked.

"Ten minutes ago, Gemma and I were in the realm of magic," Catullus answered dryly. "At the moment, our sense of direction isn't sterling. But that over there"—he pointed to the curved walls and domes of the greenhouse—"looks like the Palm House in Kew Gardens."

"That's exactly where we are," Thalia confirmed.

Catullus snorted. "Last time I was here, I was fifteen, going to see the new National Arboretum. Now this. A bloody battle in Kew Gardens." He took his timepiece from his satchel, then frowned at it before giving it a shake. "Damn—Otherworld muddled up the mechanisms. The hands are going backward." He returned the watch to the bag. "What's the hour?"

Huntley pulled a watch from the pocket of his waistcoat and consulted its battered face. "Half eight in the morning. A good thing it's so early, or the gardens would've been full of civilians. So, it's true, then," he said, replacing the watch and furrowing his brow. "You and Miss Murphy crossed over. And came back." He shook his head. "Never would've believed such a thing was possible. But there's a hell of a lot more to this world than an old soldier could ever know."

"You're not an old soldier, Huntley," said a masculine voice from the fog. "I am."

The four of them turned to see a tall, dark-haired man stride forward, with a trim, neatly dressed woman beside him. The man was dressed in civilian clothing, but an officer's sword hung from his belt. As the couple neared, Gemma saw that, though they were both healthy and fit—the man in particular had broad shoulders and an upright, dynamic bearing—they were not young. Silver threaded through the man's dark hair, and subtle lines fanned at the corner of the woman's eyes—she must smile often.

As with Thalia and Gabriel Huntley, Catullus shook the newcomers' hands warmly. He introduced the couple to Gemma as Cassandra and Samuel Reed. "Dilapidated old veterans," he added dryly. "Just like me."

Gemma looked back and forth between the Reeds and Catullus, three adults not in the first flush of youth, yet all of them were at the peak of health and strength. No one could ever mistake them for complacent middle age.

"I'm surprised you can hear anything without ear trumpets," she said to them.

Dozens of more people emerged from the fog—to her incredulity, she saw they were men and women of many nationalities. They came from different classes, as evidenced by their clothing, and from faraway shores. Asia, Europe, South America, the Near East. Some already bore injuries. All of them were armed with a variety of weapons, yet nothing was as formidable as the light of determination in their eyes. It was a humbling sight to witness this diverse group of people all banded together for a single purpose. Gemma recalled her schoolroom lessons about the founding of her own country, the supposed freedom it was meant to represent. Meanwhile, men and women of different races could not legally marry, and colored children were forced to attend second-rate schools.

What had it achieved, that dream of equality?

She saw it for the first time. Here, now. With these people. The Blades of the Rose.

Catullus introduced her to them, a ragged miscellany that knew they were outmanned, outgunned. Yet none of them seemed daunted by the steep odds. In fact, some of them looked downright *eager* to scrap with the Heirs. Crazy, the whole crew. She instantly felt comfortable with them.

Names and faces quickly flew by Gemma as Catullus introduced them to her. She met so many, she could barely keep track: Thalia's father, as well as a man from Peking, a Blade from Constantinople, another from Brazil. She shook so many hands, she felt like a bride on the receiving line.

Bride? She cast a quick look at Catullus, then glanced away as her face heated. No—she couldn't think of that now.

Samuel Reed asked, "What happened to Bracebridge? That damned magic of his cost us." Starkly, he added, "We lost Mark Brown and Stephen Pryor. Isabel Rivera's hurt badly, but Philippe Chazal is seeing to her."

The names themselves had no meaning to Gemma, but she couldn't help but be moved and saddened by this news. Fallen and injured Blades. Whoever those people were or had been, it was clear from the pain flashing on Catullus's face that they had been his friends.

"What's Arthur's progress toward London?" Catullus asked, grim.

"Nathan Lesperance has been scouting for us," said Cassandra Reed. "From him, we know Arthur's almost to West Brompton. It's our hope to intercept him in Chelsea before he reaches the Heirs' headquarters in Mayfair."

"Civilian casualties?"

"Thank God people have been fleeing ahead of him," Thalia answered. "But several suburbs have been flattened, homes destroyed. Once King Arthur gets farther into the city . . ." She shuddered.

A screech above made everyone look up. Wings flapped overhead. Astrid, now dressed in comfortable trousers and boots and armed with pistols and a rifle, jogged out of the mist. She held out her arm, and a familiar red-tailed hawk alit upon her offered perch. Seeing Catullus and Gemma, she, too, gave a brief smile of welcome, but the pleasure in reunion was quickly lost beneath the growing threat.

"Where's Merlin?" she demanded without preamble.

Briefly as they could, both Gemma and Catullus told of their journey through Otherworld. Neither decided to mention their interlude in the cottage—some things were better left unsaid.

"So, Merlin isn't coming," said Gabriel Huntley.

"No," replied Catullus, "and perhaps that's for the best. We cannot rely on anyone or anything so unstable. Not with the stakes so high. Yet he did entrust us with this." From his satchel, he produced the silver wheel, and everyone pressed closer to get a glimpse of this peculiar artifact.

Sunlight pierced the fog. The wheel gleamed, the eye of a distant god, yet held in the palm of Catullus's hand.

"Arthur will hear us with this," Catullus said. "If we cannot make him an ally, at the least, he won't be a threat. I hope."

A murmur of troubled agreement rippled through the Blades. That was all any of them had: hope. Nothing was certain. Blades had already fallen. More would be lost before the sun set. Gemma looked at their faces, each in turn, too many to count, yet too few. Who amongst them would see the next dawn? The thought pierced her heart.

"Catullus," Astrid said, quirking an eyebrow, "if I'm not mistaken, we're going to war, not a fancy dress party."

She glanced pointedly at the chivalric clothes he and Gemma wore.

"Catullus Graves doesn't *follow* trends," Gemma answered before he could, tipping up her chin in defiance. "He *makes* them."

His gaze met hers. She felt humbled and triumphant at what she saw there, in those dark depths: his pride in her, and love. Without reservation, love.

Astrid glanced back and forth between them. Slowly, she nodded, as if confirming a fundamental truth, yet happily surprised at its revelation. Catullus had changed within the span of a few days. But it was a change that made him, if possible, even stronger.

"Does that mean I get my own broadsword?" asked Gabriel Huntley. His rough-hewn soldier's features softened as he anticipated this possibility with the eagerness of a boy.

His wife rolled her eyes, but smiled fondly.

"If we make it through the next twelve hours," Catullus replied. "I'll forge swords for anybody who wants one. For now, we have to reach Arthur before he gets to the Primal Source."

Agreement, all around. A heavy silence fell in smothering waves. The upcoming battle would be the culmination of decades, centuries of warfare. Maybe they would all survive. Maybe none of them would. Gemma saw this understanding in each and every Blade as they clustered together in the middle of the charming, indifferent Kew Gardens. Those Blades that were married, or had lovers, reached out wordlessly to take their beloveds' hands.

Catullus sought and found Gemma's hand. They wove their fingers together, holding tightly.

"Before we head out," Catullus said, "does anyone have something to eat?"

* * *

Between the fifty or so Blades massed in Kew Gardens, a meal was put together for Gemma and Catullus. It consisted of slightly stale bread, a few bits of cheese, four apples, cold fried potatoes wrapped in paper, a flagon of ale, two sausages, and a partially eaten sweet biscuit.

"I didn't know the biscuit had currants in it," a Blade named Paul Street explained sheepishly. "I don't like currants."

As the assembled Blades readied themselves and their gear for their push east into the city, Catullus and Gemma sat at a picnic bench and ate. It didn't matter that most of the food tasted like it had been stored in a shoe closet. They were both ravenous, and ate with no attempt at manners.

Gemma, gnawing on a heel of bread, realized that this might be her last meal. The dry bread stuck in her throat, and she coughed.

Catullus patted her gently on the back. He offered her the ale, which she gratefully took. He resumed attacking a leathery apple.

After she drank, she found her appetite suddenly diminished. She turned the flagon around and around, thinking, mulling, her mind and heart and pulse all clamoring inside her.

"What's it like," she asked, "for mixed-race couples? In England?"

His chewing stopped. Started up again. Then he swallowed hard before throwing the apple aside. Almost conversationally, he said, "It isn't illegal for them to marry, if that's what you are asking."

"So, there are many of them?"

"Mixed couples aren't common, but not so uncommon as to provoke criticism. Not a *lot* of criticism, anyway. There are small-minded fools everywhere." He picked at the weathered wood of the tabletop, while his eyes remained focused on the Blades milling on the lawn. "My grandmother, on my father's side, is white. And my uncle on my mother's side married a white woman."

She started. "I didn't know that."

He shrugged, inured to his own history. "The number of black men to black women in England has always been disproportionate. A consequence of slavery and migration."

Gemma, too, kept her gaze on the activity in front of her, watching the men and women of the Blades prepare themselves for battle. She felt time slipping from her like ashes.

"But those couples . . . those marriages . . ." Her throat tightened. "They find ways to be together. To be together and . . . happy."

"It isn't always pleasant," he said, slowly, "but, yes, they find ways. If it is truly what they want." He turned to her, and she felt him—his presence, his gaze, desire, masculinity, and quality of mind that made him all exactly who he was, who she needed. "This isn't a journalist's curiosity that makes you ask." His words were a statement, but held a slight undercurrent of wariness, as if afraid to hope for too much.

She was afraid, too. So much could be lost, and soon after it had been gained, too. Which would make the loss even harder to take. "Not a reporter's curiosity. Ever since Mab's Cauldron, I've been pulling it apart, racking my brains. Trying to figure it out. To figure *us* out." She abandoned her pretext of watching the Blades, and faced him. Words started tumbling from her as if trying to form and be heard before they could fly away. "And I knew it would be thorny, as long as the world was . . . the way it was. But I didn't care what anyone said or did. So long as I was with you. And what you just said about what it's like here, in England, maybe . . . that is"—she gathered her faltering courage and pushed ahead—"if we make it through this coming battle . . . I want to live with you here. Or wherever you want to be or need to go." She drew in a breath. "I want you to be my husband."

He was almost motionless, staring at her. "Are you proposing?"

She thought about it. "Yes. I am."

Gemma hardly saw him move. They were both sitting side by side, and then his arms were around her, and she'd been pulled into his lap, and they were kissing. Sweet saints, did they kiss. His body was tight and solid against her, and his mouth was hot and demanding, and hers was, too, and she knew in that kiss she had her answer. And her heart didn't know whether to rejoice or break.

She knew that, as her husband, he would not try to force her into a role she wasn't meant to play. His love was for who she was, not who he wanted her to be. This wouldn't alter once they exchanged vows.

Whistles and claps finally broke them apart. Gemma managed to lift her head to see the Blades of the Rose watching, smiling. They grinned like people who knew they had only a few moments left, seizing joy before it burned away.

"We're to be married," said Catullus to the assembled Blades.

Another round of applause rose up, most loudly from Astrid. Lesperance gave his high, fierce hawk's cry as he circled overhead.

Slowly, reluctantly, Gemma and Catullus released one another and stood. She felt dizzy, buffeted by happiness and sorrow and fear and courage.

Before this day was done, she knew she would find herself either up amongst the clouds, or cast down to the depths.

Gemma had never been to London. With her insatiable curiosity and need for information, she had read about the city, its past and complex lacework of streets, each corner and alley containing a breadth of history she could hardly grasp. She once thought Chicago to be a grand and old city—though some of the oldest and most beautiful buildings had been destroyed in the terrible fire. Learning about London made her reevaluate Chicago's greatness.

It had been a city she dreamed of visiting. To see the places where Dickens, Shakespeare, and Dr. Johnson lived and worked, scribblers like her who had become more than writers. She had pictured herself wandering the tangled streets, the worn faces of centuries-old buildings all around, the sense of history palpable. She would stand on an anonymous corner and simply absorb decades, centuries of experience.

"This isn't exactly how I pictured my first visit to London." She panted this as she, Catullus, and the Blades ran along riverside embankments. The Thames, she knew that much. A thick gray course of water, filthy and regal. Names of neighborhoods, streets, these passed by. No time to play sightseer. Her views of the city consisted of flashes of parks, homes large and humble, warehouses—everything moving too quickly.

"When this is over"—Catullus ran beside her, his long legs making quick work of the miles—"I'll show you everything. The pelicans in St. James's Park. The columns of the Theatre Royal Drury Lane. Buckingham bloody Palace. Anything you want."

He said this with the strength of a vow, more serious than simply offering to play guide.

"Thank you," she answered, "but if I have to choose, I'd rather see your home."

His stride didn't falter, and neither did his steady gaze. "You will."

There wasn't time or breath to talk. Everyone ran, knowing they raced to avert disaster. Signs of Arthur's progress teemed, a path of chaos the Blades followed. A stately house's chimney writhed like an eel. Black-eyed elves leapt from rooftop to rooftop on the backs of pony-sized grasshoppers, knocking shingles to the street and punching holes in walls. Glistening green creatures, half-man, half-fish, swam through the river, causing terrified watermen to crash their boats into each other. Pixies, faeries, and goblins swarmed. Over all this hung a thick blanket of yellow fog, so that there was no way to know what was real and what was imagined.

Panicked people swarmed the streets as they fled. Carts and carriages rocketed, clattering, over the pavement. Horses whinnied in fear. Gemma dodged and wove through the crowds, as did Catullus and the other Blades, fighting the tide of citizens fleeing London. Several times, she nearly was trampled or fell underneath speeding wheels and hooves. But her reflexes had sharpened over the past week. Either she got herself out of harm's way, or Catullus protected her. A few Blades limped from collisions with fleeing, fear-maddened Londoners.

The anarchy of Glastonbury and its destructive infestation of pixies was a Sunday spaghetti dinner compared to this.

She and the advancing Blades shouldered and shoved their way through the mass of people. Gemma had no sense of where she was headed, but the others clearly did. She kept up, covering ground—though her feet ached. She wished Merlin had given her shoes that were a little more substantial. Dainty silk slippers might suit a princess for dancing or sighing over rescuing knights, but they were useless when it came time for a princess to run into battle and fight.

To distract herself from her aching feet, she took stock of her location. She, Catullus, and the Blades ran the length of an embankment. Nearly new lights blazed atop the wall fronting the river. Tall houses in a revival style faced the Thames, some in stages of construction. Walled gardens and trees also looked toward the river. A sophisticated, quiet neighborhood that spoke of wealth and taste.

Quiet. The chaos had been deafening. Now the absence of noise grabbed her attention. "Catullus," she said, "where is everyone?"

He glanced around. The panicked citizens of London

were nowhere to be seen. Only the Blades sped along the embankment. "Damn it," he growled. Over his shoulder, he barked, "Blades, prepare for attack."

No sooner had these words left him, a nerve-shredding shriek tore the air, followed by the beating of massive wings. The Blades skidded to a halt as the fog ahead swirled, stirred by an unknown wind.

Gemma gripped her derringer and her knife. Beside her, Catullus took a ready stance. The sounds of guns being loaded rose up from the Blades. *Something* was coming.

A large, dark form broke from the thick mist. It shrieked again as it landed heavily on the paved embankment, blocking the Blades from advancing.

Gemma swallowed her own yelp of horror. The *thing* defied her understanding. Human in shape, it stood almost two stories high. Though the form of its body was somewhat anthropomorphic, it had the head and wings of a monstrous red bird and taloned feet. It wore armor, dented from use, and waved a jagged sword, pushing the Blades back with each swing.

Was it some ancient English creature, summoned by King Arthur's progress?

"It's a Konoha Tengu!" Thalia Huntley shouted. "Japanese beast. Fearsome fighter."

"Japanese," Catullus muttered. He shot a glance to Gemma. "Which means he wasn't awakened here by Arthur. Which means—"

Gunfire whined above the Konoha Tengu's shrieks. Someone yelled as they went down. Blades scattered for cover, taking their wounded comrade with them. Gemma and Catullus darted toward a narrow strip of greenery and ducked behind a low brick wall. They both peered over it, careful to keep cover.

Behind the beast, the shapes of men emerged from the fog. All of them aimed firearms at the Blades. More shots rang out. Gemma ducked as a bullet whizzed overhead.

"We've got enough to contend with," Catullus growled. "Don't have time for sodding Heirs mucking things up." He returned fire. One of the Heirs screamed and fell.

"The Heirs don't share your sense of timing." She also shot back at them, even though she wasn't certain what her little pistol could do at that distance.

The Konoha Tengu stalked forward, swinging its sword. Blades tried to hold it back with gunfire, but the creature was relentless, and they struggled between it and the Heirs' barrage.

"Got to get that beast out of the way," Catullus murmured, mostly to himself.

"Ready, Graves?" shouted Sam Reed from somewhere.

"Ready," Catullus answered.

"On my count. Three, two, *now*."

Gemma blinked at the space where Catullus had been a heartbeat earlier. She peered up over the coverage of the wall. Where had he disappeared to?

There. He and Sam Reed stood against the Konoha Tengu, both of them battling the creature with their swords. The embankment rang with the sounds of metal against metal. Gemma could not look away, mesmerized by the sight of the two men fighting the beast, sidestepping and blocking its attacks, moving forward in seamless, wordless unity as they made their own assault. A savage and strangely beautiful dance.

And dangerous. Sam made no sound as the Konoha Tengu caught its blade across his shin, but Cassandra cried out when her husband faltered briefly in his steps. The beast shrieked in triumph, then shrieked again when Lesperance charged forward in his bear form. He swiped at the creature with his massive claws, tore at its flesh with its teeth.

Two armed men and a bear against a winged, bird-headed giant wielding its own sword. The kind of sight Gemma never could have dreamed, even with her odd imagination. She knew she hadn't the strength or skill to fight a creature like the Konoha Tengu, but she could do something about the Heirs.

"Astrid!" she shouted. "I need better firepower."

"Wish granted," Astrid said, suddenly appearing at Gemma's side. She tossed Gemma a rifle. Both women crouched behind the brick wall and shot at the Heirs, who fired back.

Yet no one moved. The Blades couldn't go forward, wouldn't retreat, and neither did the Heirs give or gain ground. A stalemate. Meanwhile, Arthur was somewhere in the city, getting closer to the Primal Source.

A breeze stirred the dank, foggy air. Gemma found herself inhaling deeply, trying to catch the elusive scent borne upon the wind, because it wasn't the damp, cool London stench. Something else. Something dry and warm and scented with . . . rosemary? Seawater and sun-baked rocks?

Astrid caught the scent, too, tilting her head to draw it in better. She and Gemma met each other's questioning glances. Neither had answers.

Movement over the river snared Gemma's attention. She turned, then grabbed Astrid's sleeve. "Over the water." She thought she was past the point of being surprised, but it seemed there was an unlimited amount of surprise.

A small boat steered its way through the river, navigating deftly between foundering vessels and water creatures. At the helm of the boat stood an olive-skinned man, small in height but with the stocky strength of a bull. He clenched the stem of a pipe between his teeth as he maneuvered the boat, comfortable and expert with a ship's wheel. This alone would have astonished Gemma, but what really drew her attention was the woman literally flying above the boat.

Though she was dressed in modern clothing, the woman resembled a goddess of the ancient world. Surely Gemma had seen her, or her ancestor, on a classical vase, enchanting Odysseus. Her dark hair streamed behind her as she flew; her eyes glowed with golden light. Her hands were outspread, and Gemma saw that the source of the dry, Mediterranean wind was the woman. She conjured the wind with her hands, chanting in an old language, and used it to propel herself and the boat through the Thames.

Beside Gemma, Astrid smiled darkly. "Our witch has arrived."

"She's on our side?"

"The Galanos witches are almost as important to the Blades as the Graves family. The man in the boat is Athena's lover, Nikos Kallas. Bennett says he's the best ship's captain in the world."

"I believe him," Gemma said at once. Given the expert way Kallas piloted the boat through the treacherous river, Gemma thought the man must bleed water.

"Get back," the woman floating above the boat commanded, her husky voice booming above the clamor.

Catullus, Sam, and Lesperance immediately dropped back, away from the Konoha Tengu. The creature mistook their withdrawal for retreat, and screeched its triumph as it lifted its sword above its head.

Her chanting growing louder, Athena raised her arms. The glow emanating from her eyes turned the fog to a golden haze. Below her, the Thames swelled, its greasy, glossy surface churning up white-capped waves. Kallas kept the boat steady beneath her, even when a huge wave suddenly rose up from the river.

The wave fountained up, rising up higher than the tall-masted ships on the river. As Athena chanted, the water took shape, forming into a massive catlike creature. Gemma stared, incredulous and thrilled by the magic. The huge feline was made entirely of water, its torso rising up from the river, and as it turned liquid eyes to the Konoha Tengu, its roar was the sound of booming rapids.

On the embankment, the Konoha Tengu gave a earsplitting shriek, raising its weapon. It sprung into the air, then dove at the water cat. At Athena's command, the river feline lunged, its sharp-toothed maw open. The Konoha Tengu stabbed at its foe, but the sword simply passed through the watery form of the cat's body without injury. The winged creature yowled in anger, then screamed when the cat seized the Konoha Tengu in its mouth and bit down.

Two fleshy slabs fell into the river: the Konoha Tengu's legs, and its upper body. Black blood spread in the water as the creature's severed body sank.

But the witch wasn't done. Still chanting, she directed the water cat toward the Heirs standing and gaping on the embankment. The men turned their guns on Athena, but the feline surged, blocking their shots. With one claw, it swiped at the Heirs. The force of the blow sent men flying backward, slamming into the façades of buildings or sprawling down the street. They struggled to their feet—though a few didn't get up again—and bolted.

Athena lowered her arms, and the water cat ebbed, until nothing was left of it but foam atop the river.

A cheer went up from the Blades, while Gemma put her fingers into her mouth and whistled. At the helm of the boat, Nikos Kallas blew kisses to his lover, still hovering high in the air. The witch gave everyone an enigmatic smile, though it faded quickly.

"Now is not the moment for celebration," she said. "The king is nearly to the Heirs' headquarters. Nikos and I will keep watch over the water, but you must stop him on land."

Gemma was already on her feet when Catullus ran back for her.

"With Blades all over the world," she said, "we'll never lack for places to visit."

"For our bridal journey," he answered.

"And everything after."

They shared a brief, meaningful look, knowing that they talked around the fact that the critical moment had come. But it couldn't be pushed aside forever.

Together, they ran, with the Blades at their backs.

Chapter 22

Siege

The journey from the Chelsea Embankment to Mayfair took Catullus, Gemma, and the Blades through some of London's most exclusive neighborhoods. Though he was born and had lived most of his life in Southampton, Catullus knew London, had walked its streets both sublime and squalid. Its scope never failed to awe him. A vast monster, this city, containing slums and palaces, parks and rookeries.

He wanted to show Gemma this city. With her active mind and omnipresent curiosity, she would find complex, contradictory London to be a vast treasure house of stories, and he wanted to be beside her, guide her, delight with her as she made her discoveries and explored.

"That's Sloane Square," he noted as they ran past the paved, elegant plaza. "Named for Hans Sloane, a physician in the first half of the eighteenth century. Massive collector—he bequeathed his collection of curiosities to the nation, and it became the basis of the British Museum. That's in Bloomsbury."

Gemma looked at him, incredulous. "Are you giving me a *tour*? *Now*?" She glanced at the bedlam surrounding them: terrified Londoners evacuating the city, pixies and goblins swarming over the dignified façades of Chelsea, armed Blades racing through the streets like a minuscule army.

"Thought you might want to know. New city, new sights. You like exploring."

Her incredulity softened into something much warmer. "I do. Thanks. But maybe the guided tour can wait until later."

"At your service," he murmured, and she smiled.

Later. Christ, he didn't know if there would be a *later*. No, there had to be. He refused to believe otherwise. The Blades had to succeed. They would stop Arthur from reaching the Primal Source, liberate the Primal Source from the Heirs' captivity, and, in so doing, restore the balance of magical power.

And then he and Gemma would be married.

The thought caused his already pounding heart to race in a full-out gallop.

She never faltered as they continued to push on into the city's wealthiest districts. They entered Belgrave Square, with its imposing, white-terraced mansions presenting a uniform front of British aristocratic dominance. Catullus always found the large, rational buildings of Belgravia to be cold, soulless, designed strictly to impress but never welcome. The windows became judgmental, cynical eyes, aloof and arrogant.

Now those eyes stared in shock as this center of insular superiority was overrun by chaos. Fog, people, magic. Noise ricocheted off the white-fronted mansions. Everything was anarchy—surely that wasn't what the Heirs, staunch defenders of hierarchy and order, had in mind.

"Looks like someone's been reading his Tennyson," drawled a familiar voice.

Catullus whirled as Bennett slipped from the fog with his usual skill, his wife at his side.

Bennett eyed Catullus's chivalric clothing. "Lovely surcoat. Embroider it yourself?"

Torn between embracing and throttling his old friend, Catullus settled for his usual expression when dealing with Bennett: an exasperated scowl.

"I trust your journey to Otherworld was a success," London said quickly. She seemed to have an instinctive understanding of when people wanted to punch her husband.

"We have the means of communicating with Arthur," answered Catullus.

"What about you?" Gemma asked. Blades gathered around them, eager for news.

"I managed to talk to some wives, sisters, and mothers of the Heirs," London said. She looked rueful. "A few called me a traitor and . . . other names which weren't very polite."

It was Bennett's turn to scowl. "Catty bitches."

"Bennett!" London gasped, but she wasn't especially shocked by her husband's coarse language. She seemed almost pleased at his defense of her, however crudely phrased. "Some of the women listened. Most said there was nothing they could do."

Disappointment broke in a gray wave over the Blades.

"Not all demurred," London went on. "Fifteen wives convinced their husbands not to fight. Ten others destroyed weapons belonging to their men, and nearly a dozen locked their men out of their homes." She let out a frustrated sigh. "Too many of the women are ruled by fear, and refused to act. I was once one of their numbers." She glanced at Bennett with a small smile, who returned the look with a goodly bit of heat. "None of them are lucky enough to catch their own scoundrel."

"And what of your reconnaissance, Day?" asked Gabriel Huntley.

Bennett liked having an audience, but his impulse to grandstand was tempered by the urgency of the situation. Tersely, he explained, "Investigated most of the Heirs' headquarters. It's heavily protected, as we thought. Got magical booby traps all over the place. The smallest bit of complacency or disregard will get someone killed, so stay alert."

He unfolded a piece of paper, revealing a hastily drawn map. A maze of fortifications, hallways, chambers, and secret doors. "I was able to get inside, and, thanks to you facing the Heirs at Kew Gardens, made decent headway. But I wasn't able to see everything. I do know that the Primal Source is kept within a room at the center of the headquarters. I couldn't reach that room, but I've an idea where it should be. Here." He pointed to the room in question, which lay at the heart of the building.

"Guards?" asked Sam Reed.

"An enchantment on the door. Only opens for Heirs. Barred windows. From what I understand, there's only one way in and out. It's going to take a hell of a lot to get in," he said grimly, "and a bloody miracle to get out. One would have to be mad to attempt it."

"Good thing the Blades are mad as Leonidas and the Spartans," said Catullus.

"Everyone knows how well that turned out," replied Bennett.

"We've an advantage those men never had." Catullus surveyed the assembled Blades, his gaze lingering on all the female Blades, so fierce and capable. Some of the women were less known to him, but he never doubted their skill or determination. Others he knew very well indeed. Thalia Huntley, London Day, his old friend Astrid. Each of them a limitless force never to be underestimated.

Including Gemma. The strength of his blood and beat of his heart. In her princess's gown that could not hide her fiery, passionate soul. She gazed at him now, love and spirit shining in her brilliant blue eyes—and judicious fear, too, tempered by determination to overcome that fear, which made him admire her all the more because of this determination—and he never felt stronger.

"What advantage do we have over those mad, doomed Spartans?" Bennett asked.

Catullus smiled. "We have Amazons."

Of all the members of the Graves family, currently only two had perfect memory. Catullus's sister Octavia could recall any page of any book she had ever read, and once she had traveled down a road, she would forever know each and every turn. The other Graves with this prodigious gift was Octavia's young daughter, Aurelia. The girl's capacity for recollection astounded the most sanguine members of the family, they who had seen every permutation genius had to offer.

Catullus's own memory didn't compare to little Aurelia's, but was still extensive. He knew almost every street, lane, and mews in London. Yet, as well as he knew the city, he had never once been to the part of Mayfair where Bennett now led the Blades.

It seemed impossible that an entire square could be concealed in London. But Bennett guided the Blades past Hyde Park, then up Curzon Street, turned a hidden corner, and then . . . there it stood in a square all its own. The Heirs of Albion's headquarters.

"Bugger me," muttered Gabriel Huntley. Ever the gruff noncommissioned officer.

The building would give any metropolitan mansion a bitter sense of inferiority. It loomed at one end of a plaza, four stories high, rows of columns arrayed like impassive sentries. Some ambitious architect had combined elements of medieval castles, Roman temples, and Tudor palaces into a threatening mass whose main purpose seemed to be intimidation. Towers stretched up toward the sky as if condescending to let the sun light their conical roofs. Crenellations lined the top edges of the walls. A spiked fence formed a jagged barrier all along the perimeter. Thick bars covered the windows along the lower two floors—presuming one could get past the armed sentries.

On the ground floor, up a short, wide flight of steps, stood a door. It was almost two stories high, more suited to a castle than a modern London building. It appeared to have been fashioned of solid steel. Catullus doubted any building, even the treasury or the Queen's residence, had so solid and impenetrable a door.

From the very top of the massive building flew the Union Jack. It snapped in the breeze, daring any individual or nation to dare challenge the superiority of Great Britain.

"It's sweet how bashful these guys are," said Gemma. She eyed the sentries out front and on the roof. The Heirs' guards carried the latest in firearms technology. "Why aren't they shooting at us?"

"As you say, they're shy wallflowers," Catullus answered. "Waiting to be asked to dance."

"The guest of honor is missing from the festivities," said Astrid. Her fair face paled further with strain from her proximity to the Primal Source. "But I feel Arthur is close." She turned to the alert, bristling wolf Lesperance beside her. "Perhaps if you took to the air, you can—"

Her words were lost as the streets shook, waves of power sweeping through the square. Everyone, even the Heirs' sentinels, braced themselves.

Thunderous footsteps sounded close by.

"Eternal blue heaven," breathed Thalia, at the same time her husband growled a tumble of soldierly swearing.

Stunned silence fell over the Blades as they beheld the huge figure striding from a side street. The street barely stood wide enough to accommodate the giant. He emerged into the square, then espied the Blades staring at him. He paced to tower in front of them, the Heirs' headquarters behind him. A soldier would never turn his back on his enemies, but to the best of the giant's understanding, the Heirs were allies.

Catullus would have to convince him otherwise.

The Blades gaped at the embodied legend.

Arthur.

The fabled king stared down at them, magic and myth radiating out with a golden brilliance, almost blinding. His massive stance had him straddling the street, legs braced wide, the city of London nothing but an impermanent illusion compared to his timeless might. Awe froze the Blades where they stood. Arthur glowered at them, the perceived enemies of England.

He reached for Excalibur, readying to cut them all down with one strike.

Catullus ran toward Arthur. "Hold. Your Highness must hold." He planted himself in front of the king, staring up at him. Memories of his last one-on-one encounter with Arthur flared. Catullus had barely escaped alive. This time, he might not be so fortunate.

Arthur turned his burning glare to Catullus. He gripped Excalibur, and with a loud hiss the sword began to slide from its scabbard.

In his satchel, Catullus searched. His hand kept closing around things he did not need: tools, his pipe, the Compass, a length of twine. Damn it. Where—?

The sword slid free from its scabbard. It gleamed in the fog.

Catullus started when a warm, slim hand touched his inside the satchel. He glanced up to see Gemma also rifling through the bag.

"Get back," he growled.

"You need to be more organized," she answered. "Here."

She pressed a metal disk into his palm. His thumb brushed the spokes. The silver wheel.

Catullus's gaze met hers. Despite the fact that a gigantic,

angry mythical kind was about to slice them both into fillets, she was steady and resolute.

"Someone needs a good talking to," she said, glancing at Arthur.

Catullus wasted no time. He held the silver wheel high in the air, ensuring the king could see it. "Hold, Your Highness," he said again.

The raised sword froze. Arthur looked down at Catullus with a puzzled frown, as if hearing something a great way off.

"You are being misled," Catullus continued rapidly. "The men who have been urging you on, calling you, they are not your friends. They are not the friends of England."

"Are you?" demanded Arthur.

Good Lord, he was *talking with King Arthur.* "My associates and I seek peace and the betterment of *everyone*, not merely England." He glanced toward the Heirs' headquarters. As he did so, he caught sight of all the Blades looking at him, hope and fear commingled in their expressions. Catullus was literally their only chance of survival. Gemma stood at his side, barely breathing.

Farther back, Catullus saw several Heirs gathered in the windows and on the parapets of their headquarters as they, too, waited to see what King Arthur would do.

Turning back to Arthur, Catullus continued, "If you do as those men say, follow their will, you shall enslave the world to the greedy demands of a select few. Surely that is not what the Round Table stood for."

Arthur frowned, his massive brow creasing like furrows in a field. "Your words could be idle or false. A wicked enchantment crafted to deceive."

"Merlin, your oldest and most trusted counselor, gave this to me." Catullus held out the silver wheel. "With his remarkable gift of prophecy, he foretold the disaster that would come to pass if you do not break free of these men, the destruction that shall be wrought. You cannot continue on this path, Your Highness."

Arthur appeared still undecided. An improvement, though small, from his goal of chopping the Blades into mince. Yet he did not appear convinced that the Blades were his allies, and the Heirs' plans for England meant a global catastrophe.

The king wavered, hearing Catullus's words, but not truly listening. How to break through?

"Give him the wheel," said Gemma.

Catullus stared at her.

"He needs some kind of proof," she went on, low and quick. "We know that if he touches the Primal Source, everything's going to hell. But if he touches the silver wheel, he might be able to break away from the Heirs. Two magics physically connecting with each other."

Looking back and forth between the silver wheel in his hand and the giant king looming over him, Catullus saw the reason in her suggestion. He drew a breath and, holding the wheel up between his fingers, offered it to Arthur.

"What is this?" the king challenged. "More trickery?"

"Merlin made the wheel so you would learn the truth. Take it, and see," urged Catullus.

Though Arthur scowled, he did reach for the wheel. The king plucked it from Catullus's grasp, the silver object a minuscule sequin in his enormous hand. Catullus forced himself to stand utterly still even though he knew Arthur could simply crush him, and Gemma, effortlessly.

Arthur's massive body stiffened as if absorbing a blow. He continued to stare at the wheel, horror playing across his face. Beneath his bearded, ruddy cheeks, he paled.

"By the rood," he rasped, his gaze distant, "you speak truly. I see a dark force holding the nation by its throat. I see magic fair and sinister brought beneath the yoke of servitude, and millions of mortal lives snuffed out like sighs. The fate and fortunes of all, controlled by a handful of men, who are themselves enslaved to their own avarice." He raised his eyes to Catullus and Gemma, haunted. "I am nothing but a puppet. My dream is broken."

Brief triumph surged between Catullus and Gemma as they blindly reached for, and gripped, one another's hands. They had done it! Arthur was now free of the Heirs' will. The cost, however, was high. The king turned suddenly lost, gazing around with a mystified, bereft expression. He looked out of place, out of time, an anomaly in a modern world that had marched on without him.

Of all the emotions Catullus expected to feel when standing in the presence of a mythical king, pity had not been one of them. Yet he felt it now, staring up at this creation of legend and dream, who lived in a scale much more grand than anything steam engines, gas lighting, or telegraphs could ever provide. A manifestation of chivalry and magic amidst the coal smoke. In the land that had created him, he was a stranger. And worse.

Arthur was not the King of England, its embodiment of national identity and pride, but a dupe. He knew this now. The glimmering radiance around him dimmed.

"Oh, hell," Gemma murmured softly.

Catullus took a step forward. "England still has need of you."

"Not just England," Gemma added, coming to stand next to Catullus. "But the world, too, needs you."

A bitter smile barely shaped Arthur's mouth. "As a fool, perhaps."

"As a leader," Catullus said, level. "As the people's champion."

Arthur gazed around him, his eyes lingering on chimneys thrust like dark bones into the sky. Somewhere, distantly, came the sound of a train whistle.

"Fight with *us*," said Astrid as she and Lesperance came forward.

Thalia and Huntley also strode up. "Help us take back what's been stolen," Thalia said.

"And make those bastards sorry for crossing the wrong king," added Bennett, moving close with London beside him.

Arthur's smile slowly, slowly transformed, shifting from embittered to genuine. He drew his regal bearing about him like a mantle. The air around him gleamed once more.

"'Tis a quest, is it not?" he said.

"A quest of the utmost importance," Catullus answered, his own spirits rising. "In the building behind you, the greatest power known in all of human imagination is kept prisoner. The magic is held by the same men who sought to manipulate you. And it must be freed."

Renewed, purposeful, Arthur nodded. "It will be my greatest pleasure to storm their fortress and reclaim that magic, as well as my own honor." He surveyed the Blades of the Rose arrayed before him. "You are fine warriors and knights, and I shall be privileged to lead you into battle."

Arthur raised Excalibur, and Catullus felt within himself a visceral jolt, a surge of strength to witness King Arthur ready to lead a charge. What army or nation could resist his allure? If any heart lacked resolve, seeing the warrior king prepare for battle banished doubt and bolstered courage.

Even Gemma—democratic, egalitarian Gemma—beamed to see King Arthur rallying the Blades. It had been her idea to give Arthur the silver wheel, and that had turned the tide in their favor. With King Arthur leading the attack on the Heirs' stronghold, surely the Blades must succeed.

"Onward, warriors," Arthur boomed.

A loud cheer rose up from the Blades, Catullus and Gemma's voices amongst them.

As one, they rushed across the square, toward the Heirs. Arthur took the lead, his long strides taking him to the Heirs' very door. Shots rang out from the building as the Heirs defended themselves. Blades returned fire, never breaking their advance. Catullus fired his shotgun, Gemma her rifle, neither caring that their modern firearms paired incongruously with their clothing. The battle was on.

The square filled with shouts, the sounds of glass breaking and men's cries as some of the sentries on the roof were hit and fell the four stories down. Arthur kicked down the stout fence surrounding the building as if it were made of straw. Heirs rushed to meet him, but he felled them with a strike. With the Blades at his back, Arthur reached the heavy front door. Swirling clouds of magic churned around the door. A handful of Blades stumbled back, blinded, pulling at their sparking clothes, but the rest pressed on. Heirs tried to flank the advancing Blades, coming around the sides of the building. Catullus and Gemma concentrated on keeping them back with a barrage of shots.

Bellowing, Arthur slammed his shoulder into the door. The massive building shook beneath his weight. Yet the door itself did not move. Once more, Arthur threw his shoulder against it, and again. Cracks spread across the solid stone façade. An almighty groan sounded as the door shuddered before toppling backward, into the building.

Where the door once stood, a gaping hole revealed the inside of the Heirs' headquarters. Dust billowed up, combining with black smoke from the gathered Heirs' gunfire. Most kept the line. Some fled. They braced themselves as Blades prepared to attack. Though the Heirs tried to appear stoic or fierce, seeing Arthur in the full of his fury plainly terrified them. Catullus and Gemma shared a grin. It felt good to be on the other end of the intimidation, for a change.

Giving his own savage grin, Arthur hefted Excalibur. "Now to take back what has been stolen! Come, we—"

A deafening roar severed the last of Arthur's words. The king looked up, toward the source of the sound. His face registered patent amazement as a shadow darkened him.

A huge, scaly form dove down from the sky. It crashed into Arthur. Both the king and the shape rolled, crushing everything in their path. In the middle of the square, Arthur staggered to his feet.

Only to be engulfed in a jet of fire.

The Heirs had unleashed a dragon.

* * *

"Dragon," Gemma said aloud. She stared at the beast, her eyes wide. "That's a real dragon."

Catullus could understand her shock. He'd seen scores of beasts and creatures, from the terrible to the exquisite, enormous to minuscule. Nothing quite compared to seeing a huge mythological creature in real life. The last dragon he had seen had been in a Buddhist monastery in the Gobi Desert. That beast had been made of steam, but deadly all the same. He'd witnessed it tearing men to pieces.

God knew the dragon Arthur faced in the square could easily do the same.

"The dragon must be the Heirs' fail-safe," Catullus said. "If they lost control of Arthur, they would need some way to combat him. Nothing better than the mythic nemesis of England's heroes."

Of all the beasts Catullus had seen, this dragon was by far one of the biggest. Its massive, scaled body could crush a tall-masted ship of the line, and its claws could flatten a carriage. The dragon's leathery wings beat at the air as it circled and then landed opposite Arthur. Spikes ran from its huge head, down the length of its back, and all the way to its whipping tail. When it opened its maw to roar, each tooth was a broadsword.

The dragon roared, impossibly loud, and its eyes glittered with an ancient hate. It charged Arthur. The king struck out with Excalibur.

Another roar as the blade cut across the dragon's front shoulder. Yet the beast only grew more angry. It lunged for Arthur again, and again the king used his swordsmanship to deflect the attack.

The two were perfectly matched—the height of English chivalry against a powerful, mythical beast.

"This could go on forever," Catullus murmured.

"Should we help him?" asked Gemma.

"No time. Our hosts are here."

Heirs poured from every doorway into the ruins of the marble-lined foyer. Catullus grabbed Gemma and shoved them both behind a toppled column, moments before the Heirs opened fire. Blades all took up positions as they fought to break through the first wave of defenders. The air filled with the cacophony of gunfire, shouts, and, from the square outside, the dragon's roar.

In the midst of this madness, Bennett appeared beside Catullus and Gemma, London at his side. "I'm taking a contingent to where the Primal Source is held," he shouted above the noise. He tipped his head toward a group of Blades crouched nearby: Thalia and Huntley, Astrid and the wolf Lesperance, Henry Wilson, Victoria Dean, Luis Diaz, and a dozen more.

Catullus glanced at Gemma. "Ready to push on and keep fighting?"

"Half-Irish, half-Italian," she answered with a grin. She brandished a fist. "Brawling is in my blood."

He returned her grin, then nodded to Bennett that they were primed to go.

For a moment, Bennett simply watched the volley of gunfire. Catullus had no idea what Bennett looked for, but his friend's gift for slipping into unseen spaces had gotten all the Blades out of more than a few tight corners. Bennett suddenly signaled. It was time to move out.

The remaining Blades gave cover fire. With Bennett at the lead, the contingent of Blades sprinted through the wrecked foyer, past a battalion of Heirs, up a curving flight of stairs, and into a long hallway. They could hear the fight continuing below, and moved quickly into the hall. Away from the chaos of the entryway, an almost unnatural hush descended. The Blades cautiously traveled down the passage, alert to any and every sound and movement.

"Just as understated as the outside," murmured Catullus, glancing around.

Crystal chandeliers glinted like icicles down the length of the hallway. Mahogany furniture of the finest quality stood sentry outside closed doors. Thick carpeting muted footsteps, as did the rich tapestries of fabled beasts hanging on the walls. Portraits of esteemed Heirs hung beside the tapestries, dating back centuries, all the way to pale men in Elizabethan ruffs.

"Looked like smug bastards even then," noted Huntley. "Nobody's got a chin."

Gemma took in her surroundings with a keen and attentive eye. "Is this what the Blades' headquarters looks like in Southampton?"

"Ours is a fourth the size, at a tenth the budget," Catullus answered.

"A sixteenth the budget," Astrid corrected. "Remember how we couldn't fix the east wall for three months?"

"Quiet," snapped Bennett. "Right around here should be a tr—"

A creature leapt from a tapestry, shifting from a small, two-dimensional being into a full-sized monster blocking the hallway. The front half of its body resembled a large stag, complete with wickedly pronged antlers and exceptionally sharp hooves, while the lower half of its body bore the appearance of a bird of prey, including large wings and talons.

"Holy God, what the hell is that?" Gemma demanded.

"A peryton," said Catullus. "Ancient beast from around Gibraltar. It hasn't killed yet. Look at its shadow."

Gemma swore when she saw that the beast cast the shadow of a man against the expensively papered walls.

"It's part deer, right?" She backed closer to him when the peryton snorted and stalked closer. Its antlers dug deep gouges in the walls and the carpet tore beneath its hooves and talons. "That means it eats plants, not people."

"Actually," Catullus noted, drawing his sword, "perytons are carnivorous. Have a taste for human flesh."

"Of course they do," she muttered and drew her knife.

The peryton crouched, then sprang toward the Blades. Huntley, Astrid, and Lesperance all leapt to intercept before it could reach the group. Lesperance, as a wolf, latched onto the beast's throat, but it shook him free before he could fully sink his teeth into its neck. Huntley kicked a heavy table toward the peryton as Astrid opened fire.

Neither the splintered wood nor the gunfire affected the creature. It kept moving forward, pushing the Blades back. Huntley planted himself in front of the peryton and used his rifle to shoot it right in the center of its forehead. Such a wound would have killed any mortal being. The peryton was neither. Enraged, it swung its head and caught Huntley across the chest with its antlers.

Thalia ran forward to shield him from further hurt. Her husband tried to push her away to safety, but the beast moved too quickly, and she took a razor-sharp hoof down her back. The Huntleys' blood spattered across the carpet in bright drops.

Astrid and Bennett dragged the wounded couple out of the way. The other Blades, including Gemma and Catullus, unleashed a storm of bullets at the peryton, chopping up the fine wood and plasterwork of the passage. Yet the beast itself shed bullets like rain.

"Can we find another route?" Catullus yelled to Bennett.

"This bloody place is a labyrinth," came the shouted response. "We've got to get down this hall to reach the stairs that lead to the Primal Source. We go another route and we'll wind up in a bloody dungeon."

Catullus's mind spun. The damned creature seemed impervious to harm. There had to be some way to defeat it.

A door behind the Blades slammed open. Several Heirs sprang out, guns aloft. Though Catullus recognized some of them, one in particular caught his notice. And Astrid's, as well.

She sucked in a breath, her body tensing. The Heir saw

her at the same time. Fear tightened his mouth before he deliberately assumed an insolate, smirking manner.

"How polite," the Heir drawled. "You came all the way to my door, saving me the trouble. I'm looking forward to finishing what I started in Africa, Mrs. Bramfield." He raised his pistol.

"And I'll finish what I started in Canada, Gibbs," Astrid gritted. Fury turned her eyes to sharp diamonds. "Ran Staunton through with a sword. After I kill you, Michael's death will be avenged."

Lesperance had recovered from being shaken off by the peryton and now crouched beside Astrid, growling. The Heirs with Gibbs edged back at the sight of the enraged woman and equally angry wolf.

But Gibbs's bravado held. "From men to animals," he leered. "You *are* a twisted bitch."

Snarling, Astrid charged, with Lesperance fast behind. Gibbs fired, yet Astrid tackled him, throwing off his aim. She and the Heir rolled down the hall, trading blows, as Lesperance bit and lunged.

Gemma moved to help, but Catullus held her back.

"This is her fight," he murmured. Before she could object, he added, "I need you with me."

She gave a quick nod.

An abbreviated yell caught their attention. They spun around to see the peryton biting down on Henry Wilson's shoulder. Blood streamed down Henry's arm as he thrashed, trying to pull free. Other Blades, including Bennett and London, struggled to break the creature's hold on their comrade. The peryton grew maddened by the taste of blood, eyes burning.

Catullus whirled back to the Heirs. One of them, a ruddy, burly fellow called Risby, sneered at him. "Nowhere to go, Graves," he taunted.

"There's always forward," Catullus said.

Risby barely managed a yelp when Catullus lunged and

grabbed him by his lapels. The Heir flailed, trying to break free. Catullus wouldn't allow his opponent time to gather his wits. Using his body as an axis, Catullus spun Risby around. The Heir was heavy, yet energy surged through Catullus. He whirled in a parody of a dance, and, employing centrifugal force, swung Risby about, releasing the Heir in time to send him hurtling straight toward the peryton.

Risby waved his arms, trying to stop his course, but his weight worked against him. He slammed into the peryton. The beast shrieked, releasing Henry. Bennett and London quickly pulled Henry away.

Crazed with bloodlust, the peryton attacked Risby. It clamped its teeth on the Heir's beefy neck and ripped.

Gemma and London looked away as Risby, missing the front of his throat, gurgled. The peryton tore at Risby in a frenzy. Blood sprayed across the expensive wallpaper. Heirs swore. One gagged.

The peryton glanced up from its work, its muzzle dark with gore. Blades braced themselves for another assault, but the creature only stared at them.

"Why isn't it attacking?" asked Gemma, finally turning around.

"Look at its shadow now," Catullus said.

Instead of casting the shadow of a man, as it had before, the peryton's shadow was that of a deer.

Thalia, leaning against Huntley, frowned. "I don't understand."

"A peryton can kill only once," explained Catullus.

"Not a very effective guard," said Gemma.

"It can't be hurt, either. So it can successfully repel one intruder."

"But there's more than one of us." Gemma, still pale, managed a fierce smile.

Catullus glanced over at the Blades. Henry, Thalia, and Huntley were all wounded. Then, in a display of strength that impressed the hell out of Catullus, Thalia and her husband stood, ready to battle despite their injuries. They and the other Blades faced the Heirs, who were visibly shaken by the violent death of Risby.

"We'll handle this lot," said Huntley. He issued commands like a born soldier. "Day, take your wife, Graves, and Miss Murphy to the Primal Source. It'll take all your brains and guile to free the damned thing."

Catullus almost asked if Huntley was all right with being left behind, but the grim set of the former soldier's mouth and the light of battle in his eyes left no room for doubt. Catullus had seen Huntley in battle, and knew the man was a force unto himself. If anyone ought to be concerned, it should be the Heirs.

"We'll reconnoiter at the entrance," said Catullus. *If we all survive.*

Huntley only nodded, his mind already preparing for combat. Beside him, Thalia had the same look of fierce readiness. Two warriors preparing to fight side by side.

"Time to move out," clipped Bennett.

The small group consisting of Bennett, London, Gemma, and Catullus broke away from the contingent of Blades. They edged past the torn body of Risby and the peryton, who only stared at them with disinterest. Catullus and the others darted down the hallway. Catullus couldn't spare a glance behind him, yet he heard the sounds of combat as the Blades and the Heirs clashed.

"All right?" he asked as Gemma sprinted beside him.

Her face was pale, freckles standing out like rubies in snow, yet she nodded. "I'm dandy. But I don't think I'll eat rare roast beef for a long time." She fought a shudder. "Never seen anything like that happen to a man."

"I can't promise you won't see something like that again," he said with regret.

"You don't have to."

"This way," said Bennett, ahead. He kicked open a door and waved them in.

They found themselves in a sitting room. It was a strangely domestic space, complete with bookshelves, a sofa, desk, and fireplace. A fire crackled cheerfully in the grate and filled the room with gentle warmth. If one discounted the sounds of a dragon roaring outside and gunfire inside, it could be any pleasant, tastefully furnished English parlor.

"This isn't the time for a cozy fireside chat," Catullus noted dryly.

Bennett looked provoked. "You scientists, understanding only what you can see." He strode toward the desk and pulled out and shut drawers in a sequence only he could fathom. At once, the wall behind the desk slid to one side, revealing a hidden staircase. London beamed at her husband.

"This was as far as I got," Bennett said. "And I was lucky to do so, with most of the Heirs away at Kew Gardens and then at the Chelsea Embankment. Couldn't map everything. But I believe that if we go up the stairs and to the left, we ought to find the chamber that houses the Primal Source."

"Believe, but don't know for certain," said Catullus. "Now we've a *collaborative* expedition of discovery."

"But *I* blazed the primary trail."

"You didn't go *all* the way," Catullus noted.

"For God's sake," snapped Gemma. "Enough with the schoolyard swaggering, and let's get the hell on with it."

Mildly abashed, Bennett and Catullus nodded. Everyone started toward the revealed staircase.

The fire suddenly blazed higher, tongues of flame reaching up to lick along the walls of the sitting room. Catullus pulled Gemma behind him, shielding her, and raised an arm to protect his own eyes. Bennett, too, moved to shelter his wife from the blaze.

A dark figure emerged from the fire. As the flames receded, they revealed the figure's scarred, twisted face, a visible record of cowardice and greed.

London gasped, clutching Bennett's arm reflexively.

"Welcome home, sister," sneered Jonas Edgeworth.

Chapter 23

Through the Fire

It was the face from a nightmare. Thick scars twisted the man's visage into a permanent sneer, and one of his eyelids had been fused shut so that he glared at the world with a single, burning eye. Expensive clothing hid his body, but Gemma saw that several of his fingers were likewise stuck together by a webwork of scar tissue. Though he stood tall and broad of shoulder, his whole body must be covered in the relics of a horrible burn.

Gemma had seen healed burn victims before. How could she not, when only four years earlier Chicago had turned into an inferno? Enough Chicagoans bore the marks of those awful two and a half days that Gemma did not flinch or turn away from their sadly disfigured faces and bodies. She, like everyone in Chicago, learned that a person's exterior did not reflect who they truly were. Accident, not an evil heart, marked them. Even pity was unwarranted, insulting.

The man who had just emerged from the fire—he was different. Gemma felt malevolence radiating out from him like heat from the fire. He stared at London with so much burning hatred, it was a wonder London didn't simply burst into flame.

London was stronger than that. She recovered from her shock and moved out from behind the shelter of her husband. Gemma could only admire the Englishwoman's courage.

"This was never my home, Jonas," she said, gesturing to the parlor.

"And that's why you whored yourself and killed Father," he snapped. "Why you're here now with the Blades of the Rose."

Day took a step toward the man, and only London's hand on his arm stopped him from planting a fist right into the man's scarred face.

"This isn't about righting familial wrongs, Edgeworth," said Catullus.

Gemma understood: This enraged, embittered man was London's brother and a member of the Heirs of Albion. And somehow, the fire that once burned him now gave him a power over that same element, allowing him to travel through it.

Edgeworth swung his blistering gaze toward Catullus. His face contorted even more, a combination of rage and disgust.

"The Graves species has been a blight in Britain for generations," he spat. "Thinking you're as good or better than the superior white race. Look at you, with your black skin in knightly rags, nothing but a travesty of English chivalry."

Gemma felt torn between vomiting and beating Edgeworth's head in like a rotten pumpkin. Maybe she could do both. She, too, took a step toward the Heir, only to find Catullus gently restraining her.

"Nothing is more pathetic than a name-calling bully," Catullus said calmly to Edgeworth.

This shook the Heir. "I can do more than call names," he snarled. He lifted his hands. From his upright palms, two streams of fire shot out.

They dove in different directions, Day and London one way, Catullus and Gemma in another. Glancing up from the floor, beneath the solid mass of Catullus, Gemma saw the charred spots on the walls where she and the other Blades had been standing seconds earlier.

All four of them exchanged stunned glances. Edgeworth's power far surpassed anything they'd anticipated.

Edgeworth laughed, a bleak, grating sound. "The Transportive Fire took away my life, but gave me a new one, and a new gift."

Gemma had no idea what he was talking about, and she didn't really care. All she cared about was moving the Blades out of this parlor before Edgeworth roasted them. They had to find the Primal Source and get it the hell out of here.

"The stairs," she whispered to Catullus on top of her.

He made quick calculations, then subtly nodded. "On my count," he whispered back. "One, two, *now.*"

Catullus rose up on his knees and fired a blast from his shotgun at Edgeworth. The Heir threw up a shield of fire.

Using this distraction, Catullus grabbed Gemma's wrist, and they both ran toward the stairs. Day and London immediately followed.

Edgeworth recovered enough to shoot flame after them. The banisters of the narrow, steep staircase caught fire before Gemma and London could use it for balance. Everyone ran up the secret stairs, but Catullus lingered near the entrance.

On the landing, Gemma stopped and hissed, "Goddamn it, don't fight him on your own!"

"Not planning on it," he answered. He ran his hands over the walls enclosing the stairs, then smiled tightly. "This." He pushed on an unseen panel, and the wall hiding the staircase slid shut just as Edgeworth was about to run after them.

An outraged, thwarted roar sounded behind the closed wall.

"Move your sodding arses!" Day shouted above them.

Catullus bounded up to Gemma, taking the stairs three at a time, leaping over them with a savage grace. Hands intertwined, they continued up the flight of steps together. The fire along the banisters grew, tracing the stairs with heat and light.

Husband and wife waited for them at the top of the stairs. London's face was ashen. "I had no idea," she breathed. "No idea how twisted his mind had become." She swallowed hard. "He wants us dead. He wants *me* dead. Oh, God."

"I'm sorry," Gemma murmured, placing what she hoped was a comforting hand over London's.

Day's arm around his wife's shoulders tightened. She seemed to draw strength from him, and even Gemma. Drawing herself up, a focused calm settled over her. "We have to move forward," she said.

Love and pride shone in Day's eyes—the expression seemed familiar to Gemma, and she realized then that Bennett Day looked at his wife the same way Catullus looked at *her*. Gemma's heart pounded within her ribs. They must succeed, must survive.

"I'll guess this way," Day said. He led them down another hallway, one that looked confusingly like the passage a floor below. The hall abruptly opened into a large room with parquet floors and tall windows. A ballroom of some kind. At one end of the ballroom stood a large lit fireplace. Unlit, several grown men could easily stand within the fireplace. But this wasn't very interesting compared to the sight in the middle of the ballroom.

A bear fought with a gigantic creature that looked like an unholy mix between a wolf and a man. Across the creature's face ran a white scar, bisecting its eye.

The Blades and Gemma stared at the spectacle. The bear and the beast locked together in mortal combat, claws and teeth and echoing roars in the elegant room. Every moment brought fresh wonders to Gemma's already amazed senses.

"As Huntley might say, 'Bugger me,'" said Day. "What in hell?"

"That's Lesperance," Gemma said. She had no idea how he got here, but, given that he had the ability to fly, she was sure he'd gone around the normal routes.

"And Bracebridge," added Catullus. "He and Lesperance have a grievance."

"I don't see Astrid," London said.

"Must still be attending to her own vengeance."

"No shortage of interesting views," Day noted, pointing to the windows at their backs.

Everyone turned to see Arthur outside in the square, locked in battle with the dragon. From the looks of things, Arthur wouldn't be breaking away any time soon to lend a hand to the Blades. The king dove and attacked using Excalibur, his sword flying in gleaming arcs, and the dragon countered with strikes of its claws. When Arthur lunged, aiming for the dragon's throat, it took to the air, hovering above its foe and launching a series of feints. The dragon's roars shook the glass in the windows.

Outside, two myths fought with savage determination. And inside the ballroom two massive beasts engaged in vicious combat.

"Though I'd love to hang about and place bets on the outcome," Day said, "we have to keep going. The chamber with the Primal Source must be—"

"Whore!" screamed a voice from the other end of the ballroom. "Traitors! You cannot thwart the destiny of Britain!"

Oh, God, she'd only heard that voice once before and hated it already.

Edgeworth sprang from the fire at the end of the ballroom. Heedless of the fellow Heir standing between him and his prey, Edgeworth threw jets of flame across the room. Bracebridge and Lesperance leapt apart as the fire cut between them.

Gemma again found herself diving for cover. Flames roared above her, coming close enough to sizzle across her scalp. The fire slammed into the wall behind her, and immediately began to spread. It crept up the walls in growing waves.

"Son of a bitch," Gemma muttered. "He'll burn the damned place down. With him and the Heirs in it."

"Edgeworth's not exactly thinking logically," came Catullus's dry response. He reached out, grabbed the leg of a semicircular table wedged against the wall, and dragged it in front of him and Gemma. Lamps and assorted gewgaws fell from the tabletop, shattering. Bennett Day used several gilt chairs as a barricade to shield himself and London.

From behind their fortifications, the Blades took aim at Edgeworth. At least Lesperance and the creature he fought had taken their battle out of the ballroom—Gemma heard their roars down one of the many corridors snaking off of the assembly room—so that when she and the Blades unleashed a volley of bullets, Lesperance couldn't be caught in the crossfire.

They traded fire. Bullets from the Heirs, actual fire from Edgeworth. The Heir defended himself behind shields of flame. He threw blazing streams at the Blades, until their cover began to burn.

Catullus slapped at the fire, swearing all the while. But his attempts to douse the flames couldn't stop their growth. They had no place to hide.

Everything shook violently. Plaster cracked and bricks fell as something enormous slammed into the side of the building. Catullus dragged Gemma to one side as the wall behind them collapsed inward, destroyed by the force of Arthur and the dragon ramming into it.

The mythic enemies grappled, then staggered away, caught up in their combat. They left behind a huge hole— and a useful distraction.

"Never underestimate the value of a proper exit," said Day with a grin. He and London darted toward one of the open doors opposite the broken windows.

"Always getting a line in," muttered Catullus, but he and Gemma both followed.

Edgeworth, dodging more falling plasterwork, couldn't stop their exodus.

The four of them sprinted down a corridor, this one more utilitarian and less sumptuous than the others. Open doors lined the hallway.

"Which one?" Catullus demanded as they ran.

"If my guess is correct," answered Day, "it's the second door on the right at the end, then, I believe, up another set of stairs. But those are educated guesses."

"How educated?" asked Catullus. "Harrow level?"

Day snorted. "Don't insult me. I'm an Old Wykehamist. 'Dulce Domum.'"

The men ran with athletic, long-limbed grace, while Gemma and London struggled to keep up in their confining dresses.

"Maybe Astrid and Thalia have the right idea," Gemma panted.

London made a face. "Ladies aren't even supposed to *run*, let alone wear trousers."

"To hell with being a lady."

"Forever and ever. Amen."

London bit back a yelp when her brother pounced from one of the open doors. Any question as to how he'd gotten ahead of them from the ballroom was answered by the lit fireplace in the room from which he'd come.

Edgeworth's hands wrapped around London's throat. Gemma was already slamming her elbows into his back by the time Day appeared to brutally punch his brother-in-law in the jaw. Sputtering, spitting teeth and blood, Edgeworth released his sister, but as he did so, fires erupted around him. The greater his rage grew, the more fire seemed to leap from him involuntarily. Catullus lunged forward to pull Gemma out of the way of the flames.

Edgeworth, snarling, disappeared back into the fire.

From another room, a clot of Heirs spilled out. With them was a three-armed, six-eyed giant, a club in each meaty hand. This new threat advanced.

Rather than look defeated or appalled, Day only grinned. "This Winchester man thinks it's the second door from the end, on the right. There should be stairs. Go up the stairs, and then I believe it's on your left. I'm happy to scrap with this lot while you go for the Primal Source, if you would."

"Gladly," answered Catullus, also grinning.

Gemma and London shared a look, heavy with sympathy for one another. Each of them in love with madmen. They gave each other encouraging smiles before both turning back to their respective men. Day happily readied himself for his anticipated brawl. Gemma thought about one day introducing him to her brothers.

Then she was running again, fighting to keep pace with Catullus's long legs. But he knew she couldn't match him for speed and maneuverability, and kept beside her. They entered the second room from the end on the right—someone's office, it appeared—and spotted metal spiral stairs twisting up to another floor.

She struggled not to feel dizzy from racing up the twisting stairs. When they reached the top, she and Catullus found themselves at one end of a much larger hallway than anything else they'd gone through before. This was not a decorative space, but the thickly timbered walls and ceiling revealed a far more martial purpose. At the other end of the passage stood a broad door studded with bolts. A fortress's door.

"The Primal Source must be on the other side of that," said Catullus. He glanced around with a scowl. "If we can make it down this gauntlet."

Whatever the Heirs *had* been anticipating as far as a siege, they had not counted on fire. Edgeworth's blaze had spread, so that the wooden walls of the passage rippled with flame. Fire licked along the timbers lining the ceiling, an architecture of flame that groaned as it was consumed.

Wasting no time, Gemma and Catullus ran down the passage. The structure quaked from the expanding fire. She and Catullus staggered as the building shook. Smoke filled the hallway, and Gemma bent over, coughing. As she did so, something overhead rumbled.

"Back, Gemma!" Catullus bellowed.

She stumbled backward just as a burning beam fell.

Throwing up an arm to shield herself from a rain of cinders, Gemma felt the blistering heat of the beam as it crashed down. Between her and Catullus. A portion of the ceiling smashed down with it, sputtering flame. She reared back from the fire. The flames from the beam and collapsed ceiling stretched up, forming a barrier she couldn't traverse.

Catullus stared at her from across the blaze. Lurid light reflected in the glass of his spectacles. He moved to breach the fire to reach her, but it held him off.

"Go back," he shouted to her. "Down the stairs and get the hell out of here."

She wouldn't abandon him. "But—"

"Do it," he snarled. "I'll get the Primal Source. Get yourself to safety."

Her throat ached, and she wanted to argue. It wasn't smoke that made her eyes brim and burn.

More groaning overhead. She flung herself away just before another section of ceiling collapsed. Coughing, staggering to her feet, she saw that she was now trapped between two barriers of flame. Couldn't go forward, couldn't go back.

She exhausted her repertoire of curse words, trying to figure a way out. Everything around her was heat and smoke and fire. She could barely make out Catullus as he lunged and fell back and lunged again, trying to reach her. He roared his frustration, a sound more terrifying than the noise of the burning building, hissing and moaning as fire scored its walls.

God, oh God. She truly, truly didn't want to burn to death. It ranked right up there as one of the least pleasant ways to die. But she'd be damned if Catullus burned with her. "Go!" she shouted above the din. "Get the Primal Source! Before this whole place turns to ashes!"

"I'm not bloody leaving you!" he bellowed.

Fine words from a man who was perfectly willing to let *her* abandon *him*.

He went still. Gemma couldn't tell for certain, but it looked as if he'd closed his eyes in concentration. What the hell was he doing? He needed to run, to complete the mission, not stand there, waiting to go up in flame.

Her eyes streamed, and she rubbed fruitlessly at them. What she saw made her dig her knuckles into her eyes again. Catullus had disappeared.

Her heart pitched down, even as she felt grateful that he'd stopped trying to rescue her and saved himself.

Suddenly, strong arms wrapped around her waist from behind. Gemma gasped, then coughed from inhaling smoke. She writhed in the tight grip. It had to be Edgeworth, appearing out of the fire. She fought, kicking and throwing punches, trying to land a knee in Edgeworth's groin, until a wonderfully familiar voice said in her ear, "My love, if you aren't careful, we will never have children together."

"Catullus," she rasped. Gemma twisted around to see that, yes, somehow he'd crossed through the fire to reach her. But she hadn't seen him, unless the flames and smoke were too thick. "How . . . ?"

"Like this," he said. He closed his eyes.

She lost her breath once again. One moment, they were trapped between two burning barriers, and the next, they stood where Catullus had been seconds before. Free of her fiery prison.

She spun to stare up at him. "How did you do that?"

"I used the magic you gave me." Soot streaked his face and surcoat, yet to her he appeared a stainless knight.

"But it only works on doors."

"Not just physical doors. It opens doors in space. If I concentrate, and can see the place, I can travel there." He smiled faintly, amazed at his own discovery. "Thusly." He closed his eyes in concentration.

They appeared suddenly in front of the door at the end of the burning hallway, dozens of yards from where they had stood. Her head spun from the quick movement.

"I didn't know the magic could do that," she breathed.

"I didn't either." He smiled at her, wry. "Until I was properly motivated." His smile faded, replaced by a look of such intensity, it put the fire to shame.

They stared up at the massive door. On the other side of the door, the Primal Source was held captive. The object of their long journey. The greatest magical power known. Close. They were so close.

For anyone else, such a huge, heavy door would prove an impossible, impassable barrier. The door, as Day had said, was enchanted, opening only for Heirs.

But she and Catullus never acknowledged barriers.

"Shall we, Miss Murphy?" Catullus asked. He placed a hand on the door.

She mimicked his polite British tone as she, too, put her hand on the door. "With the greatest of pleasure, Mr. Graves."

It swung inward, opening. They stepped into a large chamber, two stories high. It resembled a library, with a gallery running around its perimeter with another spiral stair connecting the ground floor with the gallery. Narrow, barred windows were set high in the walls. Instead of books, glass cases lined the shelves on the ground floor and balcony. In each case was an object. Some ornate, like elaborate crowns or jewelry, some simple, such as roughly

carved wooden figurines or battered metal trinkets. She was
no expert, but Gemma could tell that the objects came from
around the globe. They came from Africa, Asia, Europe,
even the lands of the American Indians.

There was something so forlorn about seeing all these
objects locked within their glass cases, taken from the
living, breathing world to be shut away in airless prisons.
They were throneless monarchs, removed from context and
stripped of dignity to become curiosities.

Catullus seemed to share her feelings. He took in all of
the objects in their cases, frowning, troubled.

"Never seen so many Sources in one place before," he
murmured. "Strange. I can feel their power, but it all
seems . . . muted. Bleak. Like lions at the zoo."

"Day said the Primal Source should be here."

He pointed to a case on the balcony, directly across
from the door. She squinted, trying to see what the case
contained, and started when she realized that it held just a
single, ordinary rock. It was reddish in color, roughly the
size of a human fist. Other than its color, there was nothing extraordinary or even slightly noteworthy about it.

"Are you sure *that's* it?"

"I have not actually seen it with my own eyes," he admitted. "But Astrid is very familiar with the Primal Source, and
she described it in detail to me. That is most definitively it."

"Then let's go get the Primal Source."

They stepped fully into the chamber. The door slammed
shut behind them, locking itself.

Gemma hadn't seen the small stove in a corner of the
room until it burst open, spewing flame. From the fire, a
maddeningly recognizable figure emerged and strode to the
center of the chamber. Flames trailed behind him, like the
path of a slug.

"This is where you will die," Edgeworth sneered. "Fitting—surrounded by the precious Sources you tried to cosset, and they will do nothing to help you."

"This chamber *is* a tomb," Catullus answered. "But not ours."

He and Edgeworth stared at one another. The moment drew out, tense to the point of breaking. Gemma's heart pumped, aching in its intensity, as she looked back and forth between the two men. They could not be more dissimilar. Not simply in their appearance, but in the quality of their souls. The darkness swamping Edgeworth choked away all joy, all life, wanting only dominance and subjugation. Catullus wasn't a perfect paragon—he had the fears and needs of any man—but he shone all the brighter because of those flaws. He used the gift of his mind selflessly, wanting a better world not just for himself, but for everyone, regardless of nationality, sex, or color. He represented everything Edgeworth despised and wished to destroy.

These antitheses gazed at one another, taking each other's measure, testing mettle. Catullus's hand draped over the grip of his sword. Edgeworth stood like a gunfighter, ready to unleash his fire at the slightest excuse.

Then, a blur of movement. Catullus materialized at the base of the staircase that led to the gallery. Edgeworth spun around, shocked, then shot a bolt of fire at Catullus.

Catullus disappeared, reappearing at the top of the stairs, but the flames had already caught him across his shoulder, burning through his surcoat and tunic to the skin beneath. He made no noise, even though the pain had to be tremendous.

Edgeworth launched himself up the stairs, moving with tremendous speed. Seeing that Catullus approached the Primal Source, Edgeworth threw a fireball at him. Catullus managed to deflect it with his sword, but he stumbled and the sword clattered from his grip, falling down to the floor below. He turned to the Primal Source, but before he could materialize beside it, Edgeworth knocked him down with a jet of flame. Catullus rolled, trying to douse the fire on his back.

Seizing this momentary distraction, Edgeworth leapt over Catullus's prone form. Any moment now, Edgeworth would reach the Primal Source. What he might do once he got there, she didn't know. It wouldn't be good, that she could assume.

Gemma forced herself to concentrate, staring at the place next to the case holding the Primal Source. She envisioned the doors within space itself, the planes of distance and depth, and herself, opening the doors.

She felt herself wink out like a candle. And then flicker back. She glanced around, momentarily disoriented. She stood on the gallery, right beside the case holding the Primal Source.

Her brief sense of triumph disappeared when she saw Edgeworth coming closer. He started when he spotted her.

"No manners," she said. "Ladies . . . well, *women* first." She reached for the case beside her. No doubt it would be locked, and this wasn't a problem.

A wall of heat slammed into her, throwing her back against a shelf. The shelf caught fire almost at once. If Catullus hadn't rammed himself into Edgeworth, throwing off his aim, Gemma would have been nothing but ashes and red hair. She pushed herself upright.

Edgeworth and Catullus now thrashed each other. Flames blocked her path to Catullus.

"Transport yourself away," she shouted to Catullus.

He dodged Edgeworth's fist and swung his own. "Can't. Bloody. Concentrate."

The men fought to reach the Primal Source first. They pummeled one another mercilessly. She'd seen men brawl before, but never like this. Every punch, every blow, was intended to kill. She thought herself inured to most violence, but it was one thing to watch two boxers or fur trappers exchange blows, quite another when one of the combatants was the man she loved.

Catullus didn't fight like a scientist or scholar. In the narrow space of the gallery he fought brutally, lethally. It was almost beautiful, if it wasn't so awful. In the fray, he lost his spectacles. Glass from the broken lenses cut his cheek. He didn't notice. He rained punches down on Edgeworth, and the smaller man couldn't match him. Catullus had the advantage, and hope flared in Gemma.

Edgeworth's hands suddenly blazed. They scorched Catullus, pushing him back just enough for Edgeworth to wriggle away and reach the case.

Gemma grabbed her dagger and flung herself through the flames at him, trying to keep him from opening the case. He kicked her away, winding her as she hit the railing at the edge of the gallery. Her knife fell from her hand.

Edgeworth, grinning, opened the case. His hand closed around the Primal Source.

Hell broke loose.

Light enveloped Edgeworth. The radiance blinded, yet Gemma couldn't look away. She and Catullus stared, appalled, as fire completely engulfed the Heir, turning him from a man into a living torch. All of his limbs blazed, throwing off oppressive heat, and he gazed down at himself, laughing.

"Who needs Arthur?" he cried. He held up the Primal Source. "This has given me more power than any trifling king. England will rally to *me*."

Gemma pulled her pistol, Catullus his shotgun. They both unleashed a furious barrage on Edgeworth, but the bullets melted in the heat around him.

Drunk on his new power, Edgeworth occupied himself by touching anything flammable and setting them alight. He did not care that the Heirs' headquarters would be a charred ruin; all that mattered was displaying his might. He ran along the gallery, starting fires.

As the blaze began to spread, and with Edgeworth on the opposite side of the gallery, Gemma grabbed her knife and crawled to Catullus. Smoke burned her eyes and stung in her nostrils. "There was a fire in London," she coughed, "a big fire."

"In 1666," he answered. He tore a strip of fabric from his surcoat and pressed it to her nose and mouth, then did the same for himself. "Burned for four days. Nearly destroyed everything within the city walls."

She tried to breathe through the fabric. "There was one in Chicago, too. Huge sections of the city were leveled. Both fires will be church barbecues compared to what Edgeworth could do."

His eyes narrowed, and she knew he was thinking furiously about what they could do to stop Edgeworth. Bullets were useless, and Gemma's supply was almost gone. Neither of them could get close enough to take the Primal Source from Edgeworth. They'd be burned to charcoal in seconds. He scanned the room, searching for an answer.

"Maybe you could invent something to put out fires," she joked weakly.

He froze in his assessment. Though his eyes were reddened from the smoke, she couldn't mistake the light of inspiration within them. He glanced around the chamber again, and what he saw must have met whatever criterion he needed fulfilled.

"Tell me what I can do to help," she said at once.

Thank God he didn't try to talk her out of helping. Instead, he said in a clipped, commanding voice, "Close the windows. Make sure they're shut tight."

Gemma glanced at the barred windows lining the chamber. Most of them were open, allowing smoke to waft out and bringing in a bit of welcome air. "We'll suffocate."

"It's not *us* I'm trying to smother."

"What about you?"

"I'll keep him distracted."

Smoke and rebellion made her cough. Edgeworth, deep in his madness, drew patterns of fire along the floor. He caught sight of Catullus and Gemma huddled together and smirked. Between his hands, flames wove into knots, ready to trap them in a burning snare.

"No," she said. "He'll kill you."

"He won't," Catullus answered. He leaned forward and kissed her, hard and fierce, before springing to his feet. "You look like a flaming pudding," he called across the chamber to Edgeworth.

The Heir took the bait. From the other side of the room, he directed a blast of flame at Catullus, who disappeared. The wooden pedestal Catullus had been standing in front of caught fire.

Catullus reappeared at the foot of the spiral stairs. "Down here, Guy Fawkes."

Edgeworth threw another ball of fire at Catullus, who dematerialized just before being struck.

Gemma didn't have much time. She jumped up and, darting around the flames now surrounding her, ran to the nearest window. She slammed it shut. Testing the frame, she ensured the window's tight seal.

She glanced toward the ground floor of the chamber. Catullus now stood near one of the shelves close to the door.

Edgeworth ran to the top of the spiral staircase. He grabbed the metal railings. Within seconds the whole metal structure glowed red-hot. The stair buckled as it grew molten. Bellowing, Edgeworth tore the stair from its anchors in the floor and shoved it toward where Catullus had just materialized. The structure toppled. Catullus barely managed to disappear before being crushed by the glowing hot metal.

Infuriated, Edgeworth leapt down from the gallery and landed on the ground floor in a crouch.

With the gallery cleared of Edgeworth's presence, Gemma sprinted to the windows. She banged them shut, even as she desperately craved the smokeless air.

At the noise she created, Edgeworth turned to see what she was about. He started to raise his hands to launch a burst of fire at her. A chair, miraculously intact and un-burned, flew at him, thrown by Catullus. Though the chair turned to smoldering splinters before it could touch Edge-worth, it provided enough of a distraction for Edgeworth, allowing Gemma to continue with her task.

She wouldn't allow herself to look down from the gallery, knowing that if she watched Catullus risking his life for her, all concentration and intent would be lost. So she hurried about her work, coughing, darting around localized fires.

One half of the windows were sealed tightly. She moved down the gallery, heading toward the other half of the room, when the fires blazed higher, blocking her path. *Damn!*

Then she remembered: doors. Summoning every bit of concentration, forcing herself to block out the sounds of Catullus baiting Edgeworth, the Heir's retaliation, the fire and choking smoke, Gemma willed the doors between spaces to open.

A brief sensation of a vacuum, and then she appeared on the other side of the fire. She smiled grimly to herself. This was a use of her family's magic that no one before Catul-lus had ever tried. She hoped to make it out alive, if only to quiet her normally garrulous aunts with a demonstration.

Gemma's smile, dour as it was, faded when she heard Catullus's grunt of pain. Oh, God. He hadn't been fast enough. She glanced down to see him rolling out from underneath a toppled, burning shelf. His once-white surcoat now appeared almost black, holes had been burned into his tunic, and blood streaked his face. Edgeworth shrieked with laughter.

She wanted to leap down from the gallery and plunge her knife into Edgeworth's neck.

That was impossible, so she ran to the remaining windows and shoved them closed.

Almost at once, the atmosphere changed. The air within the chamber thinned. She fought for breath and barely found enough air to even partially fill her lungs. Between the smoke and the rapidly diminishing air, her head spun, her eyes growing hazy.

Gemma reeled. She fell to her hands and knees, struggling to breathe.

Below her, she saw Catullus do the same. He shook his head to stay conscious.

She tried to stand. Her legs wouldn't work; neither would her arms. She couldn't open the windows and let in much-needed air. All she could do was force herself not to pass out.

Edgeworth, seeing Catullus grappling with consciousness, roared with laughter. "On your hands and knees," he gloated. "Exactly the way your kind is meant to be."

The flames surrounding him leapt higher with his glee. He slowly stalked toward Catullus.

"Familiar position. For you," gasped Catullus. "Father's supplicant."

Enraged, the Heir's fire blazed higher, stronger. "Shut up! I am the Heirs' leader."

Gemma fell to the floor, her arms and legs unable to support her any longer.

"Not leader. Sniveling prince." Catullus staggered to his feet. "No honor of. Your own. Pale shadow. Of father."

"Wrong!" screamed Edgeworth. "I am every bit the man he was! More!" The flames around him raged taller.

Gemma could barely keep conscious. She felt the room drawing in on itself, as if it would implode. Crushed. She would be crushed, and Catullus, too. No . . .

Then a strange thing happened.

Edgeworth's fire shrank. Sputtered.

The Heir looked down at his hands, confusion in his

face. "The devil—?" He tried to unleash a volley of flame at Catullus, but the blaze came out only as a small pop before flickering into nothingness.

"Not. The devil," Catullus rasped. "Oxygen. Using yours. Up. Then. No more. Fire."

Even the flames along the walls and floor dwindled, leaving behind black, brittle remains.

Edgeworth's eyes went wide as the blaze surrounding him continued to shrivel to nothingness, leaving him unprotected. He darted toward the door, intending to open it and let in air. Catullus threw a kick, landing a heel right in Edgeworth's thigh. The Heir went sprawling.

Catullus, using stores of stamina Gemma could barely comprehend, ran up and rammed his knee into Edgeworth's elbow, causing the Heir to yowl and his hand to spasm open. Catullus dove, grabbing hold of the Primal Source.

"No!" screamed Edgeworth. "It's mine!"

The two men grappled, rolling across the floor. Edgeworth clawed at Catullus's hand. They drove knees into each other's chests, snarling, as they scrabbled for dominance. Catullus wedged his forearm underneath Edgeworth's chin, forcing the Heir back slightly.

Using what had to be his very last breath, Catullus shouted up to her, "Open the windows."

Clinging to consciousness, Gemma staggered to her feet. She pulled herself up the wall and, summoning every last scrap of strength, smashed the pommel of her dagger through the window. Fresh, cool air rushed in like a blessing. She took deep gulps of air. As soon as she felt herself capable of standing on her own, she turned from the window and began opening the others.

Smoke began to clear. In the center of the room, she saw Catullus grab his fallen sword and face Edgeworth.

The Heir, without his nimbus of fire, was only a man. A man full of anger and frustrated greed. Catullus stood tall and formidable, ready for combat, a marked contrast to the frantic Edgeworth.

Weaponless, Edgeworth moved toward one of the cases holding a Source. Catullus's sword stopped him.

"No more magical crutches," Catullus said.

"But I'm unarmed," Edgeworth whined.

"You want mercy when you give none."

Snarling, eyes seething with hatred, Edgeworth grabbed a twisted spike of metal from the ruined staircase and flung himself at Catullus.

Gemma stood at the edge of the gallery, watching the two men clash. She had to do something—but if she went down to help, she'd wind up endangering Catullus more than helping him. She dodged flying cinders as Catullus and Edgeworth slammed together and broke apart.

"Damn you Blades!" Edgeworth screamed. "Treasonous snakes. Enemies of England."

"Not enemies of England," Catullus corrected. He blocked a strike and countered with his own. He moved with a speed and skill that stole what breath Gemma had regained. He was beautiful and terrible. "Allies of everyone. Everyone who isn't a magic-stealing bastard," he amended.

"Naïve idiots." Edgeworth launched into a series of strikes, proving that he, too, had trained in swordsmanship. "If England does not seize power, then some other nation will. And then where will your high-minded ideals be? Trampled in the mud, in chains." He lunged.

"As long as there are Blades of the Rose," Catullus vowed, deflecting the blow, "we will keep fighting."

They moved back and forth, ceaseless, brutal in their attacks.

"Because you are fools," spat Edgeworth.

"Perhaps," Catullus agreed mildly. Then all mildness fled him, and he became tempered steel, as deadly as the weapon he held. "But I'll be damned if I let some overprivileged bigot like you defile my homeland and call it patriotism."

Edgeworth charged, snarling. Then stopped and stared down at Catullus's sword jammed between his ribs. Gasping, he pulled back. The sword slid free with a wet hiss.

"No," he rasped. "Father . . ."

Despite the blood pouring from him, Edgeworth swung again at Catullus.

Gemma flinched as Catullus's sword swept out and Edgeworth's head rolled across the floor. His body slumped to the ground. The blood . . . it was everywhere. She felt sick and yet fiercely glad it was Edgeworth's blood soaking into the floorboards and not Catullus's.

Catullus left the corpse, sparing it not a single glance as he sheathed his sword. He took the floor in a few long strides to stand below her. One hand rested on the pommel of his sword as easily as if he was a warrior born and bred—which he was, a warrior of mind and body.

For several moments, they only looked at one another. She marveled at him. He was utterly filthy, covered in sweat and soot and blood, singed and weary. He'd never been more handsome. Her knight. Her champion.

Come to think of it, she'd put up a pretty good fight, too. She materialized in front of him.

"I love you," she said, because that was precisely what she needed to tell him.

He inhaled sharply, his weariness giving way to fierce triumph. He looked like a man unafraid to seize his chance at happiness.

"I love you," he answered. "Only and always."

Gemma once stood on the deck of a gunboat when it fired all of its guns at once. She'd felt the vibrations of it in the marrow of her bones. Nothing, she had believed, could ever top that force, that sensation. She was wrong.

Hearing those words from Catullus dwarfed that explosion into a minuscule pop. It was a wonder she didn't glow like a sun.

But love could not turn back the force of an inferno. The

floor beneath them groaned and buckled as the walls cracked. Sounds of combat outside—Heirs against Blades, the dragon against Arthur—and imminent collapse of the building filled the chamber.

Catullus pulled Gemma close, shielding her, as pieces of the ceiling rained down on them.

Edgeworth lay dead, and the Primal Source was free, but the battle was far from over.

Chapter 24

Aftermath

The building shook, and Catullus heard the dragon's furious roar, followed by Arthur's own bellow.

Catullus calculated exactly how much longer the structural integrity of the headquarters could last. His gut clenched when he realized it was only a matter of minutes before everything collapsed.

He had to get Gemma to safety.

"Collect the Sources up in the gallery," he said, "and I'll gather the ones down here."

After everything that had happened, and the fact that the Heirs' headquarters burned around them, he hated to take his eyes from her. But she vanished from his arms, and he fought a momentary sense of panic at her disappearance, which eased slightly when she reappeared on the gallery. She began to move quickly, approaching the cases on the second level and removing the Sources.

Catullus stepped over Edgeworth's headless body without breaking stride, registering as much as a piece of shattered furniture.

As Catullus opened each case, he felt a rush of hot anger every time. Every one of the glass containers held not only a

Source, but a tale of thievery and avarice, murder and cruelty. What would they say, these Sources, if given voice? What had they seen? Each had been ripped from its home and people, exploited, forced into servitude and hoarded.

Not so different from his own family's history.

"You are free now," he whispered to the Source he now held, an ivory hair comb taken from the East Indies. "We're all free." He heard Gemma up in the gallery, and he felt it, his own liberation, urged into being by an American woman with freckles and boundless spirit.

As he quickly opened the cases, one after the other, the power of each Source pulsed like a joyous heart. The bleak, hopeless air within the chamber dissipated, a nightmare dispelled upon waking. He set each Source, including the Primal Source, in the satchel given to him by Merlin. Here was magic: No matter how many Sources he put into the bag, there was more than enough room for all of them, and together, they weighed almost nothing, even the heavy Polynesian stone icons.

Catullus, whimsical from fatigue, wondered if Merlin might be persuaded to create a line of luggage.

"I've got them," Gemma said from above. She had removed her lightweight golden underskirt and used it as a pouch to cradle the Sources. He caught sight of her slim, creamy ankles as she moved to the edge of the gallery.

"That's a naughty grin," she noted.

"I have a very lively intellect," he said without apology. "Just a hint is enough to get me going."

"Looking forward to exploring that intellect."

She disappeared, and materialized right in front of him, her goddess's body pressed against his own. They kissed, their mouths meeting hotly. A confirmation of desire and life after harrowing trials. Trials that were not yet over. The shuddering building confirmed how much danger they still faced.

She looked down at the bundle she'd made of her skirt.

"I collected a dozen Sources. These can't be all of them. From what you've said, the Heirs have been stealing Sources for centuries."

"They have estates and property throughout England. Sources are kept in all of them. With the Heirs' headquarters in chaos, we may now have a decent shot at retaking the rest of the captured Sources."

A corner of her mouth turned up, wry. "Looks like we've still got a lot of work to do."

If they made it out of this inferno. He allowed himself a sigh. "Always."

"Good. Hate to think that we'd be bored."

His attention caught. "I have reviewed all the variables, and I can assure you that all data supports my theorem."

"What theorem is that?"

"That the collective *we* has a much greater probability of happiness than the discrete elements *you* or *I*."

Her gaze warmed further. She beamed, momentarily girlish, and it charmed him. And then she became decisive, briskly efficient. "Let's get out of this damned place so we can prove that theorem."

They moved toward the door. Before they left the chamber, both cast a final look at the room that served as a place of defilement and prison. An ugly room, made uglier by the blackened, burned walls and twisted metal lying like a skeleton on the floor. And the body of the ruined man, deformed by madness, undone by hate. The legacy of the Heirs of Albion.

They left the room without looking back.

The hallway outside the chamber was engulfed in flames.

"Aim for there," Catullus shouted above the din. He pointed to a small area at the other end of the corridor, mercifully untouched by fire.

Holding hands, they concentrated on that one little

spot. He prayed they both had enough focus to transport themselves safely.

He felt the vacuum around him, and for a heartbeat, her hand vanished from within his. Panic tore at him. When he found himself on the far end of the hallway, alone, he swung around. Then exhaled in a rush.

Gemma stood behind him rather than at his side. Her eyes were wide with fear as she searched for him; then she pressed a hand to her chest when she saw him.

"Hell of a way to travel," she gulped.

They descended the stairs leading to the hallway. Fires continued to blaze all through the massive building. Panicked Heirs choked the hallways thicker than smoke, all of them more intent on fleeing the building than fighting the Blades peppered throughout. As Catullus led Gemma through the labyrinth of corridors and rooms, not a single Heir attempted to stop them. Confusion everywhere. If Catullus hadn't memorized their route into the building, he and Gemma would have found themselves lost amidst the chaos.

In the ruins of the ballroom, they met up with Bennett and London. Husband and wife both looked decidedly scruffy after enduring God only knew what kind of obstacles. Of the three-armed giant and complement of Heirs, there was no sign. Gunfire sounded distantly. Through the hole in the wall, Catullus and the others could see a bloodied, weary Arthur grappling with an equally wounded and exhausted dragon.

"*Now* you show up," Bennett said, dragging his hands through his hair and making the whole mass stand on end. "After all the hard work is done." Bennett winced as Arthur caught one of the dragon's claws in his leg. "*Most* of the hard work."

"Are you all right?" asked London, much more polite than her husband.

"You look like a burnt roast," Bennett added.

"We're alive," said Catullus.

"And we have the Primal Source." Gemma hefted the bundle she carried. "Plus whatever Sources were kept here."

London glanced at the encroaching fire. "Jonas?"

Though Catullus was glad to put an end to Edgeworth's despicable life, he didn't relish having to tell London that her brother was dead. And by his hand. He gently shook his head.

A brief flare of pain crossed London's face, followed by something approximating release.

"I'm sorry, love," murmured Bennett, pulling her close. "But unless we want to join your brother in the afterlife, it's time to leave."

Leaving the spectacle of Arthur still battling his foe, they pushed on through the havoc, collecting Blades along the way. Later, Catullus would remember that journey as a succession of summits and valleys, spirits soaring only to plummet down into untapped wellsprings of sorrow. Blades—comrades, colleagues, friends—those that survived counted themselves amongst the walking wounded. They saw their injuries as fortune's blessing. Others, far too many, lay dead amidst the burning walls.

Blades, their faces streaked with soot and tears, carried bodies. Henry Wilson. Susan Holcot. Matthias Gruber. Renato Scarlatti. Names, faces. Catullus knew some of them well, some not at all, but as he and the other Blades met and progressed through the building, they became part victory parade, part funeral procession, all evacuation.

The building quaked powerfully, nearly throwing everyone to the buckling ground. A massive shriek split the air. It sounded like the dragon, but whether it was a death cry or triumphant proclamation, there was no way to know.

From the smoke, Lesperance emerged, partially dressed, supporting a limping Astrid. Lesperance's bare chest resembled a roadmap of lacerations, and he'd broken his nose. Blood covered his top lip. He paid no attention to his own injuries, focusing everything on the woman beside him.

Astrid, cradling her ribs, saw the Blades, and her gaze moved over them quickly, assessing who had survived and who had not. When she spotted Catullus, her unreadable expression shifted, and she permitted herself a small smile.

"Your adversaries?" Catullus asked.

"In hell," Astrid answered, straightening. With Lesperance's support, she held herself upright as she walked with the Blades.

Thalia and Gabriel Huntley met them on a landing. Hastily made bandages crisscrossed where they'd been attacked by the peryton, yet, other than that, both warriors appeared better off than most of the other Blades. They, too, gauged the living and the dead with the stoicism of seasoned fighters, yet Thalia could not hide the sheen in her eyes when she saw the lifeless bodies.

Catullus would not surrender Gemma's hand from his grip. With death all around, he needed the tangible proof of her. And she held him just as tightly.

He kept the lead as the Blades picked their way through the rubble of the entryway, meeting up with Sam and Cassandra Reed. Everyone was confronted with the sight of a giant, smoking dragon carcass. Which answered one question, but another arose.

"Arthur," Sam explained without prompting. "But once he killed the beast, he disappeared."

A ragged group, the Blades collected in the square. Each of them turned to watch the massive headquarters burn. It was a lurid sight, the stone walls charring as flames leapt along their surfaces, windows glowing like demonic eyes. Heirs escaped in fearful clumps, abandoning the structure that had, only hours before, symbolized the unbending, monolithic principles that united their numbers.

Catullus felt numb as he observed the architectural embodiment of his enemies gutted by fire. The whole roof of the building caved in with a deafening roar. Had the Blades taken any more time getting out, none would have survived.

Perhaps some Heirs were still inside. Perhaps not. Without his spectacles, he could not make out precise details, yet what he saw was enough.

He turned away. There was still so much to do. The headquarters may be destroyed, the Heirs scattered, but only a fool would believe them to be defeated. Men such as them always found ways to survive. Catullus felt so god-damned tired.

Gemma's slim hand came up to stroke his face. He met her gaze.

"This is what we do," she said gently. "But not alone."

He'd thought himself worn down to bone and little else, numb. Yet life and feeling surged through him, a little subdued, to be sure, but there, nonetheless.

Elaborate swearing in Greek heralded the approach of Athena Galanos and Nikos Kallas. The burly sailor scowled as he beheld the headquarters wreathed in flame.

"We missed the good part," he growled.

"Do not worry, my darling," Athena soothed, "I am sure there will be plenty of destruction and carnage for us another time." She turned to Catullus. "Is it done? Has the Primal Source been freed?"

"I've got it here." Catullus took the red stone from his satchel. He felt the eyes of the Blades on him, many of whom had never before seen the most powerful Source.

Athena stared at it, reverent and cautious. She murmured a prayer in Greek, and moved to touch it, before holding herself back. She clearly didn't trust herself, or her own magic, coming in contact with the Primal Source.

"It must be returned to where it came from," she said.

"I'll take it back," Astrid volunteered immediately.

"*We* will take it back," Lesperance corrected.

"Of course, you're coming with me," said Astrid, as if the idea that she might travel without him was too ludicrous to consider.

"And then there are all the other Sources we've liberated," added Catullus. "Each of them must be returned, as well."

At once, Blades began stepping forward, each of them volunteering to make the arduous journeys necessary to restore the magic to its rightful place.

In the midst of this tumult, Gemma whispered in Catullus's ear. "Say good-bye to solitude, Mr. Graves. Wherever you go, I'm going, too."

"Solitude can go rot," he whispered back. He started when the Primal Source began to glow, gleaming as if lit by an internal flame, yet it gave off no heat.

"Astrid, what's it doing?" he demanded.

"I don't know," she answered.

"The other Sources, too," said Gemma, amazed. She held her bundle aloft, and the whole of the fabric shone from the light of a dozen Sources within.

Every Blade gasped aloud as the Primal Source vanished from Catullus's hand. A fast check of his satchel and Gemma's makeshift bag revealed the same thing: Every Source was gone. Disappeared into nothingness.

No! Catullus felt a surge of anger. "The Heirs?"

"The Sources are home," said a voice, an ancient voice of profound wisdom.

Merlin materialized out of the smoky air, his robes swirling around him, his eyes dark with magic. Of all the places Catullus expected to see a somewhat deranged, phenomenally powerful sorcerer, standing in a smoke-filled square in Mayfair graded somewhere toward the bottom.

Merlin chuckled when he beheld the Blades gaping at him, though his look became more thoughtful when he glanced at Athena. Recognizing her power, and somewhat beguiled by the beautiful witch. The sorcerer's weakness. Unsurprisingly, Kallas wrapped a possessive arm around Athena's waist, and she did not object.

Kallas's rather primitive but wholly understandable

demonstration seemed to recall Merlin back to himself. He said, "All the Sources have found their ways to their homelands."

"Including the ones at the other Heir properties?" asked Gemma.

"*All* of them," confirmed the sorcerer. "Consider it a boon granted by grateful magic."

Catullus, Gemma, and the other Blades fell silent, each of them agape at the power of one man—who was not, Catullus suspected, a man, but a manifestation of magic itself.

Thank you seemed too small a phrase, respecting the fact that Merlin had just saved the Blades countless battles and decades of travel. So Catullus only nodded, and this seemed to gratify Merlin.

"To restore balance," the sorcerer added, "that magic which had been artificially enhanced by the Primal Source must, too, be surrendered."

Merlin traced a pattern in the air. As he did so, an odd pulling sensation passed through Catullus. He stared down at himself, watching in fascination as a thread of silver light unspooled from within him. He saw the same happen to Gemma. The threads unwound and drifted through the air before spiraling around Merlin and finally vanishing. Many more seemed to come from farther away, though none from the other Blades—including Athena Galanos. Her magic belonged entirely to her.

As one might test the soundness of a limb, Catullus tentatively reached for the magic that Gemma had given him. What he found was diminished, but still there. He breathed a small sigh of relief. Being able to transport oneself with the blink of an eye was indeed a most useful power, but he was more concerned that her gift, and what it represented, had not been taken away.

"So much for saving money on trolleys," Gemma said with a rueful smile. She turned to Merlin. "How did *you* get free?"

Merlin nodded toward a large figure materializing behind

him. How a giant such as Arthur could come and go like mist baffled Catullus, but myth had its own rules and force. Better to simply accept the fact that a titanic legend could simply appear at will.

"I told you the task of liberating me was not yours to undertake," tutted Merlin.

"Come, my counselor." Arthur glanced around, and in the king's eyes, Catullus saw distance, a separation that could never truly be breached. "Time we moved on."

"Where will you go?" Catullus asked.

"Back to the myth that created me," came the melancholy answer. "A cold place, this other England. A place of enclosure and brittle walls. Myths wither like leaves, blow away. This world has no need for me, no need for magic."

"That's not true," Gemma said. She looked at the assembled Blades, all of them filthy and wounded. "As long as there are hearts and minds to dream, people need magic. They'll need *you*."

A rare smile touched Arthur's mouth as he contemplated this outspoken mortal woman. "The people need *you*, my lady. And your friends. For though your enemy has been vanquished, it is but temporary, and there are always men such as them who will want power for their own ambitions."

A lowering thought, yet not unexpected. The Heirs of Albion were the Blades' most persistent enemy. Many others still existed, and would be created in the future. As long as humanity knew about the existence of magic, there would be those who abused its power.

"We'll be ready," said Catullus.

Arthur inclined his head, the closest to a bow a king would ever give. He raised his hand in farewell. Then he and Merlin vanished as noiselessly and entirely as they had appeared.

Clanging bells pierced the air. Fire brigades would arrive soon, and the Blades did not want to be around when the authorities showed up. Too many questions would be asked, questions that could not be answered.

"Everyone disperse," Sam Reed ordered. "Reconnoiter in Southampton."

In groups, the Blades broke apart, disappearing into the city. Many carried the bodies of their fallen comrades, to be laid to rest with honor. Thalia and Gabriel Huntley ran to the north, Bennett and London headed west, while Athena, Kallas, and the Reeds went south.

Leaving Gemma and Catullus with Astrid and Lesperance.

"You have your revenge now," Catullus said to Astrid. "You can let go of the past."

"Killing Gibbs was never about the past." She wiped her sleeve across her face, smearing dirt and blood. For a moment, she stared at the grime she'd tracked on her sleeve, as if studying an ancient history. With a shake of her head, she broke that study, and looked at the man standing straight and fierce beside her. "It was about moving forward. Making myself anew."

Catullus understood that. A brave woman, Astrid. He was glad, in a strange way, that the Heirs had come for her in Canada, giving him a much-needed kick in the trousers to go get her, and restore the bonds of their friendship.

Bells rang louder, closer.

"In Southampton," Lesperance said. He took hold of Catullus's wrist, the old way of taking leave, and Catullus did the same.

Then Astrid and Lesperance were gone.

"Come on," said Catullus. Hand in hand, he and Gemma ran from the square, passing the fire brigade. Into the known streets of Mayfair, where a strange peace had settled. Life had returned to normal. The usual traffic of omnibuses, carriages, genteel pedestrians, and the tradesmen who supported their lifestyle. All the pixies, sprites, goblins, and other magical creatures were nowhere to be found, though they left behind a goodly bit of damage. Catullus could only assume that the restoration of the Primal Source, and Arthur's return, restored the balance of the mortal and magical worlds.

All of this was academic, to be contemplated later. What concerned him now was getting Gemma to safety.

They caught a few curious glances as they hurried down the street, but he did not slow until they reached Hyde Park. Oddly, people were out on their usual perambulations and there were carriages and riders on Rotten Row, almost as if the utter anarchy of a few hours earlier hadn't happened. A blessed amnesia, one for which Catullus was grateful.

He had no idea where he led Gemma until he realized they had reached the banks of the Serpentine. The fog had broken, and a cool, autumnal sunlight glittered over the water like a benevolent deity. The dignified arches of the Serpentine Bridge appeared to the west, and over it strolled nurses pushing prams, and children chased one another.

Together, they stood on the banks and watched as life continued on around them.

"I can't decide if I am dreaming, or have just woken from a dream," he murmured.

"Little of both, I think," she answered. She unsheathed her dagger and stared at it. Her hand trembled slightly with the remains of fear. "I'm more than the hand that holds the pen. When I pictured my life . . . when I thought about who I was, I always thought I could be more. But I never knew what or who I was capable of being. Until you, Catullus." She traced a shaking thumb over the blade. "I've been afraid and run. I've stood and fought, and I've experienced incredible pleasure. I'm . . ." She looked up, her eyes restlessly scanning the tops of the trees as if answers and words perched upon the branches.

Her gaze returned to the knife in her grasp. "I'm myself," she said gently. "Everything that it means to be me."

He reached out and steadied her hand with his own. Beneath his touch, her trembling subsided. She looked up at him, profound joy in her brilliant eyes. "And you are . . . *you*." She sheathed the dagger, never taking her gaze from him. "The whole universe that you contain."

Catullus didn't care that it was broad daylight and in full sight of hundreds of people. He pulled Gemma into his arms and kissed her. The taste of her, the feel of her, roused him, awoke him, and in the aftermath of peril, he knew himself to be entirely alive and completely in love. His forty-second birthday was in less than a month, but it was only at that moment, with Gemma in his arms, kissing him, did he find himself in the fullness of his maturity, a man in every sense of the word.

Neither Gemma nor Catullus paid any heed to the inquisitive, and shocked, looks they received.

"It's a knight and his lady," a boy piped nearby, awed. "Not clean and jolly like in my picture books. *Real*."

"Scandalous," the nurse gasped. "Come on, now, Gerald." She ushered her charge away.

Catullus barely heard this exchange. He knew only Gemma.

"Never knew what I wanted," he whispered against her lips, "or who I could truly be." He traced his fingertips over her cheeks, along the bright points of her freckles. "Until you, Gemma."

"We still don't know everything about ourselves," she said softly. "Or each other."

"I'll trade centuries of studying magic and exploring Otherworld," he answered, "for a lifetime of discovering you."

She smiled, and they came together in a kiss. They stood upon the banks of the Serpentine, in the heart of London, learning a wonderful new astronomy. A solar system of two, each of them planets, each of them suns, warming, creating, sustaining. Perfectly balanced, and yet also wonderfully eccentric.

Epilogue

The Once and Future Blades

Southampton, England, 1876

Three letters lay before Catullus, neatly arranged on his workbench like gears awaiting installation. By some strange quirk of the postal service, all three letters arrived today, despite the fact that they each came from different far-distant pages in the atlas. He'd read them all once, but planned on reading them again. They contained simply too much information for him to fully ingest their meanings.

"Catullus?" Gemma's voice, at the top of the stair. His pulse gave a kick simply to hear her. Regardless that they had been married last March, every time he heard her, saw her, he never lost that jolt, that unfolding of incredulous pleasure. He simply could not get used to the fact that he was one fortunate son of a bitch.

"Catullus," Gemma said again, and he heard her steps coming down the stairs into the workshop. "You need a break. Cook has made Bakewell pudding and American biscuits for tea."

Turning from where he bent over his worktable, Catullus's mouth watered. Not at the offerings for tea—though it did sound tempting and he hadn't eaten anything, he realized, since breakfast. What he was truly starved for was Gemma, smiling, walking toward him with her usual, brisk stride. Heated memories of the night before trailed in her wake. His insomnia hadn't left him simply because he was a married man, but early in their union Gemma had proposed the most delicious means of passing the sleepless hours. Making love with her in the depths of night didn't put him back to sleep, but when she drifted off with a sated sigh and he went down to toil in his workshop, he did so a thoroughly invigorated man.

She walked to him now, and took his outstretched hands as he leaned back against his worktable. "I forgot to remind you to eat," she said with a rueful purse of her lips. "I got caught up writing my article for the *Times* and lost track of my own meals."

"Both of us happily buried in our work." He sighed. "Such is the price of genius."

Her laugh, low and husky, curled like incense. "Only one of us is a genius. The other is a hack for hire."

"Not a hack," he scowled. In truth, editors from several newspapers and periodicals throughout England begged for her work. Articles by Gemma Graves about the imperiled cultures of the world were highly sought. She now had the rare privilege of picking and choosing assignments. "A peerless writer in great demand."

Catullus drew her closer. She went willingly, stepping between his legs. They fit together easily. "Do you want tea? I could get a tray and bring it down," she offered.

"It's not tea I'm hungry for." He nuzzled her neck, and she murmured her appreciation, growing warm and supple in his arms.

More than a few times had he and Gemma made love atop and against this very workbench. People within the Blades' headquarters eventually learned that, before entering his workshop, they would have to knock often and loudly, then wait at least ten minutes before venturing inside. He and Gemma had scandalized a good many people, though Bennett, blast him, had simply applauded before Catullus threw a hammer at him.

"Are those letters?"

Stifling a sigh, Catullus recalled that Gemma had not lost her reporter's keen eye, even when her husband was attempting, and being quite successful at, seduction. Reluctantly disentangling himself, he said, "From Thalia, Bennett, and Astrid. Arrived today."

"What do they say?"

Catullus tapped the first letter. "Thalia says they're in the midst of foaling season, and Gabriel's been running around like a man leading a charge, making sure the herd delivers properly. She and Gabriel have been working on a comprehensive survey of Mongolia's flora and fauna—when they aren't on missions for the Blades."

Gemma nodded thoughtfully. Missions never ceased. The Heirs of Albion had disbanded after the destruction of their headquarters and loss of their Sources. But their members had found situations with other groups, other factions, both within England and abroad. Rumors of another band of men, as powerful, if not more so, than the Heirs had been surfacing over the past months.

The Blades' work was not over. Far from it.

Catullus motioned to the second letter. "As usual, Bennett and London have hared off."

"Again? We got a letter from them only two weeks ago, when they wrote to us from Copenhagen."

"This letter was posted from Gibraltar, en route to Lebanon. Seems they both have an urge to see ruins, and London has heard rumors that a tiny village in the mountains still speaks an ancient dialect of Phoenician."

"Never met two people so crazy about traveling," Gemma said, but there was no criticism in her voice, only fondness. "It makes me dizzy, trying to keep up with them."

"Nothing they like better than traveling somewhere new together," Catullus said. On the rare occasions that Bennett and London were in Southampton, they kept everyone entertained late into the night with stories of their outlandish adventures. London collected new languages the way other travelers collected postcards. Bennett was simply happy to be wherever his wife alit, eager for any experience so long as she was beside him.

"That looks like Astrid's writing," Gemma noted, looking at the third letter.

"Your eye doesn't fail you, my love. She's finally recovered from what proved to be a rather surprising birth."

"Why surprising?"

"Twins."

Gemma's hand flew to her mouth, shocked and amused. "And?"

He frowned. "And?"

She swatted his arm. "Boys or girls?"

"One of each. A bear and a wolf cub."

Gemma couldn't stop her laughter. "Oh, God, poor Astrid."

"Poor *Lesperance*, more like. Astrid wrote that he was so agitated during the birth, he couldn't stop shifting between all three forms. But the mother and children are all well, and the father's recuperating. They'll be joining his tribe at their winter camp in a month. And next spring, they'll be petitioning the government for more tribal land. Astrid is optimistic."

None of his friends had what might be considered normal marriages. Theirs was not the path of routine and monotony, of settling down into prescribed behavior. Not because of the magic in their lives, but something else. Marriage, he discovered, was a partnership, each spouse testing and finding his or her way, learning as they went, evolving together. As he did, every day, with Gemma.

Again, she nodded. "It's good to hear from everyone again. Seems like too long since we were all together."

Catullus could only shrug philosophically. "It's the way of the Blades. I believe there's some ancient pronouncement that states if all the Blades are together at the same time, one should either prepare for Armageddon or a very large picnic."

"Speaking of Armageddon, I've got to finish making arrangements for my family's visit. I still need to find bedrooms for my brothers."

"Perhaps the stables."

"Good idea. Unless the horses are bothered by the smell." Gemma rolled her eyes, but Catullus knew she was looking forward to the arrival of her family. Not everyone was coming, which cast a small shadow over the proceedings. Her father and some assorted siblings were intolerant of her marriage—she'd sent them a wedding portrait photograph along with her letter, so there was no mistaking the difference in husband and wife's skin color. Others, including her mother and most of her brothers, were glad she'd found someone as unique as herself, regardless of racial difference.

And when the Graves family of Southampton met the Murphys of Chicago . . . the army should be put on alert. It promised to be a most unusual gathering.

He expected no less for himself. His whole life had been spent in a strange, liminal existence, and, even now, he felt decidedly apart from the rest of the world. Yet this did not trouble him. As he held his wife in his arms, feeling her warmth, her spirit, he felt the dissonant threads of himself weave together. Blade of the Rose, inventor, husband.

"So, do you want to come up for tea?" Gemma asked, smiling up at him with unmistakable enticement. "Or maybe we should have a little bite—" She nibbled along his jaw. "Down here?"

"Oh, I think I'd rather take my meal here. And later," he

said, voice husky, "I can show you an invention I've been working on. I promise you'll find it more than stimulating."

Her laugh was breathless, aroused. "Mr. Graves, *you* are a most stimulating man."

Gemma was his fire, his soul. In this world of neat categorizations and preconceived roles, they were strangers. But they were not strangers to each other.

He didn't want a peaceful life. He wanted *his* life: sometimes dangerous, always interesting.

An adventure.

Did you miss the other
Blades of the Rose books?
Go back and read them all!

In September, we met a WARRIOR in Mongolia . . .

To most people, the realm of magic is the stuff of nursery rhymes and dusty libraries. But for Capt. Gabriel Huntley, it's become quite real and quite dangerous . . .

IN HOT PURSUIT

The vicious attack Capt. Gabriel Huntley witnesses in a dark alley sparks a chain of events that will take him to the ends of the Earth and beyond—where what is real and what is imagined become terribly confused. And frankly, Huntley couldn't be more pleased. Intrigue, danger, and a beautiful woman in distress—just what he needs . . .

IN HOTTER WATER

Raised thousands of miles from England, Thalia Burgess is no typical Victorian lady. A good thing, because a proper lady would have no hope of recovering the priceless magical artifact Thalia is after. Huntley's assistance might come in handy, though she has to keep him in the dark. But this distractingly handsome soldier isn't easy to deceive . . .

There was a knock at the wooden door to the tent. Her father called out, "Enter." The door began to swing open.

Thalia tucked the hand holding the revolver behind her back. She stood behind her father's chair and braced herself, wondering what kind of man would step across the threshold and if she would have to use a gun on another human being for the first time in her life.

The man ducked to make it through the door, then immediately removed his hat, uncovering a head of close-cropped, wheat-colored hair. He was not precisely handsome, but he possessed an air of command and confidence that shifted everything to his favor. His face was lean and rugged, his features bold and cleanly defined; there was nothing of the drawing room about him, nothing refined or elegant. He was clean-shaven, allowing the hard planes of his face to show clearly. He was not an aristocrat and looked as though he had fought for everything he ever had in his life, rather than expecting it to be given to him. Even in the filtered light inside the *ger*, Thalia could see the gleaming gold of his eyes, their sharp intelligence that missed nothing as they scanned the inside of the tent and finally fell on her and her father.

"Franklin Burgess?" he asked.

"Yes, sir," her father answered, guarded. "My daughter, Thalia."

She remembered enough to sketch a curtsy as she felt the heat of the stranger's gaze on her. An uncharacteristic flush rose in her cheeks.

"And you are . . . ?" her father prompted.

"Captain Gabriel Huntley," came the reply, and now it made sense that the man who had such sure bearing would be an officer. "Of the Thirty-third Regiment." Thalia was not certain she could relax just yet, since it was not unheard of for the Heirs to find members in the ranks of the military. She quickly took stock of the width of the captain's shoulders, how even standing still he seemed to radiate energy and the capacity for lethal movement. Captain Huntley would be a fine addition to the Heirs.

There was something magnetic about him, though, something that charged the very air inside the *ger*, and she felt herself acutely aware of him. His sculpted face, the brawn of his body, the way he carried his gear, all of it, felt overwhelmingly masculine. How ironic, how dreadful, it would be, if the only man to have attracted her attention in years turned out to be her enemy. Sergei, her old suitor, had wound up being her enemy, but in a very different way.

"You are out of uniform, Captain Huntley," her father pointed out.

For the first time since his entrance, the captain's steady concentration broke as he glanced down at his dusty civilian traveling clothes. "I'm here in an unofficial capacity." He had a gravelly voice with a hint of an accent Thalia could not place. It was different from the cultured tones of her father's friends, rougher, but with a low music that danced up the curves of her back.

"And what capacity is that?" she asked. Thalia realized too late that a proper Englishwoman would not speak so boldly, nor ask a question out of turn, but, hell, if Captain Huntley *was* an Heir, niceties did not really matter.

His eyes flew back to her, and she met his look levelly, even as a low tremor pulsed inside her. God, there it was again, that strange *something* that he provoked in her, now made a hundred times stronger when their gazes connected. She watched him assess her, refusing to back down from the unconcealed measuring. She wondered if he felt that peculiar awareness too, if their held look made his stomach flutter. Thalia doubted it. She was no beauty—too tall, her features too strong, and there was the added handicap of this dreadful dress. Besides, he didn't quite seem like the kind of man who fluttered anything.

Yet . . . maybe she was wrong. Even though he was on the other side of the *ger,* Thalia could feel him looking at her, taking her in, with an intensity that bordered on unnerving. And intriguing.

Regardless of her scanty knowledge of society, Thalia *did* know that gentlemen did not look at ladies in such a fashion. Strange. Officers usually came from the ranks of the upper classes. He should know better. But then, so should she.

"As a messenger," he answered, still holding Thalia's gaze, "from Anthony Morris."

That name got her attention, as well as her father's.

"What about Morris?" he demanded. "If he has a message for me, he should be here, himself."

The captain broke away from looking intently at Thalia as he regarded her father. He suddenly appeared a bit tired, and also sad.

"Mr. Morris is dead, sir."

Thalia gasped, and her father cried out in shock and horror. Tony Morris was one of her father's closest friends. Thalia put her hand on her father's shoulder and gave him a supportive squeeze as he removed his glasses and covered his eyes. Tony was like a younger brother to her father, and Thalia considered him family. To know that he was dead— her hands shook. It couldn't be true, could it? He was so bright and good and . . . God, her throat burned from unshed tears for her friend. She swallowed hard and glanced up from her grief. Such scenes were to be conducted in private, away from the eyes of strangers.

The captain ducked his head respectfully as he studied his hands, which were gripped tightly on his hat. Through the fog of her sorrow, Thalia understood that the captain had done this before. Given bad news to the friends and families of those that had died. What a dreadful responsibility, one she wouldn't wish on anyone.

She tried to speak, but her words caught on shards of loss. She gulped and tried again. "How did it happen?"

The captain cleared his throat and looked at Franklin. He seemed to be deliberately avoiding looking at her. "This might not be suitable for . . . young ladies."

Even in her grief, Thalia had to suppress a snort. Clearly, this man knew nothing of her. Fortunately, her father, voice rough with emotion about Tony Morris's death, said, "Please speak candidly in front of Thalia. She has a remarkably strong constitution."

Captain Huntley's gaze flicked back at her for a brief moment, then stayed fixed on her father. She saw with amazement that this strapping military man was uncomfortable, and, stranger still, it was *her* that was making him uncomfortable. Perhaps it was because of the nature of his news, unsuitable as it was for young ladies. Or perhaps it was because he'd felt something between them, as well, something instant and potent. She did not want to consider it, not when she was reeling from the pain of Tony Morris's death.

After clearing his throat again, the captain said, "He was killed, sir. In Southampton."

"So close!" Franklin exclaimed. "On our very doorstep."

"I don't know 'bout doorsteps, sir, but he was attacked in an alley by a group of men." Captain Huntley paused as Thalia's father cursed. "They'd badly outnumbered him, but he fought bravely until the end."

"How do you know all this?" Thalia asked. If Tony's death had been reported in the papers, surely someone other than the captain would be standing in their *ger* right now, Bennett Day or Catullus Graves. How Thalia longed to see one of their numbers, to share her family's grief with them instead of this man who disquieted her with his very presence.

Captain Huntley again let his eyes rest on her briefly. She fought down her immediate physical response, trying to focus on what he was saying. "I was there, miss, when it happened. Passing by when I heard the sounds of Morris's being attacked, and joined in to help him." He grimaced. "But there were too many, and when my back was turned, he was stabbed by one of them—a blond man who talked like a nob, I mean, a gentleman."

"Henry Lamb?" Franklin asked, looking up at Thalia. She shrugged. Her father turned his attention back to the captain and his voice grew sharp, "You say you were merely 'passing by,' and heard the scuffle and just 'joined in to help.' Sounds damned suspicious to me." Thalia had to agree with her father. What sort of man passed by a fight and came to the aid of the victim, throwing himself into the fray for the sake of a stranger? Hardly anyone.

Captain Huntley tightened his jaw, angry. "Suspicious or not, sir, that's what happened. Morris even saved my life just before the end. So when he gave me the message to deliver to you, in person, I couldn't say no."

"You came all the way from Southampton to Urga to fulfill a dying man's request, a man you had never met before," Thalia repeated, disbelief plain in her voice.

The captain did not even bother answering her. "It couldn't be written down, Morris said," he continued, addressing her father and infuriating Thalia in the process. She didn't care for being ignored. "I've had it in my head for nearly three months, and it makes no sense to me, so I'll pass it on to you. Perhaps you can understand it, sir, because, as much as I've tried, I can't."

"Please," her father said, holding his hand out and gesturing for Captain Huntley to proceed.

"The message is this: 'The sons are ascendant. Seek the woman who feeds the tortoise.'"

He glanced at both Thalia and her father to see their reactions, and could not contain his surprise when her father cursed again and Thalia gripped a nearby table for support. She felt dizzy. It was beginning. "You know what that means?" the captain asked.

Franklin nodded as his hands curled and uncurled into fists, while Thalia caught her lower lip between her teeth and gnawed pensively on it.

She knew it was bound to happen, but they had never known when. That time was now at hand.

In October, let SCOUNDREL whisk you away
to the shores of Greece . . .

*The Blades of the Rose are sworn to protect the sources
of magic in the world. But the work is dangerous—and
they can't always protect their own . . .*

READY FOR ACTION

London Harcourt's father is bent on subjugating the
world's magic to British rule. But since London is a mere
female, he hasn't bothered to tell her so. He's said only
that he's leading a voyage to the Greek isles. No matter,
after a smothering marriage and three years of straitlaced
widowhood, London jumps at the opportunity—
unfortunately, right into the arms of Bennett Day . . .

RISKING IT ALL

Bennett is a ladies' man, when he's not dodging lethal
attacks to protect the powers of the ancients from men
like London's father. Sometimes, he's a ladies' man
even when he *is* dodging them. But the minute he sees
London he knows she will require his full attention.
The woman is lovely, brilliant, and the only known
speaker of a dialect of ancient Greek that holds
the key to calling down the wrath of the gods.
Bennett will be risking his life again—
but around London, what really worries him
is the danger to his heart . . .

"Save those slurs for your grandmother," said a deep, masculine voice to the vendor. He spoke Greek with an English accent.

London turned to the voice. And nearly lost her own.

She knew she was still, in many ways, a sheltered woman. Her society in England was limited to a select few families and assorted hangers-on, her father's business associates, their retainers and servants. At events and parties, she often saw the same people again and again. And yet, she knew with absolute clarity, that men who looked like the one standing beside her were a rare and altogether miraculous phenomenon.

There were taller men, to be sure, but it was difficult to consider this a flaw when presented with this man's lean muscularity. He wonderfully filled out the shoulders of his English coat, not bulky, but definitively capable. She understood at once that his arms, his long legs, held a leashed strength that even his negligent pose could not disguise. He called to mind the boxers that her brother, Jonas, had admired in his youth. The stranger was bareheaded, which was odd in this heat, but it allowed her to see that his hair was dark with just the faintest curl, ever so slightly mussed, as if he'd recently come from bed. She suddenly imagined herself tangling her fingers in his hair, pulling him closer.

And if that thought didn't make her blush all the harder, then his face was the coup de grace. What wicked promises must he have made, and made good on, with such a face. A sharp, clean jaw, a mouth of impossible sensuality. A naughty, thoroughly masculine smile tugged at the corners of that mouth. Crystalline eyes full of intelligent humor, the color intensely blue. Even the small bump on the bridge of his nose—had it been broken?—merely added to the overall impression of profound male beauty. He was clean-shaven, too, so that there could be no mistaking how outrageously handsome this stranger was.

She may as well get on the boat back to England immediately. Surely nothing she could ever see in Greece could eclipse the marvel of this man.

"Who are you?" the vendor shouted in Greek to the newcomer. "You defend this woman and her lies?"

"I don't care what she said," the Englishman answered calmly, also in Greek. "Keep insulting her and I'll jam my fist into your throat." The vendor goggled at him, but wisely kept silent. Whoever this man was, he certainly looked capable of throwing a good punch.

Yet gently, he put a hand on London's waist and began to guide her away. Stunned by the strange turn of events, she let him steer her from the booth.

"All right?" he asked her in English. A concerned, warm smile gilded his features. "That apoplectic huckster didn't hurt you, did he?"

London shook her head, still somewhat dazed by what had just happened, but more so by the attractiveness of the man walking at her side. She felt the warmth of his hand at her back and knew it was improper, but she couldn't move away or even regret the impertinence. "His insults weren't very creative."

He chuckled at this and the sound curled like fragrant smoke low in her belly. "I'll go back and show him how it's done."

"Oh, no," she answered at once. "I think you educated him enough for one day."

Even as he smiled at her, he sent hard warning glances at whomever stared at her. "So what had his fez in a pinch?"

She held up and unfolded her hand, which still held the shard of pottery. "We were disputing this, but, gracious, I forgot I still had it. Maybe I should give it back."

He plucked the piece of pottery from her hand. As he did this, the tips of his fingers brushed her bare palm. A hot current sparked to life where he touched. She could not prevent the shiver of awareness that ran through her body. She met his gaze, and sank into their cool aquatic depths as he stared back. This felt stronger than attraction. Something that resounded through the innermost recesses of herself, in deep, liquid notes, like a melody or song one might sing to bring the world into being. And it seemed he felt it, too, in the slight breath he drew in, the straightening of his posture. Breaking away from his gaze, London snatched her glove from Sally, who trailed behind them with a look of severe disapproval. London tugged on the glove.

He cleared his throat, then gave her back the pottery. "Keep it. Consider it his tribute."

She put it into her reticule, though it felt strange to take something she did not pay for.

"Thank you for coming to my aid," she said as they continued to walk. "I admit that getting into arguments with vendors in Monastiraki wasn't at the top of my list of Greek adventures."

"The best part about adventures is that you can't plan them."

She laughed. "Spoken like a true adventurer."

"Done my share," he grinned. "Ambushing bandits by the Khaznah temple in the cliffs of Petra. Climbing volcanoes in the steam-shrouded interior of Iceland."

"Sounds wonderful," admitted London with a candor that surprised herself. She felt, oddly, that she could trust this English stranger with her most prized secrets. "Even what happened back there at that booth was marvelous, in its way. I don't *want* to get into a fight, but it's such a delight to finally be out here, in the world, truly experiencing things."

"Including hot, dusty, crowded Athens."

"*Especially* hot, dusty, crowded Athens."

"My, my," he murmured, looking down at her with approval. "A swashbuckling lady. Such a rare treasure."

Wryly, she asked, "Treasure, or aberration?"

He stopped walking and gazed at her with an intensity that caught in her chest. "Treasure. Most definitely."

Again, he left her stunned. She was nearly certain that any man would find a woman's desire for experience and adventure to be at best ridiculous, at worst, offensive. Yet here was this stranger who not only didn't dismiss her feelings, but actually approved and, yes, admired them. What a city of wonders was this Athens! Although, London suspected, it was not the city so much as the man standing in front of her that proved wondrous.

"So tell me, fellow adventurer," she said, finding her voice, "from whence do you come? What exotic port of call?" She smiled. "Dover? Plymouth? Southampton?"

A glint of wariness cooled his eyes. "I don't see why it matters."

Strange, the abrupt change in him. "I thought that's what one did when meeting a fellow countryman abroad," she said. "Find out where they come from. If you know the same people." When he continued to look at her guardedly, she demonstrated, "'Oh, you're from Manchester? Do you know Jane?'"

The chill in his blue eyes thawed, and he smiled. "Of course, Jane! Makes the worst meat pies. Dresses like a Anglican bishop."

"So you *do* know her!"

They shared a laugh, two English strangers in the chaos of an Athenian market, and London felt within her a swell of happiness rising like a spring tide. As if in silent agreement, they continued to stroll together in a companionable silence. With a long-limbed, loose stride, he walked beside her. He hooked his thumbs into the pockets of his simple, well-cut waistcoat, the picture of a healthy young man completely comfortable with himself. And why shouldn't he be? No man had been so favored by Nature's hand. She realized that he hadn't told her where he was from, but she wouldn't press the issue, enjoying the glamour of the unknown.

His presence beside her was tangible, a continuous pulse of uncivilized living energy, as though being escorted by a large and untamed mountain cat that vacillated between eating her and dragging her off to its lair.

In November, get lost in the
Canadian wilderness with REBEL . . .

*On the Canadian frontier in 1875, nature is a harsh
mistress. But the supernatural can really do you in . . .*

A LONE WOLF

Nathan Lesperance is used to being different.
He's the first Native attorney in Vancouver, and
welcome neither with white society nor his sometime tribe.
Not to mention the powerful wildness he's always
felt inside him, too dangerous to set free.
Then he met Astrid Bramfield and saw his like
within her piercing eyes. Now, unless she helps him through
the harsh terrain and the harsher unknowns of his
true abilities, it could very well get him killed . . .

AND THE WOMAN WHO
LEFT THE PACK

Astrid has traveled this path before. Once she was
a Blade of the Rose protecting the world's magic from
unscrupulous men, with her husband by her side.
But she's loved and lost, and as a world-class
frontierswoman, she knows all about survival.
Nathan's searing gaze and long, lean muscles mean
nothing but trouble. Yet something has ignited a
forgotten flame inside her: a burning need for
adventure, for life—and perhaps even for love . . .

He had looked into her. Not merely seen her hunger for living, but felt it, too. She saw that at once. He recognized it in her. Two creatures, meeting by chance, staring at one another warily. And with reluctant longing.

Yet it wasn't only that immediate connection she had felt when meeting Lesperance. There was magic surrounding him.

Astrid wondered if Lesperance even knew how magic hovered over him, how it surrounded him like a lover, leaving patterns of nearly visible energy in his wake. She didn't think he was conscious of it. Nothing in his manner suggested anything of the sort. Nathan Lesperance, incredibly, was utterly unaware that he was a magical being. Not metaphorical magic, but *true* magic.

She knew, however. Astrid had spent more than ten years surrounded by magic of almost every form. Some of it benevolent, like the Healing Mists of Ho Hsien-Ku, some of it dark, such as the Javanese serpent king Naga Pahoda, though most magic was neither good nor evil. It simply *was*. And Astrid recognized it, particularly when sharing a very small space, as the Mounties' office had been.

If Nathan Lesperance's fierce attractiveness and unwanted understanding did not drive Astrid from the trading post, back to the shelter of her solitary homestead, then the magic enveloping him certainly would. She wanted nothing more to do with magic. It had cost her love once before, and she would not allow it to hurt her again.

But something had changed. She'd felt it, not so long ago. Magic existed like a shining web over the world, binding it together with filaments of energy. Being near magic for many years made her especially sensitive to it. When she returned from Africa, that sensitivity had grown even more acute. She tried to block it out, especially when she left England, but it never truly went away.

Only a few weeks earlier, Astrid had been out tending to her horse when a deep, rending sensation tore through her, sending her to her knees. She'd knelt in the dirt, choking, shaking, until she'd gained her strength again and tottered inside. Eventually, the pain subsided, but not the sense of looming catastrophe. Something had shaken and split the magical web. A force greater than anyone had ever known. And to release it meant doom.

What was it? The Blades had to know, how to avert the disaster. They would fight against it, as they always did. But without her.

A memory flitted through her mind. Months earlier, she'd had a dream and it had stayed with her vividly. She dreamt of her Compass, of the Blades, and heard someone calling her, calling her home. Astrid had dismissed the dream as a vestige of homesickness, which reared up now and again, especially after she'd been alone for so long.

The jingle of her horse's bridle snapped her attention back to the present. She cursed herself for drifting. A moment's distraction could easily lead to death out here. Stumbling between a bear sow and her cub. Crossing paths with vicious whiskey runners. A thousand ways to die. So when her awareness suddenly prickled once again, Astrid did not dismiss it.

A rustle, and movement behind her. Astrid swung her horse around, taking up her rifle, to confront who or whatever was there.

She blinked, hardly believing what she saw. A man walked through tall grasses lining the pass trail. He walked with steady but dazed steps, hardly aware of his surroundings. He was completely naked.

"Lesperance?"

Astrid turned her horse on the trail and urged it closer. Dear God, it *was* Lesperance. She decocked her rifle and slung it back over her shoulder.

He didn't seem to hear her, so she said again, coming nearer, "Mr. Lesperance?" She could see now, only ten feet away, that cuts, scrapes and bruises covered his body. His very nude, extremely well-formed body. She snapped her eyes to his face before they could trail lower than his navel. "What happened to you?"

His gaze, dark and blank, regarded her with a removed curiosity, as if she was a little bird perched on a windowsill. He stopped walking and stared at her.

Astrid dismounted at once, pulling a blanket from her pack. Within moments, she wrapped it around his waist, took his large hand in hers, and coaxed his fingers to hold the blanket closed. Then she pulled off her coat and draped it over his shoulders. Despite the fact that the coat was quite large on Astrid, it barely covered his shoulders, and the sleeves stuck out like wings. In other circumstances, he would have looked comical. But there was nothing faintly amusing about this situation.

Magic still buzzed around him, though somewhat dimmer than before.

"Where are your clothes? How did you get here? Are you badly hurt?"

None of her questions penetrated the fog enveloping him. She bent closer to examine his wounds. Some of the cuts were deep, as though made by knives, and rope abrasions circled his wrists. Bruises shadowed his knees and knuckles. Blood had dried in the corners of his mouth. Nothing looked serious, but out in the wilderness, even the most minor injury held the potential for disaster. And, without clothing, not even a Native inured to the changeable weather could survive. He was in shock, just beginning to shake.

"Lesperance," she said, taking hold of his wide shoulders and staring into his eyes intently, "listen to me. I need to see to your wounds. We're going to have to ride back to my cabin."

"Astrid . . ." he murmured with a slow blink, then his nostrils flared like a beast scenting its mate. A hungry look crossed his face. "Astrid."

It was unexpected, given the circumstances, yet seeing that look of need, hearing him say her name, filled her with a responding desire. "Mrs. Bramfield," she reminded him. And herself. They were polite strangers.

"Astrid," he said, more insistent. He reached up to touch her face.

She grabbed his hand, pulling it away from her face. At least she wore gloves, so she didn't have to touch his bare skin. "Come on." Astrid gently tugged him toward her horse. Once beside the animal, she swung up into the saddle, put her rifle across her lap, and held a hand out to him. He stared at it with a frown, as though unfamiliar with the phenomenon of hands.

"We have to go *now*, Lesperance," Astrid said firmly. "Those wounds of yours need attention, and whatever or whoever did this to you is probably still out there."

He cast a look around, seeming to find a shred of clarity in the hazy morass of his addled brain. Something dark and angry crossed his face. He took a step away, as if he meant to go after whoever had hurt him. His hands curled into fists. Insanity. He was unarmed, naked, wounded.

"Now," Astrid repeated.

Somehow, she got through to him. He took her hand and, with a dexterity that surprised her, given his condition, mounted up behind her.

God, she didn't want to do this. But there was no other choice. "Put your arms around my waist," she said through gritted teeth. When he did so, she added, "Hold tightly to me. Not that tight," she gasped as his grip turned to bands of steel. He loosened his hold slightly. "Good. Do not let go. Do you understand?"

He nodded, then winced as if the movement gave him pain. "Can't stay up."

"Lean against me if you have to." She mentally groaned when he did just that, and she felt him, even through her bulky knitted vest, shirt, and sturdy trousers. Heavy and hard and solid with muscle. Everywhere. His arms, his chest, his thighs, pressed against hers. Astrid closed her eyes for a moment as she felt his warm breath along the nape of her neck.

"All set?" she asked, barely able to form the words around her clenched jaw.

He tried to nod again but the effort made him moan. The plaintive sound, coming from such a strong, potent man, pulled tight on feelings Astrid didn't want to have.

"Thank . . . you," he said faintly.

She didn't answer him. Instead, she kicked her horse into a gallop, knowing deep in her heart that she was making a terrible mistake.

Romantic Suspense from
Lisa Jackson

See How She Dies	0-8217-7605-3	$6.99US/$9.99CAN
Final Scream	0-8217-7712-2	$7.99US/$10.99CAN
Wishes	0-8217-6309-1	$5.99US/$7.99CAN
Whispers	0-8217-7603-7	$6.99US/$9.99CAN
Twice Kissed	0-8217-6038-6	$5.99US/$7.99CAN
Unspoken	0-8217-6402-0	$6.50US/$8.50CAN
If She Only Knew	0-8217-6708-9	$6.50US/$8.50CAN
Hot Blooded	0-8217-6841-7	$6.99US/$9.99CAN
Cold Blooded	0-8217-6934-0	$6.99US/$9.99CAN
The Night Before	0-8217-6936-7	$6.99US/$9.99CAN
The Morning After	0-8217-7295-3	$6.99US/$9.99CAN
Deep Freeze	0-8217-7296-1	$7.99US/$10.99CAN
Fatal Burn	0-8217-7577-4	$7.99US/$10.99CAN
Shiver	0-8217-7578-2	$7.99US/$10.99CAN
Most Likely to Die	0-8217-7576-6	$7.99US/$10.99CAN
Absolute Fear	0-8217-7936-2	$7.99US/$9.49CAN
Almost Dead	0-8217-7579-0	$7.99US/$10.99CAN
Lost Souls	0-8217-7938-9	$7.99US/$10.99CAN
Left to Die	1-4201-0276-1	$7.99US/$10.99CAN
Wicked Game	1-4201-0338-5	$7.99US/$9.99CAN
Malice	0-8217-7940-0	$7.99US/$9.49CAN

MAR 29 2011.